THREE DAYS IN NOVEMBER

BY T. H. ALTHOF

THREE DAYS IN NOVEMBER

St. Martin's Press

Designed by Laurel Marx

Library of Congress Cataloging in Publication Data

Althof, T. H.
  Three days in November.
  I. Title.
PZ4.A4676Th [PS3551.L79]   713'.5'4   78-3982
ISBN 0-312-80248-X

To my folks
who provided me with the refuge and the time necessary
to write this book.

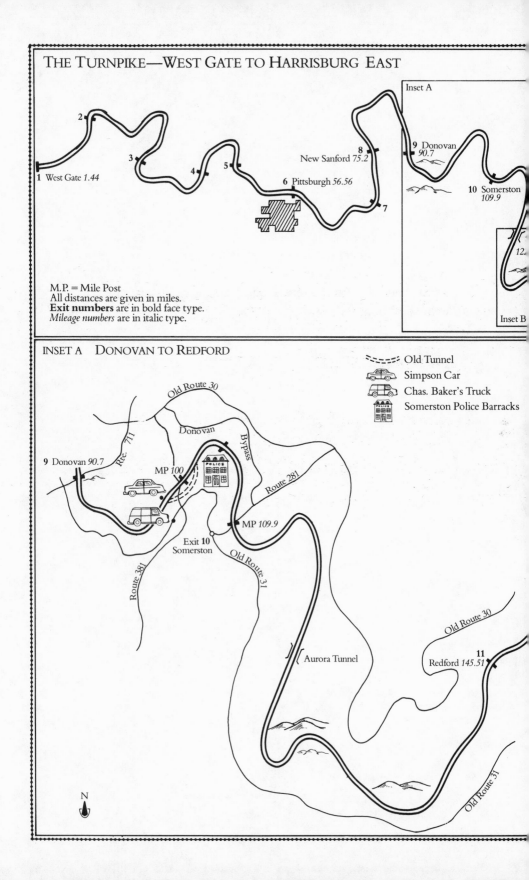

THE TURNPIKE—WEST GATE TO HARRISBURG EAST

Inset A

2

1 West Gate *1.44*

3

4

5

8
New Sanford *75.2*

6 Pittsburgh *56.56*

7

9 Donovan
90.7

10 Somerston
109.9

12.

Inset B

M.P. = Mile Post
All distances are given in miles.
Exit numbers are in bold face type.
Mileage numbers are in italic type.

INSET A   DONOVAN TO REDFORD

- - - - - - Old Tunnel

Simpson Car

Chas. Baker's Truck

Somerston Police Barracks

Old Route 30

Donovan

Bypass

Rte. 711

9 Donovan *90.7*

MP *100*

POLICE

Route 281

MP *109.9*

Exit **10**
Somerston

Old Route 31

Route 381

Old Route 30

11
Redford *145.51*

Aurora Tunnel

Old Route 31

N

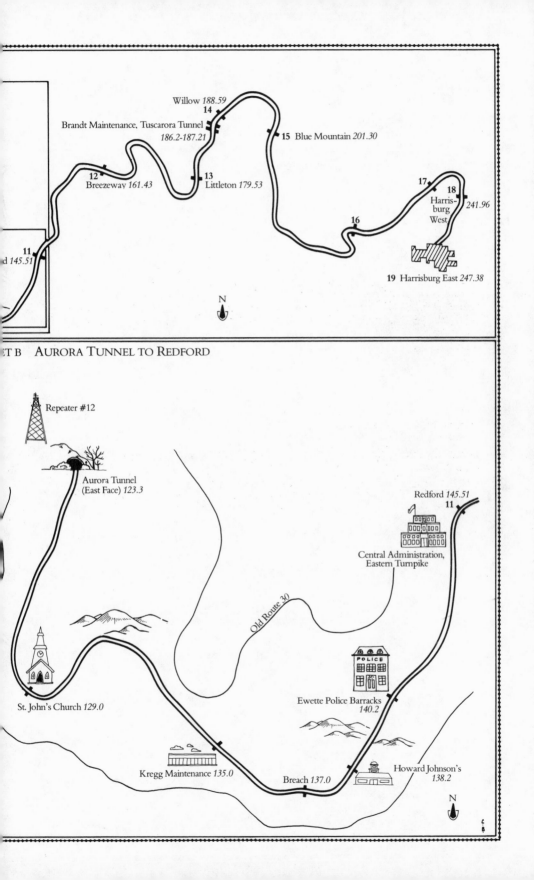

Willow *188.59*
14

Brandt Maintenance, Tuscarora Tunnel
186.2-187.21

15 Blue Mountain *201.30*

12
Breezeway *161.43*

13
Littleton *179.53*

17
18
Harris-
burg
West

241.96

16

11
d *145.51*

19 Harrisburg East *247.38*

N

ET B AURORA TUNNEL TO REDFORD

Repeater #12

Aurora Tunnel
(East Face) *123.3*

Redford *145.51*
11

Central Administration,
Eastern Turnpike

Old Route 30

St. John's Church *129.0*

POLICE

Ewette Police Barracks
140.2

Kregg Maintenance *135.0*

Breach *137.0*

Howard Johnson's
138.2

N

DAY
ONE:
SUNDAY

SOUTHWESTERN PENNSYLVANIA—THE THANKSGIVING WEEKEND—DAWN.

Sunday was like Saturday and Saturday was like the day before and two more days before. A small, late-season tropical had ground a weary way up from the Gulf across the southeastern seaboard and come to stand and stagnate off the Jersey Shore, pouring off its substance in a damp, bone-chilling rain since late on Wednesday—making mud and grayness of the holidays for the New England and Lake States. As far west as Detroit. As far south as Atlanta. And far out to sea. The little storm had been a failure of its kind, had never grown to hurricane proportions, had wandered northward losing energy into the fatal coldness and now stood locked and dying between surrounding systems. No winds. No violence. Just straight-down rain. Locked and dying. Sopping, gray monotonous days since Wednesday. Sunday differed only with regard to some sporadic gunfire in the Pennsylvania hills—a dependable constituent of the over-anxious, those unable to wait for Monday, the traditional start of the Pennsylvania antlered deer season. Later Sunday would be different, too, as millions who had traveled before the cultural imperative of the Thanksgiving holiday would hit the roads for home. By nightfall traffic densities would reach their peak, the heaviest of the year. People get away at different times but all come back at once, relinquishing their escape only at the eleventh hour. But for now the dawn of Sunday was much like the dawn of Saturday and those several days before. Another dawn broke gray and full of steady, straight-down rain that stood in lakes and puddles on roads and fields and backyards everywhere.

NEAR DONOVAN, PA.—10:35 A.M.

A young doe made her way among the barren saplings. She didn't recognize these new sounds. Maybe they were birds. They were everywhere. They made her nervous and she didn't like them.

Two men watched from the opposing hillside. The shot rang

out. The doe went down. She tumbled for a hundred yards or more down to the little creek between them, cutting a slimy scar of mud through fallen forest vegetation. The men got up and hurried forward.

They found her limp and draped around a tree, a little bit above the water. The older man got up and danced around.

"Hoo-hah! A hunert yards! You got 'er in the goddam brain!"

He pulled out a half pint of rye and screwed the cap off, he took it like mouthwash and passed it over.

"Kid, you got an eagle eye," he said. He punched him in the shoulder.

The "kid" took some of the rye and passed it back. He was apprehensive.

"Hey—Arlan?"

"What?"

"That's a *doe*, Arlan."

"Well, I can see that. I know it is."

"Did you know it at the time?"

"Hell, I dunno. What's the difference?"

"Well, it makes a lot of goddam difference, Arlan! You can't kill no doe in antler deer season—my God!"

"Seems t' me you done it. Dang thing's layin' stone cold dead there just the same."

Arlan took another mouthful of the rye, swished it around again and swallowed.

"You know what I mean; a buck is one thing, but—"

"It's poaching anyway! Nobody seen ya. What the hell?"

"Well, let's get out of here. I ain't inclined to press my luck."

"We ain't leavin' any hunert pounds goddam venison out layin' in the woods, believe me. Not the price a' meat the way it is. Come on. Give a hand, now."

"Hell no, Arlan!"

"Quit bein' such a chickenshit. Come on!" said Arlan. He killed the rye and chucked the empty to the brush. "Well, come *on*!!"

The doe was light enough to drag, so they didn't risk the

time that it would take to gut her. Arlan's cancerous old Buick was sitting on a faded jeep trail not far away. The kid and the doe stayed in the underbrush while Arlan scouted up and down the trail a hundred yards or so and saw that it was clear in both directions. He returned to the Buick and left the back door open, then went back for the kid.

They slid the carcass quickly across the clearing and threw it in the back seat, covering it with a filthy tarpaulin dug out from among the dirty tools and paint cans on the floor, then jumped into the front. The Buick cranked a large amount and finally fired to life and started off down the trail leaving a stagnant heap of blue-black smoke standing in the forest rain.

Boulders, bumps and ruts changed to asphalt, then concrete as they wound down from the hills and into Donovan to catch the Eastern Turnpike exit east for Redford—near as the Pike could get them to home. Two exits. Fifty-five miles.

The kid didn't like it. What if they got stopped by cops or something? What about the gate attendants? There would be Game Commission guys all over. Arlan wasn't having any. No way would he put up with sixty winding, roundabout, circuitous miles of potholed tar they called Route #31—up and down two of the biggest mountains in Southwestern Pennsylvania in the pouring rain! That would be the only alternative. That or #30 to the north, and that was longer. Forget it!

MILEPOST # 90.7, TURNPIKE GATES AT DONOVAN—11:10 A.M.

The kid's fears proved groundless. When they reached the gates the beginning rush of hunters had built up substantially, some early travelers homeward bound. The entry ramps were jammed. Attendants were so busy they could've ridden through on elephants. The Buick went right through.

MILEPOST # 118—11:50 A.M.

Arlan was annoyed. The drivers of the two big semis side-by-side behind him ought to have more sense. You didn't tailgate a twelve-year-old-car. Not in the rain and in traffic and in mountains such as these, you didn't. First they'd held him down to thirty-five going up the nine-mile Donovan Bypass, letting him get past just at the summit. Then they'd chased him down the other side at damn near seventy. All the way past Somerston and halfway up the mountain. They were sticking side-by-side and right behind him all the way, playing games! Where the hell was Smokey? He wanted cops, now, and they weren't there. Goddam truckers thought they owned the road!

And the kid wasn't helping any. Now he was thumbing through a battered hunting manual like he had to break the Nazi Code!

"Aw, my *God*!" the kid cried out.

Arlan tried to get his skin back on. "What's the matter now?"

"Fifteen hunert dollars! Fifteen hunert God damn *dollars,* Arlan! That's what the goddam matter is! Aw, *man*!"

"What the hell you bawlin' about? What fifteen dollars?"

"Fifteen *hunert* dollars is what they hit you for for takin' anterless deer out of season! Look! It says right here . . ."

"Never mind, never mind . . ."

"—and/or 120 days! And *or,* Arlan! You could get both! We really done it this time."

"Will you shut up?"

The kid moaned on. Next it would be tears.

"Cool it! Now just relax! Nobody's ever gonna see. Just kinda keep that tarp up nice and tight there—you know."

The kid bought that completely.

"Hell, yes! I'll sew it in a goddam bag, if need be!"

The tarp was still in place. It needed no attention. Still it relieved him greatly to be pulling here—tucking there. The kid had himself extended fully over the back seat to attend the furthest corners. In finishing, he got the tarp pulled tight across the carcass and happened to glance down.

What the hell was *that*?

Was something moving?

He froze in mid-air. Nothing. He waited. Still nothing. His muscles had begun to ache and tremble with fatigue. He shifted to withdraw into the front again.

Thump!

There! He saw it clearly that time!

Thump again.

Twice more.

A pulse. A throb from underneath the tarp. Each time stronger. No doubt about it.

Now it swelled high and settled down into a slow, spasmodic heaving, growing stronger and more regular all the time.

He sat back slowly, on his knees—his attention transfixed on the tarp.

"Uh—Arlan?"

"*Now* what?" As if the trucks and traffic weren't enough! They were getting snow, now. On the mountain!

"It's—breathin' Arlan. I think it's still alive."

"G'wan! Yer crazy!"

"I am not *either*, Arlan!"

"Yes you are."

"No I ain't! You take a look. That sonofabitch is still alive!"

Arlan was having a bad time with the big trucks and driving. He managed just to crank his head around. The tarp slid off. The doe raised her head.

Time froze solid. The three of them just stared at one another.

"We must've only grazed 'im."

"Oh, sweet Jesus!" whispered Arlan. He snapped to, just in time to keep from bouncing off the center guardrail. Just in time.

"What do we do now?" the kid asked.

"Uh—God. How should I know? Get the tarp over 'm. Hold 'im down. . . ."

"Are you kiddin'?"

"Do I look like I'm kiddin'? Hurry up—before he *does* something!"

The kid thought that over. He came up with nothing better. Ever so slowly, he reached down and got hold of the tarp and brought it up until he had it level with his chin, holding it spread out between his hands. The doe had made no move, as yet—continued to regard him with her big doe eyes. He held the tarp a long time, working up the nerve.

Arlan growled through yellow teeth. ''Do it!'' he barked.

The kid dove headlong upon the doe.

A tiny, razor hoof rent through the canvas tarp like newspaper. The kid rolled off screaming onto the junk on the floor, cradling his intestines in both his arms.

The animal was fully conscious now, and terrified. She went for the light and cracked the rear deck window. She rebounded, landing on the screaming kid, turned right around and dove into the front with Arlan. Bits of glass, upholstery stuffing, flesh and blood filled the air.

To the driver of the enormous Brockway oil transport it seemed as though the driver of that junker Buick in front of him had gone bananas—had had an epileptic fit or heart attack, or else he'd dropped his whole front end. And tunnels coming not two hundred yards ahead. He bore down on the horns—glanced over at the driver of the giant Kenworth right beside him. The Kenworth guy was white faced, shook his head and gave a shrug. What the hell could *he* do? There was a crush of traffic behind him.

Now the Buick sideswiped off the medial and slammed into an orange VW sent it flying off the mountain, over the side and tumbling down and down into the deeply forested ravines below. The Buick was all over the place, now, swerving wildly across both lanes.

The road surface bore an inch of slush. They were going downhill, now—just beyond the Aurora Summit where it drops a little going into the tunnels. The trucks were traveling too fast to brake all at once, but neither were they following that lunatic into the tubes.

Both men hit their brakes at once—a double pish of air and then the scream of tires and metal drums. Both felt the pressure of their loads build up behind them, then snap sideways into jackknife. Side by side, but they stayed on course, careening forward—bashing into one another like a pair of dinosaurs in heat, a dozen little sidelong crashes keeping each other erect and basically in line. The black maw of the eastern portal loomed.

The Buick snapped abruptly left into the medial, rebounded sideways and across both lanes. They plowed into her broadside.

Radio dispatcher Luther Green was in the tunnel observation window at the west end between the east and westbound tubes. He heard the sound before he saw it coming. The Buick had become a bouncing, rolling cabbagehead of steel, spitting sparks and ragged chunks of iron, the two rigs pounding it along ahead of them like some bizarre, nightmarish soccer ball. It all seemed a thing alive and coming straight for him. He just had time to dive beneath the counter.

The observation window above him pulverized in a crystal shower. The wall bowed out beside him like a pregnant thing. He choked in a fall of dust and masonry. Impact after impact pounded in beside him as more cars piled behind the two big trucks, unable to stop themselves. Luther hugged his knees and wondered what his wife would do with all his power tools at home. Probably sell them cheap, he had got them off other dead men's wives.

And then it quit. Just like that. He didn't move at first—not until the smoke became intolerable. When he raised his head the rain was sizzling off the concrete wall above him, turning straight to steam.

Luther Green decided to get out of there.

TURNPIKE GATES AT REDFORD, MILEPOST # 145.5— 12:00 NOON

A big, gray Bonneville swung out of the city traffic. The car was stock except for special radio antennas and the best steel radials bucks could buy. It cut across the near-deserted parking lots of the Eastern Central Administration Facility just off the Pike at Redford, sending up high plumes of water in its wake, then pulled up to a stop below huge plate glass doors, the public entrance of the somber glass-and-marble edifice.

A six-foot-two blond man in trenchcoat, jeans and tennis

shoes got out and took the steps up to the doors three at a time, not from hurry, but from being six-foot-two. He let himself into the dark interior with a private key, then crossed the public lobby to the reception booth, signed the daybook automatically, and moved to a pair of elevators, one of which required another of his keys. It opened at once and he stepped in.

When the door again slid open, he was one floor underground, and he stepped out into light and sound contrasted with the echoing gloom above.

The corridor wound to the left, then right again and through a maze of glassed-in cubicles, down another hallway lined with identical blue doors. He passed a half a dozen of the doors, selected one at last, and opened it. The din of teletypes and radio transmissions rose sharply.

He was now in a little foyer with a choice of two directions: right and out across the main communications floor or straight and up three steps into the "cage". He chose the "cage" as always.

The long and narrow "cage" was like a broadcast or recording booth, a wall of glass affording total view of the telecommunications center, the main communications floor. Door at one end only. It oversaw an arena of activity that had not been devoid of human presence since put in operation, thirty years before, long before his own time there. Directly opposite the systemized schematic map of the Eastern Turnpike that took up the whole north wall was the computer map with multicolored blinking lights and white block-bars on green background. Some six radio operator's consoles were arrayed before it like altars to a giant idol, one for each of the four original Turnpike radio zones and two more for the newer Northeast Extension. In the "cage" were also six smaller counterparts of the main consoles. From these six telecom positions it was theoretically possible to be in touch with any point on earth that could be reached by radio or telephone. The entire telecommunications center had been built below ground with civil defense in mind—during the Fifties when the bomb was having much to do with public architecture. Deeper in the complex were barracks and supply stores to maintain up to sixty men for up to sixty days and the "cage" had been intended as a contingency command point—a center where some brass might have to hole up and direct things if and when the "Big Fear" did come down. The "cage" had found more actual use for grade school and political tours and as a kind of second office for the tall man standing in it now. The fourth telecom bore his name tag: LEE DAVID RIDER—CHIEF OF COMMUNICA-TIONS and by squatter's rights the "cage" was mostly his. He didn't like his office, you couldn't see the action there. He brought his paperwork and coffee to the "cage" to watch the floor. If he wasn't home or somewhere on the Turnpike he was here.

Lee moved to stand behind his telecom, but did not sit down. He scanned the map and all its tiny lights across the floor from him.

There was a steady red light on the big schematic map in Zone 4, down east, near Philadelphia. It meant a one-lane blockage—minor or small vehicle problem—some spot construc-tion. He punched the Zone 4 button to monitor the calls from there, to catch a sense of things, to get his mind into the system.

A hundred-eighty miles to the east of him police cars were communicating along party lines of microwave beams relayed through a score of isolated robot towers.

"Three-nine-seven 'by', three-eight-four."

"What's that situation on that blue Dodge van, now?"

"Patron states it quit on him. He's out of gas. Won't admit it."

"10-4. You call it in, I'm Westbound on this other one up here at two-niner-six-point-six."

"Three-nine-seven to Redford Central."

"Redford by 397." The Zone 4 operator on the floor acknowledged the call in a routine sing-song way that told Lee that it had so far been a routine sing-song day. But it was Sunday following Thanksgiving. The day was anything but over.

"Redford be advised we got a blue Dodge van disabled down at two-nine-eight-point seven. He's off the road, no prob-lem. Lanes are open."

Each mile from Ohio marked off in numbered mileposts to make exact locations easy on the radio. Specific. Idiot-proof. 359

miles were marked between West Gate to Ohio and the Delaware Bridge. 110 more North and South on the Northeast Extension, tenth-mile posts between.

"397—10-9 on that '20'." The Redford operator hadn't caught the milepost number, was requesting a repeat. The barking VHF was anything but high fidelity, the average trooper had anything but a professional speaking voice.

"Milepost two-niner-eight point seven—eastbound. We have service coming."

"10-4, 397."

A routine call—a routine problem. As he watched the steady red wink out. He let up the button. It was time for coffee.

Coffee was behind the map—back in the electronics room with all the VHF and microwave transceiver racks, beside the police and National Weather Service teletypes, the "CLEAN" police computer terminal, the computers for the map and gate accounts. The corporal behind the state police desk near the main room door had his left hand in a plaster cast. Central was a good place for the injured to recuperate. The "Troop T" representative behind the State Police desk was changing constantly, a brisk turnover. Lee knew the fellow. The cop spoke first.

"Hello, Mr. Rider." He seemed surprised to see management on weekends.

"Hey, Del! When you gonna sell the Stradivarius?" The trooper grinned and turned back to his Sunday funnies. Lee crossed the main floor into the coffee room. Old jokes were best for cops, they understood that they were jokes. Not that cops were dumb—just tended to be literal—minded.

Judy Cochran stretched the uniform in all the most attractive ways. His sole girl operator. New this year. Pressure had come from up above to hire a broad, so Lee had interviewed. Of the few who'd actually applied, Judy was the only one who had walked into his office with an F.C.C. 2nd license and some formal training. She also had a private pilot's license—not required, but it said lots about her. Pug nose, freckles, and the wide blue eyes notwithstanding, he had felt she could do the job. Problem solved. She got it.

She was bending over the clattering National Weather Service weathertype machines as Lee moved in to make his coffee. He patted her behind in passing.

"Hiya, 'Butch'."

She jumped, startled. Angry at first. Then she saw it was Lee and melted some.

"Oh!—uh. Hiya, Mr. Rider. What are you doing in?"

Lee really didn't have an answer. Some vague urge. Just a look at things, then home. That was the plan.

"That the weather?"

The roll of yellow print-out coming off the hammering machine.

"Yes."

"When you get it, I would like to see."

"Sure."

He made his coffee, moved away to lean against the door jamb and survey the floor again. He had noted that the Zone 2 console was unmanned on his way through. Judy's for the day. It was okay. Early in the day and slow. Any other operator could take her calls.

The teletype went 'ding' and quieted. Judy ripped the paper off and brought it to him. It called for continued steady rain and overnight temps in the mid thirties. Same as Saturday. Same as Friday. Same as Thursday and the day before.

"Order wood. We're going to build an Ark."

"I know, I got three dozen more just like it." She glanced down, noticing his feet. "Sneakers?"

It occurred to him that they had never met outside of Central. She had never seen him in relaxed attire.

"I'm not staying." he said. "I just stopped by."

"Well, if this is your notorious 'Big Thanksgiving Weekend' I don't think you needed to have bothered," she said.

Lee grinned behind his coffee and looked elsewhere. That's right. Judy hadn't been here last year. Of all the holidays nothing held a candle to Thanksgiving Weekend. He wondered what she'd say by nightfall.

"Of course, it's kind of heavy westbound, but—"

"*West* bound?" It was normally the opposite, but who could say if that meant anything? Thanksgiving Sunday had rules all its own.

"Well—yes. But no problems. It's moving right along."

"Hmm." He shrugged it off. Probably meant nothing, a temporary surge for who knew what reason? Those happened all the time.

There was a little silence while Judy played with her fingers.

"You working Zone 2?" Lee broke the silence. He was looking out across the floor, not in her direction.

"Yeah," she said.

"I think you got a problem." His finger led her eyes to the reflection of the big map on the window of the "cage". A red light was flashing in the reflection. A beeper started synchronizing with the flashes as she saw it. The paging speaker blasted suddenly above them:

"Uh—Mizz Cochran. I believe you have a call?" Emmert. First Operator. Working 1 beside her. Judy scampered. Emmert's attitude about the girl had bugged Lee. Judy'd left the monitor up full and the call was very loud throughout the room. They built the audio with lots of punch. Could take your ears off if you weren't ready. Maybe Emmert had cause for annoyance, but he also could have turned it down. He could have taken the call himself. For the guys he would have.

The red was on Zone 2, all right. Lee stepped out into the room to view the map directly.

"Redford this is Aurora. We have a ten-three-three. Repeat, ten-three-three. For Chrissake wake up Redford!"

All over the room. Judy whipped the monitor control down to an endurable level. Lee pretended not to notice Emmert's expression. Emmert pretended not to have one. Lee approached the console.

"Redford 'by' Aurora. Go ahead." Judy had it now.

"Where the hell you been, Redford? Be advised—we got the worst mother-multiple I ever seen up here! It's plugged up that eastbound tube completely solid and it's burning. We are shut down eastbound all the way."

R. Fred Barger—Tunnel Maintenance Chief. Lee knew the voices. He took the mike from Judy.

"Barger, this is Rider. Tone it down and just convey your information. What have you got up there? What happened?"

"Damn if I know, Mr. Rider. Luther Green was in the west end, there. He says everything was fine and then the whole damn eastbound up and jumped right in on top of him. He don't know why. The whole west end is busted out! The maintenance on fire—we had to run all the goddam equipment out on the pavement, out the east end. We never got it all. We lost a bunch of stuff. The electric's out, and—dammit, Mr. Rider, it's a grade-five pisser we got here!"

"Injured?"

"None of us is, no. Ol' Luther Green, there—he could use about a quart of anything above a hunert proof—kinda bent him outa shape a little."

"I mean patrons."

"Oh, you're gonna have the injured there—at *least* injured. I dunno. We didn't look. We can't get over. We can't get nowhere's near it. Too damn hot in there. Look, Mr. Rider, we gotta get some help up here."

"You got it. Name it."

"Fire equipment. Everything. Anything you send had better take the eastbound west and come up this side. Nothin's getting through from Somerston, I'm tellin ya! Get Kregg. I hate to admit it, but we need 'em."

"Okay. I'm coming up there." Lee released the button. Of all the things that could happen, there was nothing to compare with pile-ups in the tunnels, especially if there was fire.

"Judy, get Redford F.D. up there. Tell them not to forget their goddam foam machine this time! Ambulances. You better let the hospital know what's coming, too. Who's on at Kregg?" Kregg was the next maintenance unit east of Aurora, between Redford and the wreck.

"Ollie Chelinski," Emmert said.

There was no one he would rather have at Kregg right now. Ollie was a rough old cob—a veteran of road maintenance since

that was smoothing mud. He had seen the Pike come and, some
believed, would live to see it go. Lee took up the mike again.

"Redford to Kregg."

"Kregg 'by'." It was old Chelinski right enough. The call
returned. Elaborately indulgent. A voice of broken glass. The
sound of half a century of cigar and chaw tobacco.

"Ollie—you been copying this business with Aurora?"

"10-4, Rider. What the hell else I got to do up here with all
my women on the rag?"

"Get your boys in gear and take your Tonka Toys up with
you. Give Aurora a hand."

"If you wasn't such a mind to stop an' chew the fat this
way, why we was halfways out the door."

"Has that eastbound cleared in front of you? That would be
eleven miles below the tunnels. It should have. Eleven miles
went fast."

"Last patrons went by us fifteen minutes back. You can
land yer Concorde any time now. Look here, Rider—gotta pull
the switch. We got a few small errands to attend to. We'll write
if we get steady work. G'bye."

Lee handed back the mike. "I'm going up. I'll be in the
car."

He started off, Emmert grabbed him.

"Lee, you got a call on 402. Tri-State. Nadel wants to talk
to you."

Tri-State was the private weather service. He knew the
weather—it was lousy!

"I'll call him back," he said.

"It's Nadel himself. He's been holding."

That wasn't typical of Jim Nadel. Maybe he'd better listen.

"I'll take it in the 'cage'," he said.

Lee slid into the well-worn chair and punched the well-worn
button.

"Rider here. Make it brief, Jim. I got a problem on the
mountain."

"Let's chat about the weather."

"What of the weather?"

"We have a fifty-fifty on a hefty drop in temperature before your holiday rush peaks out and passes over."

"And?"

"And—if that happens I suggest you move your turnpike south. The Carolinas ought to do it—northern Tennessee—"

Lee released a sigh and sat back for the rest of it.

"Hit me!" he said.

"We've had a big cold air-mass build-up over the northern territories through Saturday. Thirty-*one*-point-one inches of merc! Dynamic high. Cold. Very cold. Very Dry. This system that we're under:—28? God knows what's been keeping them apart. There's probably more water in this cloud above us now than there is in Lake Huron. It won't stay up there if it gets a chill. And there is 'the Lake Effect.' That dry air will pick up a load of its own coming down across the Lakes."

"When?"

"I don't know. At best late Monday."

"At worst?"

"Tonight. Say 6 P.M. That's why the call."

Lee let out a whistle.

"What's the probability on that?"

"Not sure. These systems just now seemed to have noticed one another. This high began to move down in our direction just within the past half hour. It's moving very slowly, but will accelerate enormously. In a little while they should be charging one another like a pair of rhinos."

"Keep me posted."

"What do you call this?"

"Okay, smartass. Keep it up."

Lee sat back and stared at the phone. Then he picked it up again.

Jennifer was a little shorter than her husband. An even six feet tall. Together walking they were like giraffes, graceful and gliding. People turned to see. Jennifer was 38, one of those whose prime came later and had been worth waiting for. Huge violet eyes, a swash of blue-black hair, graying naturally in streaks that other women had to pay for. The slender leopard cascade of a silken housedress swirled about her body as she moved from their spacious living room to get the kitchen phone.

"Hello, Lee."

"How do you do that?"

"Jean Dixon lessons."

"Listen, Hon—I'm going to—"

"—'be a little longer than you thought.' Yes, I know. We heard it on the scanner. Anyway, you're just in time to say goodbye to Charlie."

"Oh?"

"Yes. Her ride is leaving early. Just a minute, Lee. I'll get her."

Lee could hear her calling off the phone.

Charlene came into the kitchen ready to go, dressed in pea coat, muffler and beret. She took the phone from Jennifer.

"Goodbye, Dad." She was slightly taller than her mother.

"You're leaving early?"

"Yes. Clifford's heading out."

"Clifford—Clifford—"

"You know, Dad. That boy, the one you hate so much."

"Ah! *That* Clifford."

"Yes. That's the one. You really shouldn't, Dad. Actually you're both a lot alike. Hence the attraction, I suppose. Girls and their fathers. You know what they say?"

"Is that what they say? I'll have him shot."

"Relax. I'm kidding and you've seen him and you know how *much* I'm kidding. Anyway, he's leaving early. Some kind of problems at home. His Dad got drunk and shot somebody's foot off hunting. His own foot. Some kind of dumb thing like that. I couldn't follow it. I don't really know. And anyway a ride's a ride, you know."

"Good driver?"

"He's got to be. There's no brakes in that car."

"You're such a comfort to me!"

"Yes and there's more, he's flunking. Another reason I should have my own car next year." Lee could hear a car horn in the background.

"Oops! That's him! I gotta run!''

"Hey! Wait a minute!''

"Yes?''

"Listen. Skip this thing with 'Clifford' and hang back a day or two. I'll run you out myself. I've got to be in Cincinnati Tuesday.''

"Negative. I'm sorry. Got three—count 'em—*three* midterms tomorrow. Anyway, the Christmas break is in just two weeks. I'll see you then, goodbye.''

And she was gone.

"I'm sure she'll be all right,'' said Jennifer. "She's ridden with him several times before.''

"I know, it's nothing. We have an outside chance of weather. I was only thinking.''

"Oh?''

"Skip it. Nothing definite. Anyway, it's good they're leaving early. They'll be there. Or so close it won't effect them.''

"When will you be home?''

"Not long. I want to run up quick and have a look at this. If I don't do it something dumb is bound to happen. Give it—two hours.''

"The place is ours now.''

"An hour and a half.''

"A little music. A couple of martinis. By the fire. . .''

"Of course you know you're rotten.''

"That's true.''

"You have no scruples.''

"None whatever.''

"Sixty minutes. Hold the thought until I get there.''

"That's what rainy days are for.''

Lee stopped by the Zone 2 console on his way.

"What about those ambulances?''

Judy turned to face him. "I called them. They should be underway.''

"Good. I'll check in from the car.''

"10-4.'' She said. She wondered what on earth he could be smiling for.

GATE 11, REDFORD—12:38 P.M.

Rider flashed his card and went directly through the gates at Redford, milepost 145.1. He took the fork for "HARRISBURG AND EAST" and kept an easy patience going down the ramp. Then there was an end of patience. He gunned the "Bonney" and she screamed into a U that took them off and out of it—the wrong way up the now deserted eastbound toward the tunnels. He glanced into the mirror. The fellow just behind him on the ramp was stopping at the yield sign, bewildered. Lee grinned. You could build a million dollars worth of signs and steel and concrete screaming "ONE WAY! THIS WAY ONLY!" and all it took was one small act of heresy to put it all in doubt.

Ahead there would be eight whole level miles of nothing coming, nothing in the way before the winding climb began— then nine miles more up to the summit. Lee let the big car take her head and go. The Bonney rarely got to stretch it out to 90 and she loved it—she was made for running speeds that high. Maybe among the last of her kind. Who could say? The engine sang a high and even tone of joy. The man and his machine went bounding into the pouring hiss of rain—boy and dolphin in an open sea.

MILEPOST 140.2—12:40 P.M.

A "blue-and-white" swung out behind Lee and the Bonney as they passed the Everett State Police Barracks on the eastbound side. Lee resented the intrusion. He bore down. The Bonney sang a little higher. As they passed the Howard Johnson's and started up the grade at 138.4, the cop was right behind. He could read its number in his mirror. Lee reached down and took the mike.

"Hello, three-four-four. Lay off. It's Rider."

"I'm not chasing anybody, Rider. All I wanna do is get the hell up on this mountain!" John Beck, the Everett captain.

"Move over."

Lee had had the Bonney squarely in the middle. Now he took the inside lane and Beck moved up beside him. They could see each other's faces.

"What do you hear?" said Lee.

"Nothing. No one's on the radio. They're all out of their cars."

"How many units have you got up there?"

"All of mine. #337 out of Somerston got stuck in the goddam backlog on the other side. One unit out of action for us. Last I heard LaBarr was going up on foot."

"Where?"

"The car is down at 118.3, LaBarr, he can't see the end of the backlog behind him. Of course the weather's thick, but it's growing like a mother, Lee."

Lee whistled softly to himself. The western portal of the Aurora eastbound tube began at 122.18. That meant they had one hell of a problem—at least a five-mile backlog. If the Lord himself descended and they opened up the eastbound now it would still be hours till the flow could be restored. Once you broke that rhythm. Damn! Of all the days to have one in the tunnel!

Beck pulled out ahead of him and both men took the center of the road again to cut the tortured curves. Kregg Maintenance was all but vacant as they passed it on the left at 135.0. Ollie's men had mobilized and gone.

Seven miles above the valley floor the colorless terrain suddenly went white in a blanket of sodden snow. The Bonney lost her grip, began to yaw. Lee had to back her down to fifty to regain a measure of control. He was glad that Beck was not beside him.

MILEPOST 123.5

The Bonneville and patrol car 344 reached the east end of the tunnels by 12:50—or rather got as far as both of them could go together. Kregg Maintenance was there ahead of them. The Kregg machinery was strewn haphazardly across the eastbound lanes, parked on the berm and mingled with the Aurora stuff which had been evacuated from the maintenance facility between the tubes to escape the fires inside. The tunnels ended at 123.6; they still had a quarter mile to go.

Beck pulled his flashers on and signaled Lee to pull the

Bonney over. Lee ditched her well below the start of the equipment and beat it back to car 344 on foot. There wasn't anyone around but you could never tell. These maintenance fellows were a bit robust and didn't always watch behind them.

They inched forward in 344 and still saw no one. The big orange hulks stood vacant, black inside and frosting over lightly with the soggy snow. The thought was for the ambulances coming up from Redford. They must still be coming. There was no sign that anything since Kregg had gotten to the tunnels. They were forced to leave the car just once to move an asphalt roller which, with a top speed of two miles an hour and weighing tons, was a useless and impossible thing to steal and required no key. They began to encounter some of the Kregg men here and there and set them to work moving things to provide a lane for the "one-hundred" numbers—the ambulances.

Three other patrol units had already arrived at the tunnels and pulled up on the paved area between the tubes. The big barn-doors stood open. Black within. A thin, steady stream of black oil smoke poured upward from the maintenance tunnel. A thicker, blacker stream came from the eastbound tube. Whatever was happening in there was happening a mile away. There was little visible here in terms of action. Nothing but a few scattered men, the standing machines. Troopers were the action—fighting with the westbound. Judy hadn't been misinformed about the westbound. It was solid. Thirty miles an hour. Already bunching. The troopers had positioned themselves on both sides and were hustling the gawkers along. Cursing. Threatening. Screaming. Anything to keep them moving. The impacted eastbound was a sufficient problem.

They approached a quite enormous fellow at the medial. Lee stayed a step behind. It was Beck's man after all. The giant was directing with great ham-like arms and great profanity, pulling the westbound forward hand over hand like a fisherman pulling in the nets. Lee could almost sense the weight of it.

The Captain was capable of being suddenly and amazingly loud.

"Hey, Miscenic!" he shouted.

The giant shot a glance at them and kept directing. Like

something doing battle with a monster. If he quit the westbound would get him. So he didn't. He had a tiger by the tail.

"What?" he said. Then, he turned back to the westbound and he was screaming at some chinless guy inside a station wagon.

"COME ON, CLOWN! HAUL IT! GET IT OUTA HERE!"

Everyone had to get a look. Everybody had to be a gawker.

"Knock off a second," said the Captain. "We need to get over."

"Over where?" The big cop was really getting irritable.

"The other side! What the hell you think? How do we get over?"

"Your guess is as good as mine." Miscenic hadn't quit directing. "MOVE IT JERKOFF! IF YOU DON'T, I WILL!"

"Miscenic, I said knock off and I mean knock *off*!"

The Trooper turned like a mechanical man and leaned against his car. He folded up the ham-like arms across his chest and looked at them. Lee thought, Baby Huey—the cartoon Baby Huey. From when he was a kid.

The big cop said nothing. Beck looked as if he'd made a wrong first move and was thinking how to make another start.

"What's the situation on the other side?" said Lee.

"Jesus!" said Miscenic. He shook his head. He sucked his teeth and spat.

"Who's over there?" said Beck. "Let's get specific."

"Well, Prokovic and LaBarr is over there."

"LaBarr?" The Captain was surprised.

"Yeah. LaBarr was in it. Prokovic's further down in 337."

"I know about 337. Where was LaBarr?"

"In 339, on his way back in to Everett goin' off shift. Almost the middle of it. The car's at 122.05. LaBarr's okay, though. Him and Prokovic's flagging traffic on the other side. They're both on foot. LaBarr says 339 is going to take a little shop time, but it isn't totaled or nothing. He was kind of at the tail end of it."

Beck turned back to Lee.

"Correction. *Two* units out of service to us."

"What about patrons? Have you got a count?" Lee still

hadn't got the most essential information. These troopers could talk you all around a bush. A lot of semi-legalistic habits generating a lot of verbalistic semi-garbage. A Royal Pain in the Ass—an "R.P.A."

"LaBarr gave us a count of 82 vehicular involvements. That's a first estimate, though. That's nothing final. He can't see what's in the tunnel."

"How many injured?"

"Shit, I don't know! A lot, though. Lot of bleeders. He knows of two fatalities. A baby's one of 'em."

"Jesus," said the Captain.

"Who knows what's in the tunnel?" Miscenic had his eyes down now, watching his own toe shoveling slush.

"The surface was like this. No snowtreads. Who the fuck knows what went on? LaBarr was in it and all he knows is that all of a sudden it was brake lights right in front of him and then a lot of smashing into everything in front of you and getting slammed into from behind and then it quit and it's a junkyard from back about 121.9 into the tube. Looks like more'n 30 yards into the tubes. Who knows?"

The Captain rubbed his face. Behind him big machines were being moved about.

"What the hell's the matter? Is nothing obvious to you guys? What's being done about getting over there with the *one-hundred* numbers?"

"We figured they'd be coming up from Redford just like us, going through on the westbound. Pull off on the other side, right?"

"Look at that westbound, Miscenic! It would take an hour! Get some barricades and flashers and go down as far as 124 and cut this inside lane, here. Make it one lane through the westbound tube. Open it again to two on the other side, well past it. What's the matter with you guys?"

"Captain, look. I only got here maybe fifteen minutes ago. We got our problems. *You* look at this westbound. You cut down to a single lane and she'll backlog to Breezeway!"

"Forget the goddam westbound. Let it log clear back to Harrisburg if need be."

"It will."

"Well, let it. Give these ambulances the moon on rye if that's what the hell they ask for. One lane through the tunnels. Get these injured down to Redford!"

The big man seemed confused. The Captain took his arm and moved with him down the medial.

"Come on," he said. "Let's go."

Lee made his own way toward the smoking eastbound portal. Some men had come out. A small wrecker and a couple other trucks were grouped before the gaping arch. He came around the wrecker and found Ollie Chelinski suiting up into a breathing apparatus. Two other guys were doing the same and loading things onto the trucks. Chelinski was preoccupied with straps and buckles and didn't see him.

"Ollie," Lee said. "Take me in."

The wizened little buzzard of a man squinted up at him.

"Naw, naw, Rider. You best go on back and play with yer transistors. This is heavy work, here."

"Barger in there?"

Chelinski nodded, was finished with his apparatus and climbed abruptly into the truck. A kid climbed in from the other side. Lee scrambled in behind the kid. Inside, Ollie simply looked at him. The top gun looking at the young punk kid. Then he shrugged and felt beneath the seat and came up with a smaller respirator mask he tossed to Lee.

"I don't know if this will get you by. I'm out of those what got the tanks with 'em. I need 'em for my own. You better think about it."

"I have." Lee gathered up the mask and began to work the straps, to figure out the item.

"This air in here is what yer lung association considers t' be a matter of breath and *Death*," said Ollie. "Don't say ya' wasn't warned."

He pulled his own mask down and with the same hand threw the wrecker into gear in one deft motion. Lee's head hit the back of the cab. The little wrecker leapt straight off the ground and dove into the tunnel. For some moments Lee saw stars. He fought with the mask and when he finally got the thing in place and could see out through the holes, his hair was caught in buckles, his head was aching and there wasn't much to see. Ollie drove the wrecker flat out like a demon raging down into the smoking bowels of hell. The smoking gloom streaked past them, on and on.

Eventually an orangeness began to show ahead, subtle change of color which then became a growing light, a lapping, flickering, dying and resurging thing ahead of them and growing.

Then a giant shape rose all at once out of the gloom in front of them. Ollie came down with both heavy boots hard to the floor. Lee felt himself going forward, felt his face smash into the rubber of the mask against the windshield. The tires screamed and echoed in the tunnel. Lee felt the wrecker wrench sideways, tilt up and pause dead still, two wheels in the air for enormous seconds. Then he felt it coming down. It rocked once on heavy-duty shocks. Then was still.

Lee looked out his side. A wall of orange steel girders—the bedwall of one of the big salt and gravel plow-trucks. Inches from his face. So close he knew he could not get the door open, could not get out that side. He swallowed and was furious. He wheeled on Ollie, but the little man was gone. The kid was gone. The wrecker door stood open. Lee slid across the seat and out the driver's side and down.

He couldn't really see it, yet. Not clearly. Just a big orange cloud ahead. He felt the heat of it, though. He began to make his way in that direction. There was a great deal of underfoot-debris, hoses, chunks of metal, unidentifiable things and he again found cause to regret wearing sneakers. They had gotten wet outside and cold, but now were wet and hot and no defense against metallic objects. He could take it for an hour, he decided. He would have to.

As he got closer to the blaze the sides of trucks and machinery the men had brought in became too hot to touch, the heat of the fire unfaceable, even through the mask. Men were now appearing from the gloom like phantoms and being swallowed up again as quickly. All wore the masks and heavy firecoats, helmets, leggings. How would he find Barger? It seemed hopeless he would recognize the Crew Chief from Aurora.

Then he arrived behind a solid wall of men, the front line of the battle. Beyond a broiling mountain of solid wreckage, of blackened skull of truck cab, of fenders, grills and other parts of cars, of jagged chunks of God-knows-what. Wall to wall and floor to ceiling. The crewmen hadn't even started on that wall of destruction but were training hoses and CO^2 on a molten lake of oil, gas and burning rubber—forty feet of molten combustibles between them and the tangible wreckage. He caught a glimpse of where the inside wall had broken through into the Maintenance. Lee's heart sank inside him. It was worse than his worst case of imagination could have carried him. This would take weeks. He knew it.

Then he saw it—''B-A-R-G-E-R''—spelled out in big block stenciled letters across the back of an asbestos jacket. Lee stepped forward quickly and clapped the jacket on the shoulder. It burned his hand and he withdrew it quickly. The figure turned around. It grabbed Lee's face with asbestos-gloved hands and viewed it through two sets of eyeholes. Barger seemed to start. He passed the equipment that he had in hand along to the next fellow and grabbed for Lee. Fairly shoved him back and away from the fire, made broad theatrical gestures for Lee to follow. Lee had difficulty keeping up. He was regretting the sneakers more than ever. It seemed there was ten times the junk there had been before.

After some yardage of retreat the going got easier. Barger was managing a terrific pace under all that gear, but it was not so bad, not so hot now. Lee was doing no better. Then he felt a little lightness in him, a strangeness and then he couldn't feel his feet at all, the floor had vanished.

Then the floor was coming up to meet him. Darkness closed in from all sides and that was all.

THE TOWN OF SOMERSTON—1:00 P.M.

At one o'clock the mayor of the exit town of Somerston was in the Slovak Orthodox Church at his niece's wedding. Scowling. She was more than just a niece; she was a daughter. The

Pribanics had been childless. They had taken little Maggie in when both her parents had been killed some twenty years before. His brother George. So now it was the wedding, and for L. John it was a mixed day all around. For one thing it was raining cats and dogs, and for another she was making him the in-law of his foremost ideological adversary—Big Mike Mehelic—blowhard-without-grace who nonetheless owned half of the town, the highway industry, the Feed & Grain and all of it. Mehelic and his crazy progress. Twenty years across the Council Table from laughing loudmouth in his Johnny Carson suits; now his little one puts him in bed with that! And he is picking up the bills. The dour little bull of a man shifted restlessly and plopped the butt of a cigar into the corner of his mouth. The enormous woman in the pew beside him plucked the sodden object out again and went directly back to crying. What the hell! The kids were passing the Old Chalice now and it would soon be over.

Then a hand was on his shoulder and he jumped. The usher with the palsy and the growth beside his nose was at his back, looking scared and nodding toward the rear. It was better to look back there than go on looking at this usher he decided, and he turned around. A young cop of the town was standing in the narthex with his shoulders sloping down, apologetic—and his cop hat dripping rain in his folded hands. He was looking at the mayor. The mayor shot some glances back and forth and then dismissed the whole thing with a flash of stubby fingers. Moments passed. The hand was back again upon his shoulder. When he turned around this time the cop was holding up the mayor's overcoat and making big, theatrical gestures. The mayor then was on his feet and moving up the aisle with brisk, short-legged dignity. The cop and usher held the Harry Truman overcoat while thickly muscled stubby arms shot through the sleeves and set the old brown Homburg firmly over precious little hair. He pushed his way outside and waited with exaggerated patience on the sill. A roll of Tums came from a pocket and the mayor chewed a couple while the cop caught up with him. It wasn't till the door latched behind them that he spoke.

"My niece's wedding, Jimmy. As if it's not enough!"

"Sorry, L.John. We got problems."

"I assumed as much."

"Come on."

Jimmy led them around the north side of the church and out across the overcrowded little cemetery. Minor lakes of rain had formed between graves. The mayor made a mental note that he would not be buried here. The Slovak Orthodox had been built upon the highest hill in town in 1909 and seven times thereafter razed by lightning and rebuilt again. Way up high. From the wrought iron fence you could look down on most of Somerston, the county seat, a natural crossroads center. Old route #219 came down from the north, formed the main street, intersected at the central square and courthouse by old route 31 out of the west. The square was packed with traffic coming from both directions. It was a standstill. On a clear day you could follow #219 north to where it underpassed Mehelic's beloved Eastern Turnpike. It was not a clear day, but the mayor didn't need to see the Pike to know where all this was coming from.

"Turnpike!" spat the little man.

"Them cars ain't coming from Mehelic Chevrolet."

"What happened to them now?"

"Heck if I know, L.John. Half an hour back they just started rollin' in."

"They got you any state cops yet? Help you out or nothing?"

"Nothin' so far. Not unless they came since I been up here."

The mayor spat a favored Baltic curse and turned away. "Take me down." he said.

Jimmy got them to the bottom of the Slovak Hill and couldn't break into the traffic. After fifteen minutes L.John left the car and scowled his way through standing, honking traffic to the old courthouse on foot. Now he fumbled through a two-pound ring of keys at the front doors, anxious to escape the angry honking around him and the pouring rain. There was something to June weddings, he decided.

The mayor wiped his feet elaborately. The old courthouse went back as far as '86 and four times now he'd slugged it out with the Mehelic "progress" crowd just to preserve his prize. Sure it cost a fortune just to heat the place and patch the roof. Yes, it had been wired so many times that no one left alive knew all the circuits. So what if it had cost the County seven thousand dollars just last summer to remove the trees that had been growing from the roofstones and the tower, and no—they hadn't got them all. Nor the bats. Nor the pigeons. Mehelic got his Turnpike 39 years before and the only one who'd seen any "progress" from it was Mehelic. For everybody else it was the end of quiet living. L.John had seen the kind of buildings they were making now. Nothing to respect, to say that this had been there yesterday or would last until tomorrow. The marble floors and statuary, ornate clocks and banisters and water fountains—even if they didn't work no more—it was important to the people. The elegance and spectacle, like the great churches. It gave belief and a sense of awe just setting foot inside. In forty years as mayor it had never failed to do the same for him, and so the mayor wiped his feet elaborately. The foot he set inside his courthouse would be clean.

Upstairs, the mayor's office was above the public entry, where the little man could turn his chair and look out on the comings and goings, the passings by.

The mayor squeezed around the desk and sat behind it, the price a minor avalanche of papers and debris. Forty years had heaped the office with its history; the desk was no exception. Without the catalogs upon his chair the man could just about see over it. Upon the walls old photos dating back to horse and steam construction. A motto saying, "NOT ALL CHANGE IS PROGRESS," in needlepoint had hung among them since Pribanic's second term in '31. More debris had overgrown the cast iron radiators in the cupola windows surrounding the old swivel chair.

The mayor turned it with an agonizing screech to face out toward the giant limbs of elm outside and foraged momentarily among some dozen gnarled black cigar butts drying there upon a baking tin. He looked them over and selected one and lit it with a wooden match. This done, he turned back to the desk and foraged there, extracting an old upright telephone from somewhere underneath it all, then turned out to face the world again, the phone propped on his stomach.

"Hello! Yah. This is Pribanic speaking. Connect me to the

Turnpike, please. That's right. The main place. Redford. Thank you very much. I'll wait.''

Outside a little snow was coming with the rain.

MILEPOST 123.4—1:10 P.M.

By degrees Lee became aware that some kid with a moustache was above him pressing something down into his face. Everything was lighter. Light gray—not orange light, the last thing he remembered. The kid was dressed in white. It dawned on him that he was getting oxygen. An ambulance. He brushed the mask away and sat up on the stretcher. Instantly his vision tunneled in again. He held his face and waited for the whirling to subside. Then it cleared away and he looked up. Beck and Barger stood by just outside the open back hatch, watching him with sober faces. He began to speak, but all at once his whole insides welled up. He dived for the rear hatch and pitched his Sunday dinner to the snow. Beck and Barger and the kid waited patiently, then helped him get up off his knees when it was over.

"You all right?" said Beck.

"What happened?" His mouth tasted horrible. His head pounded worse than before.

"Oxygen. You shoulda had a breather. Fire like that takes out the oxygen. Smoke mask ain't enough," said Barger. "Who the hell let you go in without one?"

Lee preferred to deal with other subjects. He turned to Beck.

"You get that inside lane open?"

Beck nodded. "They're gettin' to 'em."

"You went in there with Chelinski, dint' ja! I'm gonna kick his ass clear down to 125. He knows better!" Barger said.

"Skip it. My fault."

"Still—"

"How is it on the other side?"

The Captain shook his head and heaved a sigh. Lee knew the Captain and could read him. The way Beck looked said it all. Lee turned to the paramedic, the kid in white.

"Have you got something for a headache?"

"Have I got something for a headache!"

"Can I drive behind it?"

"Contraindicated," said the kid.

"You mean to say you haven't got a simple aspirin?"

"People don't call ambulances for aspirins."

"I got asp'rins in the truck," said Barger.

"Let's go," said Lee. He hopped down and sent the ambulance to the other side. He was angry with himself for consuming one whole ambulance when it was needed.

They walked along toward Barger's truck, keeping to the center guardrail. Beck had cut the westbound as he said he would. It was moving single file beside them, bunching like a caterpillar five miles an hour.

Three ambulances came screaming from the tunnel, the newly opened access lane, spewing slush all over them as they went by.

"How long till we have eastbound, Fred?"

The crew chief didn't meet Lee's eyes. He knew his estimate would not be popular. "Well, you've seen it."

Lee nodded. "How long?"

"We ain't makin' that much progress."

"How long?"

"Mr. Rider, I can't even really get a decent start on the tube, yet. We're just keeping that in place in there, that spreading oil. All my best equipment's working in the maintenance to keep that fire off the inner westbound wall. That's all the hell we need is for that westbound wall to crack and then we're shut down *both* ways: east *and* west. Us guys figure there's a tanker in that pileup someplace. Looks like heating oil. Some kinda oil. It's away beyond the ordinary, that's for sure!"

Damn these maintenance guys, habitual defensiveness. How was he failing to communicate that he was simply problem-solving—not getting up a crucifixion.

"What about the foam machines?" said Lee.

"I got *one*. I got it in the maintenance."

"What about yours?"

"What the hell else you think is burnin' down in there?

Shit! We had it parked right where the wall burst through. Wouldn't you know it?''

"What about the Redford armory?''

"Tried 'em. They got one down there, all right—but they can't find no one to run it up here. All them weekend warriors is out in the hills gettin' ready to shoot deer!''

"Well, send somebody down and get it! Christ!''

"I did. Redford Fire Department's coming, too. Wish to hell I knew what's keepin' them!''

They had reached the truck. Barger climbed into the front and dug things from the glove compartment. He dropped down again with a thermos and a greasy quart-sized plastic bottle of industrial aspirin. He rubbed some of the excess filth off on his sleeve and screwed the cap off.

"How many?''

"Eight.'' And he meant eight.

Barger shook them out into his hand, then got the thermos open.

"Better watch that coffee. It'll burn yer mouth out.''

It did. Lee couldn't quite decide the worse—living with the migraine or the blisters forming just inside his lips. He scooped up the least dirty snow that he could find at hand and dumped some in the thermos to cool the coffee. It took three scoops more. One by one he got the aspirins down.

"They oughta make them things to where they'll cool down just a little,'' Barger said. Lee agreed. "Half the time I can't drink that shit until I'm home.''

"Fred. The tunnel. When?''

Barger shrugged. "Say—Friday?''

"Friday?"

"Maybe we'll get lucky. Maybe there's some holes in it—you know—gaps or something. But from where that is— down around 122.3—that's damn near two-tenths of a mile of solid scrap iron to the daylight, and from what we're getting from the other side, there's rear-ends all the way to 120.4. That's a junk yard over there.''

"I know about the other side. I want simple information. I

want to know how long until we get that tunnel.''

"Even if we get 'er open in an hour chances are you can't put a patron through until you rebuild that whole west end.''

"Rebuild *what*?''

"Well, a fire that hot—that heat cracks solid rock. Heat like that can turn concrete back into sand and powder. We stand a damn good chance of having it come down on top of us while we're still workin' on it.''

"But we don't know that till we try, though, do we?''

"But we have a pretty good idea—''

"We really don't *know*.''

"No.''

"Terrific.'' Lee felt a blister with his tongue and squinted at the westbound. He looked back at Fred. "You get carte blanche on this. Get back all the men you need—the entire goddam payroll, I don't care. Call 'em in. I want them here. I'll authorize it. Anything! How's that?''

"I can try—''

"What the hell is 'try?' ''

"Well, it's like them armory guys, anybody got time off is out for the deer season! Hell, I'd be out myself but what Cotchum pulled seniority on me an'—''

"Tell them that they *start* on double time. Beck is witness. I authorize that, too. Maybe that would do some good!''

"Maybe, if I can *reach* 'em!''

"*You* got ways. All you guys have got CB. Call their wives. Whatever. Just do it! That's all I got to say.''

Barger shrugged. "You're the boss.''

"You're goddam right I am.'' Rider started off with Beck, then turned again. "Another thing. There isn't going to be much left when you start pulling pieces out of there.'' He meant the tunnel.

"Not much, no.''

"Save the engine blocks. Take them down to Everett, and don't fuck up the numbers. Maybe we can find out who they were. Some of them at any rate.''

They had gone a few yards down the mountain. Lee was heading for his car. He turned to the captain, couldn't seem to think of what to say. They went several paces toward Lee's car in silence. Then he stopped and said it.

"I know what you're thinking. We'll shut the eastbound down at Somerston. Okay. Agreed."

"Too late for Somerston. *Way* too late."

"Donovan, then. But I'm telling you, John, of all the damn days of the year to route them off on #30—"

"Yes. I know. I couldn't agree more completely. We shut down at Donovan a quarter of an hour ago."

Lee looked at him a long time. The man had overstepped his bounds. A cop did not just shut down 32 miles of Eastern Turnpike on singular authority. Not even the troop captain. On the other hand, he was right. Lee had nothing to say. He turned and resumed walking. The captain followed.

"Beck, you piss me off," he said.

The captain made no comment.

"You're going to need more units. I'll call down east and see if I can scare you up some loaners."

"Thanks. We have some coming, though."

"Get a couple units down to Somerston. They'll be swamped."

"341 is there, but we could use some more. 337 and 339 are still stuck on the mountain."

Lee stopped. It was obvious he couldn't contribute much more here.

"Yeah, well, same goes for you as for the maintenance. Call back every man in Troop T. If that's what it takes, then by God we'll simply have to pay them."

"Fine."

"Clear that backlog off the bypass and open it at Donovan again. I don't want any patrons driving one more inch of #30 than they absolutely have to. We may have to run them around one mountain, but not two—nor any longer than we have to."

Lee tried to pack authority behind it but was feeling about as useful as tits on a boar.

"My sentiments exactly," said the captain. "That it for now?—because if it is, my car's back *that* way."

"Huh? Oh yeah—sure." Lee was looking skyward. Soggy

flakes were now outnumbering the drops of rain, a slight majority and mostly melting as they hit the ground but coming down the size of quarters.

"You know something I don't know, don't you?" Beck said.

"I wouldn't bet my own money," Lee said. "What is it you don't know?"

"The weather?"

The man knew what he didn't know. That had to be some special category of phenomenon.

"The word I have is not until tomorrow, but I don't like the look of this at all," Lee said. "In any case I'm glad I didn't bet my money." There was a pause during which no one knew what to say. Beck pointed at Lee's feet suddenly.

"Oh, yeah, that. Well. Not really working. Sunday. I'm going straight home."

"Right. You better get those off. They're soaking."

Yes they *were* soaking. Lee knew they were soaking. Both of them watched Lee's sneakers soaking for some moments. Then Lee broke it. "Hey. I gotta run. Keep things moving. Keep in touch."

"10-4."

Beck started back. Another ambulance came by, sending both up on the guardrail. It was getting to be automatic. Lee turned his back, but the slosh got him just the same. As he was slapping globs of it off his "London Fog," a car horn blasted near enough to anger him. He looked up in time to see an old car with college decals and the face of a vacant youth gaping at him. Behind the face a feminine hand waved vigorously. He dipped to see. Charlene! Then the car was past him as the caterpillar unbunched and surged forward again. He returned the wave, almost as if to stop it, but in that grinding westbound there just wasn't any way. The car kept moving. It was gone.

So. That was "Clifford". He could use a shave.

Lee decided he could use a milkshake. Aspirins and black coffee on an empty stomach hadn't been a bright idea.

EASTERN MARYLAND—THE BRADEN FARM—NEAR REISTERSTOWN—1:10 P.M.

A few dark ducks had come upon the old farm pond near Reisterstown to rest and feed and wait the weather out. The rain had stopped for now, but the leaden overcast only promised more and so the ducks remained content to poke and browse among the cattails and the dry brown reeds—keeping casually beyond the reach of one small boy upon a makeshift raft and an equally makeshift dog who watched the lot of them from the shore. The dog was shorthaired, black and white, fat with age and very pregnant too. She had followed boy and raft around the pond a half dozen times and now was cold. Chasing ducks was out in her advanced condition. She was bored. Now she held to one position and shivered patiently, letting out a solitary yap from time to time that said "let's go!" The boy was sopping to the knees. His claptrap assemblage of old boards was largely under water even with his eighty pounds, but he kept it moving ponderously along with growing skill and a "borrowed" laundry pole.

Then the pole stuck deeply in the bottom ooze and held. The raft moved on and out from under and the boy found himself above the water, clinging to an upright shaft of wood. The embrace was ardent. Moments passed. Then—with the grandeur of a great sequoia felled—they both went down.

There was considerable thrashing.

The boy stood up. It was an old pond, long in need of dredging, and nowhere deeper than a foot or two. He stood knee-deep regarding his disloyal craft for several moments as it glided somberly away. Then he turned and started slogging resolutely for the shore.

A thought arrested him. He reached inside his jacket, and extracted a sodden object and carefully unfolded it. A better-than-average *Playboy* centerfold. He studied it and considered elaborate techniques of restoration.

"Shit," he said. He balled it up and chucked it and continued slogging for the shore.

At 1:10 P.M. Dan Braden, Jr. was in the farmyard driveway

packing up the family wagon, both anxious and unanxious to be leaving for Detroit. Unanxious because he'd grown up on this farm. During the Thirties. The Whiz-Kid. Boy-Of-The-Glowing-Future, when technology was promising art deco-Flash Gordon outcomes to all problems. It had not turned out that way. A fragment of his crystal-set antenna still clung to the giant syca-more out front. The balsa aircraft models still hung from the ceil-ing of his room. And it wasn't only his imagination. Beneath the bed the box of *Popular Mechanics* was carefully preserved, the glowing promises still there documented on yellow pages. He had gone on and become the engineer, the competent technologist. But all the so-called advances had brought bad surprises with them, side effects which more than offset the benefits. The out-looks on energy and population he got from his job and from what life in Detroit was doing to his kids made the old farm har-der to leave every time he came. Made it tougher to resume the grind.

But he was anxious to be leaving too, to get off early and ahead of the big rush. If he had to leave a place he'd rather be in for one he wouldn't, he could at least take advantage of the sin-gle option left him—to minimize the hassle. Not eliminate, just minimize. The best that anyone could do these days. It was down to that, it was down to having to count such slender shavings as blessings. That got to him the most—everybody settling for less and less each year and glad to get it. Dan Braden, Jr. was ready, inside himself, to turn it all around and come back to the farm. The thing now was to convince the wife. Irene was just not ready to give up the dream. To let go. He was working on it. But for the present he had this single, puny option and was going to take it. Just for now.

Braden Senior had been squinting at the sky the entire four days of the visit.

"I still think you ought to let me help you get them snow-treads on. It's a long ways north to Detroit, Danny."

Fourth time he had said that in an hour. That was the other thing. The folks were slowing down. The farm was showing signs, little shabbinesses everywhere, evidences of little inatten-tions everywhere. Little, but a lot of them, as if the farm were getting old and wearing out. Farms did not wear out, people did.

It was getting ahead of them. Dan could see the time coming soon when they would not be able to keep up with it at all. His father had hinted at unloading "the old place," and that had stung Dan more than he expected. It had shaken the foundations of a boyhood sense of the permanence of home. The thought of its not being there would close the only backdoor from the "temporary" life he carried on. Dan had decided this year that he couldn't have that happen. It would cost him his last shred of personal security. He had realized just this trip that what he had in Detroit wasn't *home*. It never had been. Home was here. He had to get his family to see that, too.

"I don't want them, Dad." It was the fourth time he had said it since breakfast. "Unless I absolutely have to, it cuts my mileage down to nothing."

Irene and his mother had come down from the house with final items, the carcass of the leftover turkey balled in foil among them as usual.

"Dad, will you leave off of that?" his mother said. "Land sakes you're about to drive poor Danny crazy. We ain't had a white Christmas here in seven years!"

"Not here, Mother," said his Dad. "But Detroit is further north, you know."

They were arguing this year. They never used to argue.

"Still. We ain't had a white Christmas now in seven years." She handed him the ball of foil. "Here, Danny. Put this in someplace."

Irene started to protest. As usual. The whole routine was some kind of machine that started up and did this every year.

"Oh, now Mom, that isn't necessary. Your son makes a decent living," Irene said.

"Let's just say a living," said Dan. Irene shot him a glance that said not to start this up again.

"No, now you just take it," said his mother. "I let you talk me out of it last year and here I found the dang thing in the freezer yet Memorial Day. Dad gets sick of turkey quick as anything and you got children's mouths to feed which we do not no more so take it, now, go on! I don't want to hear another thing about it!"

That had been six years ago, not one. But why make a hassle over it? Forgive them. The folks were getting old. He found a chink for the carcass and jammed it in as always. He straightened a now-aching back and looked around. He wasn't getting any younger himself. Maybe it was just the rainy weather. He wondered when it would be starting up again.

He turned to Irene. "Is that the last?"

"I guess," she said. "I think so."

"Where's the kids?"

"Christine is in the house. I don't know about Eddie."

"You'll probably find him out behind the barn," said elder Braden. "He's been out there hammering them old boards since yesterday. Building some kind of thing the way you used to do, remember?"

"He ain't back of the barn with them old boards!" the mother rebuked the older man.

"Margaret, the boy went back there with me when I went out to help the cow this morning! He was out there yesterday as well."

"Well, I was with the chickens an hour back and he wasn't anyplace in sight. You better go and find him. That dang boy can get further off and faster than a she-cat in her time. Me and Irene, here, will go inside and try to pry your daughter off the television."

Dan and his father started toward the barn, his mother and his wife back to the house. The women had reached the house and started up the steps when Eddie and the dog came around the corner of the house.

"EDDIE!" screamed his mother. It echoed off the broad, flat surface of the barn. "WHAT HAPPENED!?"

The men came running.

Ed looked like *The Creature from the Black Lagoon*. Mud from head to foot. In his pockets and his ears. He was shivering. He had to pee. The old pregnant dog knew her limitations and retreated to a certain distance to avoid getting stepped on. She knew the sound of this and it was trouble.

"What happened?" said his father.

"Nuthin'," said Eddie.

His grandmother took him by the ear and dragged him up the steps.

"You get right into this house this minute, young man. You'll catch your death out here this way." They disappeared into the house.

Irene followed up the steps, turned back to Dan.

"Dan, will you get Eddie's suitcase out again? It's the brown one with the stripe."

"Wait a minute, Irene. How long is all this going to take?"

"Dan, he's got to have a bath. I'm sorry."

She turned and dashed into the house.

The men returned to the station-wagon and began to unpack. The brown-one-with-the-stripe was on the bottom. It all had to come out. It began to rain a little.

Braden Senior helped his son in silence for a while until he'd worked up nerve enough to try it one more time.

"Now that everything's unloaded we could get them snow-treads on," he said. "We got the time now."

Dan grabbed the suitcase and started for the house.

"Why not?" he said.

A LITTLE NORTH OF COLEMAN, WEST VIRGINIA—1:30 P.M.

Evan J. Baker was at 38 an independent trucker for the second year of his life. After twenty years of driving rigs for other guys, the eighteen wheels beneath him were his own. Second hand and mortgaged till forever, but his own. In a few more miles they'd be home from this haul to Fort Wayne, Indiana. Evan J. wasn't making out on this one, he hadn't found a load for the return. When the trailer rode empty the old Peterbilt was high-priced transportation. There were payments to be made.

It wasn't like it used to be with Em on this trip either. Em at 14, was his kid and always used to love going on the hauls, sleeping in the sleeper and eating in the places where they knew her Daddy's name and gave her extra ice cream on her pie. When the haul came up so timed to school vacation Thursday he thought it would be just fine for her to come along, but she had balked and kind of toed the ground. She finally said yes only when he broke down and admitted he could use the company.

Evan figured it was the mare, the foal so close to coming, but that wasn't all of it; it was more. She looked the same, denim clothes, the gum and all. Em had gotten solemn—serious as hell in the past year. She kept her nose inside that *True Romances* comic all the time and when it wasn't that her mind was someplace else completely. Evan J. figured he would give it one more try. He rolled the volume down on Jimmy Reeves' ol' *Blizzard Comin' On* tape that he had sent for from TV. He leaned over to see which soap opera she was rereading now. Oh. That *Gordon and Louise*. Evan J. cleared his throat. He was going a long way for a snatch of conversation.

"So how come she don't go with *him*?"

"What?" Em did not look up.

"If he can't go with her, then how come she can't go with him? That Gordon there's a doctor, ain't he? They sure as hell don't need the money."

Em flashed a look at him some way that said he had to be about as dumb as you can get.

"It ain't the money," she said.

Evan J. rubbed the stubble of his chin and thought it over. "Must be nice," he said.

"Naw you don't get it," she said. "They're the kind that cain't respect each other 'cept the only reason they're together is they wanna be and not because they have to."

"Must be nice," he said.

Em went back to brooding in the story. For a little while.

"Other folks is got their troubles, too,'" she said.

Home came into sight now, was like a lot of other places thereabouts. Tarpaper semi-farm on three-plus acres—mud yard, butane tank, a lot of automotive junk and several dogs they hadn't counted on. Em stuck the comic book back into her jeans and sat up straight. To catch sight of the mare, no doubt. All she seemed to care about anymore. Evan braked and dropped down through the gears. It was a tight trick to get the rig into the drive. As he pulled to a stop a battered old maroon Ford pickup tore out past them, fishtailing and slinging mud. The back tire screeched and threw a puff of smoke as it hit the blacktop. The truck tore off down the road and was gone. Evan J. rolled the window down and squinted after it into the rain.

"Hey, that's old Hubert. Wonder what's his hurry?"

"Let's go," said Em. "I wanna check on Molly."

Evan J. rolled the rig up by the house and shut her down. Em was down and gone across the drive yard, heels flinging up little chunks of sticky clay. The mare showed her head around the corner of the shabby barn in the adjoining small corral, nickering at Em in recognition. Evan J. gathered up a few things off the seat and went inside. What could anybody do with women?

The place was a shambles. Lights on, ashtrays heaping over, beer cans everywhere, spills on the linoleum. The radio was playing in the back—back in the kitchen. Some country preacher railing on and on about his Jesus and his lack of funds. Not a soul around.

"Hey, Jean! It's us. We're back."

She was his second wife and she had had a few of these before. Jean had been a road-stop singer when he met her. Evan J. never said too much about these parties. He let her have them. Down inside himself instinctively knowing anyone that had to make a living singing, bad as she sang, had a special need for the limelight now and then. Jean was just like him—just like anybody else—he figured. People take what they can get. Ten-to-one she was passed out on the upstairs bed right now. Evan J. checked the ground floor rooms in case, then went up to see.

Em had hit the fence flying, and her heart blew up inside her. Molly was a whole lot thinner! And she was nickering excitedly, like she had something super that she couldn't wait to tell. Em topped the fence and dropped into the mud. Molly led into the darkness of the sheltered lean-to.

It was adorable! The fuzzy little foal was dry, got up pretty good out of the straw, and was walking strong. A colt! A future stallion. It must have happened yesterday. She missed it! Molly seemed forgiving and it looked like things had gone okay, but her Pa and his doggone company!

Molly started nudging hard, kept nudging, damn near knocked Em over. Em checked her feed. No oats. No hay, no nothing. Damn that Jean! Never thought of nobody but Jean. Em pulled down a full half bale of alfalfa, a double measure each of oats and corn. Molly had it coming. Damn! She done fine! A couple apples just to celebrate. A couple more for congratulations. That horse was hungry!

Em leaped the fence again and went racing for the house, took the porch steps three at a time, and there were only four.

"Hey, Pa! She done it! She's got her foal! She done it, Pa!" She charged around the bottom floor, then bounced up the stairs. She froze solid at the bedroom door.

Evan J. was just sitting there completely still on the edge of the old bed, cap in hands like prayin'. Jean was white and gray, her blood smeared and spattered over everything, and she was dead as stone.

Evan J. spoke up after a while—hoarse and low.

"Did you know about yer Ma and Hubert?"

"He—used to come around."

"How come you never said nuthin'?"

"Didn't seem like nuthin'."

Then for a long time there was no other sound except the drumming rain, the preacher in the kitchen far below.

MILEPOST # 140—1:30 P.M.

Rider was below the snow line, below Kregg Maintenance and almost down the mountain. The snow had come no further down and for the time it even seemed as though the rain had lessened. Lee was playing with the apparatus jammed beneath his dashboard. One meter in particular had his attention. The needle would hold steady for a while, then fall and jump again erratically. He picked up his mike.

"Redford, this is Mobile 014, Lee Rider. Call me back." There was no reply. He called again.

"Redford 'by'. Go ahead." Finally an answer.

"Judy—How's my signal?"

"Five-by-five. What's the matter? Did you call before?"

"10-4. Had complaints from anybody else?"

"Not so far. You getting jerks from 12 again?"

"10-4. I'm reading an erratic carrier."

VHF radio behaves like light, it's line-of-sight and can't get over mountains well, or much beyond horizons. The Turnpike system maintained a complex string of microwave relay towers combined with robot radio repeater stations all along the line to pick up calls and then rebroadcast them from greater elevations so communications would remain dependable in mountainous terrain and intact along the system.

Of all 29 repeaters, *Murphy's Law,* of course would have it, the ones that had the "gnomes", the inexplicable and chronic problems, were in the least accessible locations. "Twelve" was perched high upon the wind-swept rocky crag above Aurora Tunnel known as "Bald Knob" and had become notorious among the techs as the foremost R.P.A. Terrain was such it couldn't be approached by going up from the tunnel. It was a trip of 39 strange, rutted miles of winding dirt road around to the northwestern face and up across state game lands—the last ten miles traversable by trailbike, snowmobile, or mountain goat. Good old Number 12 was acting up again. Without it there would be no radio communications between Redford and the western slope at all. There would be big "blind" spots along the eastern slope between Aurora tubes and Redford. Perfect timing. He was not having problems reaching Redford, but probably because he was so close, now within five miles and on the level land, not on the mountain.

"I'll check it out," said Judy.

"Any more from Tri-State?"

"Negative."

"Would you call and see if Chuck is home?" Chuck Ellis, Eastern Turnpike Public Relations Director.

"Sure." Judy broke the transmission, then came back again.

"Lee, the mayor of Somerston is on the line. He says he wants to talk to you."

"Oh, boy. Not now, Judy. Tell him I'll call back."

"I told him. He's been holding. And holding. And holding."

Lee let out a sigh. Old Pribanic had no love for the Pike. No doubt what it was all about. Face the music, Lee decided. Now or later. What the hell?

"Okay, Judy. Patch him on." Lee waited. Pops and bursts of noise came from the speaker.

More waiting. A channel seemed to open—a white-noise hiss, a clear sound. Judy's voice was modified by telephone, now.

"Okay, Mr. Pribanic. You can talk now."

"Hah? To who? Who is this?"

"Lee Rider, Mr. Pribanic. Can I help you?"

"That you, Mr. Rider?"

"Yes, L.John. What can I do for you?"

"I think we got a bad connection, Mr. Rider. You sound funny."

"I'm in my car, L.John. We're on the radio."

"What?"

"144 to 347." An ambulance had broken over their channel.

"Who was that?"

"We're on the radio, L.John. We may have to put up with some other traffic. It's kind of like a party line, now what can I do for you?"

"I got trouble down here, Mr.—"

"144 to 347. Where the hell are *you*, three-four-seven?"

"347 by."

"Well, I hope to God! We got a bleeder here. We need escort off the ramp and through the town at 145.1. We need it now."

"10-4, one-forty-four, I'm right behind you."

"Hallo? Hallo?"

"Hang on a second, L.John. Judy, are you copying?"

"10-4."

"I'm switching to the other channel to get clear of traffic. Switch L.John over, would you please?"

"10-4."

Lee set his dial and waited. More pops and bursts of noise.

"2204 to 2237. Where the hell's that generator, George? I can't get these pumps in operation without no goddam generator!"

Maintenance. Some of the boys had switched onto the alter-
nate channel. At least it wouldn't interfere as much with medical.
A few more pops and hisses, then the telephone ambience again.
Judy's voice.

"All right, Mr. Pribanic. We're set up again."

"Can I talk now?"

"Lee Rider, again, L. John. Sorry but you can hear we're
pretty busy up here. I guess you are too."

"Yes, Mr. Rider. You got problems. I can see that."

"L.John, we have a bad wreck inside the tunnels. Bad fire
You're getting our backlog now, I suppose."

"2204 this is 2237. You will get your goddam generator just
as soon as I can get the S.O.B. that left this grader parked in
front of it, that's when!"

"Hallo? Hallo?"

"Here, L.John. How long have you been getting our spilloff?"

"Forty-five minutes—an hour. Is everything shut down
completely?"

"The Westbound is still partly open. We're routing off at
Donovan, putting them back on at Redford. That's sending them
through you, I know. I'm sorry L.John. There's nothing else for
us to do."

"Not that big generator, George! How the hell'm I gonna
get a 45-K.W. in through all this shit? Use your fuckin' head!
Get me that 15-K.W. over by the access gate."

"There ain't any 15-K.W. anything by any access gate!
What the hell are you talking about?"

"L. John?"

"Yes, Mr. Rider."

"There was ten minutes ago!"

"Mr. Rider?"

"Well, there ain't now! There's an asphalt roller there now.
You want a goddam asphalt roller?"

"L.John?"

"Yes, Mr. Rider."

"Sorry. These boys are under quite a lot of pressure. . ."

"That's okay, Mr. Rider. I am familiar with men when they

work together. What it sounds like. How long do you expect this to be going on?''

"You may as well know it, L.John. We'll be lucky if we open late tomorrow. It's about the worst I've seen."

"I can see you have big trouble. I can see that. You say the west is open?''

"Yes. It's slow here, but should be fine on your side. Why?''

"Well, my niece. Her wedding today. They wanna get away. The honeymoon. You know."

"How far West?''

"Aspen. Colorado. Where they ski."

Lee let out a long, low whistle through the mike. "Boy, I don't know, L.John. Aspen!"

"They're skiers, Mr. Rider. They ski."

"You couldn't have them put it off a day and see about tomorrow?''

"These kids? Trouble enough getting them to stay for the wedding!"

Lee paused, then pushed the button on the mike again.

"I guess you ought to know it, L.John. We're getting some advisories. We could be in for weather."

"Hey, 2204, George ain't never gonna find that little generator. We got it over here."

"Hallo—hallo? Mr. Rider?"

"Where the hell is 'here'? Who is this? Who the hell is Rider?''

"L.John?''

"Yes, Mr. Rider? You said something about the weather? What kind of weather? Snow?''

"If not tonight, then probably tomorrow. But it all comes from the west, so the further west you go . . . I'd really try and get them to put it off a day if I were you. By then we'll know."

"Thanks for the information, Mr. Rider. I will try."

"I would if I were you. Look, L.John. I have to go. We're sending some of the State Patrol boys down to help you with that traffic. It's taking a while since everything's so plugged up here. I'll let you know about the weather just as soon as I hear more. Are you in your office? Is that where you'll be?''

"I'm going out for maybe half an hour, then I'll be back. I'll be in my office."

"Okay. When I hear I'll let you know."

"Thank you, Mr. Rider."

"L.John, I really wouldn't let them go."

"Goodbye, Mr. Rider. I'll see what I can do."

The mayor perched the phone precariously upon the heaping desk and stared at it for several moments. The roll of Tums came out again. He chewed a couple more, and then got up and left his office.

REDFORD CENTRAL—1:39 P.M.

Lee was pulling up in front of Central when he got another call.

"Redford to Rider."

"What is it Judy?"

"Tri-State's on the line."

"Patch it on." A few more pops, then— "Hello Jim."

"That you Lee?"

"Yep. Hit me."

"8 P.M.—8:30. It is really moving."

"Thanks. I needed that. How bad?"

"The Lakes'll warm it up some, but it'll pick up water, too. 18 inches, upper 20's."

"18 inches!?" Lee was thinking of Ohio—of Charlene. Still time. If the traffic further west kept moving.

"I don't suppose it helps to know?" Sometimes Nadel was irritating, looking to see if all his information came to any practical value.

"I don't know." said Lee. "Will you be there?"

"I'll be here. I'll keep in touch."

"Good."

Nadel hung up. Lee called Central again.

"Judy, have you got Pribanic's number?"

"10-4."

"Did you get in touch with Chuck Ellis?"

"Yes. He's home."

"Not anymore, he isn't. Tell him I want him here. It looks like we got a lot to do."

SOMERSTON V.F.W.—2:05 P.M.

More people came to drink beer than had been at the wedding. The mayor halted in the doorway of the ballroom of the V.F.W. with Homburg dripping in one hand and made note of that. He was paying for it. But he didn't waste himself in senseless outrage. That was people. That was just to be expected.

The bride and groom were gamboling across the floor. They had it to themselves. The people ringed the ballroom—clapping, whistling, stuffing themselves and making happy jibes. The first dance was for them alone. It was tradition. He would wait until the second tune when others would join in and he could cross the room without making a distraction.

Big Mike was on the other side, cutting the cake and passing big chunks out to everyone who came. Mehelic's tiny, dried out wife stood behind the tables with him, squinting through thick lenses, watching what people took and how much from the spread. Rose begrudged the sun to shine. A crazy pair. L.John had always thought so. The mayor hoped his son-in-law had met a happy middle somewhere in between.

Then there was a lot of shouts and cheering and the second dance started. Everybody moved onto the floor. L.John started for the tables, bumped into a man with a mug and got beer all down his overcoat. He had hoped to reach the cake in quietness and anonymity but Big Mike caught sight of him. Big Mike was laughing. Big Mike was always laughing.

"L.John! Have some cake! You're paying for it! Ha!ha!ha!"

The mayor had some bones to pick with God. Big Mike was one of them. He wondered why it was that God should make a man so loud.

"L.John! Have some cake! You're paying for it! Ha!

He had come to where they were now, but ignored the outstretched offering of cake. He would cut his own cake, thank you. He reached down and rolled a pickle in a slice of dark salami and took a bite. He watched the kids.

His wife came up beside him. She sat down at once behind the tables in deference to his height in public. It was nothing he'd requested or was aware of. Privately she felt her size actuely and was grateful to be married. They were married forty years and it was something that he never knew.

Mehelic kept on pushing.

"What's this? No cake?"

L.John ignored it, pointed at the dancing kids. They were joyous. Young. Rabbits in the grass.

"Little Mike. He does a lot of jumping. You know, up and down."

"Hah! You'll notice who's with him! You don't want cake, then what about a beer?"

"A beer. Okay." The mayor took the beer, ingested half of it at once. He wiped his mouth. The beer went well against the peppercorns of the salami. "Maybe you could talk to Mike. Get him not to go," he said. He rolled another pickle in salami.

"Not to go? You mean tonight?" The loud man roared. "You're nuts! What for?"

"Oh, I'm nuts, huh? You saw outside. The mess we got. What about your Turnpike, now, huh?"

"L.John, it's a wreck that's all. They'll take care of it. They always take care of it. Besides, the west is open. I heard about it. Have another beer!"

"HEY MIKE! HEY MAGGIE! YOU KIDS COME OVER! I WANNA TALK TO YOU!" The little mayor had a lot of voice inside of him when he needed it. Unlike certain of his in-laws he could keep it for the necessary times. Heads turned and couples here and there quit dancing.

"NEVER MIND YOU OTHER PEOPLE. JUST THE KIDS. THAT'S ALL. HEY, YOU KIDS! COME OVER!"

Big Maggie touched his arm. "Ssh! John." She was the only one in all the world who simply called him "John." "You are making such a noise!"

"I need such a noise. HEY! YOU KIDS! COME ON!"

The bride's face was livid as she dragged her husband off the floor.

"Okay, Pop. What is it?"

Big Maggie shook her head in sadness. They loved each

other dearly, but it always came out fights. When he zigged she zagged—like not being able to get past somebody in a hallway.

The mayor looked the bridegroom over thoroughly. "Little Mike."

"Yeah, L.John."

"Mike. You're leaving tonight, you kids. Aspen. Right away."

"Well—sure."

"You couldn't wait and see about tomorrow?"

Little Maggie's face went white. "Pop, what are you saying?"

"I'm saying stay for one night only. One night and see about tomorrow."

"You're crazy! What for?" Little Maggie shoved her hew husband behind her and took the front line of the action. Mike would have to fight to wear the pants in his new family. It was plain to see.

"We'll get you a place in one of Mehelic's motels." said the mayor. "You'll be in motels anyway. What's the difference?"

"The difference is we wanna be away. I suppose you don't understand."

"Motels is motels."

"Bull *shit*!" Her face was red, now.

"Keep your lousy mouth a secret from your mother, Maggie!"

Young Mike found his voice at last. "L.John, I got one week and then I'm back at work. It's a long way to Aspen."

"That's right. A thousand miles away."

He had to admire Mike for not working for Mehelic Chevrolet, Mehelic Feed and Implement, Mehelic Dairy Industries, Mehelic Highway Motel. Mike was on his own. It *was* asking a lot. However.

"Look. Mike. It isn't something I just dreamed up, this."

"No, I didn't figure."

"I was talking to that Rider fella at the Turnpike. *He* says not for you to go. He says we *could get* weather."

"*Could* get weather? Oh, come *on*, Dad!"

"You shut up in this. I gave you to your husband and you're his. It's up to him what he will do. I'm passing information. A word to the wise. That's all."

"What kind of weather, L.John?" Little Mike was giving him his say. Little Mike was much different from his father. L.John found that profoundly encouraging.

"He thinks it will snow."

"He thinks—he *thinks*?" Little Maggie kept on building. She was like a snapping turtle that one. She did not let go until it thundered.

"Yeah, he thinks!" the mayor thundered. "He must be thinking pretty hard. They're putting on more people."

Big Mike handed him another beer. "It's Thanksgiving, L.John. They always put more on at Thanksgiving. Shut up and have a beer. Enjoy!"

L.John took the beer and put it on the table to get rid of it. It slopped a little on the cold cuts. Rose clucked her tongue and rolled her eyes away, as if the fault were L.John's.

"They're putting on more people on top of the Thanksgiving people, Mike. I put it up to you. *He* said not to go. He said specifically not to let the kids go west. It comes out of the west. One day. See about tomorrow."

"Well—"

The bride was astounded that her Mike would even think of it.

" '*Well*?' Are you kidding? Come with me."

She dragged him back onto the dance floor. They started dancing and were talking. Mike was not wholehearted. He was on defense. Soon they quit and were exchanging words. Suddenly she dragged him back to the tables.

"Gimme a coin. A quarter. Anything."

"What for?" said Rose.

"Never mind, just gimme one. You'll get it back!"

Big Mike came up with fifty cents and passed it over.

"How's that?" he said.

His shriveled wife regarded him with shocked and frightened eyes. You would have thought it was the deed to the house Big Mike was handing over.

The bride looked set to cry or scream or kill somebody.

"Nice going, Uncle L.John. This time it's my wedding and you walked all over it. You think you owe your dead brother some kind of weirdo debt. You always tried to keep me in an incubator. You're even talking Mike into it. That is *not* the way my life with Mike is going to be! I'll give you fifty-fifty—both of you. I'm gonna take this fifty cents and flip it. If it comes up your way then we stay. If it comes up mine, we're going. That's my best offer. Otherwise we're leaving—now. Or I'm going by myself." She looked hard at young Mike. "Whichever."

Red was coming up around the mayor's collar. No one said anything for what seemed an hour. Suddenly he snatched the coin from her hand and came out from the tables. Without a further word he pushed into the center of the ballroom floor and raised his hands.

"HEY! SHUT UP YOU BAND GUYS! QUIET, NOW! EVERYBODY! MAY I HAVE YOUR ATTENTION FOR A MINUTE, PLEASE." The band wheezed down. The dancing people faded off the floor. It got quiet fast. A little coughing. The mayor waited till it settled. All the way, till it quieted clear down.

"OKAY, okay now. This is what it is. You saw the town. It's a wreck up in the tunnels—we know all about that—but there is more. I called up that Rider fellow at the Turnpike and he said to me there's weather coming."

There was a murmur through the people. "You mean like '74, L.John?" came voices. "When? I didn't hear it on the news!" came others.

"Wait a minute—wait a minute. It's not for sure. It's for maybe. But they are putting on more people. So, it's good we are together. So I can tell you. We could be ready. Not like 1950 that time. Or '74." There was a little pause, a silence. No coughing *now*. The mayor got his way with crowds; he always had. "So, I put this up to Mike and Maggie—whether they should go. This fella Rider says it's 'not to be advised.' That's what they talk like, you know—'not to be advised.' I asked these kids to wait and see about tomorrow. One day. That's all. But it's the honeymoon and Maggie she is hot to go."

L.John allowed a little smile to show, to spark little outbreaks of suggestive laughter and let them flash among the people. Maggie's arms were folded tightly, a lump of muscle pulsing in her jaw. She met his gaze unblinking. He turned back to the people.

"Mike, he can't decide. On your wedding night could you? So there's nothing to be had from him."

The mayor let the eyes and laughter fall on Mike now, let it gradually subside, then raise the stubby hands for silence once again.

"I will throw this coin where all can see. If Maggie calls it, then they go. It it falls the other way they stay and see about tomorrow. I want it seen by everyone so whatever happens our town won't be arguing forever, making blame and accusations. Everyone come closer. Everybody gather close around. Everyone must see."

Mike and Maggie came onto the floor. The ring of people tightened around the trio. The room was deadly still. L.John turned and took a long, slow look around the room, then took two steps backward, clear of Mike and Maggie. He swung the spinning coin up almost to the ceiling. It hung there briefly, then came crashing down to wheel in circles. You could hear the sound of it in every corner of the room. It roared upon the varnished hardwood on its edges.

"Step on it," said L.John.

Maggie's foot came down as though upon a roach.

"Call it!"

"Heads," she said.

Heads it was.

The people pressed in from all sides to see. L.John nodded somberly. He looked hard at his foster son-in-law.

"Mike, you take good care."

"I will, L.John."

The mayor looked at both of them, then turned and left the ballroom. He signaled to the band. It started up again. It better. He was paying for that, too.

Big Maggie shook her head in sadness.

Rose Mehelic pushed through and grabbed the fifty cents.

The people drifted back to dancing.

NORTHERN WEST VIRGINIA—2:20 P.M.

"Breaker! Breaker! Any trucker. Any brother on the road. A big 10-33!"

The West Virginia trooper poured himself a chicken soup from one of the two large thermoses and listened idly to the prattle on the CB. He had sat here in his favorite radar trap all day, catching nothing but a cold for his trouble. Nobody was making time in this kind of downpour. Nothing on CB to keep a man awake. The scalding soup brought momentary tears. "Big-10-33!" Ten-to-one one of these trucking clowns had over-loaded, busted an axle. Nothing more. They really loved to get dramatic.

"Ah, 10-4 Breaker; what is your '-33?" Some other clown was answering, of course; loved to play at "big time" emergencies. Some day they were gonna get one—*then* what would they do?

"Ah—much obliged. I'm lookin' for a '66 maroon Ford pickup with a raised suspension. Cement mixin' stuff on back. Vicinity of Morgantown, or Uffington or Dellslow. If you see him I would like to have the '-20."

"10-4, Breaker—if I lay eyeball on your guy, tell me this: why should I?"

" 'Cause the guy just cut my woman's throat from ear to ear, that's why. She's murdered. By *him*!"

Smokey choked and spurted scalding chicken soup all down his manhood. A confusion of exclamatory bursts came from the CB. The road was listening. Everybody had their "ears on" for this one.

He grabbed his mike.

"Ah, Breaker—is that homicide for real?"

"Smokey, you turn in at Coleman, R.D.#4—third mailbox north of town and see how real it is."

The cop was smoldering. How the hell did these guys always know it was Smokey?

"Is that your '-20 now?"

"Hell, no I ain't there now! I am moving, Smokey. I got business!"

"Negatory, Breaker. You turn around and meet us there!"

"Not until I catch that '66 Ford pickup, Smokey. And in the future you don't want people knowin' that you're "Smokey" I'd advise against you usin' words like 'homicide'."

"Breaker, go on home! We'll pick up your man no problem!"

"It ain't no problem. We gone by."

"Breaker?"

Silence. Not even other chatter. "Come back, Breaker—you get home, now."

Static. Nothing. The trooper put the CB up, picked up the mike for Police VHF and called his base in Morgantown.

Evan J. Baker had the hammer down. The rig was screaming east on old Route 7, empty trailer thundering behind. Beside him on the seat, a venerable old 12-gauge Remington with hardly any bluing left at all, three new busted open boxes of magnum shells. Em sat darkly in her corner watching West Virginia streaking by, keeping her arms folded, chewing gum.

"Ah, Breaker—got your ears on?"

Evan J. grabbed the mike. "This is Breaker. Big 10-4."

"Breaker, we're up here on #26 north. Four wheeler come around us just about the way you might expect he would if he done like you say. Cement stuff on the back? Raised up high?"

"10-4."

"Well then that's him I guess. Makin' northward to the Mason-Dixon Line. We can't catch him. We're on upgrade haulin' steel."

"Just provide the '-20's'. Leave the rest t'me. I'm much obliged." #7 junctioned #26 just a mile ahead. Evan J. took the left and stop sign with him, sticking like a tomahawk in the trailer's side. The truck took the corner on its right-side wheels. The 12-gauge and the shells spilled off the seat and all over the cab.

"Get them shells up! Get that gun out of my feet!" Evan J. yelled.

Em went down. Shells were rolling back and forth among the pedals. She snatched at them as Evan J. braked and clutched and fought the road. The rig dropped suddenly into a dip that wound up sharply left again and over a small culvert. Evan J.'s boots came down hard and caught her right hand under the brake pedal as she grabbed.

"Owww!!"

"What the hell?"

"Shit! Y' smashed my goddam hand, that's what! Oww!" Evan J. knew it must be bad. Em was not inclined to let you know that she was hurting. He felt it, there wasn't much to do.

"Get them shells out! Gonna blow my goddam foot off!"

"Sounds aw'right t' me, by God!"

She was talking more to herself than anyone.

"What's that?" he said.

"I said I got 'em!"

She regained the pitching seat, shells cradled in her jacket. She banged the glove compartment open with an elbow, dumped the shells in, and slammed it shut again.

"Y'd think yer out t' get the whole west end a Maryland! Amount a shells, there is!"

"What's that?"

"Nothin'!"

Evan J. grabbed the mike again. There had been nothing on the CB for a while.

"Ah, Load-a-Steel, you got your ears on?"

"10-4, Breaker."

"You see any Smokies up your way?"

"Not right now but he'll be comin', Breaker. That '-20's' out now. Smokey got his ears on, too. You know."

"10-4. I know. I'm much obliged."

Baker knew this part of West Virginia cold, knew that it was twenty miles from where he was on #26 up to the Pennsylvania Line. Smokey would most likely get on #26 from #48, the new four-lane artery going east out of Morgantown. If he could beat "The Man" through tiny Bruceton Mills and Brandonville, then Smokey had to come up from behind and could not block him at the line. There was a single cutback across further east on #48 to Glade Farms, but it wasn't much—shards of asphalt, mud and potholes. If Smokey tried that road he wouldn't make no time, so he had a chance at making it. Evan J. kept the hammer down. Hubert had to be across the line by now.

Em pulled the bandana from her jeans and wrapped it around her hand, pulling the knot up tight with her teeth. Then she sat back with folded arms and chewed the bubble gum some more, watching West Virginia racing outside, her face as dark as ever.

Several miles went under them. Then she couldn't hold her tongue a minute more.

"Yer gonna tear that rear-end out again."

"What?"

"I said yer gonna tear that rear-end out again."

"Could be."

"Could be, my ass." she murmured. "It's going to pull right out from under."

"What's that?"

"They ain't got no other second-hand ones down at Somer's anymore. You tear out this one and we're gonna have to shuck out for a whole brand-new rear-end. And *shipping*! Pay somebody else to ship it up to where we are!"

Evan J. kept his jaw set, didn't say a word, didn't slow the tractor-trailer down. Time passed. She tried again. "You still owe to Somer's for the old one. Next thing we'll be sellin' Molly just to make a stupid payment on the truck. One month after, here they come and haul it off the same as ever. Neither one of us got nuthin'. Makes all the world of sense t' me."

Evan J. came down all the way with both feet to the floor. Em hit the windshield. The truck left rubber for a hundred yards. It set the brakes on fire.

"If that's all the hell it matters to you. Maybe you had ought to just get out right here!" Evan J.'s hands were knuckle white upon the wheel. He trembled everywhere. "Your Ma is layin' dead back there and—"

"She wasn't my Ma!"

Evan J. glared out through the windshield, through the rain.

"She was my wife. That makes her yer Ma!"

"No it don't and it ain't *my* fault. I give her ever' chance. She never took it."

They sat there doing nothing for some time.

"I said it never seemed like nuthin' cause I never wanted you to know, to bust yer heart up like you got so busted up before. She had them kinda parties all the time. I'm surprised it never happened sooner."

"Shut up." he said.

"Ain't worth it throwin' over everything we got."

"Shut up!"

"You wanna know the truth I just could kiss ol' Hubert; he done you the best turn ever come your way."

Evan J. hit her hard. Her head rebounded from the window. Second time that day. And the hand, she counted to herself. She felt her face and found blood around the corner of her mouth. When she looked up again she stared at him just like a dog until he looked away.

Time passed again.

"Left rear's on fire," she said.

"What?"

"I said the left rear's on fire!"

Evan J. looked. Smoke was rising through the rain. They grabbed fire extinguishers and jumped down from the cab.

The drum was red hot and kept reigniting despite the rain and frosty rush of the extinguishers. The extinguishers were empty by the time they got it down.

Em poked a finger at the tire.

"Soft," she said.

Evan J. poked it, too. He said. "It'll hold. Ain't that bad."

They went inspecting tires all around, and all the tires were steaming. Em said the rain was on their side. She pointed out the stop sign sticking in the trailer, mentioned that it might look strange, whether or not anybody was out looking for anybody. Evan J. tried to work it free. It wouldn't come. He had to get a crowbar. When it came free at last, he flung it deep into the brush. It left a jagged wound in the trailer wall. "That was going to cost them too," said Em. Evan J. didn't say a word. He got back in the cab, fired the engine, clutched and swung out on the road and began working up through the gears again. Exactly as before.

"Yer not goin' on with this?" Em was incredulous. He'd looked as if he'd maybe come around.

Evan J. didn't say a word. He kept heading north on #26, exactly as before. He kept the hammer down.

WEST VIRGINIA—2:38 P.M.

By 2:38, the West Virginia State Police had a car turning in at the third mailbox north of Coleman on R.D.#4 to verify. The trooper prowled around a bit inside, then outside again and finally went back in and upstairs found the bloody remnants of Jean Baker. He returned to the car, confirmed the homicide, requested the county coroner. The trooper was instructed to remain there until the coroner's officer arrived. From articles of mail inside the house he was able to supply the name Evan Joseph Baker, but little more.

The State Police Barracks had better information about Hubert from the CB than about Evan J. Baker. They knew the vehicular description: '66 maroon Ford pick-up with cement tools in the bed. They had monitored the chase proceeding north on #26 toward Pennsylvania, but there had been nothing in calls to tell what Baker was chasing in. Aside from being obvious in his behavior there was little likelihood of spotting him. It would take time to run name and address through the "CLEAN" computer system to get a make and description of the vehicle. More time since it was Sunday. Troopers believed the pursuer to be a truck from the practiced style of CB lingo and the sound of what seemed to be heavy engines in the background, though what kind, what year, what color could not be known. By 2:47 Morgantown was requesting all units within the region to proceed to the state line on #26 and set up a roadblock.

REDFORD CENTRAL—SUNDAY 3:00 P.M.

Lee sat in the "cage," his feet up on the counter, staring at the solid row of flashing reds across the big map opposite. A lot of red and green, twinkling like a Christmas tree. The eastbound was a total loss from Redford west to New Sanford. Fully seventy miles, twenty more miles and it would be shut down to

Pittsburgh. Never had he seen it grown like this before. The progress on the tunnel fire was negligible so far. They were really just waiting for the heating oil or whatever it was to burn out. That seemed to be the full extent of what they could do. Sixty-seven injured and eleven dead had been brought down the mountain according to the hospital, but the tally wasn't in. There were more to come. Accumulating soggy snow above Kregg Maintenance and forty-six mile 'round trips were making things a little slow. And the hospital had unkind things to say. He was desperate to get the westbound fully open, to reopen both lanes through the tunnel. They were reporting westbound bunching as far east as 241. Harrisburg. There was little hope of having any eastbound anymore—except what got around the mountain on Routes 31 and 30 and got back on in front of them at Gate 11, Redford. But what was possible he wanted and it was possible to have a westbound. Lee was frantic to get as many of them west and gone as possible before weather. He drummed his fingers on the counter.

The plan was to evacuate the backlog from the west slope of Aurora, turn the cars around and get them down out of the way in order to attack the fire from both sides as well as having unobstructed roadway when the tube was finally reopened. The guys were saying that the wind was fanning it and giving it an unobstructed air supply from the west end. The west side was so glutted with wrecks and backlog that a snake could not get through.

"Couldn't make no headway," Barger had said. "You have a lot of company," had been Lee's reply.

Somerston Maintenance and Police Barracks at Milepost 102 was willing to go up the east slope, but the facility was on the eastbound side and there were twenty solid miles of backlog and Gate 10-Somerston between them and the fire. Berm and medial had plugged up with clowns who tried to cut out and around. No way.

The bleed-off at Gate 10-Somerston was slowed by traffic chaos in the town of Somerston itself. Somerston was getting it from north and west, from #31 and down #219 from the Pike, about a mile to the north of them. Two patrol units had, by now, made it west on #31 from Brandt Cabins Barracks forty miles east of Redford and fought to get the bleed-off from Gate 10 going north rather than south on 219 and take the northern detour thirty miles around the mountain on old Route 30, but the situation had been hopelessly advanced before they had arrived. Tempers flared. Chaos reigned. Troopers had already been involved in physical assaults, had so far survived and made no arrests—too busy to be bothered with arresting anybody.

There wasn't much to do but wait and listen to the prattle on the VHF until they had that eastbound from Aurora out to Donovan cleared out. Lee was feeling hogtied, had drummed his fingertips until his fingertips were sore. He wondered if you could get cancer of the fingertips.

"337 to Somerston P.B." It was Prokovic, the cop stuck on the western slope, out on foot and talking through his walkie-talkie. Prokovic had been out on foot all day.

"Somerston P.B."

"This backlog's cleaning up as far as—aw—119.3, I can see my car ahead. Maybe I can move 337 any day now."

"10-4, 337."

"Hey, you raise 230 or 230B, yet?" That would be Johannsen's Texaco. Two hundred numbers were the patron services. The franchised service station for the Aurora-New Sanford region, roughly the western half of Radio Zone 2, a hopeless lot of territory for today. 230 and 230B were two big tow trucks.

"Negative, 337."

"You been tryin'?"

"Affirmative, 337. Don't screw around. Nobody's lyin' to you. We got a lot of problems here today."

"10-4. You better raise 'em, get 'em up this mountain 'cause we got a few that's running out of gas, up here. Gotta get 'em down and off."

"10-4, 337. Things is tough all over."

"Sure, but if we leave 'em run out of gas we're gonna hafta tow 'em down or bring the gas up to them. Hell, we'll never get 'em off!"

"337, there is nothing I can say."

"Better have 'em bring some chains and sandbags, too. We

got about four inches here. Naturally not four out of a hundred of
these patrons got their snowtreads on. Tell ol' Louis there's a
buck to make and he'll come up, no problem.''

The door pushed open and Chuck Ellis came in. Sad-looking
little guy with glasses. Dripping rain. He spotted Lee and came
up into the "cage". He took the glasses off and wiped them, listened to what Lee was listening to.

"Somerston Maintenance to Redford." Judy answered.

"Redford 'by', S.M. Go ahead.''

"Redford we just saw the tail end of this backlog go by.''

Well! Progress! Something Lee bought into heavily. Seven
miles to go.

"10-4, S.M. We appreciate it.''

"You rang?'' said Chuck. Lee had always thought him a
curiously depressed-looking fellow for Director of Public Relations. Chuck had a back so bad the pain would've decked anyone
who hadn't built up to it over the years. Some days he looked a
full decade older and would pull his shoulders back a lot, arching
the spine. It was the only way he knew. Chuck looked that way
today. He looked sixty. He put the glasses on and arched his
back again. Maybe it came with the rain.

Lee ran the situation down, advised him about the coming
weather. They walked back to the room behind the big map, to
the equipment chambers for more coffee. Lee also wanted to find
out if the N.W.S. had started ervising its predictions to accommo-
date Nadel. It was 3:15 and should be coming now. The
quarter-hour. Chuck washed down a horse-sized capsule with his
brew, then came over to check the teletype with Lee. It was re-
vised. Eighteen to twenty inches; low thirties overnight. More
snow in higher elevations.

"Now they tell me!'' Chuck said. He took things personally.

Chuck did more than rouge the public cheek of Eastern. In
this kind of thing he had to get advisories to press and media,
make decisions about what was told to whom. Later on there'd
be the phones and people calling about relatives and where the
kids were, patrons reporting they were broken down, giving
birth, or robbed or out of gas. Whatever. There could be
thousands of those. They were getting more of them than average

already. Chuck would also have to make the calls about the list of names to come back from the hospital and morgue. Lee didn't envy Chuck the job. Lee didn't much care for his own at just this minute.

"I could use some extra people," Chuck said.

"We'll have three more operators at the shift change than we have now. If they make it in. Cochran's staying, Emmert. They just don't know it, yet. I'm keeping everybody."

"What about more?"

"We have the call out. We'll just have to wait and see what comes in."

Lee at Judy's console. "Did you get Pribanic?"

She shook her head. "Tried several times. No answer."

"Keep at it."

They walked on.

Chuck said he'd better call the little sundowner at Somerston and authorize them to stay on the air throughout the night. He better do it right away. Lee agreed.

"Have you been in touch with Turlock?" Sherman Turlock, Executive Director.

"Still in Harrisburg. I thought I'd leave that up to you."

"I love you, too." said Chuck. They parted at the outer door. Chuck gave a little shrug started toward the elevators and the upstairs office suites.

Lee went back into the "cage" again.

U.S.#26—NORTH—APPROACHING ROUTE 48—3:00 P.M.

After the first blow-up Em had given it one try; she'd said hold it down or else the burned up brakes would never stop them the next time. Evan J. had said that was fine because there wouldn't be a next time; they would not be stopping. The big Peterbilt was back to eighty-five and tearing up the potholes north on #26, exactly as before. She hunched back into her corner of the cab and nursed her throbbing hand, working gum that had gone sour, gazed out into the horizontal gray-black streaks of rain that whistled by outside her window. No use to mess with Evan

J.; he was keeping up his "pride-front", that was all. When they got like that there was nothing you could do. He was only keeping off the bottom and she couldn't fault him. Not much worse than being stuck down there.

She was pretty sure she had it figured out in her mind what happened. She knew Jean. She knew Hubert, too—Hubert was definitely one of those the rest of them kept on the *bottom*. They made it so damn awful for them when they had somebody there that it meant something to be anyplace else higher up the scale. The whole thing worked on that and nothing more. Otherwise it wouldn't. Otherwise there wouldn't be a thing to keep the country macho-merry-go-round going 'round. She figured that out for herself a long time ago. It made you sick but there was nothing you could do. The magazines kept saying all that macho pride-front stuff was over with for the men nowadays, but she wished someone locally would get the message because all the men in her world got led around by it like bulls with pinch-rings in the nose—her Daddy no exception. It kept them so caught up they never saw outside of it to other ways to spend their lives, making truth of all them old sad country songs and marveling about the truth of them. And they never ever saw.

The women were the worst of all, and Jean was queen among them. Kept up gossiping and flirting all weeklong so come Friday there'd be lots to drink and fight about, lots of ways to reestablish everybody's place on the old scale. She wondered often whether there was anything behind the Women's Lib thing. Probably it was just writers having to have things to write about. The women she knew loved the whole damn go-around. Loved to fan things up and keep 'em fanned out of pure boredom. Nothing else to do.

Em had seen it coming when poor dumb old sad Hubert came to lay the cement floor down in the barn. She never had him figured for a "bottomer." He put up some fight against it. Ever since Del Hoder walked off the water tower and bust himself wide open on the frozen ground last New Year's, everybody seemed to by trying to get Hubert to fill in the vacancy. Hubert talked about it some around the barn when Em was taking care of Molly. He had a rough idea what they were up to and he wasn't going to let them. He wasn't good with women. Hubert never got any. Being there to do the bar and Evan J. away on hauls, she watched Jean start up her teasing. Hubert was starved enough and dumb enough to be a sucker for it. Not like Del Hoder. Maybe that's what made the difference, Del wouldn't play the games at all.

So whatever happened in particular this weekend she couldn't know, but she did know Jean was fanning up excitement, having to be the star of her own soap opera. If you got burned you couldn't blame the matches. Maybe now their lives could settle down awhile, just she and her Daddy—if she could steer him through this final episode of Jean. What was needed now was mostly time. She prayed the Lord would just keep putting problems in their way.

Outside, half consciously she recognized the terrain. They'd soon be coming up to #48—the recent big four-laner running east-west out of Morgantown and into Maryland. #48 was well patrolled. She hoped for the first time in her life they'd get busted by the Smokies, but she couldn't let it look that way to Evan J. Not in his present state of mind.

"You hit #48 with this much hammer down you might as well hang Smokey out a neon sign—even if we don't get smashed to hell and gone." She did say that, smack out of nowhere. There hadn't been words between them for some time.

He shot her a look that said if she made one more crack, some trucker's little girl would be the only one to get "smashed to hell and gone." She rolled her gaze back out the window. The gum was twice as sour as before. Nonetheless, a hunderd yards before the junction she felt the tug of braking. The truck was slowing down.

Route 48—3:05 P.M.

Evan J. rolled up to a perfect stop and waited for a break in the traffic past the junction. It was heavy, the holidayers not yet rolling full tilt on the arteries, but thicker than it would be normally in this kind of weather. They waited, neither of them spoke. When the break came, Evan J. rolled across with grace and continued north on #26. He was behaving, getting crafty, now. Dammit! Em thought, but she kept it to herself.

It was five miles to the Pennsylvania line. The speed limit stayed at 35 for the next few miles, through little crossroads gas pump centers of Bruceton Mills and Brandonville; two more of those seven-building clusters that show up on the map as towns. On the other side of Brandonville, Evan J. picked up the CB mike again.

"C-Q, C-Q. Who's ever northbound #26 around the Pennsylvania line come back, if you will. We're lookin' for Bear."

The call came back at once. "Bears at the state line, wall-to-wall."

"10-4, State line. Tell me more."

"Don't know what it's for. I'm just waiting in the line, sittin' at a roadblock here. They're checkin' cars. County-Mounties, Bears, you name it. Somebody stole the pants off the governor, or something. Whatever it is, they're sure as hell out to git 'im."

"10-4, State line. Much obliged."

Baker took the little blacktop country cutback north of Brandonville. It wasn't much, but it was getting back to #48, avoiding Smokey Bear. They met no other traffic this way, but the patched and potholed little cutback and the weather were so bad the best the rig could do was twenty miles an hour. Em said a secret prayer of thanks-and-please-send-more. First time in her life that she had prayed for trouble.

It brought them out on #48, a few miles west of Maryland. Again they waited for a break in traffic. He took #48 straight into Maryland without incident, turned north a little way beyond the line again on #42. #42 would get him into Pennsylvania and rejoin #26 on the other side of Smokey—at Markleysburg.

Em went back to reading *Gordon and Louise* and making secret prayers for trouble.

3:14 P.M.—THE PENNSYLVANIA LINE

At 3:14 the West Virginia State Police apprehended Hubert at the state line roadblock. He was taken to Morgantown in custody.

Units stayed behind to sustain the roadblock for a little while on the probability that Evan J. Baker would soon follow. Not that Baker had broken the law, but simply to inform him that the chase was over.

SUNDAY 4:08 P.M. MILEPOST 122.4—INSIDE THE EASTBOUND AT AURORA

Ollie checked his regulator, his air supply was all but gone, barely time to get him out. He pulled back from the fire, got in his truck and tore out of the tunnel.

He pulled up with a screech between the tubes outside, in front of the still burning maintenance. The big garage doors of the maintenance between the tunnels stood open. There was nobody around. He jumped down from the truck and tore the mask away. The cold air felt terrific. He let the snow and rain wash some of the oil and soot away, poured out a U.S. standard ounce of perspiration from the mask. The little monkey of a guy was frustrated. They were getting nowhere in the eastbound. It was getting dark outside already. Where the hell were the Aurora guys? The Redford Fire Department? He scrounged around and came up with another tank of air, affixed it, put the mask back on and drove into the maintenance to find out just what the hell was going on.

He found them at the far end, Barger and his candy-asses, some of the weekend heroes and their big white fire trucks up from Redford, pissing around with the westbound wall. They wore no breathers. Not even smoke masks! It infuriated him. If the air was that damn good they sure as hell could spare a few machines, a man or two. Ollie tore his own encumbering breathing apparatus off, jumped down from the truck, and charged forward.

Bah! It might as well be forty guys with hoses burning leaves! The fire was down to a hibachi! To spotty licks of persistent flame. He spotted Barger standing back and chatting casually with the fire chief from Redford. The chief from Kregg saw red.

"Hey! Barger! What the fuck is this?"

"What the fuck is what?"

"What, no tea and little cakes? Did it maybe occur to you that we ain't gettin' anyplace over on the other side? Where there's a fire? I assume you heard about our fire? Holy shit! I don't believe this! What I'm seein'!"

"What you're seeing is *results* here! We fight this S.O.B. all day and here you come next to the end when everything is through. You shoulda been here back an hour. You woulda seen something!"

"How nice, let me be among the first to congratulate ya'. Then you could maybe pack up some of this and come give us a hand. Let's get our ass in gear, okay?"

Barger shook his head. "We ain't done yet. We still got that oil seeping in. We gotta keep it off that westbound wall!"

Chelinski spat and went back to his truck. He hung out of the door. "Get them pretty Redford trucks and all that other shit out of the way! I'm coming back directly." The weather-beaten monkey pulled himself inside, fired up his wrecker and was gone. Minutes passed and Barger thought no more of it. Then another and much larger truck was coming back again. Barger walked out through the stand of maintenance machines to see. A 6-axle diesel plow was coming ass-end at him with a load of salt piled high, and spilling over. Barger moved into its way and flagged it down.

The door swung open. Ollie hung out of the door.

"Outa my way, Barger or—by God, I'll drive right over ya!" Barger ran up to the cab and pulled him out by his lapels. Chelinski hit him in the nose. Five guys separated them. Barger wiped his bleeding nose along his canvas sleeve. Barger wanted to know just what the hell he thought he was doing.

"Salt don't burn, does it sonny?"

The Redford fire chief had to agree. Salt didn't burn at all.

DAY ONE: SUNDAY   71

"Move them trucks aside and let me through. Let's dump some on and see!"

Equipment was jerked around until the big plow could back through up to the fire. Ollie raised the bed. It rose slowly on its big hydraulic ram till tons of rock salt poured into the vestiges of flame, soaked up and smothered the burning oil. After that just flickers, little tongues and sprizzles at the edges. Smoke rose heavily.

Ollie hauled the big plow off and over, parked it and jumped up onto a little skiploader, a little tractor with a shovel-blade. Then in and out, back and forth, crashing gears till Barger winced in pain. Ollie spread the rock salt all around, shoveled up a pile against the inner eastbound wall, piling up a kind of dam. The fire inside the maintenance was beaten.

Ollie swung around and faced the men, stood up on the tractor like a preacher, to a congregation, an impish grin broke out of the grimy hide that was his face. He spat tobacco.

"How about that?"

R. Fred Barger's teeth were grinding. "Fifteen minutes back that wouldn't have done shit! At all! And you damn well know it!" he shouted.

"I guess you know all about what won't work, don'tcha Barger? Your ol' lady tol' me all about it!"

"W-o-o-o-a!" A little roar went through the men. And they were laughing. Fred had lost prestige on that one. There was not a solitary thing to do.

Ollie dropped into the seat of the tractor and roared past him out toward the east end of the tunnel. Barger bounced his hardhat off the cement floor. It ricocheted and almost hit him in the face again.

The Redford chief looked dismal too.

REDFORD CENTRAL—4:20 P.M.

Lee had at last reached L. John Pribanic with the confirmation of bad weather. It was too late by then to stop the newlyweds from leaving. They had left the wedding party and hopped into Mike's green MG Midget and were gone by 2:30. The mayor thanked him all the same. He would try to get his town prepared for what was coming. He thanked Lee Rider with polite formality.

The telecom lit up and buzzed Rider from the Zone 2 console. It was Judy.

"Lee—Aurora Maintenance reports the fire is out between the tunnels."

"What about the tube itself?"

"Well, it's still in progress in the eastbound. Ollie Chelinski wants you to call."

"Redford to Aurora."

Lee raised him right away.

"Yeah, Rider. Hey, look. I been tryin' to raise Somerston the last half hour. I can't get through."

"Barracks or Maintenance?"

"Either one. I can't raise nothing. What the hell is the matter? That Number 12 Repeater again?"

"We think. It's been kicking up a little. I'll call 'em on the land line for you. What's the message?" Land lines were direct wires, Eastern's private telephone system, used as back-up or for privacy. The routine traffic on police highband VHF was anything but private. Too many people nowadays had scanning monitors. Sometimes that was advantageous, but it could be a handicap. The system had to have its private systems, too.

"I got an idea about this fire inside the eastbound, Rider."

"I'm listening." Boy, was Lee listening.

Last time I was up at Somerston them guys still had that giant Fiat-Allis dozer? That 41-B with the 12-foot blade. Out sitting on that wide-bed in the back. From when they widened out that cut up on the bypass last October? You remember?"

"I don't recall." Lee didn't feel he had the time for speculation. "Get to the point."

"Naw, well if that big cat's still up there, I thought, we got about five inches snow up here right now. I was thinkin' when they get that eastbound cleared off between Somerston and the tunnels we could get that cat up there, start pushin' up that snow against the west end of that eastbound tube, cut that air off to the fire we got 'er made. Smother it with snow, y' know. See if you can raise 'em over at Somerston Maintenance and find out about it.''

That wasn't bad. "Stay by the radio," said Lee. "I'll call you back."

There was some encouragement on the land line. Somerston reported that the eastbound between exits 9 and 10 was clear. Cleared off back to Donovan. Sgt. Prokovic on the western slope up to Aurora had called Somerston Barracks also, said he wasn't able to raise Redford and was it Number 12 again? He was at Milepost 122, the wreck and reported that the eastbound from #10 up to Aurora had been evacuated, too, except for the disabled vehicles, totaling 87. Number 230B, the second wrecker unit from Johannsen's Texaco, was up there now. Prokovic had no tally on the injured, but he had a lot of ambulatory patrons wanting to get down and be with family or companions that had been taken down to the emergency station in Redford.

Yes. Somerston Maintenance still had the 41-B parked on it's special trailer in the yard. Yes, they had a tractor that could pull it up Aurora Mountain. No, they didn't have an operator for the cat. Lee told them to get underway and take it up the eastbound to the tunnel. They would find an operator.

"Ollie?"

"Yeah."

"They have the cat. No operator."

"Just have 'em get it up here. I can make it go," and Ollie.

"10-4," said Lee. "I told them."

EASTERN MILEPOST 234:—THE SERVICE PLAZA AT HARRISBURG—4:35 P.M.

Eddie Braden's fall into the pond had set departure time back two hours. The Braden family had taken Route #83 north out of Maryland to catch the Eastern Turnpike at Gate 18, Harrisburg. At Harrisburg they stopped for a variety of reasons: Chris was hungry; both kids had to pee; he had to pee. Dan was pressured by the late start and the knowledge that he would now be smack in the middle of the weekend rush. God knows what time they would be getting home. He wanted to get enough gas to make their next stop well into Ohio. It had been 4:35 by Dan's now ridiculously depreciated Accutron when the station wagon pulled into the Howard Johnson's. The kids and Irene went inside to grab a booth—Dan remained grumbling at the pump for letting himself get caught again and victimized by Turnpike prices. A blood-oath principle of doing all their fueling and trash eating prior to or after getting off the Turnpike had been broken. '76 had been a clincher, when Irene and the kids got salmonella. Today it would have to be okay. Just this once, but nobody would eat the cole slaw, he told himself. What could you do? It was a setup. It was all worked out. They got you coming and going, but sooner or later they always got you.

4:47 P.M.

Inside, it was the same depressing menu they had had the last time. Looked the same—same plastic-looking portraits of the clams and fries, taped-over prices taped again.

The place was packed—wall-to-wall, shoulder-to-shoulder. Eddie had spotted an older couple dawdling over pie and stood over them and stared at them till they became uncomfortable. Ed could do that to you. And he did. Irene was giving it to him when Dan came in, the standard lecture—this time for walking up and standing there, then asking them directly if they had loose dentures and was that why it took them all that time to eat a lousy piece of pie. Not mean or sarcastic—a straightforward in-nocent inquiry. Ed was doing things like that all the time, it was something without precedent on both sides of the family. They'd given up on Ed in this respect at last. It was something built into the package. And, sometimes it even came in handy. Dan kept to himself, but this time he was glad of Ed's unique powers. He had probably saved them one full hour. At this time and in this situa-tion Dan was glad for whatever he could get.

5:20 P.M.

Christine had watched Ed give their waitress the thrice-over throughout the meal. Chris at 13 thought about that kind of stuff a lot, speculated whether she herself would grow a pair of boobs like the pair this waitress was dangling over their table now, and if so whether it would always be what Ed was doing to the waitress now, or whether it was only your occasional sex maniac. Ed had been doing stuff like that constantly since he was five, or three or whenever. Collecting *Playboys* out of trash cans at the college, undressing Myrna Schreckengost behind the bushes at the church picnic that infamous time the family could not live down. You could tell the waitress was getting unnerved. Ed played his age and got by with stuff, you had to hand it to him. How could you accuse a 12-year-old of undressing you with his eyes. He *always* got away with it. Always. Ed was sneaky. Chris munched her second batch of fries and took it in. She wondered how she'd handle herself whenever her time came. Ed was valuable in that regard, a good subject for study. Of course it was the girl's own fault too; if you were going to drag your boobs through people's ice cream that way she did, you had to figure on some kind of reactions. Who was he kidding? Chris munched more fries. At least Ed wasn't queer. You had to count your blessings, pathetic as they were.

And all through the meal her Dad kept talking about going back to the farm. What was wrong with this, with that, with Detroit and the job. She didn't like that very much at all. God! The *farm!* No kids. No social life. *Bor*ing! God! What was so bad about Detroit? There was a lot going on.

"Well, the whole thing's crazy: Hubbard, Frazey—all the guys. Hubbard's out in Arizona, now, I tell you?"

"No." Irene picked at the tasteless bright green peas. "When did you see him?"

"Last October at the field meeting. It's what I said, Irene; the second week in New York their car got stolen. The house they could afford was nothing. Hubbard told me he spent four hours of his day just getting to and from his job. He figures that promotion cost him eleven thousand dollars. I'm not going to New York. Not the way the future looks. Not me.''

Dan glanced out the window. "God, it's *dark* already. Come on kids. Finish up. We got to go.''

"What's he doing in Arizona?'' Irene could listen sincerely to her husband hours at a time without tiring. And without any thought that it could change her own opinion. Men had jobs and wives and kids and kept them. That was all.

"Who?''

"Chris, I told you that you'd never finish those fries, besides it's bad for your complexion,'' Irene admonished. "Hubbard. What's he doing out west?''

"Well, he took a *cut*. Stepped down, that's what. They said that it was 'all they had open.' That's how they do it to you, pare off these upper-middle-bracket salaries. You take it or you're out. Hubbard is bitter, boy! An altogether different guy, I'm telling you. It's scary!''

"Well, I think you're being paranoid, a little—''

"No I'm *not*, Irene! Seriously. American business has lost sight of the basic thing. I mean, if the purpose of construction is not to sustain the lives of people—the people who keep it running, then what the hell's it for? They plug the numbers in and if it comes out three cents less profit keeping you, kiss it all goodbye. You're out! They don't take three cents off your paycheck, they just *scrap* you. Flat. The 'corporate entity'! It's got to be some kind of giant thing with a life of its own. They all bow down before it. Never question it. Throw it human sacrifices. Chris you heard what your Mother said. We're late. Let's go.''

"Well, golly, if you gave a person time!''

"You had plenty of time. Everybody else is finished.''

"Ed didn't eat his pudding yet.''

The waitress with the big endowments had come back to finish cleaning up the table, dangling them over the table. Ed was gazing at them as shamelessly as before.

"You gonna eat that pudding, kid?'' she said.

Ed didn't shift his eyes from the endowments. "It looks like something barfed up by a dog. Would you?''

The waitress took the pudding and the other stuff and went back to the kitchen. Just inside, she set down the tray and turned to peer out through the small round window. Finally! That weird kid and his family were leaving. The husband was at the counter paying.

Ed came up to the register where Dan was paying. He stood looking at the stand of trashy souvenirs and junk food just outside the swinging doors. He looked up and caught her looking at him through the porthole.

She ducked back from the door. Another waitress with trays of steaming food came up behind her.

"What's with you?" said the new waitress.

"You see that kid out there?"

"Which one?"

"That skinny little twerp beside the register."

"What about him?"

"He's been givin' me the eye since the minute they come in here. I think he wants to ball me!"

"What, that kid? You been workin' too hard. Stand aside; I'm comin' through."

The second waitress pushed out backwards through the swinging doors and stopped to look at Eddie. Eddie looked her up and down. She flushed all over. There was no mistaking it. Wanting to look as if she hadn't noticed, she spun quickly on a heel and walked tray first into a fat guy coming up to pay. Food and dishes flew. She landed on her bottom parts in hot mashed potatoes. She looked up. The kid was standing there just staring, no expression on his face at all.

Then the father came back from outside to get him.

"Ed! Let's go!"

Outside, boy and father walked together toward the car, their collars up against the rain. It was dark and seemed much later than 5:40.

"Listen, sport," Dan started.

"What?"

"It isn't nice to stare at people when they're having trouble."

"Okay," he said.

They got into the car.

REDFORD CENTRAL—4:52 P.M.

Beck called from Aurora. They had the wounded and dead evacuated from the other side. He did not have the actual count. They'd have to get the final tally from the hospital. They still had the uninjured relatives awaiting rides down into Redford. They were almost ready to reopen both lanes of the westbound through Aurora.

"Walk them through the westbound side before you open the westbound." The Maintenance between the tubes was still too bollixed up to get them through that way.

"Yes," the captain said. "I figured on it."

"10-4," said the captain. It was news that Lee had waited for. Progress! Still, he wondered how long it would take to restore the flow, and get the bunching smoothed out.

"There's quite a bit of snow," said Beck. "It's sloppy, but it's just this stretch up on the mountain. Once they got past that, westbound on the other side is pretty much wide open."

"Hey, what's your '-20? Where are *you* right now?"

"I'm up here at 122.1."

The western side. Right at the portal. How the hell could he be getting through on VHF? Well, Highband VHF played funny tricks sometimes. Maybe 12 had come back on again. Maybe it was skipping off a cloud, bouncing off a mountain. Lee had dealt with frequencies like these for twenty years and still was hesitant to predict. Maybe it would hold. Please God let it hold.

"I'm giving Prokovic a little hand. He's got this kid from Johannsen's in 230B pulling wrecks out now. Listen, I'm gonna play Pied-Piper, lead this gang of patrons through to your side. Is there anything that I can use to bring them down?"

"Talk to Chelinski out of Kregg. He's on this side some-place. Stick them in a plow-truck if you have to."

"Negatory, Lee. Ollie's over *here* waiting for something called a 41-B or D—or something. The guy is nuts. Jumping up and down. What's it all about?"

"Okay. We have a plan. Just go ahead and take those patrons over and *get that westbound open*! There's all kinds of shit on this side. You'll find something.''

"10-4. Listen, Lee, another thing . . .'' The captain's voice trailed off and faded out in static. Blotto. Zilch.

Number 12 was going to have to be attended.

REDFORD—5:00 P.M.

At 5 P.M. exactly Lee was watching as the weathertype began to pound its message. Temperature dropping, snow to begin in Pittsburgh roughly at 7:00. Traveler's advisories for Ohio, West Virginia, western Maryland, and the western two-thirds of Pennsylvania, New York and the Great Lakes. The whole bit. Wow! The teletype made it so official.

7:00 P.M.

Lee picked up the phone, called Tri-State. Charlene was on his mind as he listened to it ringing at the other end. Nadel picked up the phone on the ninth ring.

"Hey, Jim—I get 7:00 now from National. What gives?''

"They may be right. Who knows?''

"Let's try it this way—who gets *paid* to know?''

"Take it easy. The Nationals are always playing it conservative—it's policy. I still say 7:30.''

"7:30? Last time you said eight o'clock!''

"Did I? When?''

"Hell, I don't know—what was it, three o'clock?''

"I haven't talked to you since then? Sorry. Thought I had. It's been busy here.''

"What the hell's going on?''

"We've been looking at a little newcomer, an anemic little high that's risen over the southeast—the coast states and the Atlantic. We might get some benefit from that. Too early yet to tell. It's weak. It may dissolve again. On the other hand, that arctic airmass has accelerated, hasn't it?''

"Get to the point, Jim. What's that mean to me?''

"Well, I'm hoping this new southern high will push the whole business north, above you. There's a good chance it will. Looking like it all the time."

"Fine! Fantastic!"

"Not so fast. It won't shove it *that* far."

"Sum it up, Jim. Please! For me?" Nadel could drive you nuts sometimes with the scientific caution. Maddening.

"I expect you'll miss the high winds, at least where you are. The main front should pass—oh, ten—twenty miles north of the Pike at Redford. You'll get the freezing rain at first, followed by a big wet, heavy straight-down snow. The fringe effect. You'll still catch the rough stuff west of Pittsburgh where you angle north."

Lee wondered whether that was any benefit at all. At this time of year the patrons weren't expecting it, hadn't got the mental "set" for snow. Hadn't for the most part got their snowtreads on, their sandbags in the trunk. But most of all their minds weren't set for it and that was deadliest of all.

"N.W.S. says twenty-seven inches," said Lee.

"Alarmists, that National Weather Service! Twenty. At the most."

"I got five inches on the west side of Aurora, now. I'm inclined to be a little bit of an alarmist, too.

"Twenty-five up on the mountain, then. Twenty elsewhere."

"This isn't funny, Jim."

"What the hell, do I sound like I'm laughing? It's egg on my face. The thing snuck up on us. It happens! This time of year is just impossible. You never really know which way it's going to go." Nadel let out a sigh. He sounded like a doctor estimating how long you had to live.

"You'll miss the winds. That's something anyway. Let you know. See what's going on on the Lakes—up north and in Detroit right now. Real old fashioned blizzard. The good-old-days kind with everybody's old man walking four miles to school up to his armpits in the snow. But I don't suppose that helps *you* much, does it?"

"Not a whole lot, no. Let's look at it from the other side—how long before its over?"

"I'd say morning. That's a guess, now—"

"Accepted. Call me."

"Yes. I'm sorry, Lee. I guess I got sucked into my data and forgot I hadn't called you. Would it have made a great difference?"

"No."

Lee hung up and tried to figure when it was Charlene had gotten off. Perhaps if he could get the registration of the car and flag her down at West Gate. What time had she gotten off, 1:05? 1:10? The clock said 5:15. Hell, it would be shorter to her destination. She'd be past the point of no return, probably within minutes, now. Two hours to the storm.

No problem.

TIME 5:22 P.M.

5:22. Lee had just plopped on his can, propped his feet up in the "cage" and started monitoring on Zone 2 again, when Judy beeped the intercom.

"Lee, I can't raise anybody on the west side of the mountain. It's impossible."

"Good old Number 12."

"Looks that way," said Judy.

The repeater had come on again after he had talked to Beck. It seemed to be all right. Now dead again. The pattern was typical.

Lee got up and went back to the equipment chambers, to the repair benches to see who was in. Old Hondecka and the whiz-kid, Jimmy Weeks. Playing chess again. Hondecka had a transceiver on the bench, an intermittent he was "cookin". Not much else was going on.

"Hey, Jim, I got a job for you."

Jim looked up and cracked a peanut. "Number 12?"

"I heard about it," he said. "Okay. I'll go."

"I'm telling you—it's that low-pass filter," Old Hondecka said.

Number 12's chronic complaints had become a never ending debate among the technicians.

"We'll see," said Jim.

"You better take the 'Cat', " said Lee. "It's on the trailer. We got four inches on the mountain." They kept a snowmobile just for those last few miles up in the mountain.

Weeks got his parka on. Drops of water shook off the fur collar. His hair was still wet too. He'd just come in. The quiet young technician scooped up the pile of peanuts from the bench and stuffed them in his coat pocket. Once Lee asked about the peanuts—"Protein," Weeks had said, "organic." Weeks was sharp, invented slick little gadgets for the system. His fastidious and logical mind made him one of Lee's best technicians, despite short years of experience. Eastern could tolerate the peanuts.

Lee hated to send anybody out on such a night—39 miles. The last nine miles were nothing but a trail. In the summer you could make it on a minibike; winters on the snowmobile. Usually. Not always. Jim would tow the "Cat" up there with the International 4-wheel drive equipment van and test his luck from there. The van packed a pair of snowshoes among the equipment, too. Number 12 was Jimmy's unofficial orphan; he seemed to get a challenge from the "gnomes."

"We're suppose to get a load of weather after seven, Jim. Try and get back ahead of that if possible."

He couldn't make it. It took an hour and a half each way. Perhaps he could at least be back down on the level.

"Sure." He wiped his heavy glasses and picked up the tools, took the van keys off the hook and started off.

"I'm telling you, you better take that other filter," Old Hondecka said.

But Weeks was gone.

Five minutes later he was back again. He handed Lee an envelope.

"There was a guy from the hospital upstairs out front. He said to give you this." Hondecka came out with the filter. Jim

Weeks gave a little shrug and stuck it in his pocket. Why argue? He was gone again.

Lee opened the envelope. A list of names annd addresses. The tally from the hospital. 12 dead, 77 injured—3 critical. He folded it and put it back.

He took the envelope up the elevator to three, the executive floor, turned left along the marble corridor, past half a dozen glass-fronted modern office suites—his own included—standing dark and vacant.

He found Chuck Ellis in the only lighted office, lying flat upon the floor, his knees pulled up, a telephone pressed to his ear. His back must be killing him, thought Lee. Chuck did not get up, he extended a hand to take the list Lee handed him.

"Grab a phone," Chuck said. "Punch 63."

Lee did so, took one of the extensions.

"I'm on hold," said Chuck. "Turlock's on the line from Harrisburg." The big boss—the executive director.

"You have trouble getting through?"

"He called me."

Chuck looked at the sheets from the hospital while they waited. His expression didn't change. He could get no more dismal than before.

The receiver blasted suddenly in Lee's ear. "Okay, Chuck I'm back. Now what the hell's going on down there?" No mistaking Sherman Turlock.

"We had a big one in the tunnel."

"Which tunnel?"

Lee spoke. "Aurora, in the eastbound."

"Who's this? That you, Lee?"

"Yes."

"Well, come on somebody, I'm hearing all kinds of crap up here. Let's have it."

"I can't tell you that much more than Chuck. It's a bad one. A big fire. We just got the list of dead and injured."

"Hit me. I've got appointments."

Chuck glanced at Lee. 6 o'clock on Sunday? He'd *bet* there were appointments.

Chuck had it open. "12 dead, 77 injured—3 critical."

"What happened?"

"No one saw it happen. There was a little snow up there. Of course the traffic."

"Was it our fault?"

"I doubt it," Lee said.

"Could we be held liable?" Sherman Turlock was a politician, an appointee. "Were they salting? Were there plows out?"

Lee hadn't thought about it. They had probably *not* been salting. That early in the day. The snow was in the air or just in isolated patches. It hadn't yet become a recognized factor.

"I don't know," said Lee. "I will say this, if they come back to check on it tomorrow there will be no way of proving anything—one way or another."

"What the hell is that supposed to mean?" Turlock's tone was more on the offensive. That meant that he was much relieved. Lee knew what bothered Sherman, and the sort of thing that made him feel secure.

"We're going to get a snowstorm after dark."

"We've had snow before."

"A whopper. Twenty inches before morning."

"We've had twenty inches. Look. We've bought ourselves the best equipment in the world. More than's easy to justify, I'm telling you."

"We've had twenty inches, yes. We haven't had it Sunday of Thanksgiving, with a tunnel blocked, with seventy miles of eastbound out of service from the word go, with the thickest westbound ever seen. We're getting freezing rain now, just to kick things off. They're slipping all over hell and gone. Give it about two more hours and we won't have any westbound either."

"What the hell? I didn't hear about any goddam snowstorm on the news. What is this?"

"You'll hear about it on the news tonight, believe me," said Lee.

"Pretty, isn't it? We got the first word of it sometime just after noon. Half of the U.S.A. is on the road, right now."

"Where's Tri-State? Where are those weather guys? We're paying them a fortune. Jesus!"

"Well, I wonder if it would have made a difference. Storms come no matter what you say," Chuck said. He ventured further.

"Sherman, I am looking ahead to a possible shutdown somewhere during the night. I hope not, but it looks like it could get that way."

Turlock hit the fan. "I'm not hearing any talk of shutdowns, guys. To hell with that baloney! You know how we justify grossing $85 millions over $45 million expenditures? We demonstrate the service, the big Tonka-Toys, the facilities they don't get on any of the toll-free roads. And they don't! When all-other-roads-are-down-the-Pike-will-get-you-through. That's all we got to sell. We'll get them through."

"These patrons haven't got their treads on, the cars aren't winterized, they just don't have it in their minds this early in the year. What happens when it has worked itself into one big three-hundred-mile standstill? People runnig out of gas, kids pissing in their laps, the junkies, diabetics, maternities, acute appendicitises? Shutdown is shutdown, Sherm, that's all there is to that. That's gonna look terrific, isn't it?"

Lee had admiration for the little guy. Chuck didn't pull the punches.

"We'll need your authorization to shut down if and when it comes to that. I think we better have, Sherman. Just in case. We may not be able to get through to you later on."

There was a long tired sigh from Harrisburg. "Okay. You say they're on the road already, right? So there's not a goddam thing that we can do about it."

"Not *all*. I didn't say that. Some won't leave till later on. There may be a chance to stop a small percentage, but the big rush is on. No doubt about it."

"Well, get out your advisories! Then we're in the clear. If they get stuck, we'll take care of them. What more can we do?"

"Will do. Naturally. But, Sherm, a Declaration of Emergency from Harrisburg is not out of the picture. Have you got access to the governor, or to the lieutenant governor?"

"What am I, God?"

"If we really get it, I mean, if this thing stacks up to be what it looks like it could be, a *declaration* would get the proverbial ass out of the sling. The *only* thing! Then it's an 'Act of God.' We'd have the guard, the civil defense, emergency funds, etc. Most of all—public justification. I'd think about it."

"Well, I don't know. I won't work against it though, if that's what you mean."

"That's all I'm saying. We didn't want you getting any bad surprises. But you could be in touch with the governor?"

"I could be, yes." The executive director was muttering.

"Well, what can I say? Roll with the punches. Try to keep as much egg off our faces as you can, will you guys? I'll do what I can," said Turlock.

Chuck hung up the phone, stayed flat-backed on the floor. He sucked his teeth and gazed at the ceiling.

"Good old Sherm," he said.

WESTERN PORTALS OF AURORA—ABOUT—5:20 P.M.

With the heavy overcast and shortness of the days it was fully dark by 5:20, black as pitch and miserable. Beck was still amid the wrecks and stranded patrons on the westbound side of Aurora, and yet had not led them through the still closed inside westbound lane. Sgt. Tom Prokovic and Patrolman LaBarr were up-to-eyeballs in years, colors, makes, and registration numbers—every owner to be interviewed and recorded with his numbers, however briefly. Prokovic and LaBarr were not about to face their corporals without the mandatory paperwork. It was taking time, a vehicle involvement totaling 89, again, not counting what was in the tunnel in the flames. There wasn't anyone to interview for those. The slushy rain was coming even harder than before.

LaBarr came over. It was done. They rounded up the miserable hundred-odd uninjured patrons from the cars, minimizing the patrons' natural concern about losing track of their cars as best they could. The machines would be taken down to Somerston, Beck told them; they would make arrangements to get them reunited in the morning. Cars remaining, something in excess of fifty, had been pared down to those with damage such as could no longer have been driven. Some patrons elected to remain with their cars. Some cars were driven through the tunnels and down to Redford by their owners or by others who formed car pools to get down to Redford Hospital. For all of that, there was a residue of cars and people of no use to one another. The officers looked forward to the morning with enormous and familiar dread. Let the corporals tear their hair, the final paperwork was their department. It was going to be a couple days of hell just getting patrons and their cars all back together.

Beck left word that he would send a flag through with a westbound patron, signaling the sergeant that the temporary barriers still in operation on the inside lane could be take down and both lanes through the westbound tube reopened. He gathered up his dripping, shivering throng to follow and they started through the tunnel. Get the patrons out and down. That was first.

The Kregg chief had been pacing up and down, spitting and cussing from impatience. Impatient for the bulldozer from Somerston, impatient for Prokovic and LaBarr to get their goddam paperwork concluded. Impatient to clear room enough to work the giant 'Cat' up to the fire and test his theory. The slack-jawed kid named Arthur Louis from Johannsen's Texaco had come up in 230B to haul the wrecks away and had been taken captive by the roadman. The minute that Prokovic or LaBarr had one cleared, Ollie zapped in on it like a hawk and hooked it to the wrecker. The first two had been hauled down to Johannsen's in the town but the trip down and back from Somerston proved much too time consuming. The third time Arthur was back again in seven minutes with the wreck still in tow.

"The idea is to leave them there," said Ollie.

"I can't get down! Them guys is stuck *down there* at 118.4 with that 41-B of yours on that oversized trailer. Takes up both lanes. I can't get around 'em. They can't get no traction in the snow. Wanted me to help 'em pull that mother bulldozer up here.

Are you kidding? It's bigger than a house!''

Ollie spat tobacco on 230B. The kid scooped up some snow and packed it on the crawling stain.

''Hey, what the hell!'' He got a greasy rag and polished off the fender. ''Watch what you're doin'!''

''You run me down, then get your ass back up here, poke these wrecks off onto the sides.'' He grabbed the kid and jammed him in the cab. They tore down to 118.4.

The guys from Somerston had the 12-foot bladed monster chained aboard its own special tractor-trailer, were grinding futilely in low-low gear, the tractor snaking back and forth and getting no place. Ollie threw the driver out and tried himself, made giant feet of progress and got stopped again. He leaped out of the cab up onto the trailer, furiously began undoing chains thicker than his arms.

''Get that tailgate down!'' he roared.

''You can't run no 'Cat' this size on the pavement! It'll bust the road to shreds!''

''Not with me, it don't. I drive 'em on tippy-toes.''

The ex-driver from Somerston was not impressed. He stood his ground. Ollie's first thought was of decking him but he was pressed for time. He climbed up iron tracks higher than his head and when he got to the controls he was almost 15 feet above the ground. He set the heavy starter turning waste-basket-sized pistons over. The stack thundered and belched soot. Ollie stood up and yelled down.

''You gonna drop that tailgate, or will I?''

''The hell you will!'' The fellow started up for him.

Ollie threw the levers making crashing, rending sounds and revved the heavy diesel. The ''Cat'' began to strain, thick chains went taut. A terrible groaning came from the trailer. Rough oak planking tore away from the bed. The trailer bowed up in front a little.

''All right! All right!'' The guy screamed. His buddy helped him and they got the tailgate down.

Beck's march through the westbound was a trek of one full mile. The noise of the westbound traffic was deafening, the air foul and oily. The lighting system had been out from the beginning and the blinding headlights of the oncoming vehicles the sole illumination. Several of the patrons became fearful, pressed themselves against the wall, or made little progress. Beck had to get forceful to make these more afraid of him than of the tunnel. Tunnels had unpredictable effects on people, the troopers saw it many times. Unknowing claustrophobics would drive right up to the portals and stop dead. The troopers sometimes had to pry their whitened fingers from the wheel, shove them over, drive them through; it happened several times a month in one or more of the four tunnels of the Pike, a built-in phenomenon that seemed to have been there waiting when the systems opened. A given you lived with. He got one of the energetic men among the patrons to lead and he stayed behind the group thereafter. It seemed to help.

The air inside the tube was incredibly foul. Three hundred yards inside a girl of ten collapsed with asthma. He carried her from there. On the other side the Redford firemen gave her oxygen. Everyone who had come through the westbound was half sick, including Beck himself, had headaches, burning eyes and tightness of the chest. The giant ventilating fans had gone with the lights. He hadn't realized the necessity of them before.

The cold, damp air worked wonders. As soon as he had seen about the little girl, he was running down along the medial with a red flag from the Maintenance. Miscenic the giant trooper, was still working at the cut, snow piled 3 inches deep upon his hat and shoulders, alternating cars from one lane, and then the other, trying to be fair. Too tired even for obscenity. Beck approached the first car waiting turn on the inside lane, knocked on the fellow's window, asked the guy to take the flag and give it to the trooper on the other side. They gave the fellow with the flag some time to get well into the tunnel, then pulled the barriers off onto the medial.

5:42 P.M.

Beck raised Redford from the first maintenance truck he came to, advising of the time, and that both lanes westbound were now unobstructed.

The miserable clot of refugees that had come through with him hung together in a wet and forlorn herd, nothing suitable to ferry them to Redford. Most of the Maintenance and Fire Department guys were still deep in the eastbound with the fire. They would have to get them down in as small groups as they could. Together with Miscenic and two exaustion cases from the crews, they rolled an oil drum into the entrance of the Maintenance, out of the rain and built a fire. The patrons took shelter there.

He took five of them with him down to Redford, in 344, Beck's own patrol car.

TIME 5:30 P.M.

Evan J. Baker and his rig had crossed over into Pennsylvania via Maryland without any sign of state police and got onto Pennsylvania #281 at Markleysburg without incident. Nor was there any word on the CB about the old Ford pickup. Evan J. had kept radio silence till he was well above the state line, on the other side of where the West Virginia State Police would be congregated. It wasn't easy to stay off the radio. He was desperate for fresh information. He had no idea of whether Pennsylvania State Police had become involved or whether Hubert had switched off onto some new direction. He could only listen; nothing was coming to him volunteered. Maybe the detour had lost him the limelight. Maybe the CB grapevine figured it a fluke, more probably a bullshit prank. More likely he had just moved on and all those who had been in on it had now moved on and been replaced by others, unaware that Evan J. was out among them to avenge murder.

At the junction of Route 281 and Route 40, Baker stopped and thought about it. He was just a mile the other side of Markleysburg, for all the skirting round just two and one half miles above the state line into Pennsylvania. Miles behind. Which way did Hubert go? West? East? Straight north again? Should he open up on CB and possibly get Smokey on his tail? Did Pennsylvania Smokey know about it or even give a damn?

Rain. Rain. Rain. Inside and out.

"What do you think?"

Em looked up from one of Jean's old *Official Police Detective* magazines. She tried to pop another bubble but the gum gave out. Completely. She threw the gum away, rolled up the window quickly.

"Where we at?"

"Markleysburg. Hubert go for Uniontown or Youghiogheny Reservoir? What do you way?"

She dug into the glove box and came up with half a pouch of Red Man, and with great deliberation tucked a small wad in her jaw.

"Well? What do you think?" he shouted.

She stayed calm.

"I think we're gonna look about as low-down and depraved as these kind of guys they put in here whenever you catch up with him." She held up sado-masochistic rag with its depraved front cover picture to lucidate. "Won't that be fine?"

Evan J. tore it from her hands, balled it up and threw it out the door. He turned and glared at her, kept glaring at her till she felt better play along or else get killed.

She shrugged.

"I dunno—mebbe in Pennsylvania straight north up to Somerston, on #53." The numbers change in Pennsylvania. The roads kept going on, but not the numbers.

"Naw, I don't think. I think he'd wanna get off on somethin' else, now."

"You asked my opinion." Em shrugged again. She spat out the door then slammed it shut again. Tobacco was okay except for blowing bubbles. "Coulda switched off back at Morgantown. Went west on #48."

"Why west?"

"Why any place? He could be a lot of places."

They sat there several minutes saying nothing. Disconnected bullshit blatted at them from the CB. The rain poured hard and steady, dark and gray.

Evan J. smacked the wheel with the ball of his palm in sudden decision, threw the truck in gear. The diesel roared. He swung into a left and headed west toward Uniontown on #40.

"Don't know what the hell I bother askin' you for," he said.

"Me either," she said. Em kept chewing Red Man, watching rain streak by. "How would I know anymore than you?"

Baker gave it five miles more, then opened up his mike again. He raised a half dozen truckers. None had anything about the pickup, had heard about the whole affair. One guy out of Baltimore said he'd had his *Bearcat* on the whole time and neither Maryland nor Pennsylvania Smokey was making any mention of any West Virginia killers.

Another five went by.

He got a pay-dirt call.

"Hello! *West Virginia!* You copy that guy up on #381? About an old Ford pickup?"

"Negatory. Must be out of range. What is it?"

"This guy says he thinks he seen your fella. Old maroon Ford 4-wheeler there with bashed-in fenders. That's what the fella say."

"10-4. What's the '-20?"

"#381. Mile north of Ohiopyle, there; I'm 'bout three miles south of Ohiopyle m'self. Just ridin', readin' mail."

"10-4. Much obliged."

"O.K. West Virginia, just repeatin' what I copy. There's some other talk about it up this way. Could be there's somethin' to it. I ain't makin' any guarantees."

"10-4. I understand."

Evan J. was lifted up inside, a little. Maybe he was catching up with some of the original crowd again, with Hubert, mainly. Hubert was the one. They had passed the junction of #381 at Farmington three miles behind, were coming to another of those seven-building "towns" that always made you wonder who was in them and how they made a living. Baker knew there was a country blacktop north off #40 at Chalkhill coming up right away, could take it north four miles and to another "T" with another blacktop just like it, hang a right and be into Ohiopyle and #381 in another half a mile. He'd been up and down so many times between Morgantown and the Eastern Turnpike he knew them all. It was a simple toss-up as to which would slow him down the more—the rain and bad surface of that old blacktop or the rain and traffic on #40 back to the Farmington junction. Six of one and a half a dozen of the other. The decision hung until the turnoff was upon him and was finally emotional. Evan J. swung hard into the right—too fast and a little late. The Peterbilt went up on the corner opposite tearing up a corner of somebody's ill-kept yard and swung out onto the street again, roared two blocks and out of town. Whether time would be gained was doubtful by this route, but it was different turf. Not the sense of backtracking on #40. An artificial sense of progress beat a certain sense of loss by a good country mile.

Three miles north the tractor threw a tire.

Evan J. hauled her over and got out to see. Em slid out behind. The retread had come off the outside rear left, the wheel that had caught fire. They stood looking at the bald casing, steaming on the rim in straight down rain. Em kept hands in pockets, said nothing, showed not a trace of the relief flooding her inside.

"Don't you say a goddam thing," said Evan J.

Em kept her eyes on the tire, leaned over and suddenly spat tobacco. Inside she said thanks to God.

"It's on the outside wheel," she pointed out with a certain low-key optimism. She felt she could afford advantages on Evan J.'s side, now. "Something, anyway."

Baker thought about that, looked deep into it for a reason to get mad. He found none and got mad.

They stood there getting wetter. Em felt the cold and wetness reach her shoulders, but said no more. She let Evan J. make the move.

He came alive again at last. He went to get the tool chests open. Nothing for it but to change the tire.

MILEPOST 195—5:35 P.M.

An hour after setting west again from Harrisburg, the Bradens had made less than forty miles of progress. It had taken Dan a quarter of an hour just to break into the traffic, and they had just now come through the double tunnels at Blue Mountain, roughly Milepost 195, averaging under forty. He had never seen the traffic as bad as this before. It amplified Dan Braden, Jr.'s anguish; all of the diffuse anxieties, the vague and vast fears of energy depletion, population densities, the future in which his job with the major oil company marinated him each day. So he was more than normally frustrated at the slow crawl. If things did not pick up they wouldn't reach Detroit till morning. He would face the day at work with no sleep at best, late and probably un-shaven.

The kids had caught the sense of his anxiety and sat quietly just looking out the windows. The dog, Daisy, who in her preg-nancy had acquired strange appetites, hang over the back seat bumming Christine out of the remaining fries.

Christine began to moan a little, and then rolled up into a ball. Irene looked back. "Chris, what's the matter?"

"I'm feeling kinda sick."

Chris *was* a little on the chubby side. It worried Irene chron-ically.

"I told you not to eat so many fries. For God's sake, Chris, when will you learn?"

"I was hungry! Daisy got most of them anyhow! Ow!"

"Well, there's nothing I can do," said Irene. She turned forward again.

Ed turned from the window, regarded his sister placidly.

"Fat girls take what they can get," he said.

"*Mom*! Tell Eddie to shut up!"

"What did you say now, Eddie?"

"He said fat girls take what they can get. Ooooo-h!"

"Why are you always saying such rotten things all the time? What gets into you?"

"It's the truth," said Ed.

"Be quiet," said Christine.

"Look at Marsha Birnbaum in your class," said Eddie. "God! She has to be nice to *everybody*—greasy guys with giant hickeys and everything. Quit stuffing your face before it's all over and you're blown clear up to fullest size, like some kind of hippopotamus. God! It's sickening!"

"*Mom!*"

"Eddie, stop that!"

Eddie waited till his mother turned away again.

"How can a guy keep his head up with a hippopotamus sister that has got to take what she can get?"

"OOo-o-oh . . . I'm sick! *Mom*! Make him stop it!"

"What the hell's going on back there? Haven't I got enough with this driving? Settle down back there!"

"She's sick, Dan."

"What do you want me to do about it? I can't stop!"

"Marsha Birnbaum, Marsha Birnbaum—"

"Straighten up, Ed," said his father.

It was quiet for a few more miles. Ed looked out the window. Chris groaned a little now and then, remained huddled in her ball. Then, Ed got up and started digging through the stuff behind the seat. He came up with a fat manila envelope, and with an air of secrecy, hid beneath the car blanket with the envelope.

Chris watched.

A light came on beneath the blanket. Chris snatched the blanket off and Eddie scrambled to stuff the contents back into the envelope.

"*Mom! Hey, Mom!*"

"What is it *now*, Chris?"

"Eddie's got more nakeds, he's got another bunch of nakeds again!"

"Eddie! You haven't got more of those awful pictures?"

"They're in there, Mom. He's got them in the envelope!"

"Is that true?" said Dan.

"No," said Ed. It sounded lacking in conviction.

"Eddie, are you sure?" Eddie didn't answer. "What's in the envelope, Ed?" Dan was catching Ed's eye in the rearview mirror.

"Comics."

"It is not, it isn't either. He's got another bunch of nakeds in there!"

"Is that right, Ed?"

"No it's not. It's comics."

"Word of honor?"

"Yes."

"He's lying! He's lying!"

"Let's see it, Ed." Dan held his hand above his shoulder. "Come on, Ed."

Ed handed it to his father. Dan handed it to Irene. "Last chance, Ed." said Dan. "It's comics now—you're sure."

Ed paused, hesitating. "Uh-huh," he shook his head. It looked feeble. It sounded feeble.

"Okay, Pal. It's your decision." No sound or sign from Ed.

"Go ahead, Irene—open it."

Ed sank into the seat and gazed back out the window.

Chris jumped forward, gloating. "What is it? What is it?" She seemed to have lost all trace of sickness for the moment.

Irene slid the contents out.

"What is it?" Dan asked.

"Comics."

They passed the next few miles in silence. Then Chris leaned over and whispered. "You've got them someplace. I *know* you do!"

Ed kept looking out the window. Chris rolled up into a ball and resumed her sickness and her groaning.

"Fat girls take what they can get," said Ed. He went back to looking out the window.

REDFORD CENTRAL—6:20 P.M.

All maintenance facilities save Aurora and Kregg made the routine hourly report. Temperatures were in the lower thirties all up and down the line, all stations still reporting steady rain. Somerston Maintenance called in late by the land line, reporting vacant eastbound still in front of them and their inability to raise Redford on the VHF. Lee advised Somerston Maintenance to have flagmen two miles in advance of Exits 9 and 10 ready for the coming traffic. Now that the 41-B dozer had been moved and the evacuation of the eastbound between Somerston Gate 10 and Aurora had been completed he was reopening the eastbound at Donovan. They were to be damn sure that no more patrons went on up the east side of the mountain, that they were routed off again at Somerston. Lee instructed them to call the gates and alert them since radio between them was still line-of-sight and functional. He wished to God he had the Bald Knob Repeater back in service. What was going on with Jimmy? It was a blind spot over there.

The gates at Donovan didn't answer for what seemed an inexcusable amount of time. The attendant apologized profusely when he discovered who he was talking to. They were having "some confusion" there, as he put it. Lee gave the order to reopen. Things were looking up a little.

Judy had relayed the message that the tunnel lanes were open when he'd come down from Chuck's office. He now had just one segment of the eastbound down. These thoughts went through his mind and then he rebuked himself as quickly for the self-deception. With the traffic at its current density, Somerston a hopeless bottleneck and the small alternates overloaded to an absurd degree, he was really only moving the location of the backlog twenty miles. The best that he could hope for was to give old Route 31 some time to clear so Somerston would be getting it from Gate 10 alone. Before the weather. *Maybe* before the weather. It just might be possible to do that in an hour. Whether it would ultimately help he didn't know. Human systems sometimes caught you up in desperate activity for nothing. You could be aware and still you had to carry through, persist in the futility. Lee felt that was approximately the situation now.

He punched up the outside phone line just to listen, get a sense of what was there. There had been the routine calls from patrons saying they were out of gas, stuck someplace, wondering what the hell was going on throughout the afternoon. The normal. The corporal at the state police desk fielded most of these in normal times, relayed milepost locations to appropriate mobile units or the nearest franchised service operation and got them taken care of through the appropriate zone operator. He'd been with it constantly throughout the afternoon and Lee had assigned him two more operators when the shift had changed at 4:30. The rate of calls was high, but not abnormally for the weekend. The evening TV news had not yet broadcast the weather. Lee looked at the clock. The news was one third through. Give it fifteen minutes; then the you-know-what would hit the fan.

The ringing signal sounded in the monitor. Del picked it up. "Eastern Turnpike State Police, can I help you?"

"Yeah, listen," said a guy. "I got to get to Terre Haute before tomorrow."

"From where?"

"Newark. You expecting any trouble on the roads out there?"

"Yes sir. We have severe winter storm warnings. The traffic is incredible. I wouldn't advise coming west if I were you. We're having severe problems."

"Aww, *Man*! You kidding! I didn't hear anything about bad weather. Are you sure?"

"Yes Sir. I recommend you watch the evening news. It cropped up kind of suddenly this afternoon."

"I really gotta get to Terre Haute tomorrow."

"I think you would be wise to postpone that. I really do."

"Naw. You guys are always going overboard on stuff like this, I know. Ten to one it don't amount to nothing. You're playing safe, I betcha."

"No sir, this one is on the level."

"Naw. The heck with it. I'm coming." And the guy hung up. And so did Del. Lee let up on his monitor button, a familiar sense of being thoroughly helpless and disgusted.

REDFORD CENTRAL—6:20 P.M.

Phone calls began to escalate rapidly. Chuck had briefed the extra operators earlier and all were busy now. The phones were going bananas. He had made a general announcement for the systems to thoroughly discourage any plans of travel, in all phone inquiries; make it seem black as possible to those who had not yet begun to travel or had stopped somewhere they might find refuge.

Troop barracks up and down the line were receiving just about as many calls as Redford. Local areas had come to depend on them for information. For those who called to see about friends and family who had already left and now were traveling, the picture was toned down. What for? Why scare somebody uselessly? The others got the fear of God put into them.

In a sense the guy he'd listened in on had been right; the troopers tended to be somewhat pessimistic and conservative. You couldn't blame them; they did the cleaning up.

By 6:30 when the news concluded it had become all but impossible to get a call to any station on the Turnpike through the busy signal. From here on in they would be dealing with an estimated one percent of calls attempted. Even persons attempting to place calls to parties other than the Turnpike stations would experience some difficulty. Exchanges would be jammed. Lee knew it wouldn't let up before morning—maybe Tuesday morning if Nadel was right. Maybe Wednesday. Anyway the calls were coming. Chuck was doing his job. They had been warned. Lee made an "all stations directive" of his own that all maintenance units west of Harrisburg get plow trains organized and be fully loaded and start laying down salt and cinders.

REDFORD CENTRAL—6:40 P.M.

Lee received another call on the private line from Tri-State.

"Hit me, Jim."

"No news. It's as described. The main front will pass north of you."

"How far?"

"A gnat's ass. You'll get a piece of it out west of Pittsburgh where the Pike cuts north. Again as predicted. There's some electrical activity associated with this thing. Thunder and lightning. For a while it looked like the possibility of a funnel near Canton, but that seems to have relaxed, a little."

"This time of year?"

"Sure. *Anytime* you get that violent a contrast between two masses—"

Lee cut him short. "How much, what, and when?"

"Any time now. Freezing rain the first hour—maybe two—

then the snow. Same figures. You're in the fringe, it's weird. My guess is that—oh say—thirty, forty miles below you there won't be one flake on the ground by morning. Sorry, Lee. If that southern high had been an hour earlier, a couple millibars higher—''

"Skip it," said Lee. No use puddling around in things that might have been.

"Has to be," said Jim.

"Jim, you're keeping detailed record on this for us, aren't you? I'm sure we'll all be wanting it."

"We are." There was a little pause. "It may be ending earlier than estimated. Sometime before dawn." Nadel sounded distant, sort of dismal. "One advantage of fast moving systems." The gears were grinding. He had something on his mind.

"What gives? Sounds like you got a kicker in there waiting."

"Well, with this kind of setup you usually get a circulation up and around—aw, skip it; too far off to think about."

"Think about what?"

"Never mind. It's much too early. Anything can happen, just forget it."

"Right! Don't think about the word rhinoceros!"

"I think aloud. It's speculation, nothing more—a habit. Call you in a while."

6:45 P.M.

Before the tire was changed and they could get back in the cab, Evan J. and Em were as soaked and filthy as drowned rats. Em clamped down to keep her chattering jaw from spasms. Evan J. fired up the engine and threw the heaters on full blast, but that took time. Em dug out the 12-volt hot-air defroster gun kept in the truck for clearing windows, plugged it in the lighter and began to blow them dry. It was 6:45 and dark out, occasional big snowflakes in the still unceasing rain.

Em would have suffered all of this twice over. Of course she didn't think her Pa could kill a person, but he'd been in Viet

Nam and he might. He never talked about it so she didn't know. She was banking on the time lapse to cool him off. Maybe, since the tire had taken so much time, he'd give it up and go on home now. But Evan J. put the Peterbilt in gear and pulled out on the blacktop, maybe a little more deliberate and rational; a little less impulsive with the gears but still going north into the darkening storm.

A mile ahead they reached the crossing, swung right and on into Ohiopyle to get onto #381. They waited at the light. Maybe he would hang a right and roll south again for home. He didn't do that either. When the light turned he made a labored left, kept to the limit for three blocks until clear of the little junction town, then he put the hammer down.

Em let out a private sigh.

The guy who called about the pickup on #381 was long gone. No one else Evan J. raised knew anything at all, had even heard of the whole situation. The CB was like that on the road. Sometimes you got into little rolling groups or parties that you stayed with till you stopped for gas or food, and when you again got rolling it was all new company, a whole new crowd. Sometimes you could stay with someone halfway across the country and sometimes it had gotten to be almost family with a couple of them. Then you never heard of them again and always wondered what they looked like forever after. Now the miles and hours had gone by. Now it seemed the whole wide world of roads and rain had swallowed Evan J. and his little problem. She watched him from the side of her eye. He was a sad old country song, her Daddy—just like all them songs. He knew it too. There was nothing else for him except keeping on being him and up off the bottom best he could. He had to try. Em just kept her peace and let him. There was scarce chance of him catching up with Hubert, anymore.

They kept on #381 through Mill Run, Normalville, Indian Head, Melcroft, Champion—all the little six- and seven-building towns, the "who the devil lived there and what for" kind of towns. All in twenty miles of rain.

Evan J. paused at #31 junction of the old route east and west that now paralleled the Eastern Turnpike. They were a hundred miles from home and she kept thinking about Molly and the foal and how far they could go on half a bale of hay. A big green sign pointed to the left with a big white-beaded arrow, whole thing lit up in the headlights: "EASTERN TURNPIKE". Baker hesitated, undecided. Horns blared behind him. He gunned the Peterbilt and swung left—toward Gate 9—Donovan.

"You goin' on the Pike?" Em allowed her voice a touch of incredulity. What was it going to take to make him quit?

"He got people in Louisville. He said that, didn't he? Louisville?"

"Louisville!? You got to be kidding, Pa!"

"You just be glad it ain't L.A.!"

He bore down harder than before to prove there'd been no loss of conviction. Em folded up her arms and sank into the corner.

A mile west of the junction the big tractor began to cough and backfire. One mile and a quarter later they were on the shoulder. Fuel tanks dry.

Evan J. hung his hands atop the wheel and laid his face down there.

"Get out." he said.

"Wha——?" said Em.

"I said get out! Just get the hell out of here!" The second time it came with such ferocity she pulled the latch and slid down to the running board in one quick motion. She sat there a long time in the rain, getting soaked through, all over again, spitting out a little of the chaw from time to time. Above her through the doors and through the rain she listened to her Daddy cry.

The door came gently open sometime later.

"You stay with the truck," he said.

Evan J. took the gas can, CB walkie-talkie, and was gone.

REDFORD CENTRAL—7:00 P.M.

At 7 P.M. the hourly reports from maintenance had come in as before: temperatures of 35 and steady rain, high densities of traffic with the westbound averaging around 45, bumper to bumper. The bunching east of Redford had relaxed a little, but the slowing through the snow that had accumulated on Aurora and was beginning to appear on Blue Mountain now had not allowed the flow to reach anything approximating normal. Plow trains were out and fully loaded, salting and cindering as directed.

MILEPOST 30.9—7:10 P.M.

At 7:10 it hit Gibson Maintenance and Barracks. They reported that the front had passed them. They had a blizzard. It was incredible, they said. First, the rain stopped for about two minutes, then turned into a gentle, straight down snow with flakes the size of quarters. For about ten minutes it was quiet. You could hear the snow. There was what looked like lightning to the north and west. Big flashes, but no sound of thunder. Then the wind hit. It struck with sudden force enough to send some of the little minicars off into ditches. Temperatures had dropped from 33 to 25 within the last half hour. Visibility was about as far as the tail lights of the next car ahead. The westbound slowed momentarily to 35, then 25. Eastbound traffic through West Gate from Ohio was coming heavy as before, moving faster than the westbound, which they didn't understand. Irwin heard the conversation between Gibson and Redford Central and said they didn't know where the eastbound was disappearing to either. They still had the tail end of the backlog from Donovan four miles to the east of them. At least it didn't seem to be growing. They didn't understand that either. There were big, unknown areas out there where no one really knew what was happening.

REDFORD—7:15 P.M.

Judy called Lee Rider to the phone.
"It's your wife," she said.
"Jen, God, I'm sorry. I've been up here all afternoon."
"Have you heard from Charley? Did she call?"
"No. You haven't heard from her either?"

"Of course not. Why would I be asking?" There was an edge to Jen's voice that was not Jen. Then she softened, having heard herself.

"I'm sorry, Lee. I—well—I've listened to the scanner all day long until my head is pounding. Then the news tonight. For God's sake what's going on out there? How did this thing come up so all of a sudden?"

Lee let off a sigh. "Look. I—guess I'll be here. For the night."

"I assumed that."

"I wouldn't worry about Charlene so soon. How long have you been trying to get through?"

"An hour."

"Yeah, well that's really nothing, believe me. Some people getting through to us have been trying two. The lines are swamped. Charley's probably unable to get through. We might not hear a thing until tomorrow. It doesn't mean a thing except the phones are busy."

"I suppose you're right, Lee. I'm—well, kind of lonesome, that's all. The house is so—empty. It's so dark out there. It seems like 2 A.M."

"Would you like to come here?"

"No, don't be silly. I'm fine. Really. I want to be here in case she *does* call."

"Well, you're welcome if you want to. You can sack out in my office, down in the dormitories—whatever. I'm serious."

"No, no. That's crazy. I'll be fine. Forget it. I was only hoping—you know."

"Yeah, I know."

"Well, listen, I better let you go. I know you're busy."

"Yes."

"Call me if she does call. I mean if she sends a message from a station or—whatever."

"I'll send a naked runner if I have to."

"Hmm. Perhaps that wouldn't be so bad."

"You haven't seen my runner! I don't take those kinda chances with my baby."

Jennifer laughed. "I'm better now. I'll be okay."

"You'll do the same? I mean if she pulls off a miracle and gets a call through?"

"Well, naturally, you dope. You haven't seen my runner either."

"Okay, then just relax."

MILEPOST 122—THE WEST END OF AURORA—7:20 P.M.

Ollie had his first snow pile scraped up, set to go. At a top speed of some seven miles an hour, it had taken almost half an hour to drive the big Allis-Fiat 41-B up from 118.4. It had been one big screw up down below, getting the big cat down off the trailer, getting the tractor-trailer out of the way. It had been another up above. Arthur, the kid from Johannsen's at the wreck with the wrecker-truck #230-B, had made scant progress. The parking area on both sides of the tunnel and the wide turn-around between the lanes still were pretty much filled up with the initial crash. Half the kid's problem was that Jim Johannsen had him awe-struck with the preciousness of his big private wreckers. Scared to put a scratch on one. Ollie couldn't have that. He commandeered the 20-thousand-dollar wrecker and showed the boy how it was done.

"Yer takin' too much time to hoist 'em clear up off the road! Forget it!" The Kregg chief dragged the rumpled wrecks across the pavement on the towline like so many pulltoys, then turned around and shoved them in with the plywood bumper in front. The kid held his ears against the screams of metal and con- templated least offensive methods of suicide in preference to fac- ing Jim Johannsen, should Ollie damage wrecker #230-B.

As the foremost portions of the crash were reached, the indi- vidual cars had been so utterly mangled that all of them were to- taled. Ollie sent the kid back down to Somerston in the wrecker and used the big "Cat" to shove the wreckage up in piles. By the time space had been cleared, these violent activities had mess- ed up the snow so badly that he had to start as far back as 121.7 with the dozer and work the slushy snow up in piles. The "Cat's" enormous weight was making kitty litter of the pavement, Ollie knew. It was bad enough to make a single trip, but back and forth and back again over the same stretch of it with something like the Fiat-Allis was ruin indeed. They'd resurfaced Eastern so many times it must be four feet thick by now, but the top three inches or so was all that counted. That was gone. He couldn't help it. Maybe he could save the tunnel.

The fire burned visible through half a mile of incredibly lousy weather. He had a pile together now. He dorpped the 2-ton blade and started forward.

The first pass piled a mound five feet, not reaching wall-to-wall, against the burning scrap iron in the tunnel. He pulled back for a look. Already he could see it melting. This was going to take a lot of snow. He spun the "Cat" around and started back for more.

THE BALD KNOB SUMMIT—7:20 P.M.

At 7:20, Jimmy Weeks had reached the Bald Knob Repeater. There was lightning in the west and north and it was snowing, a billion little individual snowflake "pats" that you could hear, conjoining into a steady, infinite background hiss, the only sound from everywhere. He paused outside the chain link fence around the solemn little concrete blockhouse and just listened. The ambience had crushed in instantly the moment that the raucous motor of the snowmobile had been shut down, and it was lovely to him now; as he imagined the background white noise of the universe the radio astronomers found everywhere between the stars. Dimly from above, the red glow of the toplight ebbed on and off again in somber intervals of five seconds. One on, four off—paced and gentle, to sustain extended life through the long haul.

The trip had been neither uneventful nor easy. Jim had hooked the Arctic Cat and trailer to the 4-wheel drive International, started up the "Cat" to ensure its operation, then cut north through the town to intercept Route 30. Traffic coming in on #30 from the west was such that it had taken twenty minutes till a Redford traffic cop arrived to untangle traffic at the junction enabling him to move into the junction and go left and west.

The section of Route 30 west to 219 was particularly mountainous; the northern route around Aurora, a winding, two-lane
blacktop that had been a major artery up until the later '30's, was
now the province of locals with occasional detour duty for the
Pike.

Ten miles out of Redford it had gotten really sloppy. He was
well up by then. Route 30 climbed 900 feet, then dropped 500
going over to the Somerston side. Normally to save the tires he
wouldn't lock the front wheels into drive until he'd reached the
chain across the entrance to the Turnpike's private access road up
to Bald Knob. Tonight he'd had to have them five miles out of
Redford. The Turnpike eastbound being routed around the mountain had been slipping and fishtailing. He'd had to dodge a lot,
been driven off onto the berm a couple times. Road shoulder was
in short supply along this part of #30; he'd been simply lucky
berm was there on the occasions that he needed to have it.

After 20 miles of this he'd reached the chain across the dirt
road up to 12 and had to smash the ice off the padlock with the
handle of a big screwdriver. Still the key would not go in. He
warmed the lock up with a butane cartridge torch out of the van.

The road beyond was simply ruts beneath the now seven inches of wet snow, but still passable for the van for a distance of
eleven winding miles thorugh oak and cedar forest. Families of
deer appeared in the headlights several times, only to wander
casually out of the way. The deer had found the road to their
convenience and adopted it decades before. Now an eight point
buck had stood its ground, seemingly blinded in the headlights,
with his does behind him. Jim had to get out of the truck and yell
to get him moving. Amazing how bold they were up here.

There was a place some thirteen miles above old #30 where
it ended for the van, where not even 4-wheel drive would go, a
kind of landing ledge with just enough flat space to turn around.
Jim shut down the van and got the "Cat" unloaded; fired her up.
The raucous noise of the snowmobile was terribly offensive in the
night forest. However nine more miles of rocky, scarcely defined
goat-trail still lay between him the the Knob. Repeater Number
12. He spilled twice. The second time the "Cat" tipped and
temporarily pinned his foot. It hurt like hell.

The foot was still sensitive as he undid the padlock at the

gate of the repeater and then a second lock on the steel door of the shack itself. The door opened with a few small squeaks of corrosion. He made a mental note to give the hinges and the lock a shot of silicone on the way out.

Inside was a single upright rack of electronics in the center, a shelf of storage batteries along one wall, a little service bench along another. Colored panel lamps glowed dimly in the darkness till he found the light and switched it on. He set his armload of tool pouches on one end of the bench giving the place a superficial glance. A forest mouse streaked for cover in the racks as the light came on. He checked the line voltage on a nearby meter. It was within acceptable tolerances, seemed steady. A.C. line power was not the problem, the station hadn't gone on auxilliary battery supply. He hadn't expected this to be the trouble, but it was routine, the first thing you looked at up in these remote sites.

Jim could see his breath inside the shack. The equipment kept things warmer than the outside by a few degrees, but there was no intent to heat the place; electronic gear fared better in cold in any case, and human visits were but hours at a time, spaced out at as much as three- or four-week intervals. Old Number 12 was visited much oftener. Half a dozen stained and out-of-date pinup calendars hung crookedly around the walls, left by techs gone by, and an old electric coffee pot stood on the bench, a small electric space heater with its cord wound up beside it.

Jim shut the door and lifted the heater off the bench to put it elsewhere, out of his workspace. Behind it was a pile of sticks and fluff, dry grass and fuzz. It wiggled. Jim parted it with gentle fingers. Four baby field mice lay within. Their eyes had not yet opened, they were showing but a light frosting of hair. He grinned as he set the heater down and plugged it in elsewhere. He reached into his pocket, deposited a heap of peanuts by the nest. He made a workspace at the other end.

A quick check of the panel meters on the rack showed that the receiver was okay. He monitored some calls from down below to verify. Okay. That was not the problem. The transmitter's output meter showed that the energy sent up to the antenna was for the most part being reflected back along the coax line and going nowhere, a high S.W.R. Jim sucked a tooth and checked the heavy cable leading from the rack to the outside. There seemed no problem there. It looked like he would have to climb the tower.

MILE 63—7:46 P.M.

At 7:46, Irwin Barracks reported that the rain had turned to heavy sleet, that it was coating windshields, making visibility impossible. The road surface was beginning to glaze over, they were getting fender-benders everywhere. The frozen rain drops were intermingled with abnormally huge flakes of snow. "As big as gas caps," was how the desk corporal put it.

MILE 122—AURORA—7:46 P.M.

Ollie had been working like a demon for half an hour, working up the snow. His first pass convinced him that he'd have to hit it with everything at once or it would melt away to no avail. He had a pile the size of one small house standing like a minor mountain maybe fifty yards below the tunnel. He dropped the blade and plowed in.

MILE 145.1—REDFORD CENTRAL—7:55 P.M.

Lee Rider had picked up the VHF and was attempting to raise anybody at the tunnels. He was getting nowhere. He tried five calls. At last he got an answer.

"10-4, Redford. This is Aurora. Go ahead."

"What's your status? Is there any progress on that fire?" Lee didn't recognize the voice.

"Ah, yes sir. Yes there is."

That's all the guy said, then nothing. A big chunk of static open air.

"Like what for instance?"

"10-9?"

"What kind of progress on the fire, for God's sake!"

"Oh, well it's out now, pretty much. Ollie Chelinski shoved up a couple hunert tons of snow and plugged it, there, on the west end. They got it, just about. It's all but over."

"Look, lemme talk to Barger. Anybody."

Lee waited for an answer. After several minutes he gave up, let Judy know he wished to be informed if anybody called from Aurora.

REDFORD CENTRAL—8:06 P.M.

At 8:06, Somerston Barracks called in on the land line saying that the weather had hit there now too. A glaze with giant flakes of snow, turning tree twigs and radio antennas into glass. Patrons were slipping, sliding all over the place. The forward average of the westbound was down to fifteen miles an hour, twenty at most. Things were looking lousy.

Somerston Maintenance called late, 8:10; they had plow trains out. All their plow trucks. Their drivers were reporting nothing that substantial yet to plow, but they were laying salt down as best they could. The closely packed westbound made it impossible to organize into the standard 5-plow train. Plow 2229 had run out of salt at the turnaround at milepost 93 and couldn't turn around because of standing solid eastbound traffic, since the eastbound had been reopened. The bypass was a slow stampede. They had "snow up *there*, by God," is how the driver of 2229 put it. He was trying to get over to the eastbound side and down to the old two-lane tunnel that had been "bypassed" some ten years before to get more salt. Now boarded up with garage doors and used for salt and oil storage. He was basically having no luck.

Lee threw on his coat, took the elevator to the roof. He stopped by Chuck's office on the way. They went out together.

BALD KNOB REPEATER—8:30 P.M.

The first time Jimmy Weeks had climbed the tower it was not so bad, the snow was wet and you could kick it out of the triangular girder spacers and get a foot in solid. It was a straight girder type, not tapered like the "RKO Radio" towers of the old days. Lighter. Put up in prefabricated sections. The VHF arrays were physically quite small, cut to match the physical dimensions of the waves they spewed out and received from the surrounding mountainsides. There wasn't that much weight to be supported, but they had to be quite high. Jim had hooked the climbing belt around him and gone up. The foot was giving him a lot of trouble. There was no way to climb and not set his weight upon it on alternate steps, but he climbed.

Halfway up he found the problem. The cable had been bitten into, halfway through. A hunter's bullet, stray or vandal, who could tell? He'd had to go the whole way up, disconnect the cable at the base connector of the element itself, then drop the whole thing through and down then from inside the tower, haul it into the shack until he came to the rupture. He cut it there and put in a terminal connector, which had to be soldered. He cut the bad inch out and put another matching connector to the other end, joining both sections. He sprayed it down with resin, let it harden and wrapped it up with tape. Ideally it should have been a single piece of line, but that should hold, at least till warmer weather. He hadn't the materials to replace the entire feed line then and there and didn't have the time to go back down to Central and return. He checked his watch: 8:30.

He happened to glance down; the mother mouse was peering at him from behind the base of the transmitter. He grinned and went outside again closing the door behind him gently. What warmth there was would be a scarce commodity for the little mother and her brood, unconscionable to waste it.

It was altogether different outside now. Jim could barely see the red toplight above. The snowmobile was half buried in snow, and there was audible thunder to the north and west and lightning flashing. A corona of St. Elmo's fire had formed on some parts of the tower.

The tower girders were coated with an inch of glaze, the spaces barely large enough to gain a toe hold, but it was a quick job—one connection and he started up, threading the cable through the girder spaces one by one, from hand to hand.

His foot hurt badly and he noticed that the air had gotten considerably colder.

REDFORD CENTRAL—8:40 P.M.

A glaze of ice had already formed on the roof when Chuck Ellis and Lee Rider opened up the service door. Lee took one step and fell. Chuck stayed in the doorway. His back had taught him caution. The raindrops now had solid cores and struck against Lee's face like gravel.

Then it came as Gibson had described it. The rain stopped momentarily. There was very little wind. He could see lightning to the north and west. After a couple of minutes it began to snow. Big, gentle doilies of frost, like heads of Queen Anne's Lace and every bit as large, began descending. It didn't have the feeling of a snow; it had the feeling of invasion, like a billion big weird white things coming down from unseen spaceships high above the clouds. The icy roof was covered in a minute's time.

"Holy Mother! Look at that come down!" Chuck was duly impressed from the safety of his doorway.

Lee grunted something in a combination of pain and vague agreement. The Central Administration Building was one tenth of a mile directly north of the Pike itself. Normally the roof and upper office windows on this side gave perfect views of the Redford Gates. You could see it all. He had been able to see the double stream of slowly inching, grinding headlights when he first came out onto the roof. He couldn't see it now.

REDFORD CENTRAL—8:50 P.M.

Two developments faced Lee when he and Chuck got back to Central.

One: The Ohio Turnpike had called Gibson advising they would be accepting no more westbound traffic from Pennsylvania. Ohio was officially under a State of Emergency, shut down all the way, permitting whatever eastbound that could make it to evacuate through their East Gate—Eastern's West Gate—as long as they were able.

Two: The Bald Knob Repeater had come back into service. Lee at once picked up the mike to try to raise Aurora.

"Redford to Aurora Maintenance. Come back Aurora."

"Redford this is patrol car 344."

It was the captain.

"I don't believe it! John Beck on first try!"

"Hi, Lee. How's it feel to have dry socks on?"

"Where are you now?"

"138 point something. I can't see these markers anymore. I'm westbound. Heading up the mountain. Hey, I stopped off at Kregg for gas. We better get them something. They're running low."

"What's the situation at the tunnels?"

"Don't know. I heard they got the fire down. I see Redford Fire Department taking their equipment down. I've been playing taxicab the past two hours—getting patrons from the wreck down to the hospital. Going up for more. Lee have you seen these goddam snowflakes?"

"Yes, we saw them."

"It's piling up like doctor bills up here. I give this westbound half an hour."

"You have the other side of Aurora completely evacuated then?" Because of the Bald Knob Repeater no one had told Redford.

"From the west end? Oh hell yes! Hours ago. We got 'em standing round a rosy little barrel fire in the Aurora Maintenance. They better get the electric back in service there and get those ventilation fans in operation, that tunnel air is a killer. Hazard for cars inside the westbound. If it stops I think that patrons in the tube could suffocate. No illumination either. Hazard situation there."

"Better tell your boys about it. If the west stops altogether, give them gas masks and send them in to make patrons shut their motors down.''

"Yes, we've thought of that. What I'm afraid of is that one or two of these patrons could pass out even before the westbound quits moving, stop us with another wreck before the snow does.''

"Look, John. Who knows what good half an hour will do anybody? Ohio's shut down all the way. From what I hear out west, from you and Gibson and Somerston, there's nothing out there for them. Don't worry about the westbound. It's a matter of time. The only thing remaining for us to work on is the eastbound tunnel. Maybe we can get something moving east, give Somerston some relief, make ourselves some room to get in and start to clean this out tomorrow. Hell, I can't think of that much else to do!''

"I'll see what's up there.''

"Good. I got one of these laconic maintenance clowns a half hour ago. Didn't get much of a picture.''

"How's by you?''

"The phones are ringing off the walls. Executive Director's heard about it in Harrisburg. Called to make sure his ass is covered.''

"If this keeps up, there won't be much that isn't covered!''

"Tri-State thinks the snow will end sometime in the A.M.''

"What's the final accumulation?''

"Twenty to twenty-five.''

"Inches.''

"Yes.''

"The way this looks from where I am, I think I would have bought it if you said 'feet'.''

"Possibility of an emergency declaration later on—look, John, when you've gotten up to Aurora and turned around, you better get your butt down here and start delegating some responsibility. Earn your lousy pay for once and direct your men. I need you here, not out someplace playing snow queen. Got me?''

"10-9?''

"I said, 'Don't give *me* 10-9!' You heard what I said. Come straight down the eastbound into Central. Your guys are in for it. They're gonna need a *leader*. I got problems of my own.''

"Okay, Lee. I'll see about it."

9:15 P.M.

Judy flagged Lee to take a Zone 1 call. Gibson Barracks and Maintenance reported 11 inches and total stoppage at Milepost 40, now both east and westbound. Numerous spinouts, motor failures. Occasional abandonments.

"Judy, patch me up for a general directive. Zones 1 through 4."

Lee looked at his watch: 9:18. "Copy all stations, police and Turnpike personnel. We are officially shut down at Gates 1 and 2. All gates west of Pittsburgh inform any patrons entering the westbound that they will be off-routed at Gate 3 and will be very lucky to find lodgings overnight in Pittsburgh. I repeat. We are as of 9:18 P.M. officially shut down at Gates 1 and 2—all mileage west of Pittsburgh."

MILE 102—THE WESTBOUND—10:00 P.M.

The rain had started freezing on the windshield near Breezeway. The windshield fluid had run out while they were grinding up Aurora Mountain, stopping, starting, inching forward yard by yard. The very wet and heavy snow had packed the grill and radiator solid, causing the car to overheat. The windshield wipers would narrow to a 3-inch wedge until Dan would have to jump out of the car and try to knock as much of it away as possible before the car ahead would move again. That had been going on for hours. By 10 P.M. the Bradens had managed to get over Aurora, down past Somerston, and now were nudging up the bypass east of Donovan—inches at a time. Dan was getting worried about gas, two thirds of a tank gone consumed since Harrisburg. A hundred miles. Four and one half hours. They should have been past Youngstown now.

The big Camarro with the racing slicks ahead of them had caught Ed's fancy fifty miles before. Now it was ludicrous. Huge tires and engine made it impossible to control in snow. It fishtailed wildly, had crashed into whoever got trapped beside it in the inside lane a number of times now. The Camarro had so far sustained what had to be a thousand bucks of damage to it's own custom paint and body work. For his macho trip the Camarro driver sure was paying dues. At least the other guys had that for consolation. Dan was staying well behind.

"God!" said Irene. "I have never seen anything *like* this! Maybe we should stop, Dan."

"Maybe we should stop? That's great, Rene. Suppose you tell me how?" Dan was keeping close attention on that big Camarro.

"Look at that clown! Keep it in low, you idiot! Keep moving!" He glanced down at his gauges. "We're getting hot again. I've got to get stopped long enough to clear that radiator. We'll boil over." They kept passing those who had pulled off, the owners standing outside, frantically trying to get someone to let them in again. Nobody was giving anyone a break. You couldn't stop. You wouldn't dare. Dan Braden ground his teeth. His hands ached from tightness on the wheel.

The kids had been quiet for a long time. Chris had put her head out somewhere back past Breezeway, had puked the french fries down the car and ended the problem of the carsickness. Would probably remove the paint, thought Dan. Like bird shit. Maybe the rain would wash enough of it away. Ed had made exaggerated faces, complained, "Eww, God! The smell! Take a couple hundred Certs or something! Quick! Daisy's pup'll get deformed!" But that had died down soon. Last of anything approximating normal fights. Kids were like that when a crisis was authentic. He almost wished they'd kept on scrapping. Of course he surely would have killed them.

REDFORD CENTRAL—10:00 P.M.

The 10 P.M. hourly maintenance reports came mostly from fellows sitting stranded in their plows. Virtually all men were out in the storm someplace fighting with it toe-to-toe. By 10 P.M. there was no discernible movement eastbound or westbound west of Donovan. It was grinding down to nothing on the bypass, grinding down to nothing out in front of Redford Central, and as far back now as Harrisburg you could not accurately say that westbound traffic was moving. Twitching, writhing spasmodically—but not really moving. Exit towns were filling up and overflowing with travelers. At 10 P.M. Lee Rider had to make another general announcement to all stations on the system.

"Redford Central to all gates, and stations. We are now officially shut down to westbound traffic from Blue Mountain west. Westbound patrons will be off-routed at Gate 15. Westbound patrons getting on anywhere on the system are to be so advised, and discouraged from westward travel on this and all roads. We can at least say that we told them so."

In reality the eastbound was shutdown too, though not officially. Why bother? There was some hope of gathering the off-routed at the town of Somerston, perhaps opening the tunnels. Weather seemed to die off rapidly beyond Blue Mountain where the elevation dropped from the Appalachian plateau to seaboard levels losing about 600 feet of altitude. It seemed that if they made it past Blue Mountain eastbound they were golden. The eastbound from Redford to Blue Mountain was being maintained with salt and cindering, plow trains brought into service as far east as Harrisburg. Traffic eastbound from Reford Gate 11 was moving moderately—as well as could be hoped—consisting mainly of the few who were managing to get around the mountain from the Somerston side, getting on at Reford and a fair component giving up on secondary routes, trying their luck on the Pike. With conditions on the secondaries as they were, what had they to lose?

TOWN OF SOMERSTON—10:00 P.M.

The sound of cracking limbs awoke the mayor. He had slept for many hours in the desk chair, in hat and Harry Truman overcoat and the inevitable cigar. He had waited in the courthouse since leaving the V.F.W. that afternoon. At first his eyes came open and that was all of him that moved for several moments. He listened to his own hoarse breathing. Maggie knitted patiently be-

neath the dim electric candelabra on the wall across the office.
The yellowed, low-wattage gloom of the outdated room told him
it was dark outside—darker than just ordinary darkness. There
was honking from the streets, but that had been going on since
the beginning of the afternoon. It had become a background that
he didn't notice anymore.

He gave his energy to identifying the splitting, cracking
sounds, now. His mind cleared then, and it was a sound he'd
heard at times in his life before. Not often, but he knew. He remembered. The trees were breaking. He listened for wind. No
wind. So, it was *that* kind of snow.

The chair gave out a sudden scream as the mayor sat upright. His large wife jumped and dropped her knitting. The mayor
spun to face the street, got up and raised the center window. He
looked down on the Square and northward along Main Street
#219 toward the Pike. He couldn't see the Pike. He couldn't see
the first full block of Main Street. It was, indeed, that kind of
snow. A foot deep on the sill. Heavy, cakey, soggy wet stuff.
Right for snowballs. Very wrong for trees and big holiday
weekends. The jam below was a smudgy river of headlights that
faded out within just yards in billions and billions of the beautiful
gigantic falling snowflakes. A gorgeous snow. A Christmas card
snow. A warm snow. From everywhere out in the dark the trees
were cracking, breaking under the sheer weight of it, like the
rifle fire of war. A deadly snow.

The mayor watched it and listened to the cracking of the
limbs and honking and the voices of the throngs of people for a
long time before speaking to the patient Maggie.

"The kids go?" he didn't turn around.

"Yes. Hours and hours. Shut the window, John, you'll get a
chill."

He had slept in his overcoat, was overhot and sweating and
the air was, if anything, not cold enough upon his face. Still, he
shut the window.

"I'll be back," he said. "I'm going up and see about the
roof."

He took a 4-cell flashlight from the drawer and went up to
see.

MILE 101.6—10:15 P.M.

The Bradens had sat in one spot for at least ten minutes without moving. Dan had jumped out twice and beat the snow off the glass, dug the radiator out as much as he was able. His hurry had been quite unnecessary. The radio was getting just one station loud enough to hear—some clown playing *Winter Wonderland*. They switched it off. The rest of the dial was filled with heavy buzz. They must be near a power line. He switched it off, cut the motor and the lights down to parking. They sat there. Time went by and that was all that did go by.

REDFORD CENTRAL—10:20 P.M.

Lee's operators were swamped, unable to keep abreast of the radio logs, getting harried, irritable. The phones continued to be swamped without respite.

"Ah, 337 to Redford."

"Go ahead, 337." Emmert took it. He was spelling Judy on Zone 2. Judy'd worked the phones awhile, then requested to come back to where the action was and had taken 1 for Joe to grab a bite.

"Ah, Redford I'm on the westbound, 109—opposite the Gates at Somerston. Did they call you?"

"Did who call, 337?"

"The Gates. They had a pig truck topple over on the up ramp, here. Pigs is runnin' everywhere. Any other units in my area?"

"Negative 337."

"337 this is 348. What's your -20?"

"Gate 10. Well, opposite. I'm out here on this mother Westbound. Can't go forward can't get off. Can you render assistance with this pig situation on the ramp here? What's *your* -20?"

"I'm down at the junction #31 and #219 here in Somerston. Don't think I can get to you though. The weight of all this ice and then the snow. There's big tree limbs crackin' off and dropping everywhere. We got crushed houses and cars blocking up the streets and sidewalks. Everything.''

So much for Somerston, thought Lee.

He took the mike from Joe. ''348 this is Redford. What's the situation with the Turnpike patrons down there 348?''

''Somerston is wall-to-wall with Turnpike patrons, Redford. These people down here got some of the schools and churches and the firehalls open. The armory is open too. Local Red Cross is operating somewhat. It's still getting underway. You got to hand it to these local people down here Redford. Even taking some of them into their homes. But these patrons just keep on coming off the Pike and off #31. One hell of a time. We're getting wholesale vehicular abandonments everywhere. Nothing's moving. Can't get them to stay in their cars.''

''230 to Redford. Call back, Redford.''

''Go ahead 230.'' Lee gave Joe the mike again.

''I'm down at the junction #31 and #219 here in Somerboys move wreckage we pulled out of the tunnel. I'd go help out on that pig truck, but I don't know how I'd get back over, now this weather's hit and all. I can't raise my boy in 230-B. You try him. He must be over there someplace.''

''230-B to Redford or 230, either one. I ain't picky.''

''Go ahead 230-B,'' Joe was getting tired, a little hoarse. All of them were hours overtime.

''10-4, but I'm up here on the westbound—maybe mile 87. I can't tell. Hey, when the hell is anybody gonna get this backlog cleared up? I been sitting stuck damn near an hour!''

''Take it easy 230-B. They're backlogged out in front of you into Ohio, two whole maintenance units can't get the tunnel open, the whole damn town of Somerston is overrun, we got twelve inches of snow now and will be getting twenty-five before it's over. Just hang in there. Things is tough all over.''

''Ah, 10-4 Redford, but I ain't worrying about me. I'm getting fifteen bucks an hour—these patrons up here is getting cold an' hungry!''

''10-4, 230-B. What can we do? Just roll with the punches.''

''2227 to 230.'' It was Ollie trying to raise Jim Johannsen in his franchised wrecker. Where the hell was Ollie now?''

"230 to 2227. Go ahead."

"Hey, Jim. You headin' up or down?"

"Up."

"10-9?"

"Up."

"Yer gonna run into a ladder unit from the Redford Fire Department up at 138. Got jackknifed in that turn there, where them picnic tables are, just a little bit above the Howard Johnson's. You get up there straighten him around, will ya? We got a plow train trying to get through. We got everything in the world tryin' to get through."

"He tip over or just get sideways?"

"Sideways. Just get him straightened up and outa there. Got my whole train shut down."

"I see him, now. Do what I can. Where are you?"

"I'm just ahead of you at 138, ya dummy! Other side of this cockeyed fire truck!"

"Oh, yeah. Got an eyeball on ya, Ollie. I see it now."

Lee took the mike again.

"2227 this is Redford. What did you do with that bulldozer, Ollie?"

"Left it up there on the other side. Maybe we can use it later on."

"Is it small enough to drive it through the tunnel?"

"Nope."

"It better be. There's no way we can get it back down into Somerston."

"That's how it goes sometimes. Gonna pull the switch now Redford. Give Johannsen here a hand."

SOMERSTON—10:20 P.M.

The top two floors of the old courthouse had long been useless for more than storage and had been cut off from heating to conserve expenses before, but now the mayor left the doors behind him open so that heat would rise and warm the roof from underneath to melt the snow and shed the weight of it. That kind of snow collapsed old barns and modern buildings. The roof seemed okay. It showed damp in places and he could hear some creaks and groans, but what could be told from that? He let the doors stand open. He went down this time all the way to the basement.

Jake Stokes was in his office. That was good. On the telephone. That was good. Margaret his secretary was there, that was good, too. Jake, county coroner and head of the county civil defense, had lost an arm and his future as a surgeon in World War II and spent the rest of his life pulling up his coat when it slipped off the short end of his shoulder. Margaret was Jake's age. Neither had married. She had worked twenty years with Jake. The job was Jake's whole life. Everybody knew it was the arm.

Jake waved to the mayor, wrapped up his conversation quickly and put down the phone in the curiously flamboyant juggling act that screamed out to the world that one-armed guys were as good as anybody. Jake went too far with it; he made them better. Better that he just screw up and drop it now and then—it would take down walls between Jake and the world.

"L.John, here we go again, eh?" Snowstorms and the inundation of the town by travelers were nothing new to Somerston. It had just about become routine.

"What are we doing about it?"

"I just finished calling all the preachers to get their churches ready. Firehalls. My people. The armory. The Red Cross. Things are underway. We can take it."

Pribanic thought about it. Whether they could take it was immaterial. It was coming just the same. It was like your life; you got through it all the way from one end to the other no matter what, whatever happened you had lived your life. He got his Tums out and ate the remaining pair. He would have to go and get some more before the drugstore closed.

"Did you hear about a Declaration of Emergency from Harrisburg?" His town was still smarting from Thanksgiving '74 when the town had filled up like this and stayed filled up a week. They had opened up their homes and kitchens, fed people, took them in and somehow just never got repaid because they "hadn't kept clear records." They had seen times like this before. But it somehow felt different to the mayor this time and he didn't like the feeling.

"Too soon," said Jake. "These things take time."

"Jake. The trees are falling."

"I know it, L.John. The wheels of government grind slow."

Jake pulled his coat up over the shoulder again. "My people are figuring it for another '74. That's what we're setting up for. We're just ahead of it a little bit this time. Let's hope it makes a difference."

"Yes. Make sure everybody keep clear records."

"The kids, they left, huh?"

"Yeah, they left. Look Jake, when you call around, you tell people when they give out food, give out anything—write it down. Keep records. Tell them that."

Jake shrugged. His coat slipped off again, was replaced with the quick precision stroke of relfex. "I tell them! I tell them! But you think they're gonna take the time to write it down? Keep track? Baloney! Things get going too fast. Who's got the time? It's too much hassle."

"You tell them the mayor said it. This is not the fault of Somerston, P.A. We're a poor town. We can't be picking up for Eastern Turnpike anymore. They don't let us on and off for free. They can pay their own bills. Somebody's cat gets stepped on take it to the vet's and get a bill. You pass on what I say. No more Santa Claus. No more Mister Nice Guy."

"Is it the Pike's fault? That it snows?"

"It's snowing in the woods right now, but the woods aren't filling up with cars and people. We had enough of this. We had a nice life here before this Turnpike. You tell them what the mayor says. Goodbye, now. I'm going out. Get something for the stomach. Be back in a little while."

"It was a *real* nice wedding, L.John," Margaret said.

"Thank you," said the mayor. "I'm glad somebody thought so."

MILE 101.6—10:30 P.M.

"Mom. I'm cold." said Chris. "Turn the heater on."

"We can't, Honey," said Irene. "We're saving gas. Why don't you get a blanket and roll up and sleep awhile?"

Ed popped forward. "I bet we're gonna *freeze* to death, huh? Our arms are gonna get all hard and crack off when they try to get our bodies out."

"Mom! Make him shut up!"

"Well, now it won't be the carbon monoxide since we shut the motor off."

"Make him shut up, Mom!"

"We can get naked like the Eskimos and press our *bodies* up against each other in a pile to keep from freezing!"

"You're sick! Mom! Eddie's being sick again!"

"That's what they do."

"Knock it off, Ed," said his father.

They sat some more. Nothing moved at all. The windshield had covered up again. The snow was like wet rice. Dan had given up trying to keep the windshield clear.

All at once the sky lit up like daylight. A brilliant actinic blue. A thunderous concussion shook the car.

"What on earth was that?" Irene had jumped, startled to the point of pain.

"Lightning, I suppose." But it didn't sound like thunder exactly. It sounded more like the M-155 mortars he had trained on in the artillery. Dan's own answer didn't satisfy him. If lightning, it was too damn close.

Minutes passed.

Bam!

Another flash and deafening concussion. Dan rolled the window down and looked up at the sky. Nothing but giant flakes. He could scarcely keep his eyes open against them.

Boom!

Dan went blind for seconds.

Boom!

The fourth concussion followed rapidly upon the first. Dan got out and stood in the calf-high wet-rice snow, looking upward. He had no idea where they might be or what was going on now.

Then, he saw it. Another flash, this one further off—north of the Pike and not so blinding. The boom was longer in coming. Half a second. He saw it clearly. A short bolt of lightning that didn't hit the ground—a steel electrical transmission tower stood out brilliantly against the darkness. Another! Directly above. The shock was like a fist that grabbed and shook his body. Pain shot through his ears. Then his stomach. He thought about the static buzz in the radio. They had come to stand directly under huge overland high tension mains. Big ones—voltage high enough to find a path of fifty feet or more—jumping stepping-stone fashion between the dense, wet snowflakes, snowflakes to snowflakes, wire to wire.

Two more flashes and concussions in quick succession. The second strike held on. A steady arc began to burn between one cable and the steer tower. Sparks of molten metal as from welding showered from the crossarm, a sizzling, buzzing sound. Even from a quarter mile the sound was frighteningly loud, betraying the incredible amount of power there. The heavy cable started glowing dully red. The redness began growing visibly along it from the tower toward the Pike. He ripped the door open. If the cable severed it would come down right on top of them.

"Out! Everybody! Let's go!"

"What's going on?" Irene was confused and terrified.

"Never mind! Just do what I say. Get out of this car! Everybody! *Go!*"

Other people had begun to flee. Dan ran to the other side and pulled the door open, yanked his wife out by the arm, then Chris.

"We don't have time, get out and take the kids! Go up the road. Now *move!*"

The flashes and the booms kept going off overhead like the finale of a giant fireworks show. They struggled west in knee-high snow. More and more people were running too. It grew into a small stampede. A large one. They ran until they were a hundred yards or more away, then stopped and counted noses.

One short.

"Where's Eddie?"

"I don't know. He was right behind me," said Irene.

"Daisy!" Christine snapped her fingers.

"Oh, Dan! He must have run back for the dog!"

The concussions kept the sky lit up, throwing stark shadows strobelike between the abandoned cars. Braden ran desparately. It was maddening. He'd lost his car the way you do in shopping centers. He remembered the Camarro. A big truck, a big tank truck had been right behind them. He watched for these but there were lots of trucks. He became unsure as to just how far they'd run. The flashes and the reports threw sparks directly overhead again, some reaching the ground.

He saw the car!

Eddie was emerging from the back seat, cradling the whimpering Daisy in his arms. Dan grabbed him, propelled him by the collar back in the direction of the girls. The red hotness on the wire had grown across the road now, was almost white hot at it's point of origin at the tower.

Dan broke his fascinated gaze and started after Eddie and the dog, then he caught sight of an old woman staring pathetically in his direction from an aging Ford. He knocked on the window. She seemed stunned, half unaware! An old guy came around the front of the old Ford, what was it—'40, '42? One of the old bathtub Fords.

"Please, Mister. My wife. She don't walk so good and I can't lift her."

"Okay, we have to hurry," Dan said.

The woman had locked her door. She was hard of hearing or in shock. They couldn't make her understand.

"The door, Margaret. Unlock the door!" It was no good.

Dan ran around, dove across the seat and pulled the knob up. The old guy yanked the door open. She would not get out. Dan came around the car again, rolled her out and carried her. He ran. The flashes and booms confused his steps, again like strobelight. What you saw was not what your feet came down on and he stumbled often. Everything seemed to be taking hours, like dreams in which you couldn't run, like running chest-deep in the water.

"Dan! We're over here!"

Irene, Chris and Eddie and the dog. He set the old woman down. The old guy was somewhat behind, but in sight of them. Dan's heart was pounding. He was hot, sweating—shaky. He felt sick all of a sudden, spread-eagled himself face down against a car and vomited a half dozen times till nothing more was coming, then vomited some more.

SOMERSTON—10:30 P.M.

The little man stood atop the steps outside the big front entry of his courthouse, fixing up the heavy collar of the overcoat around his neck and ears, thinking of where he could get antacid tablets at this hour. Where was closest? Would they be there? He squinted up into the sky as snowflakes big as cookies tried to get into his eyes.

The great elm on the right began to bend—a long extended drawn out crackling like the summer thunder that cannot decide what kind of thunder it would be. It divided raggedly and half fell across the walk directly in his path before him. The other half remained where it had stood for eighty years, the full-flanked wound now showing yellow-whitely in the light of cars and the odd semilight of heavy snow.

The mayor looked to other trees and waited. Nothing. He at last went down the steps and through the snow, picked his way among the fallen branches he had often seen but never thought to touch and went down three steps more between the raised level of the lawn and the lower outside sidewalks.

People everywhere. Not a face he knew among them. All seemed to be looking for something. For the same thing. As if told that this is where the much-sought thing would be and all had come to get it. Some held hands and fought to stay together. Some were laughing. Others were alone and kept their faces down. He bumped and shouldered his way through among them until he was beyond the Square and heading north on Main Street through the thick of town.

Main Street and the Square were jam-packed solid and the traffic wasn't moving. Main Street had caught the main onslaught from the Pike and #31 out of the west. Off on other streets away from center some lights moved. It always seemed that elsewhere things were still going on, still moving. Maybe it was so and maybe just illusory. There was a quality about the night and light that made everything mirage-like and deceptive. He turned right on Second and went down a block. Halfway down that block the Second Street Hotel was getting business like it was a world premiere. The mayor thought he ought to laugh, although he didn't. Sleezy place for drunks and old guys that had nobody. Most of the time the Second Street Hotel was three quarters empty with the rest of the town wishing it would just fall down. The mayor was more philosophical. There would be such places as long as there were "the people with nobody" to stay in them, and there would always be those kind of people. Now other kinds of people filled the steps and lobby, a line spilling out and down the steps clear to the curbstones. Lessons would be learned by some of those now pushing, crowding to get in; lessons maybe God had sent them here to know. Fat bugs tomorrow. Fat pockets for old Vincent at the desk without whom what would the old guys do? It was the way of things.

At the corner the activity of moving lights was not what it seemed. A little bit of a bunching kind of movement, headlights and of spinning tires. Maybe someone gained a foot or two, someplace, who knows? One car here, another there. Somebody would pull up to the guy ahead of him, the guy behind would move right up behind, and everything would shut down again. Somebody would spin and get turned sideways. Then it all would happen somewhere else, some other lane, a few yards down the block. It was deceptive and illusory. Moving and yet it wasn't.

People who were walking had snow piled high on hats and shoulders. The mayor watched from the corner for some minutes, then took a left and crossed the intersection, heading north again on Maple. His legs were tiring; it was hard to get the feet to stay down where you put them and required more of the muscles in the deepening wet snow. Like walking in the sand at the shore—without the sun and warmth to compensate.

The further north he got on Maple, the closer to the Pike, the denser all of it became. Denser with people, with traffic. Papilic's Restaurant was open, the MacDonald's, the Burger Chef. All the restaurants were doing land office business. Soon they would run out of food. That's when things would start getting ugly. And expensive for his town. The mayor gave up thoughts getting his antacids. Maybe there was still some bicarb in his office. As with the Second Street Hotel, there was no way to get in. Once in, no way to get out again.

The little man kept moving and in all that time there still was not a face he knew. He fought his way across Main Street #219, went a block beyond to Oak Street and turned south again—circling back to the old courthouse. It was the same on Oak. Maybe it was worse than Maple and then again maybe Maple had worsened in the time since he had left it. Main Street #219 was impossible and he kept clear of it on the way back to the Central Square.

Maybe the kids were better off away from Somerston at that. It might be possibly so.

MILE 100.4—10:35 P.M.

Five minutes later they were still among the crowd watching the spectacular display. An inch of snow had piled upon their hair and shoulders. People began to mill around. Some had gone back to their cars, causing Irene to wonder if the arcs were really dangerous after all. Dan wondered if those people and Irene were intelligent enough to survive. He told her so. The kids were getting cold, shifting from one foot to another. They passed the dog around, afraid she might get lost or trampled with such a belly full of pups. The dog was heavy. The flashes and the noise were getting to her; she was struggling and hard to hold.

Eddie climbed a dump truck standing traffic-bound nearby, stood atop the load of gravel, looking at the long dim double stream of headlights fading quickly in the distance and the snow.

"Hey, Dad!"

"Eddie! You get down from there!" Irene cried.

"Look Dad! Up ahead. It's moving!" Eddie pointed to the west.

The driver of the gravel truck rolled down his window. A solid sheet of ice remained where the window glass had been. He punched it out with a work-gloved fist and tried to see who was on his truck. No good. He climbed out on the running board, slipped and landed in the slush. When he regained his feet he was wet and angry.

"Hey, kid! Get the hell down offa there! What the hell you think you're doin!?"

Eddie paid him no attention. "Hey, Dad! They're moving. It's getting closer, I'm telling ya!"

"Kid, you hear me?"

"Never mind!" said Ed.

"What?"

"You heard me," said Ed. "Hey, Dad! The traffic's moving."

"Ed, get down!" said Dan.

"Hey, kid! That's it, by God!" The guy went up the side. Ed ran forward, stepped onto the cab and slipped on ice, slid down the windshield, rolled off the hood, down the fender, and landed in the slush.

"Eddie!" screamed his mother.

They ran over to him. Ed was on his feet, though, slapping off the snow.

"Hey, kid. You all right?" The truck driver was suddenly a whole lot softer.

Ed didn't answer.

"What do you think you're doing?" Dan grabbed him.

"This your kid, lady?"

"Nyaa! Nyaaa! Tarzan got his butt soaked!" taunted Chris.

"I'm afraid so," Irene answered.

"You oughta teach him some respect for people's property!" The guy got back into his truck.

Chris handed Ed the dog. "Here, Tarzan, take your dog. She's getting heavy."

"You ought to know," said Ed. He was shivering.

But he had been right. The traffic movement reached them and the truck and cars moved forward about thirty yards, leaving a gap in front of the region beneath the flashing wires. The cable near the tower was still snapping, sizzling, big concussions lit up the sky.

"Dan, what are we going to do?" Irene was at his elbow. "Eddie's freezing. He'll die of exposure—we *all* will if we stay out here!"

The cable near the tower was white hot. He wondered what was holding it. Daisy flinched and whimpered everytime the flashing booms went off, she was almost yelping now. He knew exactly what she felt.

The traffic started up again and moved a few more yards. It stopped again. The gap had widened more. Dan looked at his family among the miserable crowd on the roadside. More of them had gone back to find their cars. Chris was pressing close against her mother. Ed's shivering was nearing spasms.

Finally Dan had had enough.

"I'm going to try to get the car. You wait here!"

"All right," said Irene. "Be careful."

There should have been a gap of fifty yards in front of the station wagon, but not all the cars had been reclaimed. The big Camarro was still in front of him. The old Ford too. The red hot cable overhead was clearly visible through the falling snow. He could hear the hiss and sizzle as the snowflakes struck it, vaporized to steam. He got into his car and started up the engine. The big transport truck was still behind. Liquid butane! Twenty thousand pounds! He hadn't noticed that before. He'd have to break into the inside lane somehow, slip between the customized Camarro and the Ford. He cut between them smashing out a headlight, bending up the fender of the Camarro. To hell with it, he had a wife and kids out in the middle of the boonies freezing. He gunned the engine and his rear tires began to spin and whine. There was a scraping scream as the side of the station wagon dragged across the Camarro's newly ragged fender. Dan knew that he was probably devaluing his car a thousand dollars, but he was in the inside lane now, moving out from under all those volts and amperes. It was worth it. It had to be.

Ten yards further he was stopped again, flashing booms seemed close as ever. He was driving with his head out of the window, there had been no time to clear the windshield and the wipers wouldn't budge it.

A car door slammed behind him. The guy who owned the Camarro had apparently come back and got his car and now caught up with him. And was coming after him. The traffic moved again. Thank God! The guy got back into his car. Dan thought about the tire iron in his trunk and wished that it were in his hand. He was half afraid of having an altercation, more afraid of staying near the high powered wires.

He was also stuck in the inside lane. Moving at about two miles an hour he managed to reach across and roll the passenger window down. It was difficult to see out the passenger side. He was afraid he'd miss the girls and Eddie.

The whole thing converged on poor Daisy and welled up inside her all at once—the booms and flashes, the cold and running, the being held. At a moment the entire thing became too much. With a yelp she wriggled out of Eddie's arms and sped back the way they'd come, toward remembered warmth and safety and familiarity and was gone among the trucks and cars.

Ed went running after before Irene could stop him.

Dan still couldn't get into the outside lane. It seemed more impossible than before to see through the darkness and snow and standing cars in the outside lane between him and the berm where his family would be. Would they see him? Would they recognize the car? And there was the factor of the guy behind him and what that might come to. He bound forward in a dozen little starts, then at last caught sight of Irene. She had seen him first. She was yelling something—pointing back in the direction he had come. Chris spotted him and grabbed her mother's arm and urged her toward the car. The girls tripped carefully among the ruts and cars and reached the station wagon. Chris dove into the back at once. Irene paused at the open window. "Dan! Eddie's run off after Daisy!"

"Which way?"

"Back there! The way we came!"

"You drive. I'll catch up with you."

The traffic had surged forward just a little more. Dan wished now that it would quit. Irene slid in and across from her side and took the wheel. Dan got out, crossed to the outside lane and started back toward the booms and flashes assuming Ed and Daisy had gone down that way. He didn't need to waste time in confrontation with the guy behind him either!

Daisy had reached the point beneath the power mains where the car had been and didn't find her refuge. Another big arc struck across the sky, frightening her all the more. She ran even faster. Ed had caught sight of her, was now some twenty feet behind, but couldn't close the gap and was getting mad. He was going to pound the shit out of that goddam dog. If he ever caught her. They ran past the butane truck and on.

Dan saw it go. The white hot junction at the tower lit up like a supernova, sparks shot out a hundred feet, an incandescent fountain of molten drops of metal, a tremendous buzzing "snap"! One end of the thousand-foot span, the eight-inch steel and copper cable, parted at the tower and began to come down—slowly in the first few moments, almost slow motion—like a drooping whip of licorice in a child's warm hand.

Dan froze in his tracks. People who'd not left or returned to their cars began to dive directly in the path of it—stampeding, diving, screaming, falling in the snow. The cable draped itself across the earthen cuts on either side, and sank some more, leaping like some incredibly ferocious serpent-dragon, whipping back and forth and spitting bright actinic blue-white flame as it slid down the embankment and across the broad round back of the gigantic butane tanker.

For an instant there was a brilliant pinpoint, a fallen star of blue-white light, so intense it struck his retinas with needlepoints of pain—and then the truck exploded.

Eddie had caught up with Daisy on the other side, grabbed her and hadn't had the time to straighten fully up again. The force knocked him flat upon his face with daisy under him. He felt a fantastic rush of cold as the first wave of liquid butane expanded into gas, then heat that seared the exposed flesh at the back of his neck.

In silhouette, Dan had just caught sight of people coming past the tank truck as the first wave of expanding gas caught them. They were frozen solid in their tracks, microseconds before the ball of flame engulfed them. Dan turned his face as the concussion lifted him and threw him headlong in the snow. The shock wave passed over him like an express train, blew his overcoat and shirt up over his head. He felt the frost and then the heat like cat-o-nine-tails on the bare skin of his back.

Then it seemed to all be over. Eddie got up stiffly, turned around. The heat had him stumbling backward instantly, until he reached an endurable distance. He saw people standing rigid at the edge of the flames, some with arms upraised as if made of stone. The frozen people. The cable was still whipping back and forth spitting, snapping—louder than machine guns. Streaks of blue shot through the snow upon the ground and then there was no snow, just bare channels and big, rising clouds of steam. One frozen lady came into the path of one of these. He saw her arms burst off and fly in opposite directions. Then there wasn't any lady at all.

Dan got up. He couldn't turn to look until he'd stumbled back another fifty yards. He didn't see the car. He didn't see his son. He saw the big fire and bolts of power shooting through the snow, hurried to be out of reach of them. He saw two such electrocutions. He saw the ball of butane flame mushrooming hundreds of feet into the air. He stood there thinking nothing. Then he thought there wasn't a prayer for Eddie. Then he thought there might have been. He could have been blown out ahead of it, the same as he. Kids had green bones that bounced and didn't break. He could be on the other side. He might have got that far.

Dan stood there looking at the fire. A lot of people stood there looking at the fire while snow piled up upon their hair and hats and shoulders.

REDFORD CENTRAL—10:44 P.M.

"Exit 10 to Redford."

"Redford 'by'."

"You got anybody to come take care of these pigs? There's jillions of 'em here. They're everywhere!"

"Hang in there, 10." The operators could not supress a little laughter. It broke the tension. That was fine with Lee.

Then the lights went out, a brief interval of black confusion. Lee heard the big relays drop in, the auxiliary power generators starting up. The lights came up again, jerked a little, then leveled out. That hadn't happened in a while—not in Redford. Lee wondered just how widespread this might be. He thought about Jennifer.

"Hey, Del!"

"Yes sir, Mr. Rider."

"The phones still alive?"

"Yes sir, they are."

"See if you can rach my home—I mean, when you get a chance."

"I'll try," he said. He gave a little shrug.

SOMERSTON—10:44 P.M.

As the mayor reached the courthouse square the lights went out in Somerston. He didn't notice it at once. Most of the illumination in the streets was coming from vehicle headlights which of course remained unaffected. He was not aware the power had failed until he entered the courthouse and his people in the offices had gotten out the candles. They were lighting candles everywhere.

MILE 100.9—THE WESTBOUND—10:50 P.M.

Dan had watched the fire some fifteen minutes. The butane ball itself had burned out rather quickly, leaving wrecks on fire, an area devoid of snow across both east and westbound. He'd tried to approach it looking for a possible way through, but the live power cable continued to whip around wildly, spewing bolts across the wet road surface. It had to be one of the phase lines, a major overland main, probably the output of an entire power station. He knew these to be anywhere from 350,000 to 740,000 volts. Nothing to play with. It lashed the bodies of the blackened hulks, vaporizing steel with blinding sprays of molten metal, continued to shoot bolts across the pavement through the snow. At last he gave it up and went back to find the women and the car. Somebody would have to cut the power on that line before too long. He could go for Eddie then.

REDFORD CENTRAL—10:50 P.M.

Power outages were reported from Somerston Barracks, Maintenance, and the town of Somerston almost immediately. Radio communication and the telephones were so far not affected. The repeaters all had auxiliary generators and the switch-overs had taken place with no noticeable impairment to communications. So many lines were falling everywhere from the weight of ice and snow, the fall of the big mains across the Donovan bypass had not been diagnosed at Central.

By 11 o'clock though, the westbound had stopped dead past Somerston Exit 10, up the west slope of Aurora, through the tunnels, and all the winding miles on the east face down to Redford and beyond. The back was growing sort of in a reverse velocity in excess of fifty miles an hour, since the vehicles had already been so close together east toward Breezeway. The flow had been so irregular and worsening through the past hour that the traffic would have to stand quite a length of time to draw attention. If anybody noticed no one bothered to report it.

MILE 109—10:50 P.M.

Sgt. Tom Prokovic had gotten car 337 freed and brought it down the westbound to Milepost 109 at Gate 10 at Somerston some time before and brought Patrolman LaBarr down with him. 339 was still up on the mountain—damaged and pushed off on the side half a mile below the tunnel. They'd had to leave 337 on the westbound shoulder and walk over to the gates and had been there to assist with the pig truck on the ramp when the problem arose. Prokovic returned to 337, now. Wet, tired, angry and upset from running down and shooting pigs. State law specified that livestock thrown out on the highway in accidents had to be destroyed upon the site, a task that fell within the province of the troopers and one Prokovic hated. He hadn't got them all and didn't care. Run, Pigs! Break for freedom!

In crossing over to his car, he noted that the westbound wasn't moving. Not at all. He had to radio the pig thing into Central for the books in any case. He'd mention it.

"337 to Redford."

"Redford by, 337."

"Ah, about that pig truck down at Exit 10—Patrolman LaBarr and myself destroyed nineteen animals. Couldn't get them all—lost a lot of them in the storm and traffic. They're still trying to get that truck righted on the offbound ramp. Offbound ramp is closed.'' He gave the make and registration on the truck.

"Say, this westbound here at Milepost 109 hasn't moved an inch in half an hour. Anybody west that knows about it, call me back. What's happening?''

"Aurora to 337. We have standing backlog up here too. Don't know anymore than you do.''

"Somerston Maintenance to 337. We have a patron here, come in on foot, says there was some kind of big explosion up behind him on the bypass. We heard something up there, too. Thought that it was thunder. We have no units in that area. No way to get up to it—roads and berm impassable.''

"Any maintenance up there now?''

"Negative, 337. Nothing.''

"10-4.''

Prokovic let up on the VHF and swtiched his CB on. Lots of chatter on 14, mostly truckers asking if things were better in ''-20s'' other than their own. They were not—there were no greener pastures.

Then he caught a call of interest.

"Ah, hey there, Silver Fox. You still on 19?''

"10-4, good buddy. Only game in town.''

"I been standing here at 101, you know, on the bypass, since that big fireball up west y'know, got sick of waiting, walked up to have a look. Mercy! That's it for the westbound! All you westbounders east of Milepost 100, just forget about to-night 'cause that is all she wrote! Get off, go sleep, write letters to yer lady loves, whatever. Nothin' coming through 100 from the west neither. Everythings all over both ways at 100.''

"What's the problem Tulsa? This is Troop ''T'' Smokey. You got a '-33 up there?'' Prokovic broke in before the Silver Fox had time to answer. .

"Not me, good buddy, but it's deep six for a lot of folks, I'm tellin' ya. Looks like them big 300,000 volt overlands come down across the Pike up there. Musta come right down on toppa something righteously inflammable. That's a regular crematorium up there at Milepost One-Double-Oh. That big cable's still alive, whippin' all over . . . shottin' voltage through the snow, fryin' people in their tracks. Somebody better cut the switch on that one. You better call that in.''

Prokovic picked his mike up. ''10-4 Tulsa. Is that a definite affirmative on Milepost 100?''

''10-4, Smokey. It is. They'll be needing help up here. Medical and people standing out there in the weather—no place to go. Where are you guys?''

''First we heard about it Tulsa. Much obliged. You have a time on when that happened?''

''As it happens I was givin' 'Thunder Joe' a time check when she blew. My digital said 10:48 and stuck there. Must've been a lot of electricity got loose in the air or something. It just keeps saying 10:48.''

Prokovic compared that with his own 10:56. Tulsa's digital was about a minute slow.

''Ah, thank you Tulsa. I'm much obliged. We'll appreciate it if you render what assistance you can for people till we can get some help up there. It may take us sometime, things being what they are.''

''Do what I can. Lot of folks out on foot up here. Some people are taking other people in.''

''Keep an eye out for people with small babies, medical emergencies. Give them preference. Old folks. And keep on 14 and listen for me. You be our contact up there, will you?''

''10-4, Smokey.''

''Much obliged.''

Prokovic radioed the report and time to Redford.

REDFORD CENTRAL—11:00 P.M.

Lee looked at his watch. 11:00. He might just have time. He left the Telecommunications Center and buzzed Chuck from the ''cage''.

''Chuck, get a late bulletin out on TV right away. Can you make it for the news?''

''Major markets anyway. Shoot.''

''We're shutting down everything westbound from Harrisburg, eastbound from Redford.''

"Okay. Anything else?"

"You have Turlock's number in Harrisburg?"

"No guarantee that I can reach him." Chuck nodded affirmatively with doubt.

"I'd rather he got it from us first, wouldn't you?"

"That's a toughie," Chuck said.

REDFORD CENTRAL—11:40 P.M.

Chuck was on the phone when Lee reached his office. He waved Lee into a chair, to shut up and sit down. Chuck was wrapping up a conversation with somebody scary. It was not his normal attitude on the phone at all.

"I think it *is* in order," he was saying. "Thank you. We will."

Chuck hung up and arched his back without lifting either elbow from the desk top.

"Lieutenant Governor, no less. Wanted our opinion on whether we should have a declaration of emergency. Seeking emotional support for the decision, I guess. It's supposed to be coming down the wire soon. Save it for me I want a copy."

Both of them sat several moments without speaking. Both rubbed their growing beards.

"How we doing on notifying radio and TV?"

Chuck snorted. "I got through Pittsburgh, Harrisburg and Philly. That took two hours. Mostly there is nobody to reach. Ma Nature really pulled the plug."

"What do you mean?"

"Two thirds of the state's in a power blackout. All the goddam wires are down. They're off the air. It's just that simple."

"We have a problem along those lines up on the bypass," Lee said.

"Was that a pun intended or are you as tired as I am?"

"I was here two hours sooner. I'm even tireder."

"What about the bypass?"

"Report about some kind of big explosion up there. Relayed by CB. Somerston's blacked out. One of those big West Penn

Overlands came down. It's on our turf. You better get hold of them.''

"Yeah and maybe there's a Easter Bunny.''

Lee shrugged. "Maybe there is, who knows?''

"I'll try,'' said Chuck.

Lee got up to go. "What did you tell them in Harrisburg—about us, I mean?''

"I told them we were shut down. We are, aren't we?''

"Westbound west of Harrisburg. Eastbound west of Blue Mountain.''

"Harrisburg says the westbound backlog extends well east of them now. They can't get on at Lebanon-Lancaster.''

Lebanon-Lancaster? Gate 20—Milepost 266.45! Lee didn't like that kind of information coming at him from this source. It was a bad surprise.

"What the hell's going on? We gave out a general address at 10:30. 11:00. Every fifteen minutes now! Are those guys still letting people on the westbound?''

Chuck still had his elbows on the desk. He unfolded his hands and made a helpless gesture without moving them. "Beats hell out of me. Communications are *snafu*. Who knows what's going on? Anywhere!''

"Well, get hold of the power company. I better get downstairs and see about all this.''

"I can try.'' Chuck said.

DONOVAN BYPASS— MILE 100.8—11:40 P.M.

Eddie Braden had stood back from the fire and watched it for more than half an hour. He was soaked and chilled and shivering and his arms were aching from the weight of Daisy. He couldn't put the dog down where they were. The snow was still too deep and wet and in any case he didn't want her running off again.

The fire had died down a lot now and he edged closer looking for a way through but found, as had his father, that the big cable was still live and thrashing violently, spitting blue-white flames and vaporizing what the blue-white flames touched. The sight of the people caught at the fire was still vivid in his mind, the people who had frozen then exploded. It kept him cautious about getting close.

He found both sides of the Pike impassable, cars burning on both sides of the medial, the overpowering smoke of burning rubber, plastics—powerful and sickening smells, like feathers. The big wire was a science fiction menace, a zapping, buzzing 60-cycle ray. Deafeningly loud. Ferocious in its power.

"Hey, kid!"

He turned around to see. A guy about his dad's age was leaning out of a camper just behind him. A heavy pickup with big knobby tires. Just behind him.

"Yeah. You better watch it. Stay back from that wire."

Ed nodded and turned back to the fire.

"Hey kid."

Ed turned around again.

"You better get back to your car. You better get back with your folks."

Ed nodded and turned back to the fire. There had been a lot of other people watching at first. It was the same as being the short kid at the old parade. By this time most of them had got cold and gone back to their cars. And bored too, he guessed. He was. A little. He was one of a few dozen forlorn-looking stragglers now. He and the dog. The snow was melting in his hair and running down his face like sweat. It was piling on his shoulders.

Time went by. He heard a car door open, footsteps squishing up through the slush behind him. A hand grabbed his shoulder and spun him around. The guy from the pickup was face to face with him in the flickering light of the smelly fires.

"Hey, kid! You don't listen so good, do you? I said go on back to your car. Where is it?"

Ed nodded toward the fire.

The guy's face softened. Ed saw he was dressed for hunting. Coats and belts with thousands of pockets like army clothes. The guy's face looked kind of sick and sorry for its own big mouth.

"Naw. The other side," said Ed.

The guy swallowed, looked a little less wiped out. He noticed how wet the kid and the dog were and how much they both were shivering, the snow piled on his shoulders and his hair.

"Come on back and get in the camper till this fire dies down and you can get back over."

Ed didn't leap for it. He seemed hesitant. He let the guy start back by himself. He let the guy get all the way back by himself.

"Come on," said the guy. "None of us is queers or nothing if that's what you're thinking." The guy waited by the door a second.

"Okay, kid. I made the offer." He got back in his camper.

Ed let five more wet, cold shivering minutes go by then took the guy up on his offer.

REDFORD CENTRAL—12:00 MIDNIGHT—MONDAY

At midnight Lee was back in the equipment chambers supervising the replacement of the 24-hour reel of recording tape. All radio and telephone traffic through Central was recorded 24 hours a day, 365 days a year, on eight tracks, six for the radio zones, one for telephone and the last for U.S. standard time signals. Tapes held 24 hours—one day each, and each tape was preserved one full year for legal purposes.

Murphy's Law dictated that since this, of all tapes that year, would be the most significant, something therefore had to happen to it. Lee wanted to run it over into Monday long enough to catch the hourly status reports from the various facilities without interruption. The reports were coming in now and for a change they were worth preserving.

"Gibson Maintenance reports no east or westbound movement, heavy snow continued with high winds west of Pittsburgh. We are unable to proceed with maintenance or police activities. Spinouts, illegal turn-arounds, disabled and deserted vehicles have most shoulder and rest areas congested and impassable. We are backlogged from West Gate through Gates 5 and 6 Pittsburgh. State and municipal roads are for the most part closed. Evacuation into Pittsburgh is proceeding poorly, if at all. Electrical power is out for about half the Pittsburgh area, most surrounding rural districts. Gibson Maintenance and Police Barracks both are filled to capacity with patrons and cannot take in more. We are getting numerous reports of patrons running out of gas, boil overs, and various mechanical failures. Both Gibson Maintenance and Police Barracks are on local auxiliary generator systems. The time is 12:03 A.M. Monday. Mark.''

"New Sanford State Police, routine hourly—12:04 A.M. Monday. We have presently no movement east or westbound. Approximately 18 inches of wet snow accumulated and continue heavy. Not much wind. We have no means of access either through or around on secondaries. Troopers are on foot going car to car in search of medical emergencies, infant problems, and the like. We are also crowded with patrons afoot. Desertion of vehicles is widespread. We are on auxiliary electrical power.''

The reports from Donovan and Somerston Barracks were much the same. Standstill. Aurora reported westbound standstill, continuing to cut away the wreckage from the eastbound tube. Kregg Maintenance reported failure of their auxiliary power system and, of course, Aurora's electrical system was a total loss, no power coming in or out. Aurora, Kregg, Everett all reported influxes of patrons on foot seeking shelter. Wholesale vehicular desertions.

By the time reports were in, Lee had his picture—one solid unmoving backlog from Harrisburg now, at Milepost 234 on the westbound still growing. The reported backlog at Gate 20 Lebanon-Lancaster had proven temporary or inaccurate. They were now off-routing them at Harrisburg and accepting no more westbound. Period. Small comfort in any case. The eastbound remained one solid pack from West Gate to Somerston. Vacant over the Aurora Mountain, then solid again from Redford to Blue Mountain. Past Blue Mountain there was still just rain, but troopers were of the opinion that many of the evacuations from the westbound had been finding there was no place for them where they got off and were just getting back onto the Pike, going east again and getting stopped. Thus doubling the gate influx for the eastbound east of Redford. The patrons were having ''fuel problems'' with so many of the restaurant-service areas without power. There was gas below ground, but no means of pumping it up to them. Gas pumps are electrical.

Lee remoyed the tape himself, put it in its steel canister, and labeled it with masking tape. Old Hondecka put the new reel up—actually an old tape, recorded one year ago to the day. Once in a great while they got them mixed up somehow. Lee wasn't taking any chances with this one. Should it ever come to actually examining one, the guy who did it had his work cut out for him because to hear it all would be seven tracks times twenty-four hours: a hundred and sixty-eight continuous hours of VHF noise, laconic bursts, long periods of nothing followed by perhaps a half a word—a check in. But for Lee the present situation was unprecedented. He had missed the big snowstorm of '50 naturally. A few old timers still around told stories of it, but like fish that grow post-mortem with reach retelling, Lee had felt that a great deal of it was pure exaggeration. Now he wondered.

"Jimmy should've been back down b' now," commented Old Hondecka. He was finishing up the threading of the tape. His left eye was in continual paroxysms from the eternal thread of smoke pouring upward into it from the Lucky in his mouth.

"Traffic," Lee said.

Old Hondecka nodded, somehow, without agreeing. Dark old guy. You couldn't read him.

Lee stopped by the Zone 2 console on his way out. He wanted the tape upstairs in Chuck's office or his own.

"Judy, did that Declaration of Emergency come off the ' type'?"

She handed it to him. He glanced over it. The standard thing with the specifics of the situation interjected at the appropriate lines "signed" by the Lieutenant Governor. It should have made him feel better but it didn't. It was awfully fast for official recognition of a situation. Too fast. So fast that it was scary. Lee tacked the sheet into the canister with the tape of Sunday.

"Judy, what time did the Bald Knob Repeater come back on?"

"Before 10 sometime. Not sure *exactly.*"

Lee took the tape upstairs.

REDFORD CENTRAL—12:22 A.M.

Beck called. Lee was near the console and he took it. By the sound of it Beck was using a base station and not a car. The tone was brassier and there was noise and talking in the background.

"Where are you now, John?" asked Lee.

"Everett. Listen, Lee. There's been a fracas at the turn-around at 137. Have there been any calls from Jim Johannsen?"

Lee quickly scanned Judy's logs for the past two hours. Nothing from 230 since 9:41. Lee told him that and asked what it was all about.

"Well, his wrecker's sitting there at 137 with nobody in it. He was helping haul the junk out of the mountain, wasn't he?"

"He was helping on that firetruck from Redford Volunteer F.D. It was stuck someplace near there."

"And you haven't heard from him?"

"Not since 9:41."

"Damn."

"Out of gas?"

"No. The wrecker is terrific. We checked a radius of maybe forty yards in all directions. He could be lying ten feet away in this snow and you would never see him. You're absolutely sure you haven't heard from him?"

"Nothing written down. What about this 'fracas' at 137?"

"Oh, some of these patrons on the inside discovered the turn-around and cut over onto the eastbound for God knows what reason. Hit one of the Kregg plows coming down from the tunnel. There were about nine other vehicles from the westbound involved. A small stampede, but we have that eastbound clear now. We shoved the cars off, got the plow rolling again. Nothing serious, just fender-benders. We brought the vehicles down to Everett and the patrons. I don't know what we're going to do with them now that we're here. The place is overrun."

"Well, what about Johannsen's wrecker? How did it get into the picture?"

"I have no idea. As we were pulling this mess apart we found it standing there. Right on the eastbound headed toward the tunnels. Unattended. Beats the hell out of me."

"Me, too. Listen. Did you do anything about that turn-around. Block it so this can't happen again."

"We took care of it."

"Have you been up to Aurora?"

"Negative."

"You've heard nothing about what's happening up there?"

"The fire's supposed to be out. That's all I know. I'm going to try to make it up there after a while."

"Listen. If you do hear anything from Johannsen call me, will you?"

"Sure. You call us too."

REDFORD CENTRAL—MONDAY 1:00 A.M.

At 1 A.M. there had been no more from Beck or Ollie Chelinski. There had been no more from Jimmy Weeks or Barger. No one. Shortly after midnight it had gone quiet, almost entirely. Lee drummed his fingers on the counter of the "cage", then punched up the private line to Tri-State. The sound of ringing at the other end was comforting. At least *something* remained intact.

"Tri-State." It was one of the underlings.

"Eastern. Get me Jim Nadel." Lee drummed his fingers more, looked at his watch for the six-hundredth time since midnight. 1:03.

"Hello."

"Jim? Lee Rider. What's the news?"

"I'm blind. We're on the darkside of the planet now. I have to wait for infrareds."

"When?"

"Hour maybe. Looking at Arabia right now. It's not snowing in Arabia, in case you wanted to know."

The National Weather Service teletypes had held pretty much to what Nadel had said before—estimating that the storm should abate around 3 or 4 A.M. for southwestern Pennsylvania.

"Then you don't know if it's on or not?"

"Huh?" Nadel sounded weary, didn't have his usual sense

of banter. Nobody had much bounce left. It was grinding everybody down.

"This 3 or 4 A.M. end of the storm, you're telling me that no one knows?"

"Oh, *that!* I thought you meant the other thing—"

"What other thing?"

"This second system, the one that everybody's watching. No that's 3 A.M. on this present storm. That's all but history. You can expect an overcast and even a warm morning, temperatures above the melting point. Sun by 10 A.M., I think."

"What if it doesn't? What's going on Jim! For God's sake!"

"That little southern high that shoved the hard core blizzard north late yesterday afternoon—the big winds—the possibility of drawing more warm air up from the gulf, a second chance of letting that very cold air come further down as it moves out to sea. Bunch of stuff going on, but I'm in the dark. Bad mixture. I need infrareds to see if it's moved east."

Lee let off a sigh. "What time tomorrow?"

"This is *if,* now, remember—"

"Yeah, yeah—*if.*"

"Two to 5 P.M. Sometime in there. *If* it goes against us."

"If it doesn't?"

"Well, if this high stays where it is, it ought to hold things off. Continue with the melting trend and so forth. Then we'll get *floods.* Ha. Ha." Nadel wasn't laughing.

"Ha. Ha." Lee wasn't laughing either. "Call me," he said.

Nadel stretched out his assurance through a crushing yawn. They hung up. Lee went back to drumming with his fingers.

He surveyed his operators, the wet and soaking police and volunteers and people, coming in and going out. Everyone seemed to have plenty to do, to keep them busy, save him. The place was hopping while he drummed. He thought about another cup of coffee. No, he had the shakes already.

He got up and went for coffee.

REDFORD CENTRAL—MONDAY 1:26 A.M.

Beck came in with Ollie and a skaggy-looking truck driver and about four dozen skaggy-looking kids and skaggy-looking mothers. Everyone of them was wet and snowed on and dragged-out looking. A pack of flood rats. Skaggy.

"You're not telling me you brought these in a snow-plow—not this many!" Lee found himself yelling to get above the din of it, the bawling and the caterwauling.

"Naw, hell no," said Ollie. He thumbed at the truck driver. "We off-loaded Macon Henry Gruber here. Throwed off his flatbed load of Christmas trees down there at 137 where that fracas was. He was on the inside of the turn-around and we was able to get him over on the eastbound and bring him down that way. Behind me. We picked up these kids at 137 and at Everett and some other places on the way."

"Hey, I'm gettin' paid for them trees now, don't forget that," Macon Henry Gruber said.

"Make me out a voucher," said Beck. "We'll take care of it. We said we would."

"800 trees—twelve bucks a tree," said Gruber.

"Make up a voucher!" Beck repeated.

"And shut up about it!" Ollie said.

Macon Henry got out a receipt pad from his jacket and went to the wall to write against it.

Lee scowled at his pair. "What the hell, you guys! That's a $9600 hayride! There's got to be some kind of limit on this kind of thing!"

The captain looked guilty. "We couldn't leave them there at Everett. The place is an absolute madhouse. It's crawling to the walls! They're little bitty kids, Lee."

"And we used them Christmas trees," said Ollie. "We piled 'em up there at the turn-around for a barricade. It ain't as if they're goin' to waste for nothing."

"You might as well have piled up money! You had a snowplow! Plow up snow!"

"The main thing is we needed that flatbed," said the chief. "The rest is gravy."

"Gravy!" Lee glared at the big police captain with a laser-powered look of reproach. Big softy should have been born Santa Claus. A bachelor and a sucker for kids.

"Jeez, Lee. They're little, bitty kids!"

"I noticed that," said Lee. "It's entirely audible. Well, what the hell can we do with them?"

The captain shrugged. "We got more room here than any-place. We got lights. It's warm." He shrugged again. He looked like a kid himself, caught red-handed in the cookie jar.

"Oh, all right." Lee gave in to it. What else was there to do? "Open up the cafeteria. Get some of those army blankets out of Civil Defense stores, we'll do something."

Lee leaned into the Telecommunications Center door and called for Judy. She came right away.

"Get somebody to spell you for a while and help out with these kids and mothers, will you?"

"Why me? I'm no good with kids! I suppose because I'm a woman?"

"If you hate it that bạd go in there and find one or more of these mothers with a little leadership and let them take it over. I don't care. Let them get their own thing going. They'll probably do better."

Judy shrugged and went back in to find someone to take the Zone 2 Console. Lee turned to see Macon Henry and the captain and the crew chief from Kregg walking off.

"Where do you think *you're* going?"

The captain shrugged. "Back for more."

They rounded the corner and Lee found himself left among four dozen kids and mothers. He put his head in through the Telecommunications Center door again. Judy was sitting at the Zone 2 Console as if none of this had happened.

"Hey!"

She looked at him with a kind of nondescript defensive blandness on her face.

"What's with you?"

"I couldn't find anyone to take the console," Judy said.

"Just get out there!" Lee strode across to where she was. "I'll take the stupid console!"

MILEPOST 109—2:00 A.M.

Sgt. Prokovic had called "Tulsa" up on the bypass and received a report that was, if anything, more dire than before. The thrust of the urgency was injured patrons. Most of the simply displaced seemed to have been taken in by others or found other shelter, but there were still fires and people in agony and why the hell didn't somebody get the power to the line cut dead? No telling where it was going to jump to next.

The Sergeant called Redford, Everett and Aurora—all to no avail. Somerston Maintenance on the eastbound between Gate 10 and the bypass explosion was unable to assist. The eastbound in front of them solid backlog. All of Somerston's Maintenance machinery was out on the Pike trapped in the backlog. It was very dark and quiet where they were. Patrons in the cars seemed for the most part to have cut lights and engines and be sleeping. Somerston did not see how passage could be made by anything short of helicopter. Most of the shoulder and medical had been filled with sideslipped, backwards vehicles. The Turnpike immediately before them was in reality more like eight lanes than four. They had no idea what the two men they had left at the facility could do about the situation on the bypass.

Prokovic called Reford again and asked if they could reach the armory in Somerston proper. He was told they had made repeated tries and been unsuccessful. They had tried the civil defense and the courthouse. Busy signals. They too had thought perhaps the armory or town fire department volunteers could be more resourceful at the local level, would have some equipment and be closer. They would be taking casualties to the Somerston hospital in any case. Redford had been trying since Prokovic's first report but had been so far unsuccessful.

Prokovic then called 348, the car that had come up from Brandt Cabins that afternoon to help out with the traffic in Somerston, and got no answer after several tries. He called Redford to see if they could raise him. Redford tried and couldn't.

At last the sergeant called Gate 10 again.

"Is Patrolman LaBarr there?"

"Just a minute."

"Have him call car 337."

"LaBarr to 337?"

"George I need somebody to stay with the car. I'm going to need to walk down to Somerston."

"What for?"

Prokovic ran the situation down for him. Somebody was going to have to alert Somerston authority by word of mouth.

"What about it? Are you free?"

"Why don't I walk into Somerston?" said LaBarr.

"Beats hell out of me," said Prokovic. "Why don't you?"

"10-4."

REDFORD CENTRAL—MONDAY 2:10 A.M.

At 2:10 Lee called Chuck on the building interphone.

"What's up with that power line on the bypass?"

"I got through to West Penn. Can you believe it? They didn't know!"

"No, I can't believe it."

"They say they have so many lines down in so many places that it didn't show. I don't believe that either, but it's their electric company. From the way they sounded, I bet I could've made it mine for a dollar eighty-six. Maybe they have problems."

"Yeah. So?"

"So, they said it might be a while. They're having trouble with manpower. Guys can't get in and then they can't get out to the wire-falls. Said they couldn't reach lots of guys who'd gone out of town for hunting and things like that. We had those problems too. The National Guard is out now assisting with power line restorations, but there's a lot to do."

"They didn't ask if their goddam power line fell down on someone and maybe fried a few of them to crisps or anything?"

"No. They asked the location. That was all."

"You're kidding!"

"No. They did say thanks for the location." Chuck paused to see if Lee had further comment.

Lee did not.

MILEPOST 100.8—EDDIE BRADEN—2:10 A.M.

When Ed got into the camper he found three other guys besides the guy who'd come out and got him. They were hunters on the way from York to Greene County, wherever that was. They had three guns each. Two of the guys had pistols. All of them were squashed into the camper with the guns and bullets and a lot of tents and Coleman stoves and stuff like that. The guy who came out and got him had stayed up front in the cab and put Ed and the dog in back with the three other guys and all the junk. Now he came back too and squeezed himself in with everything and everybody. There was a lot of grunting and bad language. It was hot and stuffy and you could hardly move at all. They had a Coleman lantern on and it was getting stuffy.

"What's it doing out there?" One of the back guys asked the front guy.

"Snowing. What the hell. Hey, kid. You may as well take it easy. They still haven't cut the power on that big main line."

"You're kidding!" said another of the back guys.

"Right. I got a lot to gain by saying that the wire's alive when it ain't alive," the front guy said.

"It ain't that. It's what the hell's going on? Who's watching the damn power company! Jesus!"

"Probably all gone hunting like old Jerry here." The front guy nudged another of the back guys. The new guy looked kind of sheepish and dropped his eyes. "You work for West Penn, don'tcha? Sure!"

Jerry shrugged and didn't say anything and kept looking at his thumbs and then said how the heck could *he* know?

Nobody said anything for a while. Then the front guy turned to Ed.

"Hey, kid. Where you from?"

"Detroit."

"Detroit! Whew!" All four of the camper guys shook their heads and sucked their teeth. Then the front guy curled up crookedly among the junk and guys to sleep. "You ain't going to Detroit for a while. Aw, the hell with everything. I'm gonna get some Z's."

One of the back guys cut the lantern off so they all wouldn't die of carbon monoxide. Ed sat in the dark for a while listening to sounds from the outside. He could hear the big wire zapping and exploding kind of at a distance. Now and then somebody would walk by. Daisy was sleeping warm and dry. After a while Ed drifted off and slept too.

SOMERSTON—2:56 A.M.

By 2:56 the mayor had been everywhere inside the old court-house except in his office which had filled with weeping, hand-wringing relatives and "oh-we-should-have-listened-to-you-L.John" till he was sick of it. He'd left the sniveling pack of them with Maggie and had not come back since midnight. He was worried to the heart about the kids himself, but what to do? The Mehelics would be finding ways to make the buck off of this like always. The kids were probably as good off there as any-place. Count the blessings and hang on. It was late now to be crying.

At 2:56 he was up in the courthouse attic underneath the roof again, had been there since two, repositioning the pots and jars that caught the drips that scores of patchwork roof repairs had been unable to subdue. He was up there looking north along Main Street #219, just as the snow quit falling, out one of the north gable windows through the old brass field binoculars his father brought back with him from the war. When it happened it was like what happens when the Alka-Seltzer in the glass stops fizzing and the water clears. The night stopped being full of white swirlings and went clear. The dull smudgy river of lights below came into sudden focus. And it grew. Now within a space of maybe a minute, maybe two, it extended into the blackness beyond the town, a mile up to the Turnpike gates and spread from the gates along the Pike making a red and gold and glowing "T." Beautiful. And not so beautiful. Through the binoculars he could see down close among the cars there the people were by the thousands. Lost. Confused. Upset and miserable. By the thousands.

Now boots were coming up the stairs behind him. Two pair, or was it three? Heavy. In a businesslike way of coming up the stairs—even after seven floors.

"L. John! You up there?"

It was Jake Stokes. The footsteps came up the last narrow flight of stairs into the attic and across. With the coroner was Patrolman George LaBarr.

"L.John," said Jake. "We got a problem."

"Oh. Is that right?" said the Mayor.

Jake pulled his coat back up onto his stub of shoulder.

"This is new. Trouble on the bypass."

The coroner and Trooper LaBarr filled L.John in as the trio clattered down through the upper floors to the inhabited ones by the light of flashlights. It was decided they would best go at this from the armory, to make their way there and find what kind of equipment was on hand. Jack wanted to gather his Civil Defense boys and see who had snowmobiles. L.John would see about the fire department guys. LaBarr felt that with a heavy truck to plow it, it might be possible to clear a shoulder lane as far as the gates. Beyond that it might have to be by snowmobile. It might be a damn good thing to have some available.

L.John stopped briefly by the office to tell Maggie. The office was still full of relatives and cigar smoke. He told them he was going with Jake and the trooper to the armory. She picked a thread off his lapel and knocked some attic dust from his sleeve and said be careful.

There had been no calls.

She went down to the first floor with them. A lot of people had been coming in from the streets for refuge. They were sleeping on the stairs and making it difficult for them to get down.

"Go downstairs and get one of the cops to help out," said L.John. The police station was in the basement of the courthouse. "You let the kids and old folks in and kick the big bums out," he said.

She said that she would do that.

And she did.

MILE 100.4—THE BYPASS—3:30 A.M.

Dan Braden woke from fitful dozing. It was pitch black now except for vague smudges of what had to be a random fool or two keeping headlights on, the light showing dimly through the foot thick snow on his windshield. Irene slept against his shoulder. He tried to raise his wrist to see the time without disturbing her. She murmured and snuggled closer, then sat up.

"What time is it?" she whispered.

"3:30."

"Have we moved?"

"No."

"No sign of Eddie?"

"No."

"What's happening to us?"

"We're getting cold, that's what. I'm going to run the motor just a little."

"Do you think you should?"

"Just a little." Dan started the engine carefully. Both watched to see if Chris would awaken, but she didn't. Dan switched the radio on and brought the volume up with care. The static buzz was gone. It looked as if the power to the fallen line had been cut. He searched the dial, picked up KYW, the Philadelphia 24-hour news station. They sat through a science news topic on the spread of roundworms through the feces of dogs, an item on a strike of local dairy truckers, a promo for boat owner's insurance, then the weather story. Pennsylvania, Ohio, Indiana, Michigan and New York virtually shut down in an unprecedented record early snowstorm. In the western two-thirds of the state, all roads including the Eastern Turnpike were shut down; two-thirds of the state of Pennsylvania and most of Ohio were without electrical power. The Lieutenant Governor had issued an official declaration of emergency, the emergency expected to be declared federal before morning. Dan switched it off.

The car was warmer. He shut down the engine. The two of them sat looking at the buried windshield for a long time. Finally . . .

"I'm going back and take a look. Hand me the flashlight."

She dug it from beneath the seat and gave it to him.

At first the door would not open far enough to let him out. He pumped it back and forth until it had beaten a sufficient wedge into the snow outside. Small avalanches from the roof went down his neck, over his clothing. He regretted having run the engine now instead of after his return, much of the warm air had escaped in simply trying to get out. A waste. A stupid waste!

Outside at last, he found himself above his knees in snow and that the snow had ceased to fall. There was no moon, no stars but a strange luminescence about the night and snow. At some distance there were headlights burning, here and there a motor running. He felt like tracking down those people, slapping sense into them. If enough ran out of gas they'd never get the roadways clear. It didn't help to be intelligent—the stupid would always be there to bring everyone down with them, a staggering futility. He might reach the first half dozen, but statistically there would be a definite percentage, a certain rate of "clowns-per-mile," and he could pursue that to Lake Michigan and they'd only turn them on again the minute he was out of view.

The site of the explosion was unmissable. A clear demarcation of perimeter where the prior snow had melted away and only post-explosion snow remained. A crater. Three feet deep, 6 inches of new snow on the bottom. Here and there a car still smoldered, a stench of burning rubber, a stench like burned feathers and like pot roast, like charred steaks on the grill. He played the flashlight over blackened hulks with mantles of new snow, then stepped in and toward the center of it, slowly.

The steel medial barrier was gone. Gone. Wreckage had been flung askew. There was no distinguishing the eastbound from the westbound, just one confusion, a scrapyard. That was all.

He swung his flashlight casually. It penetrated to the inner blackness of a hulk still vaguely shaped like a car. The bodies sat there gazing out, except they had no eyes. No hair. You could not tell what sex they were, what race. There were two in front, two more in the back. No sign of struggle, they just sat there, almost serene except they were black as coal. A little dusting of snow had settled on them.

In other places, other struggles had been more vigorous. A corpse had shot headlong through a windshield in another place—whether from a moving impact or in desperation to escape, he couldn't know. The head and upper torso protruded through the glass down to the waist, burned to blackened crust like all the others. An arm was missing, lying just beneath the snow on the hood of the demolished car. From some cars arms or parts of arms or hands with or without fingers protruded from half-rolled window ventilators.

Something rolled beneath his foot, he slipped and went down hard, the flashlight spun away. Went out. He grabbed widly for it beneath the snow, coming up with bits of junk debris.

Then his hands hit a dead body. A small body. He froze momentarily, then he tore with even greater urgency through the snow, desperately hoping not to find a dog. He found the flashlight. At first the light would not come on. He banged it on his palm and cleared the snow away, twisted both end caps and somehow got it lit. He made his way back to the small body.

It was charcoal, like the rest. Eddie's size. About. How could you tell? How much had burned away and what remained? There was a vestige of the leg of one blue jean. A lot of kids wore blue jeans. The beam found the belt and he realized at some length that it was face down. He turned it over. No face. He played the flashlight down the front of it and came to the belt buckle.

It wasn't Eddie.

He searched the area a little more and it was everywhere the same. Finally he gave up and went back to the car feeling kind of sick and crazy.

"You didn't find him."

"Someone took him in, I'm sure. You know Ed. If they said no to his face he'd climb in anyway."

"Yes. He would. And he would have."

"It's pitch black. Everything's covered up with snow. I wouldn't be able to see him three feet away, especially not if he got in someone's car. People are asleep now. Ed, too, I wouldn't doubt it. we'll find him easy in the morning."

"What's that smell?"

"Huh? Oh? Well, tires and things. Still burning. You know."

Irene was quiet for a long time. "It was very bad, wasn't it?" she said.

He nodded.

REDFORD CENTRAL—4:20 A.M.

In the hours beween midnight and the dawn a strange and kind of drowsy dormancy had settled on the system. Calls were infrequent now, occasional small bursts of people a hundred, two hundred miles apart telling each other they had nothing much to tell. The snow had quit just a little ahead of Nadel's schedule at 2:55, Redford a little short at 22 inches. The night was dark and not too cold, the overcast still blanketing the land and holding in the warmth from the black vacuum of space. To listen to the brief laconic bursts of chatter one might think that nothing beyond normal was going on. For the people in the Telecommunications Center it was an eerie silence, unlike anything that any of them had experienced before, a sound like the slowest normal times in contrast to their knowledge. They were shut down. Nothing left but talk and nothing much to say. Everyone had worked more than two straight shifts and was bone weary.

Even Beck's caterwauling kindergarten in the cafeteria had settled down. They'd brought up blankets and floor mats from the inner dormitories for those who overflowed the bunks available. Red Cross locals had come in with formula, milk and blankets. They even had real mother's milk for kids that couldn't take cow's milk or formula.

4:20 found Lee Rider nodding off in the "cage" behind folded arms.

Judy came to shake him by the shoulder.

"Punch up the interphone line, Lee. Mr. Ellis is on the line to Harrisburg. Wants you in on it."

"Turlock?"

"No, it's the governor's mansion."

That shook a lot of cobwebs out in a hurry. Lee lifted the telecom handset from it's cradle.

"Lee Rider, here."

"Yes, Mr. Rider? My name is Kent. I'm aide to the governor. We wanted to inform you that the governor has arranged for a party of various relief and military agency personnel to make an inspection tour of the Turnpike early tomorrow. The governor would like you and Mr. Ellis to join them. Can you?"

"Uh—certainly. What time?"

"We're not certain of the exact time. It should be shortly after sunrise. You have a place to land a helicopter there, I hope?"

"Yes, police helicopters land on the parking lots, but—" Lee started to make some cautionary statement about the snow.

"Fine. We'll radio you on our way in, then. Thank you very much, both of you. We'll see you in the morning." He hung up.

Both of you? Then he realized Chuck was on the phone too.

"Chuck?"

"Yeah."

"What about that?"

"Beats hell out of me. Looks like we go for a plane ride in the morning." Chuck yawned broadly. "I think we better get some Z's," he said. "We're going to need them."

Lee agreed. He tried his home phone number one last time and got the busy signal. He left word with the operators to wake him at seven, whoever was on shift. They had set up a rotation. Judy was off sleeping somewhere too.

He laid himself full length on the counter and out like a light bulb.

MILEPOST 100.6—5:10 A.M.

Patrolman LaBarr, Jake Stokes, and L.John Pribanic reached the site of the explosion on the bypass at a little after five with four army trucks, half a dozen snowmobiles and about twenty National Guardsmen and fire department volunteers. The Guard was shorthanded and could spare only a few men for this. Two thirds of the roll could not be reached or get to the armory for duty on account of road conditions. The same with the fire department volunteers. Some of the men belonged to both and it was limited to those who actually lived in the town itself. Anybody else just couldn't make it. The town could not be left any less attended than it was.

Two hours since they'd left the courthouse. In LaBarr's opinion that was damn good time. LaBarr had been right about the possibilities of clearing a shoulder lane from Somerston up to the gates. And by the same token Somerston Barracks Maintenance had been wrong about the shoulder of the eastbound on their side. What they were able to see was as described, a hopeless, chaotic jumble. It was far less congested on either side of their immediate vicinity, just occasional spinouts every now and then.

Now at two hours before the dawn the Pike was strangely still and silent and asleep, unnervingly so. With the exception of the natural gathering places of the gates and the Somerston Barracks Maintenance facility halfway up, it had been almost completely dark and dormant all the way. The little convoy had fought its way up along the outside of the eastbound, stopping to check out vehicles in its path and found them occupied four times out of five. Almost always the occupants were sleeping, had given up, snuggled up, and decided to see what the morning light would bring, and had to be aroused. If places could be found to drive or shovel their cars into, the cars were not pushed off the side. Otherwise they were. The declaration of emergency had come into the civil defense office and Stokes had brought it with him. The armory was thereby on active call and considered these actions to be justified in view of the necessity of reaching injured people and opening a work access to restore a major overland energy line. The huge army trucks just shoved them off and over. If there were people thus displaced, they offered them a ride. That was the best that could be had for now. Without exception people took it.

The handful of troopers and volunteers dismounted from the trucks and waded thigh-deep with rifles ready into the circle of the blast. The patrolman and the coroner and mayor too. They saw what Dan Braden had seen an hour and a half before. A couple of young guardsmen got sick and went back to the trucks. They saw no other people, no walking or otherwise visible injured. Either there had been none or they had been taken into nearby cars and trucks. Obviously it had been the latter.

As they were wading through the snow and junk and going across the medial to the westbound side some figures ducked and bolted through the wrecks, were caught in the flashlight beams and lost again.

"Halt! Police!" LaBarr was unsuccessful. He didn't stop them. There had been two, maybe three. He didn't bother giving chase. Looters. Perhaps the curious. Based on what they'd seen of cars and bodies, what could the ghouls have taken? They hadn't routed them up again as they reached the far perimeter. LaBarr and a couple of the older guys were surprised there weren't more.

Stokes grouped them all.

"Cordon off this area," he said. "We'll have to keep people back away from this, at least till bodies and parts thereof are out of here." His job as coroner said he had to examine and make determinations of death at the scene of death before bodies were removed to storage. "Christ, what a mess," he said.

They went looking in the nearest cars for the injured and they found them. And orphaned kids. And emotional shock cases. Three of the big trucks got loaded quickly with the worst of them. L.John went back down to Somerston with the three trucks to try to raise somebody from the local office of the power company. Stokes and LaBarr and eight armed guardsmen stayed up at the bypass.

DAY
TWO:
MONDAY

DAWN MONDAY

Dawn broke gray and silent over the seemingly endless continuum of white; a muffled overcast of gray above a vast blanket of soft angora. Stifling quiet. 31 degrees. Twenty-two inches. Not as deep as had been predicted but sufficiently so that five more inches would not really have been noticed. The effective damage had been done in the first eight inches. Eight would have been enough to that weekend of all weekends. The rest was numbers for the number books. That much accumulation in that amount of time was now an all-time record for southwestern Pennsylvania. It beat January '77 and '78. It beat Thanksgivings '74 and even the legendary 1950 "Great Thanksgiving Snowstorm." But it was different from the "Great White '50" in more than snow. That one had hit Friday, the day after. People were where they wanted to be, the long weekend, and not traveling. This one had hit Sunday when everyone that had gone visiting was on the road for home. And the hunters. The timing could not have been more perfect.

A view from a Tiros satellite at the moment revealed only the northeastern two-thirds of the massive cloud cover protruding from beneath the edge of night into the morning obscuring totally what would have been the eastern seaboard of the U.S.A. and the Atlantic Ocean. It was either larger or much farther out to sea than yesterday. How far inland it still extended could not be seen. From so high above the cloud was white and later in the morning when it would move away the view would not appear so different as the whiteness of the underlying snow simply replaced it.

It was a lot of snow.

MILEPOST 100.8—BYPASS—6:50 A.M.

Eddie Braden had awakened in the van not knowing where he was. It took a couple of seconds. Then he raised himself to one elbow and took a look around. All four of the camper guys were sleeping, snoring horribly. There was a faint gray light showing through the snow stuck to the back windows. Somewhere off outside he heard the sound of heavy motors and crashing noises. At least he thought he did. Maybe it was just the snoring.

Daisy, cradled at his stomach underneath him, raised her head questioningly and stuck her cold nose directly in his mouth. He spat and pushed her down, then wormed his way with utmost care to the back doors of the camper, untangling his cramped legs from the legs and equipment of the camper guys. Ultra slowly so as not to wake them. The latch popped loudly. Eddie froze and waited. One of the guys murmured and rolled over but didn't wake up. Eddie let himself out and down into the snow.

A guy was standing on the roof of his car nearby outside, taking pictures with his wife yelling for him to get a-shot-of-this and be-sure-not-to-miss-that. Neither noticed the small boy stomach deep in snow. Ed cleared a space in the deep white stuff and relieved himself, taking pleasure in the power of warm urine as it burned a yellow hole deep in the snow. He lifted Daisy out and super gently closed the camper doors and didn't let them latch and make that terrific noise again.

Plenty was going on at the site of the explosions of the night before. Two army trucks went past on the eastbound going the other way. He could hear a lot of work going on now that he was out and away from the snoring.

Ed fought his way along until he found a rut that had been made by someone else, then pushed along it until he reached the crater. It was like a crater, the snow a good two feet deeper all around than where the fire had been. He stepped into it and out of the deeper snow. The walking was a great deal easier.

He had progressed about three yards into the circle, passed a gaping window of a wreck and happened to glance momentarily into the black interior. A corpse lay face down against the wire skeleton of what had been a steering wheel. The body was ashes. There was no hair. No ears. No anything. Cracks of pink alligatored through the black surface. Hot dogs on a grill came to his mind. It was an arm's length from him. Over powering revulsion and curiosity brought his hand up slowly and he touched it. He withdrew the hand at once. Held it in mid-air for a second, smelled the fingertips just very delicately, then wiped it quickly on his jeans.

"Hey, kid! Get out of there!"

Ed jumped. It startled him so bad it made him sick a little.

Two guys were running at him—an army guy with a gun and some other guy, some kind of worker. Eddie stood his ground. They grabbed him and carried him back to the east perimeter.

"What the hell's the matter with you, kid? You stay back outa here until we're finished," the worker guy said.

"Gotta get over to the other side," said Ed. They set him down. "Folks are over there."

"Sorry, kid. You can't get through. Can't let ya. Not for a while."

The one guy looked at the other. It was obvious to Ed they thought his folks were burned up in there someplace like that roasted guy, same as with the camper guys.

"Naw, they're not in there with them dead people. They're on the other side! I have to get over."

"In a while, kid. You stay out of here now."

"I'm cold! I got to have some place to go!" Ed said.

"In a while. You can't get through. I'm sorry."

Ed took his dog and climbed the medial.

"Hey kid! Where the hell you think you're going?"

Ed paid no attention. They crossed the medial to block him. He cut through the cars and reached the outside eastbound berm and sprinted across the open channel. They blocked him there. Ed climbed the high bank of plowed snow and went over the guardrail. He found himself confronted with a steep, snowbound hillside sloping down and down. Below and past the naked trees there seemed to be another, smaller road with trapped cars too. Sitting there like lumps of marshmallows. One of the guys climbed to the top of the snowbank and stood in his way. The other stayed in the open shoulder access lane.

"Give it up, kid. Do like we say. It's for your own good I'm telling you."

Ed did not so much as look at him. He started down.

Fifty feet below the guardrail he turned and started trudging west again. The guy was following, was keeping abreast of him above.

"Think you're smart, huh kid? You come up, I'm gonna grab you."

"Stick it," Ed said.

"Oh yeah? You wait, kid. You just wait."

Ed didn't look up. He just kept trudging. The redneck kept pace above him. Ed kept trudging, pushing waist deep through the snow. His feet were hurting and the snow was getting down his pants. He didn't let discomfort show. He'd never give them the satisfaction.

Then his foot came down on a rotten branch and slipped. He went head over heels, gathering small avalanches around him. He saw nothing but the alternating rapid flashes, white and gray, and whirling. He was conscious of spray-burn of snow on his face going down his neck. He lost hold of Daisy. He just kept going down and down and down.

MILEPOST 100.4—BYPASS—6:50 A.M.

The pounding jolted Dan severely, ramming an initial stuporous awareness into his brain. He had slept, his head against the window that was being pounded on. The snow fell away, revealing a state trooper and a highway workman peering in at him. The trooper pounded on the glass again. Dan rolled the window down.

"Is everyone all right in here? Do you have any sick persons, any babies?" The trooper asked it in a tone that bespoke a thousand repetitions.

"I—uh—we're okay. Look, my son got separated in the night. We couldn't find him."

The trooper took Eddie's name, Dan's name—a general description.

"Mr. Braden, can you move this car? Do you have gas?"

"Some."

"Good. Then we're going to have to ask you to move it."

"Where?"

"We're moving people down away from this accident site. We're making access to the work, to restore the power lines."

The workman brushed a foot of snow from Dan's windshield. There was an open lane ahead with ruts where other cars had moved on. The cars were gone.

"Look, I'd rather not. In case my boy comes looking for us."

"Sorry, sir. We've got to have the room. You won't be going that far. Half a mile at the most. We'll keep a lookout for the boy."

The men began to move away.

"I'm not going anywhere," Dan said. "I mean that!"

The trooper turned around. "Sir, you either move that car or we will. The choice is yours. I'm sorry, but that's how it is." They went directly to the car behind.

It was closer to a mile before Dan came to the backlog again and could go no further. He shut down the car despite Chris's pleading for some warmth. He didn't know when he'd be able to get gas again. He left the car and started back up to the site of the explosion. It was uphill. He hadn't noticed they were on a down-grade the night before, hadn't thought about it while moving the car this morning. You noticed it when you were walking up though, you really noticed it.

Other cars were coming down behind the station wagon. Nothing moved across the medial on this side. He assumed the working crews had come up from the other side of this mountain. Obviously there was a town in that direction. That was good to know.

U.S. ROUTE 31 WEST OF SOMERSTON, PA.—7:00 A.M.

Old Route 31 is within a hundred fifty yards of Eastern Turnpike Milepost 100, summit of the Donovan "bypass". Neither can be seen from the other. Route 31 is a hundred fifty yards of almost straight-down pine forest hillside below the Pike. The slope and forest conceal an obsolete and disused two-lane turnpike tunnel as well, the deep land cuts and six-lane pavement above having years before "bypassed" the old bottleneck tunnel, now boarded up and used for rocksalt storage. Thus, while Em Baker had spent the night in the Peterbilt so close to the Pike, had heard the profanity and chaos on the CB and knew that she was somewhere near it she had no idea how near she really was. She had spent the night alone and listened and wondered about her Pa and horse and the new colt at home until it seemed so late and dark that she had taken the old 12-gauge and curled up with it in the sleeper. During the first few hours the traffic had been incredibly thick, but then it all bogged down in the snow and everything got quiet and she balled up in the sleeper to wait for morning or her Pa, whichever came first. She drifted among her thoughts and listened to the sounds until the silence was the biggest sound of all and drifted off to sleep.

She felt the cab shake and came instantly awake. She didn't move. She watched the ceiling of the sleeper bunk and waited. It came again. Then scraping, clambering sounds. Somebody was climbing up onto the cab. Then a dog yapped. Small dog. Worried dog. Em kicked the blankets off her legs and sat up. She reached for and found the shotgun. Whoever that was it couldn't be her Pa. He would've unlocked the truck with his keys or even if he lost his keys, he would be pounding on the door and setting up a hollar—so it wasn't him. She took hold of the gun and slid down into the cab.

Early light diffused through the caked snow. There was a scrape-track up the windshield on the right side, a crack of sky and tree tops showing through was all that she could see of the outside. She got closer and peered out through it, could see the lumps of white that were cars on #31 beneath the snow, some kicked up snow on the motor hood, but that was all. The dog yapped again, somewhere below her on her side. It was a small dog. Sounded like a kind of old one too. It was absolutely still for some long moments.

Then metal buckled overhead. He was on the roof! Above her. On the cab! She slid stealthily into the driver's seat. Once there she stopped and waited, thought it over and waited for the sound to come again. She waited for a long time. She began to think almost that it was left over from a dream and then it went clump again, above her. Just a little, but real as it could be.

She pulled the button of the door lock slowly, then reached for the handle and turned it slowly down until it had come all the way down and could turn no more and still it didn't give. Frozen! Damn! Let it up and brought it down again and this time leaned on it with all her weight and more.

The latch let go with a terrific bang. The door swung out and wide and over open space with her still hanging on and stretched out over virgin snow that came up higher than the running boards. Avalanches of it poured down onto her in sticky clums. It was a wet snow. It wasn't cold.

The 12-gauge had fallen from her and she saw a hole where it had slipped beneath the snow. Still hanging to the door she carefully looked up and saw nothing, then she let herself down, feeling with her foot for the running board. She let herself down with the stealth of legendary Indians and felt for the old Remington and found it. She brought it up and got the snow out of it as best she could and tried to get it dry.

Then she pushed out from the cab. The snow was stomach high and fought against her like in water when you can't run, except worse and wet her jeans with ice water. She turned backwards to face the cab and raised the Remington and pushed back further till she had come out far enough to see.

"Hey, kid!"

A kid! A stupid kid up walking on the cab!

"What?" Eddie Braden looked down defiantly from his high place.

"What the heck you think you're doing up on my truck?"

"*Your* truck? You ain't old enough to have a truck like this. Who the hell you think you're kidding with that old gun?"

"Before you scratch the paint! Get *off!*"

"What kind of a gun is that, anyhow?"

"It won't matter what it is. It'll be all the same to you. Get *off!*"

She stepped back menacingly and raised the gun and slipped in the wet snow.

Ed felt the charge pass right in front of him, a whoof of

wind into his face. He slipped, too, and tumbled awkwardly. In stages. From roof to hood and down the other side.

Em collected herself, got up and slapped off the sticky snow. It stuck like powered sugar to a doughnut. She looked up and scrambled up into the cab and across the seats and rolled down the window fearing that she'd shot him. There was ice and snow caked on the window and it was trouble getting down, but she got it down, making avalanches of the ice and snow that broke away.

"Hey!" It was the kid. Shouting from below.

Em poked her head out. He was down there yelling because the avalanches were coming down on him. She looked for blood. There wasn't any.

"Aw. You're okay," she said.

The boy said nothing.

She was right about the dog. A small, old, fat dog. The boy was sitting on his pratt, the dog licking him in the face. He pushed her off and got to his feet and never once throughout it looked up at where Em was. He had snow down his neck and in his coat and was soaking, but he made out completely as if there were nobody but him and the dog for miles. Keeping up the pride front. Like the rest of them. She watched to see how long he'd keep it up and he did; he kept it up. He beat out a place in the snow on the running board of the truck and set the dog down and never once broke out of it, never looked her way. Not for a second.

"Hey!" said Em.

"It's for the dog," he said. He knew she would say something. "She's too short for the snow."

Em said no more for some time. She could see the wetness and cold was getting to him. He was dancing, shivering and looking every direction in the world, like nobody in the world was watching, expecting a bus to come along or something. He was turning blue. Em kind of smiled behind her face and let him turn blue for a while.

"Hey, kid!"

"What?"

"What happened to your folks?"

Ed pointed up the hill whence he had fallen and she saw the track he'd made down through the trees, a couple of big snowballs that had grown beside him as they rolled.

"What's up there, the Turnpike?"

He nodded.

"Far?"

He shook his head and danced a littler harder. Stamped his feet.

The dog slipped off the running board and he retrieved her and set her up on it again. She was wetter and colder than before. It struck Em the dog was pregnant, too.

"You can bring the dog up if you want to," she said.

"What for?"

"How old is that dog?"

"Eleven."

"Same as you."

"I'm thirteen." It was a lie. Ed was twelve.

"Anyhow a dog eleven—that's like leaving your great-grandmother pregnant and naked in the snow."

Ed looked at Daisy. She was trusting, optimistic as long as he was there, but she was shaking like those heavy-duty vibro-massagers at the barber shop, the ones that make your whole head numb.

"By the time you get your mind made up, the dog will be solid froze," said Em.

Ed handed up the dog. He didn't talk. He didn't want to talk. His teeth were chattering so badly he was afraid that if he tried to talk he'd stammer.

Em reached down through the window and took Daisy.

"What's her name?"

"Di—Di—Di—Daisy."

That was it. There went the dignity.

"You let this dog get pregnant, didn't you? You ought to be ashamed, a dog that old. How many did she have the last time?"

"Ti—ti—ti-ten."

Em got an old towel and began to towel Daisy dry. Daisy whined and watched Ed from the window.

"It's too tough on them when they get this old," Em said.

She looked out the window and regarded him with a stern and reprimanding eye. "Don't you dump 'em in the woods. I'm sick of city people ain't got the guts enough to own up to their animals. I shot more baby cats and dogs than I can think of till I'm sick to heart. Little babies out there starving and cryin' in the woods. Easier to shoot the people if I even catch'em doing it. Whole lot easier."

Daisy barked at Ed. She whined more vigorously and pranced her front feet on the ledge of the cab window.

"I'm gonna roll this window up now, I got no heat up in this cab, but we can get you both dried off. You want to come, you best come now. The dog is lonesome for ya."

Em got the defroster out and began to blow them dry. She kept the doors and windows tightly shut so heat from the defroster would not be lost. They listened to the radio part of the time. The radio announcers were having a high time about the storm and the vast shutdowns and how many people had got stuck out on the roads. The radio announcers pretended to be grave and serious, but they loved it having something big and worth the telling for a change and you could tell. It got through all the grave and serious.

After a while Em shut the radio off and at once confinement crushed in on the cab. She ran the windshield wipers so they could see and that helped a little but not much. It was nothing but white lumps on the road in front of them and black branches piled high with more snow and that was all. No people were out. Nothing moved at all.

The defroster took a long time. It didn't do much to get the cab warm. Ed's toes hurt like hell. He took the shoes off and tried the defroster on them and that helped a little. He blew the defroster into the shoes and got them hot before he put them on and that was great. Em dug into the glove compartment and came up with half a bag of stale Doritos for their breakfast. Daisy ate her share.

"She eats anything because she's pregnant," said Ed.

"She eats anything because she's poorly trained," said Em.

"Naw, she don't eat crazy stuff between. She eats regular dog stuff in between."

Then they didn't talk for some time and when they talked

she asked him about his folks and what had happened and he told her. Em had turned to caring for the old shotgun after drying Daisy, now, resuming her effort to get it dry before it started rusting, but it was too late already. A thin dusting of bright orange had begun to frost the barrel. The old Remington had long since lost its bluing and most of its sharp edges. Ed watched the process fascinated, seeing what she did and at each step tried to determine why inside his own mind without asking.

She asked him how he planned to get back up to where his folks were. He only shrugged.

"Well, at least you know they ain't goin' anyplace," she said.

They talked about the big explosion and the things that Eddie saw and especially about the lady that had blown apart and Em let him continue to do the talking as she ragged a thin coat of oil over the gun with great deliberation. He quit talking and at some length his last words hung in the air as she thought over what she'd heard him say. She kept polishing the shotgun for a little while.

"You never saw nothing get killed before?" she said. She kept working on the shotgun.

"I had another dog once that got hit by a car."

"Was that as bad?"

"Worse. It didn't die. It just got kind of half-killed and it dragged its back legs around and around on the street and screamed and screamed and screamed and God it hurt your ears and was just completely sickening. You can't believe it."

"And you let it? You just left it suffer on and on like that?"

"After a while the Pollock's old man came out in the street and shot it with this gun he has left over from the army, except he didn't hit it right till the fourth time. God!" The memory of it made him sick. Every time he thought about it, it always made him sick.

"You let somebody shoot your dog?"

Ed shrugged. What was he going to say?

"He had the gun. And then he was there already."

"Still, you don't let somebody shoot your dog. You shoot your own damn dog. You should have stopped him."

Ed shrugged again. He thought about the Pollock's old man

and all the adults that came out and everything that was going on and the horrible screaming of the dog and all the arguing and loud concussions from the pistol—not even in the slightest like you see it on TV.

"You got to shoot your own dang dog," she said again.

Em seemed satisfied about the gun now. She laid it aside. "You should not have told about the lady either, I don't think."

"What lady?"

"The one that got her arms blowed off. I don't think you would have if you knowed her personal."

Ed thought about it. No matter what you did this girl would find some way to make you feel like shit about it. He didn't say anything for some time. Both of them just sat there staring out the windshield.

"He wasn't my dog really," Ed said. "He just used to come around a lot."

MILEPOST 100.6—THE BYPASS—7:10 A.M.

Jake Stokes M.D. and county coroner had found the situation on the bypass grislier than even he could have imagined. The living injured had been located and sent down to Somerston. They thought they had them all. What they would do with them in Somerston was anybody's guess though. They had taken them down in army trucks and in some cases even snowmobiles because there were no ambulances. No route had been opened to the hospital. It didn't look as if one would be in the near future. The town was so completely packed and overrun a pigeon couldn't shit and hit the ground. Someone had come back up from town and told him they were putting up a temporary hospital in the A&P and some other stores too. So be it. He would worry about that when he got back down. Jake Stokes M.D. and county coroner pulled up his coat onto the amputated shoulder for the hundred-millionth time since 1943 and heaved a sigh. They had finished with the quick; it was time now to see about the dead.

It was getting to be a problem. Motorists outside the area

had had to be awakened to be moved and now were getting curious, leaving their cars and coming up to see. Stokes had called for more men and got a few. He walled the public out with armed National Guard and used his civil defense volunteers to literally hand shovel all the snow out of the area to make sure all bodies and all parts thereof were found. Where he was going to put the grisly artifacts was another matter. The county morgue at Somerston had a capacity of twelve. He had thrice that number at hand within forty feet in any direction. All beyond recognition. What was needed was frozen storage to keep them until he could get around to the more subtle aspects of this occupation, identifying things that had been people. Essential first to get them out of sight. It was not the kind of thing you let the uninitiated walk unsuspecting into. That fit into a category of experiences which leave one forever changed. But where to put them?

LaBarr came up to him with stale news that the wounded had all been sent down to Somerston. Stokes said yes he knew. What he did not know was what to do about the bodies.

LaBarr thought about it, started to give up on it. Then the idea of the abandoned tunnel struck him.

"What tunnel?" said Stokes. Then he remembered. Of course! The bypass! Bypassing the old two lane Donovan tunnel! My God! That had been twenty years! Thirty! He hadn't thought of it in years! Was it still there? LaBarr assured him that it was. You could drive past it every day for a hundred years and never guess there was a tunnel there—just below where they were standing now. The cops knew. And the maintenance guys. Mainly just the zone cops and maintenance and that was it. Little hidden gates at Mileposts 98.2 and 101.4. If you didn't know exactly where to look you'd never seem them. Stokes had just two words to say:

"Let's go!"

MILEPOST 99.4—BYPASS—7:10 A.M.

The waking of patrons on the westbound and moving them downhill had kicked up general activity and Dan Braden found himself on foot among a growing pilgrimage back up to the summit after having moved the car. The western slope of the Donovan bypass had come alive much earlier than most of the rest of the Pike and secondary roads. The rutted and refrozen slush made it hard to stay erect. His legs were cramped and aching from thirteen hours sitting in the same position and would only obey approximately. His face was waxy and demanding to be shaved. He looked like hell and felt like sixty. It was a long, uphill mile.

At the top the crowd had formed. A parade wall of people had piled up against the barrier of Somerston police and guardsmen letting no one by, entertaining no pleas of exceptional circumstances. He gave up after walking back and forth across all six lanes a couple times and went down to the car again. He got in and sat with cold and aching feet wondering what for. It wasn't any warmer. Irene at least had sense enough not to make some kind of inane remark like "What happened?" or "Did you see Eddie?"

Chris was moaning softly in the back, rolling slightly.

"What's the matter with her now?"

"I don't know, Dan. She says her stomach hurts. What happened? Did you see Eddie?"

"Of course I didn't see him! If I saw him would I be back here alone? For heaven's sake!"

Chris moaned in the back again.

"What's the matter Chris? Where does it hurt?"

"All over. Ooohh! Where's Eddie? Why didn't you find him?"

"I don't know." Dan and Irene waited and said nothing.

"Can we have some heat? I'm freezing! My feet are freezing," Chris complained.

Irene looked at Dan. "Could we? Just a little?"

Dan looked at his gauge, about an eighth of a tank. His watch said seven-ten. There ought to be some news somewhere.

"I guess for a while. I want to see what's on the radio anyhow." He fired the engine.

The dial was mostly stations too distant to hear clearly—motorboating, overlapping, going in and out. French Quebec,

Montreal. At the high end of the dial he hit a loud one—very clear.

".. . story of the hour continues to be the record-breaking over-night snowfall which has left parts of Indiana, all of Ohio and the western two-thirds of Pennsylvania virtually shut down. Travel advisories are—well it's rather beyond the advisory stage, the word is simply—DON'T TRAVEL with almost all state, county, and municipal roads impassable and uncounted thousands of motorists already stranded. The wet and heavy snow, which is officially re-corded at twenty-two inches, but also as much as thirty-six inches in some places, was responsible for large numbers of fallen power lines, creating additional hazards and leaving many communities throughout the northern and central portions of the state without electricity. West Penn officials say that efforts to restore the power lines are being greatly hampered by the impassable roads and by large numbers of employees unable to get in to work. The state is currently under Proclamation of Extreme Emergency. Na-tional Guard units and local communities have been called up to assist with restoration of the lines and road clearing operations. Penn Department of Transportation crews which have been out trying to keep roads open since late last afternoon, report that many stranded and deserted vehicles left on the roads and high-ways are prolonging efforts to open lanes and restore traffic also. They also report that sizable numbers of their own machines have become immobilized in the stranded traffic.

The Eastern Turnpike is shut down from Harrisburg west to the Ohio line, with Pike officials reporting similar conditions and are not expecting to be able to make significant headway before the second storm, due sometime this afternoon, drops temperatures into the low teens and brings high winds and a possible additional accumulation of up to twelve inches.

There has, as yet, been no estimate of fatalities, but Red Cross . . .''

Dan snapped it off. Chris moaned softly.

Irene stared into the jam ahead of them. Dan too. "What are we going to do?" she said. She wasn't hysterical, but she wanted answers.

Chris moaned again. Dan turned to see. She was lying on her back across the seat, holding her stomach.

"Chris, is this for real or is it just another belly ache? We can't fool around with little aches and pains."

"Nooo-oh. It hurts! My legs are hurting too."

Maybe it was another of her cases of food poisoning. She seemed to get them more than any other human being could manage and survive. Maybe it was gas and cramped legs for sitting in the car, like his were. A combination. Maybe it was appendicitis too.

"What are we going to do, Dan?" Irene was more insistent.

"I don't know. I think we'd better get into town."

"What about Eddie?"

"We'll leave a note. Tell him to come to the town. There's a town back there. There has to be. A lot of Guard and local cops are up there at the fire. Chris, can you walk?"

"I don't know."

They pasted the note to the inside of the window on Dan's side. With an arm about each of their waists, Chris got halfway up the hill. Dan carried her piggyback thereafter.

They reached the crowd at the top, pushed through and were at once accosted by a young redneckish looking guy in army clothes. The guy held up a rifle, sideways, as a barricade against them, like something he had learned from old TV movies.

"Hey! Get back."

"Look. I've got a sick kid here. We need to get to town."

"What's the matter with her?"

"I don't know. She's got stomach pains, leg pains. She can't walk. Maybe food poisoning. Maybe appendicitis. How the hell should I know? There's a town down there, isn't there?"

The kid looked at Chris. She did look bad. He had orders about the sick and injured. He thought about it, looked beyond them for a possible wave of crashers in their wake, then let them by.

"Keep off on the right of the westbound, go over to the other side of this. You'll see some army trucks and ambulances."

They crossed the no-man's land of burned machines. Some had been pushed off to make room for live ones, working monster army trucks and an assortment of civilian 4-wheel drive pickups and vans. Up the mountain of the westbound side, men and machines trailed upwards toward the big steel tower, men were climbing with tackle blocks, ropes, tools. Guardsmen and civilians too—hardhats. Guys were shoveling the snow by hand, right down to the pavement. He didn't understand that. A lot of yelling, barked orders. He hurried through. Chris was heavy. It was getting to be all that Dan could do to hold her, but he hurried through, remembering the things he's seen the night before and hoped neither of the women would see them too.

When they had reached the other side it took a little searching to find what the army kid had told them about, a kind of waiting area. The cases remaining were all ambulatories, a handful standing about with bandages and tags tied to their clothes. The more serious having gone first. A civilian van had just been loaded, a guy with a Red Cross armband shut the back doors and gave it a signal and it took off.

Another guy with an armband came up to them. He looked at Chris.

"What's the matter with her?"

"She's got stomach pains. Leg pains. How the hell should I know?"

"Okay," said the guy. "Wait here with the rest of them."

He made out tags for them and tied them to their clothes and they waited with the rest of the waitors with tags on their clothes. Dan felt like every kind of refugee story you ever saw on TV. He watched the van that had left disappearing down the steep single channel on the outside eastbound like a bobsled in a long, straight downhill run—a small black cube getting futher and further down.

"Chris."

"What?"

"If I let you down do you think you could stand on your own for a while?"

"I guess so."

They helped her down off Dan's back and over to a nearby truck and leaned against it with the girl between them. They stood there with their tags waiting for their turn.

MILEPOST 101.4—THE BYPASS—7:20 A.M.

Stokes and the trooper had of course found the access road down to the old Donovan tunnel under two feet of unbroken snow and had had to go back to the explosion site to get some kind of machine that would get them through. The 4-wheel drive van that had brought them down would not make it without damage in the opinion of its owner. Stokes wanted a look at the tunnel before investing a machine, the time and the manpower it would take to plow out a lane. It was nearly two-thirds of a mile from the small access gate down to the west end of the tunnel. He couldn't see it from the Pike at all. At the explosion site the only thing available had been a snowmobile. They took it down to 101.4

LaBarr drove because he knew how to get in and where. Stokes fell off once. It takes practice for a two-armed man to remain a passenger on a snowmobile. Stokes had never ridden one before.

The ends of the tunnel had been sealed against casual entry by animals and weather with big wooden garage-type doors— truck sized doors with a regular door built into them. The smaller door was not kept locked. What for?

When his eyes adjusted to the dark, Stokes liked what he saw. The stockpiled salt and drums of machine grease and fuel did not begin for several hundred feet. It was cold and empty and out of view. It would do.

They left the tunnel and returned to the Pike. They would begin the job of prying out the bodies and recording what kind of car, and numbers and license plates they were found with. If any.

Stokes did not fall off on the return trip to the gate.

REDFORD CENTRAL—7:10 A.M.

The call came from the governor's party at 7:05. It was Chuck who woke Lee Rider. The operators had shifted breaks and duties around so much and were getting so punchy from the long hours that his request to be awakened had simply gotten lost in the shuffle. They called Chuck Ellis rather than awaken their chief. Chuck found him laid out like a stiff on a slab on the oak counter of the "cage", sneakers and all, just where he had stretched out a few hours before.

Chuck shook his shoulder.

"Let's go. They're coming."

"Who?"

"The Governor of Pennsylvania. Come on. They're landing in ten minutes. They're in the air right now. They called us from the chopper."

Lee looked blank and stupid for a minute. Then it all came back to him.

"Jesus!"

He sat bolt upright and rubbed his face and felt the stubble. He looked at Chuck. Chuck needed a shave as bad as he did.

"Do I look as bad as you do?"

Chuck handed him his coat. "Worse. Don't change a hair. Looks like you've been busting ass all night. It's great public relations."

Lee fought his way into the sleeves of the heavy trenchcoat mumbling vague protests.

"Don't argue," said Chuck. "They'll be here in ten minutes."

Judy Cochran appeared from somewhere with hot coffee. She looked frazzled, tired and miffed. She shot dirty looks at both of them.

"Thanks," said Lee.

"Don't thank me. I did it under protest." Her dirty-look laser eye-ray was burning holes in Chuck, now.

"All I asked was would you make Lee a cup of coffee! Because we're in a jam! Is that so terrible?" Chuck was exasperated.

"Because I'm the woman," Judy said. "Say it isn't so."

"As one human being to another, I appreciate it," said Lee.

Judy cast her eyes down. She shrugged a little.

"Well, I guess that's better," she said. "At least a little, I suppose."

REDFORD CENTRAL—7:25 A.M.—THE HELICOPTER

At 7:25 Lee and Chuck stood knee-deep in the parking lot as the helicopter came low out of the east following the Pike and then swung off and over, blasting out a crater in the snow in front of them. Lee gulped the last of the coffee, jammed the cup into his pocket. They climbed aboard. The chopper lifted off, swung out and over the Pike again and headed west, exactly as before.

The governor was a little man with an ice-pick nose who needed a shave as badly as Lee did. Everybody in the helicopter looked like they'd spent a heavy night in hell. Stubbled jowls, red bagged eyes, undone collars and tobacco smoke. Lee felt better. Chuck was right. It would have been terrible to show up here looking shiny bright. It would've set the rest against him, he was sure.

They were handed headsets and told to put them on and shown where to plug them in—little jacks at each position and the seats were plush for helicopter fare. A custom setup. Obviously someone had a lot of need for airborne conferences. The jacks and headsets were an interphone within the ship. It didn't matter how plush you made them, choppers made horrendous noise, inside and out.

Once in their headsets he and Chuck took their first good look around. The headsets helped a lot. They cut the noise and sealed you into a private inner space of tinny, electric-sounding intimacy. Eight other guys were breathing in your ear. It took some getting used to. Also you couldn't tell where the sound was coming from. You had to look and correlate the words with lips and when it fit you knew who to look at.

Their boss Sherman Turlock was there, looking even sourer than usual. Sherman introduced them to the governor and to his aide, a nervous, over-groomed fellow with glasses who scribbled on a pad. The guy who'd called last night on the phone. And J. Archer Reese, Regional Coordinator of Civil Defense whom Lee had met before. The other two he didn't know—an older, possibly retired, military type and the only man within the helicopter who had shaved. A brigadier general. The brigadier general was looking down at Lee's feet and because of that Lee looked down at his wet sneakers too, then up again and met the fellow's gaze until the fellow looked out his porthole. Window. Whatever they were. What the hell. He wasn't military. He didn't have to wear a uniform. To hell with you, pal! Lee wasn't going to like the brigadier general, he could tell.

The last guy in the fuselage seemed out of place completely. Young. The perennial grad-student. English major. Tweed sport coat with leather elbows, vest sweater over Hathaway shirt and undone tie. The whole thing. Curly dark hair and pipe. Most of the smoke inside the fuselage was his fault. He puffed and worried at a gnarled pipe with half the stem gnawed off. Smoking it upside down then sideways or aright. Lost in thought out of the window. A lot going on behind those blue-gray eyes. Twenty-eight. Thirty maybe. They were looking younger to him every year.

Other than that it was just the two pilots, Chuck and himself. Eight guys breathing in the interphone. Everybody staring out the portholes. Windows. Whatever they were.

The pilots were keeping them low, about a hundred feet above the Pike, still above the flatland now and coming to the long, tortuously winding, ascent up to Aurora. That would come soon. Everett Police Barracks were passing on the left now. The double mole track of white lumps that distinguished the turnpike from the surrounding white blanket fanned out and enveloped Everett's several buildings. People were out of cars at Everett. There was a great deal more activity than on the road. Elsewhere it was just the endless file of the white lumps, the cars beneath the snow. Dormant. Sleeping. Thousands upon thousands of them. It seemed to be three lanes below them now, the westbound and its shoulder completely filled and solid. The eastbound showed only an occasional isolated lump—some abandoned car or machine. The eastbound also showed the tracks of movement. The Kregg and Aurora crews were still at it in the tunnels. Everett apparently had been overrun by the breakout at the Milepost 137 turn-around the night before. He saw that below them now. The high snowbank barricade that had to be filled with Christmas trees. John Beck had not come in as ordered. He regretted that. The captain should have been along on this.

They were going up, now. Ascending to Aurora. It remained

the same. The eastbound showing an occasional plow truck or wrecker coming down with some item of debris from the tunnel or going up for another load again. The westbound remained the steady and unbroken triple lane of lumps. At Kregg Maintenance halfway up the mountain the westbound lumps widened out again and enveloped the buildings at Kregg like a primitive organism enveloping some particle of prey, the same as at Everett. Kregg was one of the few maintenance facilities that stood separate from the police barracks. It was justified by the incredible ascent up to Aurora and the difficulties that arose on the mountain. Extra fuel and salt and cinders were stockpiled there, extra machines, extra manpower. Especially in winter. The western slope was not so bad. Somerston was some seven hundred feet higher that Redford. The next police-maintenance was Somerston on the eastbound at Milepost 102—7 miles beyond Gate 10—the town of Somerston. Thus there were maintenance yards at Everett at 140.2, Kregg at 135.5 and Aurora between the east- and westbound tubes of the big tunnel—122.18 to 123.32. A huge, mile-long garage. The greatest density of facilities within the system and still not adequate in the opinion of a lot of the guys. Lee included.

Now they were rising sharply. Lee felt it in his stomach and in his forehead between the eyes. The G's. The forces of acceleration. A rocket-powered elevator ride. The chopper had reached the eastern portals of the Aurora tunnel and was going straight up the sheer rock facing of the mountain to top the Bald Knob Summit and go-over. The rock wall seemed to be going down outside the port-hole windows like a waterfall of rock in front of him. Lee looked away and braced himself and waited till his stomach would catch up with the helicopter. The others in the chopper looked a little queasy too.

The chopper leveled out abruptly, almost as bad as going up. Stomachs were in throats all around. The pilot thought himself some kind of hotshot and after twenty hours of instant coffee nobody appreciated it.

"What the hell is *that?*"

The voice was tinny in the earphones. Strange. He could not tell where it came from.

The governor was aghast at what he saw out the window.
He was white-faced, literally ashen. Lee half rose from his seat
and leaned to look out that side with the others.

It was the Bald Knob Tower, the antenna of the Repeater
#12. From it hung the body of a man, by one foot, upside down
some fifteen feet below the toplight. The other leg stuck rigidly
out and down a rag doll angle. The arms hung down, above the
head, and rigid too. The body had accumulated snow.

"Pilot!" It was the governor's voice again. "Circle that antenna, will you?" A little squeak was happening in the voice that
was new as of the last few moments.

The chopper swung around the tower several times and came
in closer. It was Jimmy Weeks. Who else could it have been?
The chopper came in close enough that Lee could see his face
and it was. It was Jimmy Weeks.

"God," said Lee. He didn't shout or anything. He said it
softly.

The governor's eyes flashed about to see who'd said it. The
eyes hit Lee and stopped.

"Do you know about this?" he demanded.

"Yes," said Lee. "I know the man. One of my technicians."

The chopper continued to circle round and round the tower.
Nobody said anything for two complete rotations. They just
looked out at Jimmy with his hands up, like some kind of pathetic upside down victim of a stick-up.

The governor was nonplussed. "Should we stop? What
should we do?"

"Sir, there's no place I could possibly put down," the pilot
said. Nobody said anything to that. The chopper just kept going
round and round. "Do you want me to keep circling?" the pilot
asked.

"No," said Lee. "Go on. I'll see to it when I get back."

The chopper broke out of the circle and went west again.
They resettled in their seats. Nothing was said for some moments.

"I suppose it may seem an insensitive thing to say," a voice
said," but he'll keep. The cold has some advantages."

It was the young guy. Lee got the last of it connected with the face. The guy was knocking out the ashes from his pipe against his shoe and now repacking from a pouch and lighting up again with a big cowboy wooden match. Plumes of smoke billowed as he got it going.

"You should have been in Guatemala. Whew!" He shook the match out and extended a lean hand to Lee. "By the way, you're Lee Rider, aren't you?" Lee took the hand and nodded. "Mark Woods. We've spoken on the phone."

They had. Woods was regional director of disasters for the Red Cross out of Pittsburgh. There had been a tornado that hit Irwin and crossed the Pike some years before. And some other things at other times. These contacts by phone had caused Lee to envision a much older tougher looking man. The physical appearance was a surprise. The hand was hard and warm.

Woods reached under his seat and came up with a thermos. He poured a capful and offered it to anyone. There were no takers. Woods sipped it himself.

"The cold is preferable to heat," he said. "I'm sorry if that offends anybody but it's true. The other can be really ghastly."

They were over the summit now and dropping steadily toward Somerston. It was the same below them on the west side of the mountain, same unbroken snow except for some piled up heaps just at the tunnel. The great bulldozer where Ollie had left it, standing huge and solitary and mantled with snow at the western portal of the eastbound. After that nothing. There was no activity on the eastbound between Aurora and Gate 10.

The shock of Jimmy Weeks and the passing of time had Lee's head almost clear. Finally. He felt in his pocket and brought out the coffee cup and held it out to Woods.

"Can I change my mind about that coffee?" Maybe another shot of the caffeine would finish up the job. Woods poured.

"Maybe I will, too," said Reese.

Woods let him use the thermos cap. They seemed to know each other well. That would make sense naturally. Regional director of disasters and the civil defense commander? How could it be otherwise? Now that Lee was awake he was beginning to see the implications of the group assembled in this helicopter. It had the little hairs on the back of his neck beginning to rise. The Red Cross? the C.D.? the Guard? the turnpike director? The governor himself? And no press. That was *scary!* Well, Chuck was there. But that was not the same. This thing was looking heavier and heavier all the time.

They were passing north of Somerston along the Pike now. Woods had the pilot swing off and spiral upward in a climb and circle the town several times from about a thousand feet. Again the rocket-powered elevator ride, the hotshot stomach sag. Sommerston inundated, glaciated from all sides at once. There was a great deal of darkening of the snow in the streets among the cars and buildings where people had trodden it to slush. They could see the people. By the thousands. Dark ants among the cars and buildings. There was a dark plume of smoke rising from the south end of town. Some kind of fire which did not seem to be intentional.

The governor remarked about it, about what a mess the town was. Lee pointed out that Somerston just seemed to be a natural catch-all for the turnpike's winter problems, situated as it was between the bypass on the west and Aurora Mountain immediately east. Somerston was on the Cambria Plateau and had the severest winters of southwestern Pennsylvania along with Johnstown and Altoona and so on. Everything just seemed to funnel down on them from the mountains on either side. Somerston was squarely in the middle. They got if from both sides and north and south from #219. It was unavoidable. An unfortunate circumstance of topography.

The pilot broke out of the circle and continued west again. More people were out of cars on both the east and westbound on the way up to the bypass. The activity, the cleared lane on the eastbound shoulder, was visible through the movment of vehicles along it and lines of people walking into Somerston. The activity had doubtless caused the patrons to awaken sooner than they might have. Elsewhere on the Pike it was still deadly silent. And it was brighter now. The sun was threatening to burn through the overcast in places.

The summit of the bypass was a big, black circle, fringed with the hundreds of people who had come to watch, looking from the high vantage of the helicopter for all the world like ants around a lollipop. Lee started to explain, but the governor knew about it. The subject of the electric companies was a point of sensitivity with the governor.

"Two-thirds of the state is out of power," he said. "A thousand communities and hospitals and nursing homes. Two million private dwellings. This is the worst thing that ever hit us. We're going to have fuel crises everywhere within a day or two if we don't get some roads open. What about it, guys?" The governor looked more than just a little overwhelmed.

Nobody answered his question. Everyone kept looking down at the white world below. Beyond the black spot on the bypass was all white again. There was nothing moving, nothing going on. An occasional individual or clot of three or four were waving at them here and there, but otherwise the Pike was largely dormant, largely still. It showed white and lumpy down through the pine forests west of the bypass and on out onto the broader and more open, level and endless pull of taffy that had draped down across the rolling hills and settled there into shapes and crevasses and become a part of everything.

"What is the length of your average car, Mr. Rider?"

The question came out of no direction, out of the headsets. Lee looked up. Arch Reese and Woods were looking at him. Reese had a pocket calculator in his hand.

"Pardon?"

"A car. What's the length of the average vehicle? How much space does it take up? Bumper to bumper?" Reese was talking. He and Woods had got involved in something. Clouds billowed from Woods' pipe. He was intense and absorbed.

It caught Lee off guard just for a moment. "Uh, trucks and everything?"

They nodded.

"Right," said Woods. "An average."

"Cars are smaller now. This is not my field, it's just a guess." It was, but when you worked around this kind of stuff you did pick up some numbers.

"It's all right. We're only racking up some quick figures, approximates," said Woods. "Would you say—16—18?"

"Twenty," said Lee.

"I like that better," Reese said. "With the trucks and gaps and everything let's make it 22. I work from worst case figures. That way you only get the good surprises." He adjusted himself above the calculator, shifting in his seat as if the way he sat restricted his button-punching finger.

"Okay. We got 5,280 feet per statute mile divided by 22 gives 240 cars per mile. But that's just single file. I see almost six lanes down there, with only minor exceptions, all the way along. 240 times 6 equals 1440 cars per mile. How far back did you say this thing goes? Harrisburg?"

Lee hadn't said anything. But it was Harrisburg as per his most recent information. Maintenance and hired men and machinery and armories east of Harrisburg were working at evacuating the westbound from that end, but had been making only slight progress. The toughie in the whole thing was where to put the abandoned and broken down cars once you had got them to transport fuel enough to refuel them even with a gallon and get them moving. The eastbound was being cleared more easily. Once they woke them up and started them, most of the cars were simply able to drive on. They would clear the eastbound to a turn-around, then use that turn-around to U-turn the westbound and send them back toward Philadelphia. That's what was taking time. And the abandonments. And the dead batteries. And the arguments and fights and all of it. The backlog was probably a turn-around or two west of Harrisburg. You could fit a lot of cars between turn-arounds.

"Say Milepost 225," said Lee. "Take off a mile for Milepost 1. We don't begin with zero."

"Okay—224 times 1440 equals—322,560 vehicles."

"Try that again," said the governor. He didn't want that to be right.

Reese ran the figures through again. It came up the same—322,560 vehicles.

"What would you say the average occupancy is?" said Reese. "Per vehicle?"

Chuck fielded this one. He was the man with the statistics.

"Ordinarily it runs something like 1.5, but this is

Thanksgiving. *The* big family day. It runs more on the order of 3.7.''

"322,560 times 3.7 equals 1,193,472. Round that off to one point two million people. That's on the turnpike alone. Gentlemen, I'd say we have a problem.''

Everyone sat silently for what seemed an immense span of time, just little crackles in the earphones, the motors off and away outside someplace.

The governor turned to his aide.

"Kent, be sure you have those figures. I'll want to have them when we call Washington.''

"I have them, sir,'' he said.

ROUTE 31—THE BYPASS—8:00 A.M.

By eight the cab of the truck had exhausted itself for both kids. They were less cold and they were dry and they were hungry. The girl's concern for the mare and the foal was getting like a smoker's urge and wouldn't let her be. The mare would be out of food unless the Hoders down the road had seen the goings on and came by to look in on the place. Maybe they would and maybe they wouldn't have. The Hoders were half and half on stuff like that.

She scratched through the glove compartment for things to write a note with.

> Pa—
>
>   I have satten here all night. The truck can not be stold the way things are. You have to do what you have to do and so do I which is taken care of my horse which needs me and her colt among the living. I took the shot gun down to Somerston to sell for money to get the bus and go on home. I am sorry about the shot gun. It is all I got to sell that would sell right off. Somebody got to be to home to keep things up.
>
> Em.

She taped this to the wheel with electrical tape, pulled the CB transceiver from the rack, wrapped the mike cord around it and handed it to Ed. She took the shotgun and climbed down from the diver's side. Ed slid over, made a quick scan of the note, then dropped into her tracks. She had the tool chest open and wanted the CB. He handed it to her.

"How much can you get for that gun?" said Ed.

She stuffed the CB in the box, put the lid down with a bang and locked it. She didn't answer.

"How much will you get?"

She shrugged. "Twenty?"

"Twenty dollars?"

"They don't make them kind no more. Them old light-weight pumpers is collector's items now. It's more than fair. It's a bargain out of necessity."

To Ed it was more than fair. His BB gun cost $27.95 plus state tax. The stocks were plastic. It shot down and to the left and wasn't powerful. Half the time the BB rolled out of the barrel when you pointed the barrel down. Junk.

"I'll give you twenty." He saw her look. "I mean it."

"You got twenty dollars?"

"Not *on* me."

"No. I didn't figure."

"I have eight." Daisy whined from the edge of the seat above him. He climbed up to get her then dropped into the snow by Em again.

"Eight ain't twenty."

"My old man is holding the rest of it for me. Twenty-six fifty. My vacation money."

"You take twenty-six fifty with you on vacation?"

"It was 54.50 before we started. No one gives it to me. I earn it myself."

Em carried out some final chores, locking up the truck and other things whose purpose was less obvious to Ed. She picked up the shotgun and started off without a word. East. Toward Somerston on #31.

"Where are you going? What about me?"

Ed chased after. Trying to carry Daisy. It was cumbersome. He would not be able to keep it up for long.

"That's up to you. I got a ways to go."

"What about the gun?" Ed followed in her rut. A few yards only. It took hard struggle to push through the snow, fighting with her knees and kicking her way into it. Her jeans were wet at once and the cold becoming painful.

"I thought you wanted to sell that gun."

He was keeping right behind her, letting her do all the hard work.

"I will," she said. She didn't turn around. She was fighting the snow that kept packing up in front of her like hard, wet snowballs. The air was pretty warm and it was soggy, a good packing snow. A snowball snow.

"So?"

He never quit, this kid.

"You got eight bucks," she said.

The shotgun stayed across her shoulder in a T-bar. She carried it that way to keep it up off the snow.

"I said I got the other! All you got to do is come up to my car we'll get it."

"Your old man will never give it to you."

"Sure, he will!"

"Never in a million years."

"It's mine. He has to."

"He'll say, 'What on earth are you going to do with a gun like that in the city? Where are you going to shoot it? What are you going to shoot at? How are you going to?' And he's right. It's a 12-gauge. It ain't a kid's gun."

"What about you?"

"It's not my gun. It's Pa's."

"He doesn't know you're selling it."

"Nope."

"He'll probably kill you, huh?"

"I generally don't do this kind of stuff. I wouldn't know."

They had pushed another fifty feet and barely got around the trailer. The going was no easier. Her legs were giving out. A scattered few of the cars nearby showed signs of life, now. A couple of them. People had gotten out to have a look. The rest remained the same silent mounds of white. It was yet largely still and silent in the early cold. Just the sound of distant engines up above them on the turnpike. Daisy shivered in Ed's arms. She was getting heavier. This wasn't going to work at all.

Em stopped, studied what was up above them. Steep and bare trees.

"You've been up there, what is that?" She pointed at the sound of the engines up above.

"Construction guys and army guys. From the explosion."

"The road plowed open?"

"For themselves is all. A bunch of rednecks. They won't let you through."

Em's jeans were soaking through. She was aching from ice water. She couldn't do this seven miles to Somerston. Maybe they would have to wait until more people tramped the snow down. She turned around and was face to face with Ed for the first time since the truck. Ed was in her rut and in her way.

"Go back," she said.

"I can go where I want," he said.

"I'm going back to the truck. If you don't want to, then step aside or else lie down and I will walk over you."

In the truck again Em again dried herself with the defroster. The defroster was turning out to be an indispensable thing to have. She had a map out and was looking.

"Well, what about it?" Ed had come back too. He was first to break the silence. He noticed she was disinclined to initiate conversation, markedly unlike the other girls he knew. Sparing with words as if she had a certain number in a box and when those were gone she'd be a mute or something.

"About what?" She remained deep in the road map. She made him feel intrusive by the way she sounded, made him feel like he was dipping too deep into her box of words.

"You coming up so I can get the money?"

"Where's your car?"

Ed pointed vaguely west. Vaguely up.

"How far?"

"The other side. A couple city blocks. I don't know."

Em shook her head once. It didn't sound that promising. She lost herself into the map again. Several cars ahead of them had opened and some people stood out in the snow looking forlorn.

The sun was burning through the overcast in spots. The light was waking everybody now.

"I got a seven-mile hike to Somerston ahead of me. No time for going on side excursions."

"He'll give it to me. It's my money."

"I'd have to have assurance."

Ed thought about it. She continued drying off her person. A sober face.

"I'd give you the eight bucks in advance."

She looked up with a business eye.

"Supposing we get up there and he doesn't let you. Then you want the eight bucks back, I guess."

Ed was undecided. It was a risk. Ed was jealous of his money. "You'd do better if you went up to the turnpike," he said. "They got a lane cleared."

Em lowered her eyes to the map again.

That was worth thinking about, but she wasn't going to let it show. This was horse-trading now.

"I'd be out an hour's time and looking like a fool, my legs froze off."

"He'll give it to me."

"Cain't believe that. Got too much experience to the contrary."

"Okay. If he doesn't then you keep the eight dollars. Okay?"

She didn't look up. Nothing changed about her face. She must have that stupid map memorized by now, he thought. She spoke low and solemn now, keeping her eyes down all the time.

"What is going to happen is just exactly this," she said. "We get up there, your old man will have the common sense to tell you *no*. And he should. If I was your old man I would. So would you. If he has any kind of sense at all he will. You'll start feeling this big ache now. You'll be bawling about how I clipped you for eight dollars. Your old man will grab me by the ears and shake me up and down and wring them eight dollars out of me. I'll have trouble with them ears forever after. Ever' way that can be thought of I will come out behind."

"I wouldn't bawl. I don't bawl."

"Dealin' with kids is bad practice. I found that out before."

"I don't bawl," he said.

"You think you wouldn't, but you would."

He came up with a fist of crumpled ones and put them on the map in front of her. She set the map aside and with grave deliberation took up the bills. She unfolded and smoothed them soberly while counting. Then she folded them in two and held them up in her bad hand, the bandana hand. They looked more valuable in her hand somehow, now that she had them they weren't his any more. She looked him level in the eye.

"Last chance to back away." The way she said it, it was like a blood oath that you had to die to get out of it.

Ed shook his head. No. He was sticking by it.

She extended her hand. He didn't understand at first, but then he shook it. She deposited the folded bills in a breast pocket. She softened up somewhat. Her face got less full of authority.

"I wouldn't ask it except that time's against me."

Ed did not know what to say. She took things awful serious. He shrugged and still had not thought of what to say.

"It might work out," she said. "You never know."

He said nothing to that either.

"What do you want it for?" she asked.

"I can sell it. Make money. You can get a lot for guns where I live. I know some guys that buy them. I can get a lot more than twenty dollars."

"I guess you can," she said. "I wouldn't be doin' this if it wasn't worth it to me."

She folded up the map with the same sober care she gave the dollar bills and put it in her jacket. She folded up the map the right way on the first try. That impressed Ed. He'd never seen it done before. Maps drove his Dad bananas.

Em said nothing more. She climbed back into the sleeper and emerged again with a canvas satchel, like a bowling satchel sort of, with leather loop handles. She packed it with the same sobriety which attended everything she did, putting a flashlight and some items from the glove compartment in the bottom, then a blanket over these. She set the bag open on the seat between them.

"The dog," she said.

"What for?"

"Put the dog in the bag," she said. "So you can carry her without her busting water!"

He lifted Daisy around and they fit her into the bag. Her body filled the bag exactly with her face sticking out one end and tail protruding from the other. Em brought the leather loops together at the top and held them up for Eddie's hand.

"Here. To carry."

Ed took it.

"She's smiling," Em said soberly.

She was. She looked worried but secure and trusting that Eddie was there. Very snug. And definitely smiling.

Em unplugged the defroster.

"We have to fit this in." she said.

The dug around beside Daisy and lifted part of the blanket. Em slipped it into there and Ed restored the dog and blanket to their original positions. Daisy rode a little higher on one side but still retained her smile, her hopeful trusting. Em dropped from the cab and stood in the snow reaching up for the bag.

"Hand her down," she said. "And be careful. That dog loves ya."

Ed handed down the bag and then got down himself. Em handed back the bag with her good hand. The bag was heavy. She knew that she would wind up carrying it soon. The boy was obviously not accustomed to things of the rough and physical nature.

Ed had been watching this girl's natural proficiency with things.

He wondered how she was when she had two hands. She stood looking at him, now. Expectantly.

"What?" he said.

"Go on," she said. "You lead. You know the way."

They went a few yards west in the unbroken snow. Soon Ed felt the cold and effort of it. The ice-water came through his jeans.

"I'm not leading all the way!" he said.

"We'll switch off," she said. "If I'm nothing else, I'm fair."

They went a few yards. More sun was shining through the clouds. More people coming turtle-like from inside the cars.

"You talk like a cowboy," he said at last. It was all of her that he could think up words to say about.

"I know it," said the girl.

They continued plodding through the snow.

HELICOPTER—7:55

Below them smoke rose from a bonfire. Several dozen patrons had banded together and torn down a wooden billboard, piled up the boards and got them burning. They waved cheerfully as the helicopter passed overhead. Since the bypass it was the first activity they'd seen. The turnpike below had just gone on and on and on, the endless mole track of the white and silent bumps in endless snow until it had become frighteningly monotonous. Everywhere the same. This first sign of life below them lessened the "last man in the world" feeling for Lee. It wasn't quite enough to make him want to cheer.

Woods smiled a little Mona Lisa smile that was not a smile at all. Not really. He smiled from behind Arch Reese's binoculars watching the bonfire.

"Party time," said Woods. He gave Reese back the binoculars. "That'll often be the first reaction. They slowly poke their heads out turtle-style and have a look around and find themselves unhurt and basically okay. Then it's the "we're-all-in-the-same-boat-brother" syndrome. The normal everyday social barriers break down. A wonderful euphoric atmosphere takes over. A thousand stories of warmth and openness and human interest and heroic generosity will be generated and all of them will be absolutely true. It happens every time. It ought to keep them busy for a while. It ought to hold out for the rest of the day."

Woods was puffing up the pipe again, looking a little cross-eyed as he watched the match flame bob and dive into the new tobacco. He shook the match out and straightened up a little in his seat, addressing all of them generally now.

"By the way, what's the freshest E.T.A. on that second storm? I have 3:30. Has anyone got information to the contrary?'' Nobody had. Woods simply nodded and sat back and puffed the pipe. He was a fiend of one-man air pollution. The darting eyes said that the mind behind them was going a mile a second.

The brigadier spoke, "What do you intend to do?"

"What would you do, general? The general was Brigadier General George R. Brand, commander of the Pennsylvania 28th, the state's national guard regiment, Lee had found out. Three quarters of the Pennsylvania 28th was immobilized in all that snow however, just like the turnpike and all its gear, just like the Pennsylvania Department of Transportation and all of theirs, and like Duquesne Light and West Penn Power, and on and on and on and on and on.

"Why, contain them," the general spluttered. "It seems to me we have the classic refugee thing here: a chunk of the population has broken off, separated from the body and become displaced. An entity unto itself. A tumor. When it gets desperate— even a malignancy. It's got to be contained. For the sake of the surrounding population."

"I agree with you completely," Woods said. "Exactly how do you intend to do it?"

"How?" The brigadier got faintly apoplectic, spluttered more. "Why, troops! Naturally. Contain them around the perimeter!"

"The perimeter, General?" Woods' tone was not derisive. The facts he brought forth made it seem that way, however. "You mean to enclose an area 225 miles long? 1.2 million people? With troops? I don't believe we have that many in the standing army, do we? Even if I'm wrong how would you get them into position in time to do any good? How would you get them into position period?"

The general was more than just faintly apoplectic now, he was getting purple. A little quick to temper, Lee could see.

"Don't be absurd!" he said. "We don't have to surround every single inch—just at the off ramps and places where they see towns and naturally easy places to walk out. We can depend on natural barriers for most of it."

Woods remained calm and serious, busy with the pipe.

"Remaining with your approach for the moment, that might hold true until the snow melts. The refugee has been known to cross the Himalayas barefoot out of necessity or *belief* that the necessity exists. It makes no practical difference which, the resultant behavior is the same. And as for natural escape points, who knows where they are? It would take a year's research to catalog them all. This an enormously large object we're dealing with. It has a great many unobvious features to it. They start showing up at times like these."

The general was purple now, as though he might explode.

"I don't have to sit here and listen to this kind of . . ."

"Shut up, George," the governor said gently. He put a restraining hand on the braided sleeve. The governor had the intense black ferret eyes on Woods. Woods had him.

"Go on, Woods—whatever you were saying."

"All I'm saying is yes. They need to be contained. Especially at the towns. We saw that at Somerston. It's the towns that are in the most critical danger."

"Guys, we can't be too careful with this," Woods said. "We could not contain them with force no matter how badly we wanted to. Even given time to organize. The only things that are going to keep them where they are now are *one*: seeing no place better to go; *two:* the value of their cars, both monetarily and psychologically; and *three*: what they themselves believe about their current circumstances. That last—what they believe shaping their view of what is happening to them—is the only thing we have any control of right away. They have radios. A lot have CB. Everything. Keep light. Keep it calm. Quell any rumors that those cars and somehow do it low key. Play the whole thing down in such a way that we don't create a monumental panic. They will only stay if they believe there are no greener pastures, that they are better off staying where they are simply because no place they can go is better than what they have."

Woods focused on Chuck and Lee.

"I wanted you communications guys along to help us get a handle on this right away. Your state troopers—most of them have CB in their cars. Get them and any truckers or volunteers they can organize just to soothe them, hold them down, keep the whole thing calm. You know what it's like. It's a hell of a lot like the old cowboys singing to the cattle nights to keep them calm. That's what we have to do. Keep up a constant sing-song, let them know we're there. Whether we are or not is immaterial. If they believe we are that's what counts. So we keep a calm, and unified face to the public on the media, the telephones, the CB. Everything. Keep light. Keep it calm. Quell any rumors that might cause people to want to leave a place for someplace else. No greener pastures. Anywhere. That's what it's got to be.''

"Most of the radio and TV stations are shut down. No power," Chuck said.

"The big clear channel outfits are still operating. KDKA in Pittsburgh—only about half of Pittsburgh is without power—WOWO in Fort Wayne, WRVA richmond. KMOX St. Louis. You can get these on the Pike. I know. I've heard them myself. Especially when the dial's not cluttered up with all these cheap little top-40 sundowners. We'll talk to them from the outside, that's all. KYW Philly. That's another. Our people in Philly are working on it there. We may be able to get cooperation from the C.B.C.—Radio Toronto and Montreal. They're very good about this kind of thing.''

"The main thing is to quell the rumors. Keep things calm, which is why we can't be flying over like God's Holy Angels dropping goodies from the skies. How would you appraise the situation if you were down there and saw that happening? You'd think it was the end of the world. It is not a conquered country to be occupied with force; it's a million-point-two ordinary people full of pumpkin pie and private problems. Their minds full of jobs and money and the coming Christmas rat race. Confused. Not expecting anything like this at all. You start dumping armies with big black ugly guns on them and they will stampede, I promise you. Then you'll find yourself mowing them down in never ending waves like attacking North Koreans. Then when it was over you would turn away with a grim set to your jaw, convinced you "did what had to be done." It would be a classic situation, all right, the classically neurotic self-fulfilling prophecy. There's a classic for you.''

The chopper swung off the Pike and northward at Gate 6,

the second Pittsburgh gate, went overland in the direction of the downtown districts, the "Golden Triangle." Woods had asked to be let off on the helipad atop the U.S. Steel Building and simply take a chance the elevators were running. The group had decided not to continue all the way to the West Gate. It would just be more of the endless white desolation there and beyond into the white forever of Ohio. Nobody spoke. They watched Pittsburgh beginning to come in below them, the suburbs and the hills. Most minor streets remained unbroken by even a single track through the snow. Elsewhere there was furious activity. Some electric lights showed in the yards of factories and businesses.

"Fabulous," said Woods.

It was starting in the electric microcosm of the interphone. Everyone seemed to have drifted off into the worlds of their own and were jolted back by the sound of the word.

Lee looked in Woods' direction. Almost a twinkle in Woods' eye. Not mischievous, but dazzled. Excited and enthralled. Busy in thought.

"Absolutely fabulous coincidence," Woods mused. "Of course all disasters are. Astronomically improbable long shots, confluences of circumstance no one can afford to stay prepared for. And they happen everyday. Somewhere. This one has a difference."

"How so?" asked Reese. They were Holmes and Watson. A long history of communal musing showed.

"The first cultural disaster. Cultural. It's really just a heavy snow. It wouldn't have happened like this Saturday. Not even today. It had to happen Sunday. Sunday night, to boot. The culture has set up this holiday and things and systems have become arranged about a *date*. An arbitrary date when a genuinely substantial proportion of the population is culturally dictated to be on the move for strictly cultural reasons. Celebration. Kinship ties. The sudden availability of extra leisure. A bunch of Indians and Pilgrims get together two hundred years back. A time of year when it could conceivably snow. It very seldom does so early and in such degree, but it is *possible*. And because of that? Pow! The timing was incredible. Fabulous is the only word that can describe it."

Lee didn't know exactly how he felt about this Woods guy. Woods *was* impressive. His psychological immunity, his distance was incredible. It almost made your skin crawl. The guy was a pro. You had to give him that.

"Yes. Nor could it have waited fifteen years until the world ran out of oil," said the governor. The governor was something of a pro himself.

They were coming down onto the top of the huge, rust-colored building now. The target of the helipad had been cleared of snow. Some life was evident below them in the streets. Lee felt the contrast. Woods slid the door open and hopped out. The downdrafts from the blades blew flaming sparks and ashes from his pipe and tore his hair this way and that. He beat the sparks and ashes off his clothes and shoved the pipe into his pocket.

"I'll see you in a while," he shouted.

Lee pulled off his headset. "What's that?" he yelled. The helicopter made a tremendous racket.

"I'll see you in a while. We'll bring you a load of toilet paper."

"Toilet paper??!"

"Yes. People can go days without any food at all, but the other thing—it gets to be a problem rather quickly. Need I say more?"

Woods backed away. He kept low until he was beyond the blades and then straightened up and disappeared into the stairwell door.

The chopper lifted off again and swung them back toward Redford.

ROUTE 31—8:35 A.M.

Half a mile west of the truck Em Baker spotted what seemed to offer a small promise of passage up the hillside. Something had come down, something larger than a car, a van or panel truck or something which now lay buried at the roadside beneath another mound of snow. Up from this was a wake of sorts—a kind of velvet channel leg up the hillside through the trees—the snow was not as deep, the slope more gradual. It was the best possibility of getting up to the Pike they had come across, so far. As promised, she had spelled the load, had blazed more than her half of the trail and said nothing. The boy was younger than herself and she was taking eight dollars of his money, even though a deal was a deal and money didn't come as hard to him.

She pointed at the track up through the trees. Some of the trees were broken.

"What about up there? What do you think of that?"

The sun had burned through the early overcast and haze and it was brilliant all around and warmer and she could hear a lot of trickles running.

"Where?" he said. He had missed her gesture. In his hardship he was tending to look down.

"There." She pointed to it till he saw. "You want to try?"

"No! I'm going to stay down here and die! What do you think?"

She started up. He followed close behind.

The drainage ditch was shallow. The panel truck or van or whatever was inside that mound was right down in it. Em began to wade around and through and hopefully to more shallow snow beyond the ditch. There was no sign of life inside the van, no windows to see into without digging and they made no attempt at that. It was scary near the van.

The snow got shallower again beyond the ditch and van. They ascended hand by hand, by little trees and bushes, pulling themselves up one item of vegetation at a time.

Halfway up the slope Ed wanted to exchange the bag with the dog for the gun. His arms were giving out. The dog was getting bounced around. As much as anything he wanted to possess "his" gun, to feel it. What it felt like. A real gun. She agreed. For the sake of the dog. She agreed to take her to the top and after that no more. He agreed. She handed him the gun and took the dog.

"Careful with it. It's loaded."

"Don't you have the safety on?"

She shook her head. "Safety's wore off. Been wore off since nineteen fifty-nine."

"How would you know "1959!" That's before either of us was born! Don't give me 1959!"

"Pa shot three toes off of his foot with that gun in 1959. Because the safety broke. Part of the foot too. He remembers 1959. It's his gun and he told me. Any more questions?"

"You'd think he would've got around to getting it fixed by this time."

"He was goin' to. Then after that he noticed he was bein' so careful with a gun he didn't need no safety anymore. So then he didn't."

They climbed again. Ed was in deep thought. He did not seem to enjoy the gun in proportion to his prior eagerness.

"Was that a joke? About the foot, I mean."

"Nope."

They climbed some more in quiet.

"If the safety's bust the gun ain't worth as much," he said.

"Price takes that into account already," Em said. "And then some. Worth more."

Ed shrugged.

"You know it is," she said.

They resumed the climb.

"What does it look like?" he said after a while. "Does it have the bones sticking out and like that? The foot, I mean."

"No. The skin's folded over. Looks like a candle that got melted off. It hurts him in wet weather."

The hand-by-hand and bush-by-bush process got them to the shoulder of the Pike eventually and at a price. They danced in agony from wetness and the cold. The girl knocked snow off the nearest guardpost and sat high on it. Ed took the next one for himself. They gave the muscles of their legs some chance to recover. It was poor relief because the muscles were going taut with spasms from the cold and could not relax to recover much, but they took what they could get. The legs just wouldn't go.

A lot of people were afoot on the turnpike, motors running here and there, people standing out. Much greater activity and noise. A line of people stumbled past going uphill to their right where the machines were working.

"Do you see your car?"

He didn't. The drift of people was all uphill, toward the sound of the machines where Eddie pointed.

"It has to be up there someplace," he said. "We weren't going downhill."

For the first time she realized that his car might have been included in what had happened at the top, the things he had told her. He might be in for a terrible surprise. There was a big commotion going on. Something pretty big had happened. He didn't act as if that had occurred to him. She dropped herself from the guardpost and signaled him to do the same and for him to lead because she wouldn't know his car.

People had the snow tramped down, a good rut through the snow, and Ed let Daisy down. She was trading comfort in the bag for wet feet and a rut that she could not see out of, but he couldn't carry her anymore. They kept the dog between them and went single file uphill through the rut along with all the others in the trudging line. The going was a great deal easier than it had been down below.

In half a mile the line broke up against a wall of people, like for a parade. The wall was growing thicker all the time. From the other side came shouts, invectives to stay back, profanities about the government, the sound of big trucks and machines. When would the roads be opened? What the hell good were the police? People were either in a light spirit or completely up tight and bananas. There didn't seem to be an in-between.

They crossed over to the westbound. Ed tried to push into the crowd and got ejected. Hard. There was nothing here for them. They could obviously not go east. They looked back and saw the westbound almost devoid of cars as far below as they had come. The westbound wasn't visible from the other side as they came up because of people, piled up snow, standing traffic, and a medial island 60 feet wide up on the bypass. They had not noticed this till now.

"What about in there?" She meant behind the wall where the destruction was.

Ed shrugged, said nothing. He just danced and shivered. He had given up at getting through.

"Further down?" She tried again. He was in a bad way.

They'd have to get in someplace warm and soon. Why not? They started down the westbound.

It was easier going down. Less people, less gravity. The snow had been more completely trodden down. No cars to pick your way among.

They found the station wagon shortly after reaching cars again and found the note pasted to the window telling that the family had gone to Somerston. Ed threw the bag down with outrageous force into the snow. He assaulted the wagon with feet, fists and body, then sank into a sullen heap beside it in the snow. But he didn't cry.

Em gathered up the bag and put the contents back. She took out a pocket knife that had an especially thin ground-down blade and fiddled with the door latch.

"Never mind that," Ed said. "The back hatch won't lock. It's broken."

They climbed in and plugged in the defroster. It worked despite the dashing to the ground. They went through the process for the third time in two hours. Maybe now that there were ruts to walk in they wouldn't have to get their jeans so wet. By and by they got to feeling better. All except their feet and toes. The feet and toes took time. Em took out her pouch of Red Man and stuffed some in her cheek and let it make her gum begin to ache the way it does when you just begin to chew tobacco.

"Chewing tobacco?"

"Yes," she said.

"Let me try it."

"You'll get sick and puke and feel humiliated. This is something that is best to learn when you're alone and other people don't have to look and see you."

"What about you?"

"I've chewed before."

"Your Dad would kick the crap out of you if he knew it. I bet he would, huh?"

"He's the one that steered me onto chewing."

"He put you onto chewing tobacco? Your Dad?"

"To get me off of smoking cigarettes. That's how he done it."

"You smoke cigarettes?"

"Nope. I quit."

She folded up the pouch and replaced it in a pocket. She sat back and scanned the outside for a while, chewing hugely. Ed watched to see if anything incredibly adult would happen. She opened the door a crack and spat auburnly into the snow, then shut the door as quickly as she could so as not to lose what heat the defroster had been making. Neither of them said anything for quite a long time.

"Where the hell is 'Somerston'?" Ed said. He tore off the note left by his parents and was reading it again.

She jerked her head to show it was behind them. Up the hill again.

"East," she said.

"Seven miles?"

"Six miles—seven. Don't know how to get around that crazy crowd thing up there. Probably have to go off the side and back down the way we came. Two hours nothing gained."

"What about the gun?"

Em spat into the snow again and shut the door again exactly as before and went on chewing. She looked upward through the windshield into the sky. He did too. They watched a helicopter go over.

"I didn't get my other money."

"They're in Somerston, that's all. You're going to Somerston. Well, so am I. I have to."

"Way things look its going to be a crazy place to be—most crowded, overrun situation that you have ever come into. I don't have the time to wait around until you find them."

"I'll find them. Don't worry."

"Eight bucks will get me home. I'm hanging onto it. As per the deal. No hard feelings?"

"What do you mean 'no hard feelings?'"

"Hard feelings then. Whatever. I give you ever' chance to back out from the start. I got living animals at home to think about."

She repacked the bowling bag and got set to leave.

"I'm going. You coming now or in the future?"

"If I get the other money do I still get the gun?"

"Up until the time the bus leaves. I stick to my deals. I ain't that kind of person."

"There probably won't be buses today anyway," said Ed.

"It don't have to be a bus. Whatever ride I find I'm taking. I ain't waiting."

Daisy got up suddenly and began to whine and root among the luggage in the back.

"What's the matter with the dog?"

Ed crawled into the back and pulled her out; then saw what she was after. He came up with the aluminum foiled carcass of the turkey.

"What is that?"

"Half a turkey." He handed it forward.

They were hungry. It tasted good cold. Especially the stuffing.

REDFORD—9:30 A.M.

The sun was fully out and it was warm and very bright when the chopper again set down in the parking lot at Redford. There had been more activity since they were gone, a few more ruts cut through the snow for them to follow, a greater assortment of vehicles in the lot. More staff appeared to have gotten in. Lee hopped down first when the pilot cut his engine. The snow was wet and thick and heavy and soaked his sneakers through at once. He could hear the snow around him melting everywhere, but it was still up to the knees, still a lot colder around his feet than the air.

He led the way into the building. Everyone inside the chopper wanted to come into Redford, wanted to get to a phone. Chuck took the governor and the rest upstairs. Lee broke off on his own and headed for the Main Communications Room.

He tried the "cage" phone, tried getting through to Jennifer again. All four special numbers, the unlisted numbers. He could see the switchboard through the door into the rear equipment rooms. The secretaries were unceasingly busy; no sense to even try the listed turnpike numbers. The four lines were dead. No busy signal. No dial tone. Nothing. General overload. The whole exchange. He gave it up.

Judy came across the floor, a sheaf of papers in her arms. He intercepted her below the "cage". She looked tired and dark around the eyes.

"Haven't you guys set up some kind of schedule for relief?" He'd instructed Emmert to set up something last night.

"Sure," she said. "I'm next. Whenever that is."

"Who came in? Who's new?"

"Nobody for us. Cops. Couple secretaries. Some Red Cross volunteers from Redford. A lot in and out. Small net gain."

"What about Tri-State?"

Judy shrugged.

"Give me the weather sheets."

She foraged through the stuff in her arms, logs and teletypes and memos, handing him the teletypes until he had a little pile. All said about the same: essentially, a blizzard at 3:30. 3:30! That's when you got out of school, not when you had a blizzard!

"Oh," said Judy. "This came for you."

She handed him a scribbled memo in handwriting he didn't know. It said his wife had called and would he please call back? It was neither initialed nor timed.

"When?" he said. "Who got this?"

Judy shrugged. "They don't know," she said. "One of the secretaries. Could have been anytime all night. They took a lot of messages."

Lee stuck it in his pocket. It made no sense to do that, but he stuck it in his pocket.

"Have you heard from Beck?"

"He's in. About twenty minutes. Came in with Ollie. That truck driver is with them."

"In here? Where?"

"The back. The dorms I guess. I guess they're sleeping. The guys go first, of course. They have a place to sleep, of course."

"You can sleep there. No one will bother you."

"They snore. I can't sleep where there is snoring."

Lee got out his keys and took one off the ring and gave it to her.

"Here," he said. "Use my office."

"Are you serious?" She looked at him as though he'd lost his mind.

"What's the matter *now?*"

"I can't go up there and have him see me looking like this!"

"Who?"

"The governor of the state! I mean that's him that you came in with, isn't it?"

Lee placed the key in her palm and folded her fist over it, patted the fist gently.

"Work it out your own way, Judy. I've done everything I can."

He found them not asleep but in the showers amid clouds of steam. Macon Henry Gruber slept wet and naked on his feet in one corner snoring. Ollie and the captain regarded Lee, continued to lather and luxuriate. It looked so delicious that Lee stripped down then and there.

9:42 A.M.

The governor and entourage, led downstairs by Sherman Turlock, pushed into the Main Communications Room in search of Lee. Nothing had worked out upstairs. Nobody had gotten through by any means with anything to anyone. Perhaps the communications chief could come up with alternate means of communicating, some professional mysticism of the trade. After all, it was his job . . . .

Judy saw them coming, tried to disappear into the equipment rooms on busy work, but Turlock caught her, demanded to be taken to Lee. She led them to the inner dormitories, pushed through the door ahead of them and led them down a hall lined with metal lockers. She was tired, the sound of running water did-n't register. She turned the corner to confront her boss and all the others in their altogethers, did an about-face in stride and left the wet ones and the dry ones staring at each other. She went directly out, banged her shin on one of the benches, swore, did not stop and was gone.

The governor inhaled the sight and steam, tossed his hat onto a bench nearby and began to get his coat undone.

"This is the best thing that I've seen today," he said.

9:55 A.M.

A second helicopter set down beside the first outside at Redford. A side hatch opened. Two large canvas-tarpaulined bundles bounded out. Mark Woods bounded out on top of them and followed the same ruts as the others to the outside stairwell. It was good to get inside. The sun was fierce and blinding.

When his eyes adjusted and he could see, he saw Judy regarding him from a certain suspicious distance.

"Yes?"

"Uh. I'm—is Mr. Rider here with the governor's party?"

Judy thought about it. "Yes, but they're really busy. If you want to help I think that if you'd ask any of the Red Cross people in the cafeteria they could tell you what to do."

Woods fished out I.D. and showed her.

"Oh, I'm sorry—"

"It's okay. I get that all the time."

Judy took him to the door and stopped and it was obvious wild horses wouldn't take her further. It made Woods apprehensive, as if ghastly death awaited on the other side.

"In there," she said. She walked away.

Woods found them in the showers, except Kent, the aide, who sat nearby with pad and pen, paper getting slightly puckered with humidity. The showers looked as good to Woods as they had to the rest. He started to undress.

The governor looked like a baby bird, the kind that falls and dies naked on the sidewalks in the springtime. Gray with blue veins, skinny legs, a bulbous paunch.

"Before you get in here find yourself some soap," he said. "I'm governor of the state. I don't share soap."

Woods shrugged palms up, a gesture that said look at me,

I'm helpless, was told to scrounge the troopers' lockers by the captain, came back with two more bars, three razors and some towels and was out of his clothes and under the hot streaming water in a flash. He let out an orgasmic sigh. The rest of them grinned. They knew the first rush of ecstasy. It was nearly indecent, it felt so great.

The governor was surprisingly quick in performing acts of self-maintenance. He was already finished and stepped out. He took one of the towels and the best of the razors with an efficiency and an automatic opportunism that bespoke decades of political road life. He had retained his bar of soap. He wrapped the towel around himself and lathered with the soap and began to shave.

Lee was next to leave the showers. When the governor saw that Lee had left his soap for the others he passed the bar along. There had not been enough to go around. He was finished with it now. Lee lathered and began to shave.

The governor met Woods' eyes through the mirror. "You're back," he said. "I presume you've more to say."

"Let's look on the bright side," Woods said.

The governor turned around and looked at him directly and not a little bit incredulous, but then turned back to shaving. He seemed to know and to expect that sort of thing from Woods.

"All right," he said. "For the sake of argument. Let's look at the 'bright side.' "

"This second storm is probably a blessing in disguise. Depends on how you look at it."

"Keep talking. Don't make me prod, Mark. It's annoying."

"Okay. No way in hell that Washington is going to get a federal declaration together, call up the army, assemble the magnitude of manpower and supplies it's going to take to make the slightest dent in this in anything less than—what—two days?—36 hours?"

Brand snorted. The brigadier seemed to have been through dozens of such things before, or at least wished very strongly to appear as though he had.

"36 hours? Maybe there's an Easter Bunny!" He snorted much louder than necessary.

"Maybe there is. Let's look at this. What you and I agree on, general, is keeping them in place—out on the roads, I mean. For entirely different reasons, but the net result's the same, not so? You're afraid of the damage they'll do to the surrounding areas. I see that occurring, if at all, on just a very limited scale. At exits or where the Pike passes right through towns. An occasional farm. My experience tells me ten-to-one what *won't* happen even in these places is riots and destruction, but that local people will take them in and give them shelter till it all blows over. For a few days at least. It's the millions or so out in the 'boonies,' where they're *not* within walking distance of anything at all that worries me. Those could be in trouble. On a percentage basis they're a whopping majority. Most of this road is flanked by forests or open country. If the 'boonies guy' just wanders off someplace and gets caught out when the other storm hits, well, it's going to be the wind that does it. Wind chill. Could be heavy tolls if they abandon in large numbers."

"*We* want them with cars," said Beck. "No one there to drive the cars off when we get to them. Pain in the ass."

"You getting many abandonments?"

"Yes, we are. A lot."

"Where do they go? What do they expect to find?" the governor was every inch a practical man.

"Who knows?" The captain shrugged, stepped out and grabbed a towel, began to towel off. "One thing I figured out about this road though, it's deceptive. Miles are abstractions to people. Numbers. Minutes. Hours. Gallons of gas. A board game on a road map. A mile is nothing in a car. They lose sight of just how *big* things are. The world is still big. A *mile* is a big thing. Cars make them forget that. Petroleum has given an artificial view of size and distance, like looking through the wrong end of binoculars. But a quarter of the population couldn't walk a mile on a bright spring morning and we have hundreds of them. The other thing is that they get the idea that since everywhere along the road they see steel signs and concrete they are near civilization. That's an illusion too. It's rarely so. All those miles are still there waiting for the second that the traffic stops moving. We kind of help to keep them papered over with our patrol facilities, but we don't have that now. Where they are is where they are and we can't get to them. If we don't get there within a certain length of time and help them they get mad and take off on foot, looking for someone who will, believing in Santa Claus, or something. When we do get to them they go for our throats. Where the hell were we? They've all got their expectations way up in the clouds about the forces of society and the protection it affords them. I think it's these 'paramedic-rescue-hero programs' on TV. They get saturated with all of that and just automatically assume that if they get hurt, the ambulance is there, a team of super guys appears from nowhere. Mommy kisses and makes it well. Those shows may be accurate in some of the close-in technicalities, but they give a bent perspective. You ride with the hero guys, not the victims, you only see the cases that they get to. Naturally you don't see the 95% they don't get to. Naturally you are where the action is, not where it isn't. People get some vague notion that that's how things will be. Lots of action. They don't identify with the victims. They don't expect to be the guy that lies bleeding with busted legs in the hot sun three hours waiting while somebody finally comes along and finds out about him. They don't show that on TV. It's the action that you see; not the *in*action. It takes more guts to deal with the *in*action believe me—but it doesn't show up good on TV.''

"Exactly," Woods said. "I'm not sure it's all to be laid at the foot of TV, but you're right. I otherwise agree completely. There is a vaguely defined, but strong, pervasive kind of parental expectation there. People have it. It's in them. Built in. A vague kind of reliance on something that if you tried to force them to name it you'd get nothing. *God. Santa Claus. Mommy kiss it. Something* will come along. You encounter it in almost all populations, cultures, individuals. We can use it.''

"*Use* it?" The governor was pulling on his socks now. Nearly dressed.

"I'm saying we can use it. Sure we can. We have an interval of time before the sense of chaos sets in. It's going to take a while to hit them that the society 'they knew and loved' is, for all intents and purposes, gone. Nonfunctioning. Does not exist. Not for them it doesn't. Not where they are. That kind of thing takes time to dawn. Maybe time enough to hold them down until this blizzard pins them down and freezes further social deterioration as it were. Give us 'great forces of society' the time it's going to take to get our act together. Maybe we can stretch it out a little, maybe get ourselves a day. Or two. Maybe not. Even a day would help a lot. The point is your John Doe Patron is in fair shape if he stays in his car. We all agree. He can weather out a blizzard, a couple days of storm. He can do it standing on his head if he keeps out of the wind. We know that. We know from some of the things that happened as recently as the January '78 hurricane in Ohio it's no trick at all. Truck driver that stayed buried seven days, punched a hole in the roof of his cab. All the Boston stories that same year. Stories like that coming out our ears. It can and has been done. No problem. If they stay near radios and in their cars we can tell them exactly what to do.''

"*If* you can get them to stay with their cars," said Brand.

" '*If*' is exactly right. Look. The whole point of everything I've got to say is we know that we can't get in there with anything even approximating meaningful help before this afternoon. We're caught flat-footed. We couldn't even begin to offset the damage we would do by scaring them, by letting them get the idea this thing is really as serious as it is. They would hit the rails in droves, every man for himself. Let the other fellow tough it out in the car and to hell with us and all our fond intentions. It's always the *other* fellow. We, ourselves, can always do better than the other fellow, can't we? Well, no we can't and we cannot allow things to reach that point any sooner than it absolutely has to.

"Form and Nosow delineated three stages to disasters in their study of the Beecher Michigan Tornado of '53. STAGE ONE seems obvious: *pre*-disaster. *Before* it happens. The *norm*. Where everybody lives most of the time. Everyday life with all its social systems is functioning at the standard 11% efficiency. Don't quote me—that's my own sarcastic figure." Woods heaved a sigh and swung back into gear again. "Anyhow. We relief types are the only ones who are aware of this so-called STAGE ONE state of being. Paid paranoia. It's our thankless job. STAGE TWO is the disaster itself and it persists until STAGE THREE when—

tadda!—we, the relief agencies, have gotten there and begun supposedly to restore vital services and supplies. What's odd about this is we've got a prolonged STAGE TWO. An earthquake lasts what—forty seconds?—a minute? A tornado levels Lubbock, Texas in a minute's time or less. This is still in *progress*. The danger here lies in the possibility of having masses of them perceiving that enough time has passed that they should now be in STAGE THREE; time for us to show before STAGE TWO is even over; what the captain said about their expectations.

The chaos—the sense of chaos—doesn't set in all at once. What happens is that when it's over those who have survived will raise their heads and look around and see that it is over and pick themselves up and dust themselves off. Immediately the uninjured tend to revert to predisaster social roles, in other words, the men go out and rescue and fight little fires and so on, while the women stay at shelter and care for the young, old and disabled. The strong will lead, the weak will fold. Of course that only carries them so far. After a time they begin running up against things they can't handle. No medical facilities, no lights, no power, no santitation systems or drinking water. Then they start to look around for us and—if we haven't shown up by the time a critical percentage thinks we should have—that's when chaos strikes. That's when the warm and open 'we're all in this together' thing comes apart like cheesecake and the 'to hell with you I'm getting mine' thing takes over. The danger *here* lies in that happening before STAGE TWO is over. Before we can get organized and get in there. I'll tell you something else. The size of this in terms of sheer mathematics tells me we don't have a showball's chance in hell of doing it. Not in time. It can't be physically done.''

Everyone was out of the showers save Woods and Macon Henry Gruber who remained naked and comatos as ever in the corner. Woods stepped out dripping, grabbed a towel. He went dripping to his clothes and lit his pipe still dripping. Only when the clouds of smoke were rising did he towel off.

''All of which just brings us back to what I was saying before. The 'singing cowboy' thing. We can't be there, but they don't have to know that. We can do the next best thing. We can *appear* to be there. We can *talk* to them, make all kinds of helpful and official sounding noises on the radio. Coo to them. Relax them. Send out the 'helpful handy hints for cold mini-survival in a car.' What to do and how to do it. Got a million of them. Radio. TV. Mass saturation. Never let them get the feeling they're alone. Keep it light, keep it mellow. It's probably as good as if we were right there patting hands. Belief is everything. If they believe we're there it has the same effect of behavior as if we were.''

There was no talk for a couple seconds. Woods' pipe had gone out again. He relit it. A single shower was still running over Macon Henry. His snoring rang in the tile shower. Ollie Chelinski reached over and shut the water off. The snoring rang even louder. Ollie turned the water on again.

"What's the matter with the guy?" the governor said.

"He ain't slept in two and a half days," said Ollie. "He coming down from whites.''

"From what?"

"From bennies. Uppers. Truck guys use 'em.''

"What should we do about him?"

"Leave him. He'll be okay. He needs sleep, that's all.''

"You can't do that. What if he falls? He'll crack his skull!''

Ollie and the captain took the trucker, laid him out on one of the benches, spread him over with some towels. It made the governor feel better. At least he looked as if he felt better.

Everyone looked better. The group came from the inner barracks looking shiny, except a little blue around the eyes. Woods had not finished dressing and was temporarily behind. He caught up with them again in the equipment rooms, the coffee rooms. The sugar was gone, the phoney cream was gone. There was only coffee. A quarter of a jar.

Nobody was talking. Woods broke the ice.

"Well, what about it?"

"It's thin," said Brand.

"Sure it's thin. It's thin as hell. We have to thicken it a little. Nobody's saying they'll just sit there listening to prattle. It has to have a limit to it. A time when it will end. If you have a definite end-time you can endure. No matter what it is. They'll hang on longer then, if they have a goal.''

"When?" said the governor. "How long?"

"Not forever, but more than they would have. Wednesday, I think."

"What are you promising?"

"Clear weather. The end of the storm."

"Wednesday? Can you promise that?"

Woods shrugged. The teletype had begun to rattle. Lee glanced at the clock and the clock said 10:15. Probably the weather sheet from the National Weather Service. He tore it off.

"Is that the weather? Does it say Wednesday?"

"Yes," said Lee. "It says, "high winds expected to last *through* Wednesday.'

"Yes," said Lee. "It says, 'high winds expected to last *through* Wednesday.' Whatever that means. Wait a minute." Lee picked up the private line to Tri-State. He waited. They all waited. Jim Nadel picked it up on the eleventh ring. Nadel sounded dead asleep.

"Jim."

"What?"

"When is this blizzard thing due to pass over? The N.W.S. sheet says through Wednesday, whatever that means."

"Too soon to tell."

"I thought you'd say that."

"What do you expect from me? I can't get information. Half my phones are down. This time of year it can go any way. You just can't tell. I say Wednesday too, but I don't think *all day* Wednesday. I think daybreak. Maybe before. That's as good as I can do."

Lee hung up. Nadel had beat him to it. Nadel was really out of it.

Lee shrugged. "Wednesday. Before dawn he thinks. He doesn't know. Too soon to tell."

There was silence for a time. Woods shook his head. "Well, it's Wednesday anyhow. It's got to be. It doesn't matter what they say. They wouldn't put up with it much beyond that. Wednesday's what we tell them. Wednesday's what we say. We promise them the world for Christmas Wednesday morning and we better be there."

"Suppose it isn't Wednesday?" said the governor.

"Suppose it isn't? We've bought some time. We'll figure something else by then."

There was silence. A little time went by. The air got thick.

"Look," said Woods. "Despite their trusting expectations, none of this is our fault. We didn't cause it. Keep that in mind. We're not responsible. We can only do the best we can." He paused a moment and relit the pipe. "And this is it, I think."

The governor shook his head.

"Forty miles south of here there's nothing on the ground," he said.

BYPASS—MILEPOST 99.4—9:30 A.M.

The kids had gotten reasonably dry and warm again. Em packed the bag. They abandoned the Braden station wagon as it was found, letting Daisy hoof it on her own as long as they were able to remain on the Pike where snow was beaten down and reasonably shallow. They backtracked half a mile up hill. As many people were coming down from the summit as going up now. It was half a mile of dodging through a crowd. They stayed on the westbound because it was free of cars until they reached the top, the sight of the explosion the night before, the wall of people, and crossed over to the eastbound there. Em surveyed the outside railing for about a hundred yards until what seemed a suitable departure point presented itself. They packed the dog into the bag for deep-snow passage and went over the side again and down.

Same story: the waist-high snow, wet pants and ice-water-aching cold all over again. They plowed ten yards straight down the slope, then rested on a tree, leaning their backs against it, against the pull of gravity. Ed was not able to keep Daisy and the bag above the snow. Em tried it with the same result. The snow had turned out to be much deeper and much rougher going than it had appeared from up above. They took a horizontal course east-ward, tree to tree for ten yards east, but it wasn't working. The dog was getting the worst of it, the bag was getting full of snow. Em then fashioned a system of carrying the dog between them with the shotgun resting on their shoulders and the bag suspended from it by the handles. From shoulder height the bag cleared the snow by inches. The weight was shared by two. Em faced about and prepared to continue the trek eastward.

"Wait a minute!"

"What's the matter?"

"What about the gun?" The muzzle was at his end, just beyond the ear.

"What about it?"

"What if it goes off or something?"

"It won't go off."

"It might. No safety! What if either of us slips?"

With enormous forebearance she turned the gun around, the muzzle at her end. He still wouldn't move.

"What's the matter now?"

"It's only going to kick my tongue out," he said. "I'll only be deaf for life, that's all."

Em lifted the muzzle off her shoulder, let the bag with dog slide down to her hand and caught the bag and hung it to a tree, suspended from the stub of a broken lower branch of pine.

"You never shot a gun your whole life, did you?"

He shrugged. He made it look like shrugging was the hardest thing to do, like his shrugging shoulder had begun to set like plaster or epoxy and was hardening—into something very difficult to move.

"You better find out what it's like then. While there's somebody around knows what they're up to. Take the gun." She held it out to him.

"What?"

"Come on. Take it."

He took it by the middle as her way of handling it caused him to do.

"What should I do?"

"Shoot down that way. Nothing you can hit there."

He didn't move.

"Let's get it over with," she said. "I'm cold."

Ed raised it to his shoulder, let it down a little, raised it up again. He aimed and aimed.

He aimed and aimed and aimed and aimed and aimed.

"What's the matter," she said.

"It's loud," he said. "It's really bad, huh?"

"Well, it's loud. It *is* a 12-gauge after all."

"How loud?"

"You heard it once already. You ought to know."

Ed raised the gun again and aimed some more.

"Shoot the stupid gun," she said. "They'll find us there, our legs froze down."

Still he hesitated.

"Is it going to knock me down?"

"Is what?"

"The kick. What if it knocks me down?"

"You'll get back up again. Same as anybody."

"Suppose I slide clear down the hill?"

"You'll climb back up again. Same as anybody."

"Wow," said Ed. He said it softly, reverently. The last 'wow' he'd ever get to say.

Em reached for the gun. "Look. Mebbe this whole thing is really no idea at all. You obviously ain't ready for no 12-gauge gun."

"I'm ready. Tell me what to do."

"What do you think you do?"

"Pull the trigger?"

"Sounds like it's worth a try."

Ed raised it again, then let it drop. "My arms are tired."

"For the sake of God! Gimme back my gun!"

"Do I get my eight dollars?"

"Four."

"Hell no."

"Then lift it quick and get it over or I'm taking it and going my way. I'm tired of this and I'm tired of you."

Ed raised the gun, braced for the end of everything he knew and loved, and with squinted eyes pulled the trigger.

Nothing.

He pulled harder, but it wouldn't go. He let up and pulled it back and forth. Nothing. He looked up amazed.

"Helps if you cock it." She spat into the snow. "There's a

dead shell in the chamber. The one I shot this morning. Shows how much you know.''

Ed had let the gun drop. He looked down at it desolately.

"Do I have to?''

"Mainly I just wanted you to know. There's nothing safer than a spent shell in the chamber.'' There was a little pause. Em spat again.

"Well, you think it's safe enough to try going on or do we homestead here, build ourselves a cabin in the pines and spend our life, here, makin' up our mind?''

They made progress, tree to tree, going horizontally along the hillside below the Pike, on top the old Donovan tunnel without suspecting it was there. They listened to the sounds from the Pike above trying to determine by the sounds whether they had gone far enough and could go up again. They came to Ed's track down the hillside, where he had fallen and slid down to #31 hours before. They could just make out the standing traffic on #31 below, could see her truck as they had left it. She seemed disinclined to talk about it.

They moved on, worked up the hill a little further to where Ed had come over the rail originally, beyond that place a little further and then up to regain the Pike.

They were coming up and over the outer rail and snowbank as the last pair of army trucks from Somerston went by. Ed didn't see his dad and mother in the first truck, didn't think to be looking for them there, assuming they had long since made it into Somerston and so the trucks went by all but unnoticed. They waited for the trucks to pass, then dropped down the embankment, fell in behind them for perhaps a quarter of a mile. They had Daisy down again and going was easier, but keeping up with the trucks grew tiresome and seemed pointless, so they let them get ahead and further down the hill.

BYPASS—10:00 A.M.

Nor did the Bradens catch sight of their son. The evacuation had been a long slow process, involving radio coordination of arrivals and departures between the bypass and the terminus in Somerston. The single channel lane between high banks of snow and pushed-up cars permitted travel in one direction only. To meet another vehicle head-on meant the uphill traveler was forced to back the entire distance down, no place between the ends to turn around. Trips had been averaging forty minutes each way. Patrons abandoning the Pike for town found the emergency channel the best going afoot and filled it wall to wall in places, had to be honked and shouted up the banks on either side to let the trucks go past and then would drop down immediately and close in behind as in the wake of a ship. The coroner and local civil defense had all the bodies stowed and the injured down. The determination that nothing could be done about the fallen line for the time being had been made and they were abandoning the site, leaving it open for the patrons to explore as they would surely do. The Bradens were among the last group to be taken down and were loaded into the leader of the last pair of the massive brutish-looking canvas-covered troop trucks leaving the bypass site for Somerston. They sat facing inward and did not see the kids as they went by. All remaining guardsmen and volunteers piled on one truck or the other and came down with them. Guardsmen rode the running boards and fenders, shouting the people out of the way.

Christine seemed no better no worse. The joltings of the stops and starts and potholes caused her to wince a little. Perhaps it was just as well the trucks were forced to go slow. The trucks were hard and stiffly suspended, made Dan's own flesh and body seem even less substantial than they were. Softer. Much more fragile. It seemed a stupid thing to do to soldiers possibly en route to combat, to make them feel more delicate and damageable than normal. The beds of the big trucks were high. They were near the tailgate and could see much of the turnpike on the way down. The Pike was wide awake now. Everyone was out and looking. People out there seemed to be having a great time throughout the length of it, to be enjoying themselves wherever he could see. Snowball fights. Constructions and sculptures out of snow. Here a nude, there a giant bear. An igloo. Snow fort walls between the cars. A carnival frivolity to it, no sense of gloom, no face betraying any idea that things would work out otherwise than well. An appreciable proportion had taken to the roof tops, had set up folding canvas chairs and spread blankets. A pair of blondes sunbathing on the roof of a black Lincoln, it looked like, perhaps a Caddy. Half-buried it was hard to tell.

People with camping equipment, hunters primarily, were doing a lot of cooking. Breakfast smells came to them.

"Smell that bacon," Irene said.

"Yeah," said Dan.

"Take it *away!* It makes me sick," Chris groaned. "The smell of it!"

Irene shot Dan a glance. That wasn't Chris at all.

They rode and watched the people in the bogged down lanes. The others in the truck were not as badly hurt as some of those who had gone earlier. The air of things stayed light and jovial outside the truck, out on the turnpike, but nobody spoke much in the truck itself. The people outside waved cheerfully as if the people in the trucks were some kind of heroes or especially entertaining fools parading by. A couple snowballs pelted off the windshield of the truck behind. Kids. The guard guys cursed and threatened. Getting by with something. After a time a feeling of being too much on exhibition overtook them and they stopped looking out as much and then not at all and spent their attention counteracting jolts and waiting out the ride.

Behind the second truck their son and his companion followed for a time until the extra effort took its toll and ceased to seem worth while.

REDFORD—10:34 A.M.

The governor took off for Harrisburg with Turlock and the brigadier. He left Woods and Reese putzing about somewhere in the bowels of the Redford complex, checking out the civil defense stores there. He left Lee and Chuck standing in the parking lots with icewater feet and sun aching eyes. The air was like that final day of winter, that first real day of spring when you just know the worst is over, that the really heavy cold and snow is gone for good. If you didn't know from scientific sources what the afternoon had in store there was nothing in this morning air to tell you. It would come as a surprise.

They sloshed back through standing puddles, kicking the thick slushy stuff out of the way. The snow was a foot and a half deep everywhere, still thick on the pavement, but heavier and grayer, full of its own melt. From everywhere the sound of trickling water. Horns honked randomly, almost gayly on the Pike below them. Like a Sunday wedding. It was a relief to get inside, to get the sun out of the eyes.

The governor had been anxious to get back. The inability to communicate by telephone had been just so much intolerable bullshit to him. He left with the promise that a military team would be there to set up a radio link with Harrisburg before the storm. The brigadier—Brand—had assured them that it could and would be done. Back inside and disentangled from big brass and their egocentric focuses, Lee had priorities of his own. He split up with Chuck and went straight back to the equipment chambers. He went the other way, through the service door at the north end of the hall rather than squish through the communications room with sopping sneakers. He was going to have to do something about that soon. As a joke it was wearing thin. As a matter of practical necessity it was becoming urgent and it was beginning to appear that he would not be home for quite some time.

Old Hondeka, the old technician, was still at the bench where Lee had left him the night before and seemed as if he hadn't moved. The ashtray had grown into a higher small white mountain, mounded high and overflowing. Otherwise there was no sign of change. Hondeka was still cooking the same intermittent set. Probably had nothing else to do. The chess board was undisturbed as he and Jimmy Weeks had left it last night too, and it was Jimmy's move.

A quick check of the generator room revealed that half the 240-gallon tank of diesel fuel had been consumed. Hondeka thought they had another 55-gallon drum in storage in the van garages, but would have to check. Drum or no drum they'd better get some more.

At the current rate the generators would run dry sometime

before midnight and Redford would go dark. It might stretch it out a few more hours by cutting the lights, saving the power for communications gear. But if that's what they were going to do, the sooner the better. They'd do it now. About two-thirds of the system's repeaters were on their own local auxiliary generators too, and unless the power came back on, would also run dry sometime during the night. Nothing could be done about that. The long, serpentine body of the turnpike system was progressively falling under mechanical paralysis, piece by piece going silent and numb. Lee was determined to keep the brain alive, at least to keep the system conscious of as much of itself as possible, if for no other reason than the psychological. Maybe Woods was right. His reasoning was seductive. For those who managed to call in there should be someone there to answer and make noises that said the world was still alive. Maybe pass out the boy scout survival junk advice from the pamphlets that Woods had spread all over Central. Maybe there was something to it. Maybe not. In any case he had that much he was sure of. That much was within reach of his own hands.

They left the generator room, came back into the repair area. Lee foraged among lockers, drawers and under benches for boots, galoshes, whatever might present itself. Nothing did. He made another stab at calling home and got the no-tone, nothing dead-wire sound again. Zilch. It figured though. In the southwest corner of the most heavily populated region of the country at the most heavily traveled holiday of the year. Extended. Kept on ice. There would be hardly anybody anywhere who was not either in the thing or had someone who was. Himself included and his entire staff. He thought of what the governor had said, this thing not waiting fifteen years until the world ran out of gas. Nobody had any idea of what *that* was going to be either. He hung up the phone.

"You didn't get no calls from Weeks or nuthin'." Old Hondeka said.

"No," said Lee. "No calls."

"12 come back on though."

Lee nodded.

"He musta got hung up someplace," Hondeka said.

Lee nodded.

Chuck Ellis, Beck and Ollie had congregated in the "cage", were pouring over pages of a yellow legal pad as Lee came by. He joined them. It turned out to be a list compiled of smaller lists taken on one of Lee's own orders by the radio operators throughout the night. Numbers of police cars, maintenance vehicles and what mileposts they were near. Beck had his own list, knew that he had twenty police patrol cars in it someplace—out of service for one reason or another. Trapped. Disabled. Wrecked. It included his own car 344, which had burned on the eastbound on the way up, 6 miles below Aurora. The wiring had caught fire and burned the car. He had caught a ride in Ollie's plow, been picked up afoot at Milepost 129. They had used the plow to shove the burning car off on the shoulder and they had stayed together through the night thereafter. There were still five cars Beck could not account for. He was able to make a fair assessment because there were 48 cars in the troop. A manageable number. There was at present no way of telling how many or exactly what pieces of maintenance were actually missing or destroyed. There were too many. Too much had been moved around. Nobody had been entering the new changes in the computer. There had been a lot of changes. That a number didn't show up on the list meant only that no call had been received from it or written down by one of the operators. What they had, then, was a working list of isolated outposts; eleven with which they could communicate—mostly the big gravel-salt trucks that doubled as snowplows—standing in the vast length of the backlog, able to give or receive information, to relay calls up and down the line. That could have great value when repeater service began to fail. So far the electronics had functioned well. That wouldn't last forever.

The backlog had been cleared as far as the turn-around at Milepost 196, just east of the Willow Tunnels. 38 miles in 8 hours? 10? A bishop's chance in hell of reaching Redford, Milepost 145 before this afternoon. It was slow, the block method of clearing one three-mile stretch of eastbound between turn-arounds at a time, then bleeding the westbound over and sending it back east. Lee asked why they didn't just let the eastbound run itself off free and bleed itself empty, then worry about the westbound later. The captain had two reasons. One: the westbounders stopped long before the eastbounders, had seen traffic flowing free beside them and had made or attempted U-turns, creating pileups and blockages at almost every turn-around. Two: between these pileups and blockages on the westbound patrons sitting in their cars had run themselves out of gas, about 4 out of ten, and ten percent abandonments. Empty unattended cars. Where had they gone? Anybody's guess. In any case, they had given up trying to refuel them, trying to locate owners. Patrons with gas were being sent east. Those without were shoved into the outside lanes and onto shoulders. East and westbound. Only the inside lanes were open. The outside lanes were storage for disabled vehicles. There wasn't time to tow them off. They were doing a lot of towing, but just as far as finding space in the outside lanes to stick them into. That was complicated by finding old people, sick people, passengers, pregnant women and all. The storage on the outside lanes had grown past Harrisburg again. The turnpike or the troopers or the army or whoever would have to come back at some later time with gas when there was gas and time in vast quantities to be had. To say that the backlog had been cleared to Milepost 196 was a misnomer then. It could be said that there was some *movement* as far west as 196, some opening of single lanes, but the east and westbound both were anything but *clear*. It was messy. Limping single channels. Nothing more. Chuck said they were getting flack from towns and cities to the east about all this back routing. Carlisle, Harrisburg and York had been filled to overflowing by as early as eleven the night before. There was some kind of cock-eyed second Battle of Gettysburg, off-routed patrons being met with roadblocks and guns at roads into the little city. Nobody killed or injured. Some windshields broken, tires shot out. The re-routed were finding themselves unwanted and going on and on, winding up in Philadelphia, Jersey, and the Chesapeake, even Washington. Some were running out of gas again and getting stranded on the way. Gas pumps were simply running dry, had been drained normally by the holiday and were unable to get restocked in time—even where the lights were on and the ground was clear and dry. Incidents of price scalping were not unknown. Actual violence was so far rare. Amazingly rare. All things considered.

Woods and Reese converged on the "cage" simultaneously, but from separate directions, each with lists of his own, the civil defense stores, supplies on hand. They traded lists to see what the other had.

"What's this?" said Woods. "Seventy-two *radiation survey instruments?*"

"Geiger counters. You know what they are. Those little yellow kind."

"I know what they are," Woods said disgusted. "But, *seventy-two?*"

"Sure," said Reese. Reese was a rather placid fellow. He had an amiable smile.

"Does anybody ever *use* the damned things?" Woods demanded.

"Be glad they never have to," Reese smiled placidly and amiably.

"I hate that kind of thinking," he said. Woods thrust Reese's list back to him. He turned his attention to four men in the "cage", to Lee especially.

"I'm hopping down to Somerston. Who's coming?" he said.

"What for?" said Lee.

"Your little exit town has gotten clobbered. Overrun. I thought you knew."

"We knew," said Lee.

"You think you ought to put in an appearance?"

"And have that little Slovak mayor walk straight up to me and bite me on the stomach? I think not. We must be really popular in Somerston right now."

"*Confession time,*" said Woods. "I *need* you. Your appearance with me puts the turnpike stamp of approval on me and my spaced-out ideas. With the problems they have now a talk-campaign is going to sound ridiculously thin. The more prestigious the company, the less thin it will seem. And I need introductions. I've got to lay a crash-course in rumor control on the town Dads, there—a handful of trinkets for the natives. Immediate stuff. Same kind I brought you. Toilet paper, insulin for diabetics, morphine for shock and junkies.''

The captain raised an eyebrow.

''Captain, when you've got them packed in like sardines and the wind is howling and they're stuck someplace a thousand miles from home, the only thing is to tide him over rather than have him going bananas, knifing people, shooting up the place, creating stampedes and all like that, you know? Really don't have time for questions. All we know is that it happens and that we don't want it to.''

''Look, the scene in Somerston is critical. Worse on the Pike. The soup is thin; they've got to buy it. If they don't, I wouldn't give much for the future of that town. Their predicament is partly—well let's face it—it's a lot your fault. I'd come if I were you.''

''You don't mind wielding the 'sword of compelling guilt' much, do you?'' Chuck said.

''I don't mind at all,'' said Woods. ''It's a game of percentages, now. We salvage what we can. Whatever boosts the odds is fine with me.''

SOMERSTON—10:45 A.M.

The emergency channel from the bypass ended at Johannsen's Texaco at the north edge of town, amounted to no more than a turn-around, a bivouac for armory and volunteered vehicles adjacent to the white frame United Church of Christ— across the street from the armory at the north end of Main Street #219. The streets of Somerston were utterly impassable. The trucks could go no further.

They pulled up and parked and everyone got down. The Bradens along with others were taken into the Church of Christ where a sort of halfway hospital had been set up with cots and Red Cross volunteers and a couple of paramedics with a radio linkup to the local hospital. People with minor injuries were staying in the church and being given first aid there. Only the worst cases were being sent on. How they were being sent on was not immediately apparent. The last group had been small, the injuries more or less minor.

One of the paramedics came up to them.

"What's wrong here?"

"Pains in her stomach," Dan said.

The medic had Chris lie down and probed the abdominal area and found it tender. He radioed the symptoms to the hospital. He wore a headset and seemed to be talking to himself. Half of a conversation. They couldn't hear what the hospital was saying. The drift of talk involved appendicitis as Dan had anticipated. Then the paramedic pulled the earphone off his ear and spoke to them again directly.

"Well, the hospital thinks they better have a look."

"Is that what it is? Is it appendicitis?" Irene had to know.

"I don't know, lady. They don't either. They think its worth a look, that's all I know."

"Where is it?"

"The appendix?"

"The hospital."

"Clear the southeast end of town," said the guy. "Don't worry about it. We got a thing set up. We'll take you there."

The "thing set up" turned out to be a kind of sled train, stretchers on dogsled-trailer affairs, pulled by snowmobiles that arrived and departed from the back door of the church, took them north across the open fields and then turned south at the east end of town and then due south through more open fields to the extreme southeastern edge of town. The halfway center at the United Church of Christ was getting down to the last of urgent cases. There was room on the sleds and both parents were able to go along. There were two sleds behind the snowmobile locomotive and the track was well defined. Fences had been cut and bridges of compacted snow spanned ditches or formed stiles over various barriers. Irene rode with Chris in the middle sled and Dan rode with the driver on behind. Aside from the nagging hollow sense that the world as they had known it was forever gone—that chaos had set in—the ride was fun, felt like powerboating. They hit the bumps and rises in familiar lifting little bumps, small impacts and then went over like a boat hitting waves. Not violent, but solid. Chris didn't seem to mind. Dan looked back and she had risen to her elbows, watching, shielding her eyes against the sun and snow-spray flung by the belt and runners of the train.

They came upon a little pack of dogs that seemed to be waiting at the trail side. The dogs came out and chased them for about a hundred yards and then most of the dogs began to drop away in pairs and threes until a single raw-boned, rangy individual persisted. The driver reached down and then swung around with some kind of large pistol, shouting for Irene to duck. She flattened face down in shock as he pulled off a concussive round, then two more close together. Then he stopped the sled and got off, stood up and shot five more times at the fleeing dog, bullets kicking up a little snow. The dog disappeared over a rolling mound and did not reappear. It did not seem as though any of the shots had hit him. The driver got back on and they were rolling south again.

"S'um-bitchen dog been chasin' us all night," said the driver.

"Far to the hospital?" said Dan. In case the guy was crazy and they had to walk.

"Not far," said the driver.

At the hospital it was the same as at the United Church of Christ, the same as everywhere. Packed to the walls. Whatever urgency the radio conversation between the hospital and paramedic at the church had held was not reflected on arrival. There they found cramped spaces in the hall and told to wait among hundreds of others waiting to be seen by a doctor. Staff of all kinds was vastly outnumbered, actually quite rare and when you saw them, they seemed dead on their feet from fatigue.

It was going to be a while.

MILEPOST 105—10:40 A.M.

There were a lot of fires. People had built little fires from everything that came to hand, trash and roadsigns, Christmas trees and bales of straw, and built them in hibachis and turnpike trash receptacles. The kids and their dog had made it five miles down the broad slope from the bypass toward Somerston, from fire to fire. Coming up from the woods they had been wet and stayed wet, finding no place like the Braden station wagon to get dried off again. They fell into the march of all the other people down through the outside emergency lane, trudging along until cold or the need for rest overtook them and then dropping out of line at one of the little fires, finding a place to sit, perching up above it all on some turned up car to see. These surfaces had turned into prizes of great scarcity. As they got further down the hill the crowd increased and it became impossible to get next to any of the fires or to find anything to sit on. The march had turned into a thing of pure endurance, and though the sun was high, the warmth was only on their faces, the cold and wetness from their legs creeping up into their spines and bodies. Real warmth seemed unattainable, a thing gone out of the commonplace forever. It was a grinding, squishing awfulness that just went on and on forever. Ed quit suddenly, stumbling out of the thick lines to lean against a truck, an abandoned turnpike snowplow. Daisy was enormously glad and looked up expectantly, wet and shivering but smiling. Anything was fine with Daisy as long as it wasn't walking. Em had gone on a little before noticing, turned back then, and fell in beside them. It was cold in the shadow of the truck. They missed the sun but it was the first place they'd found to stop in almost two miles. They leaned in the cold shadow watching the endless trudging of people going by.

"How long is this going on?" Ed said.

"Couple miles."

"More *miles?* How many have we come already?"

"Couple miles."

Ed sank back against the truck, collapsing in a pout.

"This ain't the way to any town; this is the Death March of Bataan! At the end of this there is a grinding-up machine that chops them all to pieces and cheap cat food comes out at the other end."

Em got out her pouch of Red Man and refreshed her wad.

She continued to watch the refugee line trudge by. She got the
fresh wad broke in and spat the first excessive gob into the snow.
The first gob was enormous. Always. Tobacco was a thing you
had to get experience with or it could overwhelm you. Not unlike
the way you dealt with horses. You had to show them who was
boss.

"Gross!" said Ed. Her technique fascinated him.

But she wasn't thinking about that. Her mind was working
harder than her jaw.

"If all of these is goin' down into Somerston, it's going to
be in tough shape down there," she said.

"Where else would they go?"

Em spat exactly where she had before. "That's right," she
said. "My point exactly. Downhill all the way."

There were some kids and young adults on top of the truck,
perched there like a mob of sea birds on ice. A dozen. Maybe
less. Ed went around the rear end, squinted upward at the pen-
guin people looking for available spaces and found that there
were some. It was a high truck, eliminating all but kids and
younger people whose parents were staying nearby. It was the
same kind of truck he'd climbed the night before. Exactly. He
found the same little ladder step and made his way up again
exactly as before. Below him Daisy worried to be left behind.
She barked once just to remind him she was there and not to be
forgotten. Em watched with hands in pockets till he disappeared
over the rim. She collected the gun and bag and kept them close
and watched for him to reappear and presently he did. He leaned
over and beckoned her to come. She climbed up halfway, handed
him the gun, then came up all the way, leaving the dog to whine
and prance below and watch the edges of the truck against the
sky.

The plow truck had not had a chance to spread its load of
cinders and was nearly full to the brim. People there before had
kicked off most of the snow or packed it mixed with cinders.
Footing was stable and there was room to stand. None of the
other people seemed inclined to talk. They looked as if they
might at any second but didn't and it made Ed nervous. The line
wound on for miles below them and in the distance curved off
gently to the left and out of view. It had no end they could see.

Somerston was visible in the valley. Five miles across the brilliant and almost unbroken snow, a clustered bunching up of faint straight lines in the whiteness. Faint details and smoke tails. Perhaps from chimneys or small smokestacks. It was a town. That much you could tell. And it was still a long march away.

Closer was the Somerston Maintenance and State Police Barracks facility on the eastbound at Milepost 105.2. A hundred yards below them, down the road. Big main building. Several out buildings. Tin sheds and stockpile shelters. Heaps of rock salt, sand, various materials and strange machines. The yards were full of cars and wandering people bunching around them in small groups. No sign of official activity, of authority in action. It was just a wide place off the road with more fires and more people. Like the Pike, but wider, but it seemed promising in terms of buildings and more fires and people—more chance of getting dry. They got down off the plow to the delight of Daisy and rejoined the march. The line soon caught them and locked them back into its old, familiar rhythm and they let it trundle them along. You did what the line did. Like a river. Nothing that you did could speed it up or slow it down.

11:30 A.M.—MILEPOST 105.2

They had worked their way across the line to be on the outside when the maintenance barracks came by. It was hard to see anything from in the channel. Pushed up cars got higher and junkier and more pushed-up looking, more packed together, and the evidence of the increased density of people thickened. Slush got filthier, more trampled and mixed with grime. Finally the outside wall of snow and cars gave out altogether in a ragged breach and they moved through it into the yard of the facility.

A lot of minor cooking was taking place on the many little fires. A lot of smells. Daisy approached various people cooking begging food, got kicked and shooed and sometimes a morsel for all her earnest hunger. They walked among the cars and people and their little food fires, being available in case something might turn up.

"Hey, kid!"

They looked around.

"You guys, yeah."

Some kids were gathered around an oil drum, a fire inside. Hot rippling air poured over the top of the drum like liquid and a little smoke, the drum sides orange with heat waves. The kids were bundled up in everything they could possibly wear, had sticks and were roasting marshmallows. They had an entire case of marshmallows beside them—a big box with many plastic bags inside. Ed stepped into the open downwind gap of the circle and immediately got a vicious waft of hard smoke in his eyes. He backed out and ground his knuckles into the sockets squishing out tears that flooded the smoke out, until the pain swelled, peaked and was gone. He dried his face as best he could on sleeves and came into the circle from another side. Em had half a dozen on a stick and held the stick up with the marshmallows burning with the blue marshmallow flame that you can hardly see. The skins were black and crackly, burning black and crunchy ashes.

"Take 'em," she said. "They got more'n they can handle," like bodies in the cars up on the bypass.

He watched the marshmallows burning, then shook his head and moved away.

"Naw."

He drifted to another oil drum, another fire where they weren't cooking anything and warmed his pants against it for a while.

Daisy stayed where the food was and ate marshmallows until presently the sweetness turned her off. She came to Ed and stood by his legs. Em came too. She had an entire dozen on the stick with her, still on fire with that invisible blue. She blew it out and turned it smoking and gnawed the end one off with great care that she touch it only with the hard part of her teeth, not letting the flesh parts of her touch it till it had had a little chance to cool. Ed watched how she kept it separated from the tobacco with a certain admiration he held for anyone who did the difficult, however valueless the feat might ultimately be. She held it out to him but still he shook his head, turned away and would not look at it.

"Best take what you can," she said. "You might not be gettin' nothing for a long time."

But he wouldn't and they drifted from that fire and began wandering to other fires throughout the yard, making their way at last to the main building, a two-story brick affair with no frills. Very square. There was a guy in construction clothes who stopped them at the side door and wouldn't let them by. There were guys like that at all the doors.

"You can't get in unless you're sick or got babies," said the guy. "We ain't got room except for sick and babies."

They could look beyond him into the room, a big garage, and see that it was full of people that had little kids. The guy was probably on the level. They could hear a lot of babies crying. They could smell soup and coffee too, and a lot of smoke from cigarettes.

"Maybe my folks are in there," Ed said. He told the guy about his separation and his sister. He gave the guy his name.

"Wait a minute," said the guy. He disappeared inside and called out "BRADEN" very loud. He waited and he called it out again. He came out with the corners of his mouth further down than was necessary and shook his head.

They screwed around in the maintenance yards behind the building a while to see what there was to see. Nothing but little fires and the people and the endless ice-cold mush everywhere underfoot. The fires were stable and the people transitory. And the new people would feed the fires with trash they brought or lumps of coal from the big piles in the yards and keep the fires going till they in turn moved somewhere else and other people came and took their place. The kids explored the yard a while and found it was pretty much the same all over, warming themselves from fire to fire until their jeans were dry, then got back out into the channel. Em still had marshmallows far down on the stick she hadn't finished. She tossed the stick with the marshmallows and Daisy chased to see about it and then didn't want them either. She rejoined the boy and girl and hastened to keep up with them at the line's edge and avoided being stepped on more than was absolutely required. At least it was downhill. She was very glad of that.

11:20 A.M.

Lee and the captain wound up going with Woods to Somerston. The captain had lost track of a car and man in Somerston
and had a few other reasons to want a way to get there. Since the
westbound had been reopened then subsequently bogged down,
the mountain had become a great wall between Redford and the
western side. No one on either side had been able to get over
since before midnight. Lee found himself admitting inwardly that
some of Woods' guilt trip had penetrated, that he was vulnerable
to the degree that he would come along—maybe if for no other
reason than common courtesy. There was no rational reason why
he, Lee David Rider, should feel responsible for Somerston—he
hadn't built the turnpike where it was, hadn't caused the town of
Somerston to be established in the high Appalachian pass, along
the route of natural pioneer trails that would inevitably evolve
into this passage of the interstate-turnpike system through the
hard-winter Cambrian Plateau. He hadn't made it snow with such
rotten timing, and yet he felt responsible. They all did. Poor little
Somerston regularly got clobbered by their spilloffs, and their
economic and political imperatives. Pike people and Harrisburg
shrugged it off because it ''had brought the town a lot of
economic benefits,'' but Lee had never been that sure of that
rationale. It always seemed that the town's adaptation patterns
had been more in terms of pure survival than of chosen growth.
It was not the town it was. Another side of Lee just wanted to
get out of Central and be moving, to shuck the sense of being
trapped, to see what it was really like in Somerston. For a variety
of reasons then, he now found himself in Woods' helicopter, rising up the rock wall toward the Bald Knob summit with his
stomach about a hundred feet below him.

Jim Weeks hung from the tower as before. The same position. The snow had melted on him, no longer perched in the
obscene little pile on his crotch but he was otherwise the same.
They all looked at the floor. Woods pointed to Lee's sneakers,
shook his head in disapproval. Talking necessitated shouting, so
they didn't. Lee shrugged. Woods shook his head again. Same
thing as before. The captain shook his head with Woods. Lee

waited for the pointless interest in his feet to pass, hoped that it would happen quickly. He had already decided that if businesses were open in Somerston and if there were boots to fit him, he would pay. He didn't care how much. He'd pay. It was getting to be both a serious and a stupid problem—one he was getting tired of.

Above Somerston now there seemed no place to put down. Lee and Beck were having difficulty picking out the armory from among the whited-over buildings. North of the courthouse several blocks on Main Street #219, on a corner, Beck said—almost to the gates at 109. The streets had darkened into trampled slush, but the rooftops still carried virgin snow and were just so many sugar loaves. Woods' chopper was Air National Guard and had a military radio aboard. The pilot made half a dozen calls, finally raised the armory, and was advised that the armory building had a rooftop helipad, but that since no one had come by air since last July, no one thought about the roof with all of the confusion on the ground. It had not been cleared of snow. The armory advised that it was located directly across the street from the United Church of Christ. Beck knew the church, was able to direct. The pilot put down blind against the glare from the snow, guessing that the pad would be in the area of the roof that had the least obstructions. The chopper sideslipped slightly on contact, whacked off some kind of small radio antenna, but otherwise came to rest upright and intact and did not fall through the roof. That was good enough for Lee.

The snow was a full six inches deeper in Somerston than in Redford. Woods jumped out first. Lee followed, found himself crotch high in the heavy, sopping, ice water slush—so heavy that he wondered that the armory had not collapsed beneath the weight of it. They stood there momentarily with their family jewels on ice.

"This is bad," said Woods.

"No kidding," said Lee.

Woods began to forge his way forward toward the stairwell door. Lee followed in his rut. The captain jumped down behind him, now that space had been made.

"No," said Woods. "I mean about this blasted 36 degrees.

Better if it had stayed below freezing. People will get wet. Be ten times the hypothermia and frostbite we would have had at 20; even zero. Got to stay dry. It's the main thing.''

Lee believed him. He'd pay two hundred dollars for a good pair of rubber hip boots now. Three. Three fifty. The door was open. They went down.

The life game in the huge armory garage was immediately apparent. The floor had become premium real estate, cut up into a thousand shrunken residential city lots. People without floor space sulked about the circumference like vultures waiting for any of the fortunates to vacate one of the grave-size positions. Red Cross and local women had a "soup and coffee line" going at the end. A jumbled line extended two-thirds of the way around the perimeter. Another smaller line was an appendage of the rest-room doors. Unless you had family or an alliance with a trusty neighbor to look out for your position you either had floor space or physical relief and sustenance. If not, you stayed where you were, starved and held your water. The air was full of people and garage smells, soup and tobacco smells. Axle grease. Thick and smokey. Kids cried. Dogs barked here and there. There was a lot of scattered coughing. A handful of young guardsmen stood about, two more armed to the teeth stood by each door. There was a check-pile of hunting weapons behind an older guy at a card table who was keeping them listed in a ledger. Hunters taking refuge were admitted only upon interim surrender of their guns. Several hundred weapons in the pile, a lot of irridescent orange showed in the armory, the hunting caps and brilliant vests stood out against the everyday drab clothing. A guard sergeant and a civilian with a Red Cross armband approached and made them show identification. Woods gave instructions to unload the bundles from the helicopter on the roof, gave a little inventory of the contents, asked directions to the courthouse. They were taken to the Main Street door and told to go six blocks south on Main.

The air outside was better. Fresh and good and welcome. But there was little else to recommend the streets of Somerston: a sloshy medieval carnival sort of atmosphere; a gold rush of the Yukon quality. The cars had flooded in and got stuck backwards, crosswards, everywhichwards then got buried in the continuing fall, as everywhere, except in Somerston it had happened in spades. A pathetic kind of boom town or Berlin, Winter '45, Lee could not decide. There were no sidewalks. Cars had flowed up to the building walls and been fossilized in place like cockeyed cobblestones in some gigantic mockery of paving. Anything that moved from one place to another was afoot. Not even snow-mobiles could pass among these cars. The streets were thick with people picking their ways gingerly among the maze of close-packed hulks, but oddly at a distance. Not immediate in front of them, before the armory door. The three exchanged unhappy glances and plunged in.

It became at once apparent why there were no people. Sur-viving animals from the pig truck accident on the ramp the night before had regrouped and wandered into town, or wandered into town and *then* regrouped, and now were keeping in a herd among the cars, invisible until you tried to go through. Then you found yourself knee-deep in a little sea of pigs.

They went forward with great care. The pigs were hungry. Irritable. Would not move out of the way until just at the point of contact. The pigs watched them closely. Lee remembered the old jungle pictures he saw as a kid—paddling down some murky river in deadly silence, inscrutible looking savages lined up solid on the shores, staring hippos on all sides.

"Look out," said Woods. "They bite, I think."

The pigs were clearly in command.

"I thought your guys shot them all," said Lee.

"Not *all!*" The captain was as touchy on the subject as the pigs. "Blizzard! Couldn't see your hand before your face. There was hundreds of them. More than Prokovic had bullets."

"Okay," said Lee. "Forget it."

"Easy piggy," Woods said. "Nice piggy piggy."

"What are we supposed to do?" said Beck. "Go shooting little piggies in the town in front of kids and women? Even if we didn't kill somebody with a ricochet we got problems with our image now."

"I said forget it," Lee said.

"Don't get them cornered," Woods said. "Always leave them an out."

"Like pigs like people," said the captain.

Inevitably they met the porker who squared off and stood its ground, directly in their way. The captain fumbled with the hammer loop to release his .38, but in the window of a car beside him the parents snored in the front seat while a preschool girl and boy watched the confrontation wide-eyed from the rear, noses pressed against the glass. The captain relooped the leather thong, gave Lee a helpless look of resignation. The three backed up a little and ducked into separate cracks between cars, out of the main channel. Seconds passed. The pig came forward intelligently, peeked around the cars until it had located each of them. They held still. The pig was assured that there would be no treachery intended. It charged past them and was gone. Not long after that, the pigs got scarcer and they were beyond the herd and pushed past people. Woods broke the paper package he had carried from the chopper over a knee and passed the contents out with instructions to fan out and distribute them to passersby, stick them under windshield wipers and so on. People were accepting them, even amiably. There was an open feeling, the barriers were down. A feeling of community was strong and they accepted pamphlets almost jokingly. Even so, Lee was relieved when they were gone. He felt like some kind of religious street corner hippy. They were out of them within two blocks and Lee was glad. Beck was even gladder. The captain pointed out that half were simply tossed aside, stuffed into pockets without a glance. Woods didn't care. They'd use them to start fires, line their shoes and wipe their asses. As long as any kind of useful purpose had been served, what did it matter? The captain promised to write him a citation for littering when they got back.

Half the cars stood vacant; when they were occupied, it was by haggard, linty-looking sleepers rolled in blankets. A number had been left with vicious dogs locked inside. Beck was furious. An absolutely stupid thing to do. If the dogs did not die of cold or thirst, troopers would have to shoot them to move the cars eventually. Not a thing was gained; how could a car be stolen from such a mess as this? It was rotten for the troopers and the dogs would die.

They passed only one car that seemed to have been stripped

and looted, windows busted, interior torn out and another that was burned. Other than that just a lot of bumped fenders. Some cars with families had a sense of squatter's rights about them. Homesteaders. Little inter-auto neighborhoods had arisen. Kids built snowmen on hoods of family cars. Camp stoves and hibachis sat on others, frying breakfast, filling the bright air with smells of eggs and bacon. A guy was selling apples from his truck, another canned beer from a van. A buck a can. Fifty cents an apple.

"A thing to keep in mind," said Woods. "*Resources*. Food. Fuels, Merchandise. Pantyhose to rutabagas. They've already got tons of it with them. It is there already." Lee cast about for somebody with a truckload of stout shoes. His feet were almost paralyzed, so numb he was having difficulty feeling sound footing.

Some of the businesses in Somerston appeared to have opened and been overrun. That or simply crushed in from the front, from the sheer weight of pushing crowds. All down Main Street #219 the travelers slept in windows—shop windows, restaurant windows—piled against one another like so many bags of laundry. An auto showroom had become a glassed-in campground. Stores were filled with standing crowds so closely packed that none could have got down or worse—got up again once fallen. Broad rough lines fanned out into the street from the dark inside. Whether any business was actually going on Lee could not tell. It didn't seem likely. In any case it didn't matter. He didn't have a full half day to stand in line to get inside to find out, then not to be able to get out again. He gave up the idea of finding boots in Somerston, resigned himself to living with what his feet were doing to him. Woods was right about the wet thing though. It hurt. He thought about Charlene and hoped wherever she might be her feet were dry.

The courthouse was dark inside, surrounded by activity. People in and out, the rack and growl of chainsaw engines ripping the air and rebounding from the flat facades of buildings on the square. Men worked at cutting up the great elms that had split and fallen. The courthouse had escaped the fate of other buildings, the inundation of traffic, by virtue of a lawn built-up three feet above the level of the street inside a stone retaining wall. The chainsaws tore their nerves as they fought through the branches on the walk up to the entrance, the kind of racket that made you furiously angry. There was no respite from it till they were inside.

It was warmer in the courthouse. They could feel it on their faces. All three were trembling from soaked trousers from the ice bath on their legs. A chill shuddered up Lee's spine. When his eyes adjusted to the darkness he could see that some elderly people and little kids with mothers had been permitted refuge on the stairs and in the hallways. Candles, kerosene and Coleman lanterns lit the halls and offices. Offices were open and kept clear for workers, seemed fully manned and briskly busy. Phones rang. There was typing. The people who had taken shelter in the halls looked tired and rumpled; dirty, sleeping in grotesquely awkward and uncomfortable positions on the stairs and floor and wooden benches. Those awake were doing little talking and looked at things with dungeon eyes, as if every object of this limited environment had been looked at so many times there remained no detail yet to be discovered. Beck knew the courthouse, led them up the stairs, picking their way among the refugees.

The upstairs corridor was darker. There were no people on the second floor, at least not in the hallways. The mayor's cramped and cluttered office was full of sleeping men and crying women and a lot of handkerchiefed and somewhat old-worldish looking older people, but no mayor. Lee recognized the mayor's enormous wife as she rose to meet them. She knew him too. She ushered them outside into the hall "where they could talk," she said.

"It's good to see you, Mr. Rider."

Lee took her other hand. The gentle giant looked inquisitively from Woods to Beck and Lee introduced them.

"You'll be wanting to see John," she said.

"Yes," he said. The shyness of the woman always amazed him. She had an inferiority complex to match her size. She could have picked up any man among them and broken him in two. Nature struck odd balances sometimes. Likely for the best.

She led them back as they had come, back through the

darkwood hallways to the stairs and pointed up where more stairs
wound up through further floors.

"You'll find him up there, Mr. Rider. Just go on up."

"Up there?"

"Go all the way. He's underneath the roof. You just go up
as far as you can go."

"Is it all right? You're sure? What is he doing up there?"

"He's just up there. I don't know. It's nothing special, don't
you worry." She looked down. "Forgive my saying, Mr. Rider;
you should get some other shoes."

The floors above showed progressively less evidence of habi-
tation as they went upward. Trunks and boxes, shelves of crumbl-
ing books and ledgers stood in dusted gloom. Old furniture,
desks and pictures. The fifth floor in particular had broken windows boarded from within, showed evidence of bats and pigeons.
An upright piano stood frontless with exposed, rusting strings and
droppings in the wooden mechanisms. The stairwell ended there.
Another final flight up to the attic, much narrower and in a sort
of closet, began at the south end of the hall. They found it by
following the mayor's footprints through the dust and droppings
on the floor.

Lee found the roof low in the attic. Pots and jars and cans
sat everywhere to catch the drippings. The heavy burden on the
roof was melting, a test just within the limits of endurance for the
old slate roof. They found the mayor in the northern gable with
the window standing open, looking out across the town and Pike
through the old binoculars. The mayor lowered the binoculars and
turned to see who was coming up behind him. He recognized Lee
as soon as he came out into the light. He knew the captain, too.

"Who is this guy, this young guy here?" Pribanic did not
know Woods. Lee explained Woods briefly, then took the field
glasses from the extended hand, followed the mayor's unspoken
inducement to look out the window. Pribanic stood aside. "Take
a look at that," he said. "It's quite a thing to see."

Lee could see up Main Street #219 the way they'd come,
part of the bypass and the west slope of Aurora until both became
obscured by land and trees. Then he followed #219 down into
Main Street, again past the snowmobiles that were working up

and down, across the open fields north of the town and up onto the Pike. Long lines of people trod steadily down from the Pike along #219 and into town. Lee followed the line and could find neither end nor origin. It seemed a little late for Woods' plan to keep them in the cars. They were pouring off in streams.

"Hell of a thing, huh?" said L.John.

"Take a look at this," said Lee. He passed the binoculars to Woods. Woods looked a while at the things Lee had seen and then the mayor took the glasses again, shut the window, led them to another gable on the west side. The windows were dirty and had to be swung open to see anything at all. Pigeons fluttered off the sill. The mayor handed the glasses back to Lee. For some reason Lee got the feeling it was important to Pribanic that Lee Rider be the first to see.

It was not as bad as what was coming down from Gate 10, but not that much of an improvement either. Streams of people trudging into town from #31, making their way among the stranded cars. Same ant-like stream. Abandoning their cars in a steady little river. Lee passed the binoculars to Woods again, who looked and handed them to Beck who had been passed over and was chafing just a little.

"Never saw so many people in my life, did you?" said the mayor. "Did you guys ever see that many people in one place?"

"I can't argue with you, L.John."

"You wonder what the hell the world had got for all those people. What are they when they're not here? It makes you start believing in that stuff, all that worry stuff that comes out of the papers and TV. I don't like it, Mr. Rider. I don't think it's good for the kids in the town to see it with their own eyes."

"Lot of people, L.John."

"I hate for the kids and old folks in my town to see that, you know? It's different when you see it with your own eyes. It's never what you think. It changes the way everybody looks at things from now on, I bet. I bet I got a town that's worried sick forever, now. I bet I can sue you for it, maybe. I bet I should."

Lee could only shrug. Maybe he should.

"Come on. We'll go downstairs, dry you off before you freeze and then I got to do all this myself."

He shut the window and repossessed his brass binoculars. He led them down the stairs through all the gloomy floors again.

MILEPOST 107—11:30 A.M.

Two miles below the maintenance yards at Milepost 107 they came to a really big fire in a cleared out area with a lot of people. Half were singing campfire and semi-raunchy songs and passing beers around. The other half were standing at the fire with tight mouths and minds and folded arms. Some hunters and older folks who couldn't walk to town. Young people sang the songs and passed the beers around. Not everyone was leaving their cars and not just because it was too far to walk. Most people cared about their cars too much to leave them. An actual majority. Still there were a lot of people leaving, walking into town. There were a lot of people period.

The kids had seen more and more of these group fires as the morning wore along. Local areas in the standing backlog had become like neighborhoods—the cars their homes, the big fires the nuclei, the *El Centro's,* the hub of the activity that defined the hasty social units, and the people who came down to them, who organized around them from the nearby cars brought trash and papers and anything that would burn to keep the fires alive. This was the biggest so far, the loudest and most cheerful sounding and they edged into the periphery to check it out.

Ed found himself beside a stack of magazines. Fodder for the fire. All kinds of newspapers and magazines, *Playboys, Hustlers, Ouis,* and sundry pulps more lurid and depraved than even he had seen before. At once he started thumbing through them, rooting through the pile.

"Hey, kid!" A hunter and a fattish-looking lady in her fifties grabbed him simultaneously.

"What do you think you're doing?" the woman screamed. She looked the type that was full of Jesus waiting to bust out all over any kid that tried to see a dirty magazine. It showed in her face and the kind of glasses she wore. Ed felt super-dumb, like he had walked into a setup, a booby trap. A bold-faced sucker

who had walked right into it with eyes wide open. He hated himself a lot for several moments. He looked back and forth between
the Jesus woman and the hunter and tried to keep his face together. Em and Daisy stood nearby and when he glanced at them
Em was looking elsewhere. She spat into the snow and kept looking elsewhere and for some reason Daisy stayed next to her legs
and neither of them seemed to have any connection with him
whatsoever. Ed felt thrice denied.

"Uh—I'm looking for electronics magazines," he lied.
There were some in the pile. He caught a glimpse of one or two
among the others.

"Electronics magazines. Oh, sure!" the hunter said. "What
are you, kid—some kind of wonder-sicko?"

"Well, what are you?" the Jesus lady said. She was glaring
at the horse-faced hunter and his beer. The hunter was caught off
guard. She was a Jesus lady, alright. Ed was right as rain about
that. They were always going to turn on you no matter what side
you took. This time it was the hunter who walked into the web.
Ed was glad of it. It was a big turn in his favor.

"Let's ask whose magazines they are in the first place,"
said the Jesus lady. "This young man certainly didn't bring them
with him, now did he?"

"No," the hunter drawled. "I don't guess so. These college
kids, more'n likely. They're the ones."

"More than likely," said the lady.

"Well, can I have them?"

They both looked down at him. They had forgotten him.

"The electronics magazines," Ed refreshed their memories.

"What do you know about that kind of stuff?" the hunter
said.

"I'm interested in it. I'm studying up on it."

"Well, skip it now," he said. "We need 'em for the fire."
The hunter killed his beer under the steady laser eye of the Jesus
lady and chucked the can into the blaze.

"It's for my future," Ed said. "I can't afford them new. I
have to get them second-hand."

"Field is overcrowded," said the hunter. "Be a veterina-
rian,"

"Give them to him," said the Jesus lady. "Here when a

young person tries to get serious on something worthwhile he's up against a person such as you just waiting to defeat him!''

"Whaaddayou mean—'a person such as me?' '' the hunter said. "What do you mean by that?''

The Jesus lady had her eyebrows high and eyeballs looking down.

"Your whole behavior toward this boy. If you don't know, it won't be me that's able to undo what no one did for you.''

"I only want a couple,'' said Ed. "Two or three.''

"No telling how long we're going to be stuck out here like this,'' the hunter said. "This could go on for days.''

"A silly magazine or two is not going to make much difference either way,'' said the Jesus lady. "If it comes to that it won't make much difference either way.''

"They're hard,'' said Ed. "You have to exercise your mind.''

"Them half-minutes add up,'' the hunter said weakly.

"For heaven's sake,'' said the Jesus lady. "Give them to him.''

"Just a couple,'' said the hunter.

"Four?'' said Ed.

"You said three.''

"Okay. Thanks a lot.''

Ed began to sort down through the pile, separating the periodicals into separate piles per category. As he came to the electronics magazines he stuck them further down so as not reach the limit before the choicest lurids had been found.

"Wow,'' Ed lied. "This is really great!''

"I hope you find some that are worthwhile, young man.''

"What are you lady?'' The hunter snapped open another beer. "You sound like a school teacher to me.''

"Well, I did teach school at one time. Long ago.''

"I knew it,'' said the hunter.

Ed soon had a stack as large as he could run with, jammed them quickly into the canvas bag and tore away with Daisy barking after. The hunter and the Jesus lady saw the electronics magazines still sitting there, saw the boy's heels flinging chunks of slush up in the air, saw him disappear into the line.

The hunter gave a token chase but had not lost sight of him.

He purused halfheartedly a couple dozen yards, then gave it up and came back to the circle and the Jesus lady.

"I'm not surprised," she said. "I'm not surprised at anything these kids will do today at all."

The hunter thought of several devastating things to say, cracked another beer and didn't say any of them.

SOMERSTON COUNTY COURTHOUSE—11:30 A.M.

Woods was right about one thing, the soup was thin. The mayor had them in the basement, listened to the spiel in the furnace room where the old coal furnace roared red hot again beside the gleaming modern electrically controlled and useless gas unit. Jake Stokes was there, down off the bypass about an hour, bodies all hidden in the storage tunnel, the injured down in town. Everybody sat with feet propped up on old wood crates to catch the drying heat from the old furnace, listened patiently with steaming shoes and pantslegs as Woods went through the whole thing again. The talk of media campaigns and CB campaigns and keeping people where they were—what they were going to do everyplace but Somerston. The mayor shook the ashes down through the grates, a big iron lever on the side with a spring for a handle, made a lot of noise a couple of times but didn't speak. He listened and kept his fire until presently Woods ran out of things to say. The things he *had* said. The soup seemed even thinner in the talkless room.

Lee pulled off his socks. Looked at his toes. Stokes and Woods and Beck looked at them, too.

"You feel them?" Stokes inquired.

"They hurt like hell," said Lee.

"Good," Stokes said. "You'll be okay."

The mayor shook the grates again, harder than before. "In other words the help from you amounts to nothing."

Woods shrugged. "At least until Wednesday." The old guy had him cold.

"What makes one so sure about Wednesday?"

"Nothing," said Woods. "It's the best that anyone can do."

"That much I expected."

"Good!" said Woods. "You won't be disappointed."

The mayor was on his feet in a flash.

"Listen, Mr. Smart Guy. This is not the first time we had things like this. These people flood in from everyplace. Wreck things. Steal things. Eat things. Take and take and somehow we always hear all this terrific crap about the Red Cross and the army and the state and the government, this church outfit, that church outfit. Bologna! It comes out of our pockets, sucks the blood right out of our veins. We pick up the tab. We always wind up paying for the ride, somehow or other. Well, not this time. This time we're keeping track of everything. You guys are gonna get a bill like you never saw. You wait and see."

"Fine," said Lee. "We want you to."

The mayor slumped suddenly. He sat down in a sudden little heap. "Ah, who am I kidding? It gets all mixed up, gets lost. It's forms this, approvals that. Bureaucrats. It's bullshit. We wind up getting stuck again." He gave his head a little shake. He looked at Woods, almost appealing. "You got to send us stuff," he said. "It's bigger this time. We don't have it to give. What are these people going to do?"

"They'll hang on until Wednesday. Wednesday it will rain down from the skies," said Woods. "Red Cross, army, Salvation Army, all those church groups. You are right about it being bigger, Mr. Mayor. It's really big. When that happens you find yourself getting so much help and stuff you won't know what to do with all of it."

"But that comes Wednesday."

"The end of the storm—whichever comes first. The thing now is to get through all of this till then. It's too late for any kind of radio campaign to keep your town from being overrun." You were worried about what all this is going to cost your town, Mr. Pribanic. I'd say take advantage. Tell your people to milk this thing for all it's worth. I have no doubt you're right about the state and federal bureaucracies and you certainly must know your own history with these things. Jack up your prices. Don't be so altruistic. The prices of some things will inflate astronomically and that's good in one sense—in the sense that it assures the really scarce and vital things will not be squandered or wasted.

There's something comfortingly normal in good old American price scalping and exploitation. It'll make them feel at home, feel as if the day-of-doom is anything but nigh. We and all the other relief outfits will start dumping on you later. Businessmen will donate all kinds of bullshit—stuff they can't unload for tax write-offs. Sell it. Hustle it. Let your people make a buck. In the long run it's the best thing you can do, and why should you be any different? Tell them.''

"What about the people that can't pay?"

"You'll know who they are. You can tell and they'll be taken care of. But by God you'll know the asshole too, and shove it to him. Let the fat guy make up for the thin. Take it from him in exchange for what you have. Don't let your people be victimized. Between us here, this thing is going to take a long time to unscramble. The logistics of it aren't even calculable right now. The numbers are staggering. We haven't even had the time to write them down.''

There was silence for a while, just the roaring of the coal inside the cast iron inferno. Then Lee spoke.

"Does anybody know about that business on the bypass?''

"One phase of the West Penn overlands came down last night,'' said Stokes. "Right on top of some kind of liquid gas fuel—L.N.G. or butane. Blew it to hell. Froze 'em, then fried 'em. We have twenty-six cadavers stored in your old Donovan tunnel: nineteen complete, seven partial. Hope that's okay. There's nowhere here in town to put them.''

"What chance of getting power back?''

Stokes shook his head. "The local office doesn't have that kind of heavy cable on hand, not a thousand feet of it in one piece. That's not your everyday stuff. It has to be shipped on a rail car out of someplace up in Michigan. It's their own *Titanic*. They didn't think it could happen. Has it got you blacked out too?''

"We're blacked out. Whether that's it or not, who knows?''

Lee looked at his watch. It said noon. They all had things to do, he said. Beck would stay behind with Stokes and Pribanic's local men and help them get the barricades set up. The group got back into its socks and footgear. Pants legs were hot and burned them when they rose. Woods yelped and smacked his ankles. Lee was not entirely dry. The sneakers were warm. If only they would stay that way.

Big Maggie Pribanic met them on the first floor, on the way out the front door. She was helping with the people there, and broke away to approach them. She had a pair of workmen's green galoshes. She held them out to Lee.

"Take these, Mr. Rider. See if they fit you."

He took them in kind of numb surprise. She pointed at his sneakers.

"You need something more," she said. Then she dropped her eyes demurely. Extremely shy.

The rest of the group had stopped at the door. Woods and Beck and Stokes and the mayor in the Harry Truman overcoat and saturated cigar. Waiting for him.

"Go ahead," said Lee. "I'll catch up in a while."

The group went out into the sunshine and were gone. Lee flopped against the wall and pulled one of the galoshes on over the sneakers. They went on easily and were too large, but beat plain sneakers by a country mile.

"Maggie, I could kiss you! Where'd you get boots this size?"

She blushed. "They're mine."

They had to be size twelves. The astonishment must have showed on Lee's face. She blushed a little more.

"I can't get nothing in my size for a woman," she said. She turned her face away. "I'm pretty big. You know."

"Well, I can't take—"

"Oh, you just go on and take them, Mr. Rider. I'm staying here. I don't have to run around all over everyplace like you do."

"Well, I—"

"You can bring them back sometime if you want to," she said.

"Maggie, all I've got to say is that you're not big enough to hold the heart that's in you." Lee bent and kissed her on the cheek. He didn't have to bend far. She blushed some more.

"I've got to run. I'm sorry. I'll get them back to you."

He started off but she caught up with him. She pressed a slip of paper in his hand. He unfolded it, the year and registration number of a green MG Midget.

"The kids, Mr. Rider. Little Maggie. Little Mike." Her eyes betrayed a slight worry behind the shy smile. That meant there was a lot of worry to make her overcome and ask the favor. Then she tried to take the paper back, but Lee did not allow. "Oh, it's silly Mr. Rider. So many cars and people. How could you find them? I wouldn't even ask. So many relatives. I told them I'd do something, but it's craziness, I know."

"No, it isn't. It's a long shot, but it isn't crazy. I'll put it on the wire. You never know."

"Of course, we know not to expect nothing, but if you would—"

"I have a daughter out there too," said Lee.

"Oh, Mr. Rider! I'm sorry! I didn't know."

"Too soon for being sorry. Most people are doing okay. Thanks again. I'm sorry, but I've got to go."

"Sure. I know."

And he was gone. Down the steps and out into the sunshine. To catch up with the rest of them.

MILEPOST 108

Em caught up with Eddie and the dog about a mile down from the magazines and the Jesus lady. From her point of view it didn't matter if she saw either one again, except he had the canvas bag and the electric defroster, neither of which would have amounted to a loss worth serious pursuing. But she had the shotgun and his money and the kid was more than ordinarily tenacious about things like that and she figured she'd see him again. A greedy kind of kid.

She looked up at him, sitting up high and dry on another turned up car, going through the magazines with fever, the dog beside him. She climbed up on the upturned car and stood up tall to have a look around and saw the town was pretty close now. Maybe a mile if they left the turnpike and went across the fields, maybe two if they stuck to the roads. There were a lot of snow-mobiles and a lot of snowmobile tracks crisscrossing the white fields between them and the town and it might be worth it just to bust out of the crowd and cut across directly and maybe catch a ride. But the snow would still be deep and she remembered the aching cold of wading through it. Maybe they could catch a ride on one of the snowmobiles, but that was hoping for a lot. None of them seemed to be heading close to them, all going further west or circling south around the town like toy racing cars, razzing on the blinding snow, a faraway sound of little Jap gas motors, like model airplanes or distant chainsaws.

She sat down with him between her and the dog. He hardly noticed. He was so busy with the naked pictures. She gave it a little time.

"Howdy," she said finally.

"Hmm," he said.

"Ain't that far to Somerston, no more."

He didn't answer. He was studying the pages fast and taking stock of something, tallying, appraising.

"You got a knife or anything?" he asked.

"What for?"

"What do you think?"

She shrugged. "I seen enough of you that I'm not venturing no guesses anymore."

"I wanna cut these out. I don't want to have to be carrying any thirty pounds of paper everyplace."

"There's scissors in the bag."

"There are?"

"Well, I put them in. Unless you dumped them out or something. In the bottom, there."

He rummaged through and came up with scissors. Just like she said.

"Decent!" He began to clip the pictures out and slip them between the pages of one of the periodicals selected to survive, to function as a folio, a wrapping. "What were you going to do with scissors?" he asked finally.

"They're mine. I saved up and bought them and they're good ones, cost me seven dollars."

"That's not much."

"It is for me."

"What do you need with seven-dollar scissors? You don't look like the sewing kind to me."

"Clip stuff out of magazines, same as you. Not *them* kind, though."

"What kind?"

"All kinds."

"What for?"

"Send off for junk. See how close it is to what they make it look like in the pictures. You know."

"Like what?" Ed was stripping out the nudes like an old time Chesapeake waterman shucking out the tender flesh of oysters, working fast and clean—a total pro.

Em paused to reach into her mouth and remove the chewed out cud of tobacco, grasped in a delicate and slim pinch between thumb and forefinger. Ed watched from the side of his eye concealing horror. She dropped it carefully straight down in the snow, having the manners not to take the chance to let it fall on anybody. She shook the worst of the juice off her fingers with similarly considered aim, then wiped them on her pants. She did not as yet replace the cud with fresh tobacco.

Ed went back to cutting, vaguely nauseous.

"What do you send off for?" he repeated, his mind returning to the former track of things.

She shrugged and stuffed her hands into the pockets of her jacket and appraised the sky. "Stuff. I dunno. Whatever."

Ed had finished with the first of the magazines, had flensed it like a hapless whale and flung the tattered remnant backwards off the car, over the embankment behind them down into the snow.

"All that stuff is junk," he said. "A waste of money."

"Something to look forward to. If all else fails ya you can at least be watchin' for the mails."

"Dumb," said Ed. "If that was true of me I wouldn't tell it. Not to anybody."

"Preferable in many ways to whatever this is you got here," she said. "Sorry regard of the female of the human beings for sure."

"I don't spend my money on it."

"Costs you though."

"Like what for instance?" Ed just kept clipping, clipping.

"You ought to see yourself. All feverish and consumed. That guy was right up there—a pretty sicko hobby."

"It's a business. I'm a businessman."

"And I'm Olivia Newton John."

"It's not a hobby." Ed looked up from his work for the first time and the face was serious. She could see that whatever he was saying he believed. "I don't have time for hobbies," he said. "Nobody has time for hobbies. That's baloney. You don't either if you know what's good for you."

"Try that on me one more time."

Ed stood up and got her to stand up, too. He waved over the chaos of the endless turnpike jam, the people and the cars and all of it.

"See that? Pretty soon you'll never see a thing like that again. It's not going to be able to happen like that anymore."

"Dadburn shame," said Em.

"In a couple years the world is going to run completely out of gas and then nobody will be able to drive around and get in scrapes like this. It's going to be real historical. And they won't be able to harvest the crops or feed anybody and the population just keeps piling up in heaps and the results is that they'll all be dying off like flies. The only chance is if you're super super rich. It's going to take a ton of money just to stay alive."

"It does that now."

"This is nothing, now. Nothing."

"You believe in all that news junk, do you?"

"Yep. So does my old man. He works for oil. He sees the facts and figures every day and he believes it. He says by the end of the century that the world will have undergone more changes faster than in the entire history of mankind and the whole thing comes back down to overpopulation every time. Supply and demand. I saw it someplace on TV that in the year 2000 a dozen eggs'll cost $8.40. $8.40! Gas and electricity and land and food and houses and clothes and just the basics will cost so much money that only the giant corporations will be able to own it and everybody else will have to work night and day for them to just let you have a crust of bread and a hole to crawl into. It will be the same as communists but for money reasons instead of torture and secret police and junk like that. They'll be running everything by money. You won't ever have enough to keep in the clear no matter what you do. You'll have to be a Rockefeller just to live ordinary. It's happening already.''

Em was stuffing a new wad into her jaw. It looked like the black, stringy stuff that came out of compost by the garden. She munched it a while. She tucked the foil pouch back into the hip of her jeans and spat the first huge rush of new tobacco and saliva out and just generally took her time.

"You must've smoked a lot,'' said Ed. The attraction of the chewing habit was fading rapidly inside him.

"Two packs a day,'' she said.

"You probably got cancer anyway,'' he said. "It wouldn't make much difference if you smoked.''

She shrugged and looked out over the fossil traffic, the cars, the trudging people and the whole affair. From where they were standing now, the kid was making sense about the future, if not about tobacco. She'd paid twelve dollars for her last pair of jeans. On sale. They didn't fit good; they weren't the usual kind. She had to sew them up a couple times. You couldn't miss that stuff on TV and the radio and school. They kept pushing it into your face and in your ears and everything you read, ate, burned, drank or slept about. She really didn't want to talk about that bullshit now. It only thickened up the knot inside her stomach and there wasn't any in the worry room down there.

She shook her head again, her cowboy way.

"All that's kind of goin' the long way 'round the mountain to explain about a buncha dirty pictures.'' She spat gigantically and with concern for passers-by, waited for what he would say.

"I don't go for these,'' he said. "I sell 'em.''

"To who?''

"Kids at home. Down at the grad school. Around the Catholic school. Especially the Catholic school. God! I used to go for them at the beginning but no more. It's like pictures of food if you were starving. Who needs that?''

"Always seemed like that to me," she said. "But these guys pay you for them? You get money?"

"Heck yes! Look at this!" He sat down as before and started going through the magazines and showing her. "Centerfold—two bucks—three if it's a good one. Buck for little color shots. Black and whites—fifty cents. A buck on top of anything that shows a beaver."

"Beaver?"

"Yeah."

"Oh."

"These guys are fools, I'm telling ya. They're nuts! They pay anything! I cut out twenty bucks already. I'm on the second magazine."

"What keeps them from just going down and buying them like everybody else?"

He shrugged. "Scared. They don't sell these kind of magazines to kids around our place. Maybe in Flint but not near us. Kids are scared their folks'll catch 'em, the nuns'll catch 'em. Anyway they're fools. They buy 'em. What do I care?"

"What if you get caught?"

"I take the heat and keep the money. I got caught before. You survive it. What are they going to do to a kid? It's a big advantage. You got to start young. I'm behind the way it is. I should've wised up years ago. A million isn't what it used to be. You got to make four or five. It takes more and more."

"You really gonna haul them things all the way to Detroit, huh?"

"You bet I am. That's gold. At home I'm watched. Lotta people got the same idea, y' know. Getting rich, I mean. It ain't what you'd call scarce thinking."

"So what?"

"Thought I'd mention it for the effect, that's all. Most people will never do it because they don't know they have to. They still think it's somekind of a dream out of the movies. They don't think it's do or die, but if you don't have a lot of money in the future you'll be holding down three jobs and living at the riverside in shacks and picking garbage like a pack of rats. I'm just getting ready for it, that's all."

Em chewed soberly and thought about it some and then spat gently and straight down again so as not to hit the passers-by.

"Well, anyhow I'm moving on," she said. "I wanna get to Somerston before the bus fare gets above eight dollars."

"Wait a minute! Lemme get these things cut out!"

"All those? There's a blizzard on the way. I'm leavin'."

She hopped down off the car and started away, taking the shotgun with her. Ed scraped up the magazines into a stack and shoved them in the bag and jumped down too. He lifted Daisy down and hurried to catch up. The magazines were heavier than the old fat dog and slammed against his legs if he went too fast, which wasn't fast at all. But eventually he caught up with the girl.

"You're gonna clip a lot of pictures for a million dollars," she said after a while.

"That's only one that that I do. I got to get my working capital built up. It's not going on forever."

"Your life to do with as you choose," she said.

"No, it isn't, but I'm working on it. You'd be too, if you knew what was good for you."

"Who says I ain't?"

They walked without doing any talking. Em spat again with easy expertise—avoiding all the people around them. He studied the way she did her spitting: soberly and very well the way she seemed to do things generally, avoiding raising any feelings of offense.

"What are you doing about it, then?"

"Well?" She paused for cowboy emphasis and squinted at the sky with one eye squinted shut entirely. "I'm the one that wound up with your dollars and your gun for all your schemes it seems to me."

"I'll make them back. I'll make them six times over."

They walked a little more. Em kept looking to the sky. There seemed to be a dullness to the west down close to the horizon. Nothing that meant a whole lot now. At the moment it could go a lot of ways.

They walked a long time before anything was said.

"I don't get it." It was she who broke the silence again.

"What?"

"What's so greatly interesting about a 'beaver'?"

"Gets a dollar more; that's greatly interesting enough for me."

12:20 P.M.—SOMERSTON ARMORY

The chopper took off for the Bald Knob Summit leaving Pribanic and the captain and the one-armed man standing in the pigs and slush and people. The thought of having them go south around the mountain occurred, but Lee said nothing. When the chopper topped the crest the body still hung from the tower. They passed it silently and dropped toward Redford. It was a thing to be abhorred, indeed, but not shirked and dishonored. Had to get Jimmy down. Had to.

SOMERSTON—12:20 P.M.

Stokes, Pribanic and the captain wound up at Johannsen's Texaco within minutes after the departure of the helicopter bearing Woods and Rider back to Redford. The Texaco was no longer operating as a Texaco. Jim Johannsen and his young helper Arthur were nowhere around, had not been seen by any of the local armory or civil defense guys hanging around with the trucks and snowmobiles. The place was open, the doors were open and it was filled with local guard and volunteers. The Texaco had become an unofficial motorpool, a rendezvous point, a headquarters for the local emergency operations such as they were—a hang-loose little knot of men awaiting leadership. It was a small matter of a few brief exchanges of conversation to find out that the town had been ringed with snowmobile trails to the hospital proper and to the temporary hospitals set up in various buildings around the edges of the town. Trails existed to the Pike and one or two supply dumps, town guys had found out about the vacant eastbound and the market for food and gas up on the turnpike—were hauling food up, hauling sick and pregnant people down. It took no time at all to recognize that the emergency channel that had been forged up to the bypass the night before was more than half the problem—standing unattended, an open invitation to the people on the bypass slope to walk into town, pouring them into Somerston like cattle down a chute. No one had thought to plug the lane after the work was done. It had simply been abandoned. Stokes was boiling mad—as mad at himself as much as at the situation. It had to be reversed if possible—that channel shut down totally and as of now.

Beck had his doubts. The channel was an ongoing thing. Established. He doubted it could be stopped at such a point of advanced development.

Stokes collared one of the guard, a young corporal in a group of three and two more locals resting on their snowmobiles having smokes. The fellow thought there was a PA set in the armory that would take its power from the trucks and was sent to get it. Pribanic, Stokes and Beck ran down the situation for the other guys, asked that the snowmobilers go out, round up their comrades and meet at the Turnpike gates. They would drive the big trucks up the channel, pushing people back if possible or at least out of the way. They were going to need all the help at the barricade they could get, help turning people back, help using the CB. The snowmobilers seemed doubtful of it all. They had been talking with CB people on the Pike almost from the beginning— all night, all day. They had told them it was overrun in Somerston and not to come. They had told them essentially everything that Woods had said. It seemed so obvious and commonsensical out here, the mayor felt a fool for having said it. The snowmobilers shrugged and said that indeed, a lot were staying up there on the Pike, but then a lot were coming into Somerston as well. Pribanic asked what the trouble was: didn't they believe about the storm? Some did, some didn't. Same story as before. The fellows pointed out that at this same time yesterday no one was hearing one damn thing about a twenty-two-inch snowfall. The weather people's credibility was somewhat down. The mayor thought about it, found that he could see that side better than what officially must be his own. He decided to say nothing further on that subject either way.

"You get the idea," said L. John.

"Sure," the snowmobiler said.

"The idea is to keep them out of town and whatever works and does that then you *do* it. Use your judgment." The young snowmobiler was a blond kid with a reddish beard and black teeth when he smiled. Vaguely familiar. L.John thought he knew the people, the protestants north of the interstate, maybe, the Turnpike. The pike had always sliced the region, cleft it in two like a Great Wall of China. The northern families had been always more off on their own.

"You say you're selling stuff to them; you clipping them good, or what, you guys?"

The black-teeth smile went under. Defenses in the face went up. The kid squinted in the sun, uncertain what to say.

"It's okay," the mayor said. "I'm not gonna ream you out. I'm told that this is fine, to get a blackmarket going quick and make a buck so we don't come out short like before. Good for everybody; keeps them occupied."

The smile came out, the black teeth in the sunshine—the face brightened.

"You tell all the guys. Just don't—well—just don't shove it hard to anybody that can't pay, that's in trouble. You know."

"We been hauling sick and pregnant all day. We're doing a lot of good up there," the snowmobiler said. "Now that you think of it."

"Sure. It's fine. Tell all the guys what we said here."

The black-teeth kid took off on his rackety steed. North. Across the fields toward others. They waited. In a couple minutes two guys in fatigues and army coats came across the street with army boxes, an army-colored mobile loudspeaker setup and began to wire it into one of the big canvas covered trucks. Stokes, the mayor and the captain continued waiting until L.John became impatient. They left instructions with the guard guys in the truck to bring it to the gates as soon as it was ready and took off ahead of it on foot.

REDFORD—12:30 P.M.

Plumes of smoke were rising from Redford, four distinct black columns stood crookedly in dog's legs on the snow, from the northeastern and more modern residential section, where his home was. Where Jennifer would be. He gave instructions to the pilot to pass over Central and look more closely at that part of town. Woods looked momentarily as though he might object that they hadn't time, but privately decided that it wouldn't hurt to size up the status of Redford.

REDFORD—12:35 P.M.

Redford wasn't as bad off as Somerston. It was within one exit of the tunnel just as Somerston, but the breakdown had been Redford's favor, had actually drained the town of a proportion of the normal eastbound stop-offs before weather precipitated the heavy westbound spilloff later on. Redford was bigger, laid out more broadly and on flatter land. The streets were wider. City street crews even had a few of the more crucial streets open now. Given one clear day ahead and they'd have at least this one town opened up and working. One clear day.

The fire was not at Lee's. Lee had them hover low directly over the house and neighbors came out on their porches, fat with extra clothes and sweaters, curious about the noise, but no one came from Lee's. Lee had the pilot hold position for a minute more and then requested to put down.

"Your place?" Woods didn't look surprised. Lee nodded.

"What's the size of your front yard?" It looked okay, but it never hurt to have hard information. The pilot never hesitated with questions like that.

"Sixty by sixty-two." Lee knew exactly because they had built that house two years before and he and Jen would be getting close to old before the trees grew up enough to give them shade. He regretted that about the place.

The skids sank deep. Lee jumped down and waded toward the door. Woods jumped down behind him. Maggie's galoshes made one hell of a difference, but he was going to grab his heavy camping boots while home and take every advantage of the visit. No telling when he might get back again. No telling what might lie ahead.

The front door was unlocked and when he opened it the choking acridness of gas bloomed into his face, into his eyes and mouth and nostrils and hit him in a swooning rush. He backed away, leaned against the railings of the porch.

"What is it? Oh! Gas! Jesus!" Woods had caught up, the invisible malevolence had spread further out and down the steps and reached him. Woods got out a handkerchief and put it to his face, a useless precaution that surprised Lee. Woods seemed to know so much about so many things that killed you. Lee didn't feel inclined to take the time to explain to him that gas was not particulate and could not be strained out; he gulped a lungful of fresh air and held it. They charged inside.

Afghans lay in disorder across the couch. The TV stood wheeled out on its cart for viewing in the middle of the living room, martini glass and shaker on the table, the Sunday papers strewn about—a set up for an all-night vigil—but Jennifer was not here now.

In the dining room the dinner Jen had promised sat untouched upon the table grown stale beneath unlit candles. The gas was all but pure and overwhelming. Lee threw the inner windows up and punched out the storm windows with a gloved fist, returned to the living room and set the phone receiver off its cradle lest someone should call and blow the house to smithereens with the small spark created in the ringer. Maybe that's what happened where the fires were. So many things that could have happened. He dashed through the kitchen knocking out more windows, threw the back door open wide. Jennifer was nowhere on the gound floor. He called out and at once regretted filling his lungs with the atmosphere inside the house. There was no answer and he was getting sick again, the hot headache and the pulling eyes as before, like yesterday outside the tunnel. He heard the sounds of someone moving upstairs, bumping into things. It had to be Woods, was not the way Jen moved and sounded, but he had to get good air. He rushed out the back and gulped it in, waiting for his head to clear to make another dive into the denatured methane atmosphere that had yesterday been the common things of home. Glass shattered above, an upstairs window rained in splintered shards around him. Lee stepped back a few paces and looked up. Woods' head appeared from the window of Charlene's bedroom.

"No one up here," Woods choked. He gagged about to vomit.

"Did you set the phone off?" Lee called. Charlie had a separate number, a line all her own. An absolute domestic necessity.

"What?"

"The phone by the bed! Set it off the cradle!"

Woods disappeared then reappeared some seconds later.

"Good idea," he shouted. "Where's this gas from? Furnace?"

Lee shrugged and nodded vigorously. It had to be. It was the only gas appliance in the house.

"Get outside before you pass out," he shouted. "I'm going to the cellar—shut the utilities down."

Lee gulped down a new chestful of the new, cold air and dashed back inside. He clambered through the kitchen again and down the cellar stairs, holding his lungs tight. Worse below—as thick as fumes from down in the cellar, and dark—only the faint light penetrating the snow-buried cellar casement windows. He groped through the downstairs den, the laundry, trying not to knock down anything of metal that might make a spark against the cement floor. In the laundry he at last found the fuse box, felt upward along conduit to the smaller box above the main one, the box with the big master lever on the side and pulled it down, disconnecting all incoming power lines from the house. It would be disaster should the power come back suddenly with all this gas still in the house. Now behind the furnace to shut the gascocks. Finally the water. The pipes were going to freeze, nothing he could do about that now, but at least it wouldn't flood the house.

Where the hell was Jen? Where could she have gone? He had to breathe. He couldn't hold it anymore. At once he fought the need to cough, the yellow, green, and purple lights again sparkling at the edges of his vision and his legs shaky under him—as if he'd come up several flights of stairs at a full run. He felt hot and sick and couldn't stop it, couldn't fight it down. The coughing came in torrents as he clawed his way back out through the den and somehow up the stairs again.

The light hit him in the eyes and stomach. He puked violently with one arm hung around a pillar of the porch and sucked in the good air, waiting for his tunneling vision to widen out again, waiting till he knew for certain up from down, till the air tasted good again and didn't make him ill.

When a little normalcy returned he saw that Woods was outside too—across the yard and climbing into the chopper. From the porch of the adjacent house the Norweds watched like penguins, fat and stiff-armed in their extra clothes. The Riders didn't really know the Norweds. Both he and Jen had tried to make the usual chit-chat over the back fence from time to time and each time found them humorless, obscure. But when Lee came into a little strength at last he waved to them. Perhaps they knew something of Jennifer, of what was going on.

"Mrs. Norwed?" There was no response at first. "Mrs. Norwed! It's Lee Rider."

The woman moved forward to the railing of her porch and shaded her eyes. "Who?"

"Lee Rider!" He and Woods might just as well be burglars cleaning out his house in full bright daylight. All the Norweds would do is stand there stupidly and watch.

"Have you seen Jennifer?"

"Who?"

"My wife! Mrs. Rider!"

Mrs. Norwed shook her head. "When will we be getting the electric back?"

"I don't know. You're sure you didn't see her?"

"No. We didn't see anybody. You don't know anything about the electric then—you're sure?"

"Power's out statewide. It's gonna be a while. That's all I know."

The Norwed woman waved him off disgustedly in a manner which as much as told him he was lying or that the whole thing was his fault. If there was a Heaven in an afterlife it had to include a place where for a nickel you could spend an entire day punching people like that in the face until you'd had your fill. All of them. Everyone you'd ever met throughout your life with none excepted. Perhaps the Norwed place would soon burn down— some day when he was home and watching and there was nothing good on television. And then the sickness overwhelmed him once again and sent him wretching and the Norweds were forgotten.

Woods was on his way back from the chopper—face in one of those effeminate-looking little clear plastic oxygen masks. He brought it up to Lee and pressed it into his face.

"Take a couple hits of this. Does wonders."

Lee let himself slip down to sit on the edge. Woods hauled up and sat beside him.

"Where you think she could've gone?" Lee wasn't having thoughts. He was pressing with the full force of his mind against the blackness trying to close in, drinking deeply of the oxygen, waiting for it to start to push the clouds away, relax the pulling of his eyes. He held his hand up, asking for time.

It was dead quiet for a while. Dead quiet. No sound of traffic in the background. Nothing but the sighing of his own breath in the mask. Lee thought back for some other time in the past when he'd been outdoors without some kind of traffic, however distant, as a constant background roar—a seashell roar. It had always been there. Always. For the first time in his memory it was gone and that was louder than the roar. He could hear the blood in his own ears, squishing like footsteps in the snow. The strangeness of it was unnerving, creepy—as if something fundamental had gone wrong—an apprehension, a sudden silence that at any second would blow up the entire universe right in their faces.

Woods got out his pipe again and slung it in his jaw. His hands got out a pack of matches. He stopped himself just at the act of striking, remembering the gas. He conserved the match by lodging it behind the others. He put the pack back in his pocket and sucked at the pipe upside down and cold. One of the Norweds went inside, letting their aluminum storm door fall shut with a bang. Echoes of the crash came back from every house along the drive in clear and separate reverberations. They listened, trying to connect each building with each reverberation till the impulse traveled on to other streets and neighborhoods beyond view and multiplying into so many that it became swallowed up and gone into a fading multiplicity and then the void pressed in again. The unearthly quiet.

Woods cocked an ear. "What's that?" he said.

"What's what?"

"Listen."

Lee's ears reached deep into the stillness. Something there. Something. What? Radio? Radio. Static. Voice sometimes. Murmury and dim and electronic.

"Radio," said Woods.

"Ssssh!" said Lee.

They listened ten more seconds. Lee got up abruptly and went straight for the garage.

Jen was on the front seat of her car, the garage extension telephone beneath one hand upon her lap. The ignition was still on. Red lights showed from the dash, the radio was on just very softly, some distant station that had faded with the sun. The gas showed empty. The car had been running and ran out of gas. How long ago? Woods came in, smelled the fumes and threw the garage doors up and open. The exhaust that still hung in the air was heavy, but not suffocating. Lee reached across the seat and took her hand. It was gloved, but underneath the fingers were not stiff. Jen's hands were thin, he felt the normal movement of familiar bones—alive not dead. Then she moved her head and grimaced slightly and made small complaining noises when the light and noise from the garage doors struck her.

"Go back and get the oxygen. I left it on the porch," he called to Woods.

Lee raised her upright from behind the wheel and got the door open on her side. She moaned and murmured his name, then drifted off again. He shook her and she fought him vaguely, not wanting to be wakened.

"Jen! Jen! Come on, Baby."

Woods was back and handed him the respirator. She fought that too. Lee held her head and forced it to her face until she'd gotten some good breaths. She seemed to relax a little, fall back to sleep, then her eyes opened—a violet glistening through narrow slits. She looked at him blankly for a moment before recognition showed.

"Lee."

"Correct," he said.

"I have a headache."

"I believe it. Here—" He put the mask up to her face again. "Breathe some more of this."

"What is it?"

"Oxygen. Come on now."

Jennifer took three more breaths, then pushed the mask away, startled—much more awake, now. "Oxygen! What for? Where am I?" She sat up on her own and looked about. Recognition, memory coming back in great rushes. "Oh, my God!"

"What were you doing out here? Are you crazy? You know better than to run a car inside a closed garage! You're nuts!"

"It was so cold inside the house. I wanted the radio—"

"But Jen—to run the engine—!"

"It was cold. I had the door up partway. I guess I drifted off—"

"I guess you did. It's lucky you forgot to gas up Saturday." Lee reached down and cut the ignition, took the keys. "Can you walk?"

"I don't know."

"Let's try it." Lee helped her slide across the seat and get feet to the floor. Woods assisted. Jen was shaky, but between them she could make it. Lee let her take a few more bits of oxygen before attempting the yard and the chopper.

"Who's this?" She had not met Woods.

Lee made hurried introductions. "We've got his helicopter waiting out in front. We're short on time, Jen. We have to get back now."

"I'm—kind of sick. Watch out for me in case I—you know—"

"Yeah. Let's go."

They got her across the yard and up into the chopper. Lee held her. "Where are you taking me?"

"Central."

"What if Charlie calls? What about the house, Lee?"

"Charlie knows the Central number."

"What about the house?"

"The Norweds can look out for it."

The motion of the chopper lifting off, the sudden brutal noise of it, brought sickness back at once—to Lee, not Jennifer. Jennifer passed out again, drifted off. Lee couldn't tell. She seemed to be taking it all very peacefully. It was all that Lee could do to hold his stomach down. Woods bent over Jennifer and held his fingers to her throat, asked whether she had a history of heart or respiratory problems. She had not.

"The oxygen should do it then," he said.

The chopper had stopped rising and was traveling across the town now.

"You want to take her to the hospital?" Woods asked.

"I wouldn't mind." Lee knew the usual thing for monoxides was pure oxygen. The wartime airman's cure for a hangover. Not much more. She seemed worse than might be expected. They might want to keep her overnight for observation. One of those things. But this was Jennifer. Why take chances?

"Show us where it is," said Woods.

SOMERSTON—12:45 P.M.

Pribanic had become annoyed with the tedium and delay of the installation of the PA set into the armory truck, had had them set off for the Turnpike gates with the unit half-installed; they could complete the job up there. Jake Stokes and the Troop T captain stayed with him. All three piled aboard the fenders and, with a couple guard guys, rode with rifles and uniforms clearly showing. The guard guys had those little bullhorns with them anyway. What had been the reason to delay? They nudged and bullhorned their way into the channel and from then on it was upstream against a river of people, people convinced that what was being shouted at them through the bullhorns and the waving arms was precisely counter to their own best interests. It was a grudging, inch-by-inch grind, the full three-quarters of a mile between the Texaco and Exit 10. The people would jump out of the channel or up on the sides, the snowbanks or the upturned wrecks and wait until the truck was past and drop back down again and simply continue on their way into Somerston. They were not turning around and going back, that's for sure.

On their left now, they had come abreast of the Mehelic Highway Restaurant and Motel and outside a large mob seemed more than unusually restless, a mood there that bothered Pribanic. The motel was hard beside the Pike, huge sign on the roof to catch the business, drag it in off the Pike—just below it at the foot of the ramps. Pribanic waved the driver to pull up and jumped down from the fender. He told Stokes to go ahead, to take the truck up to the gates and get set up there. The captain had seen the crowd and was staying with the major. The mayor agreed. The uniform would be an asset. Perhaps it was. The crowd, though brooding and hostile, gave way to them. No trouble. The hostility was focused on the inside of the place, not on them. L.John's anger increased as his distance from the door diminished. There were a lot of old folks and young folks with babies standing out front. It had the familiar smell of the Mehelic character of business to it somehow. He didn't know how, but he knew that smell. It came up smelling like a rose—Rose Mehelic. The mayor lived in town and wasn't familiar with the interior of the motel. He knew enough to know it shouldn't be this empty though. Hardly anybody in the lobby. Well, two-thirds full, but two-thirds full was hardly anyone today.

"Hey, Mister. Accutron watch. Five dollars."

A guy inside the door. He needed a shave and sleep—like everybody—but his clothes weren't the clothes of a bum. Good clothes. The captain looked at the watch in the outstretched hand. Accutron all right. Practically an antique now, obsolete in the flood of digitals and transistors of recent years. The transistors were taking over everything, but it had cost a bundle one time. Maybe a collector's item now. The watch was running too.

"Where you get it?" said the captain.

"Mine." The guy turned his hand over and showed him the watchprint in his suntan. The watch fit the white space just exactly. Of course the guy could have stolen it *before* Miami. The captain switched his paranoia off abruptly, derided himself for having too much automatic cop's mentality.

"Why you selling it?"

"Feed my kid. They're not taking credit cards. I'm out of cash." The guy thrust it out at them with renewed urgency. "Look. Don't do me any favors. Take advantage. I need cash."

"You wait here," said the mayor.

The man was right. Both the motel registration desk and entry to the restaurant section displayed big cardboard standup signs that said "CASH ONLY—NO CREDIT CARDS OR CHECKS ACCEPTED."

"Whose idea is this?" L.John demanded.

"Whose idea is what?" The girl behind the register was snippy. You could tell she'd had a bunch of this already. The restaurant booths, like the lobby, were about three-quarters capacity, the counter somewhat fuller. It didn't reflect conditions on the outside at all. Pribanic was surprised that there should be such a shortage of cash. He heard that everything was credits now, dits and blips in the computers, but he hadn't seen it quite as tangibly manifested before. He got the same sick-scaredness in his stomach that he got from seeing the actual presence of so many people yesterday.

"This not taking credit cards." He took four rolls of antacid tablets from the wire thing by the register and laid a dollar down.

"It isn't up to me, sir." She rang up the sale. "That's a dollar forty-eight with tax, sir."

He counted out the change exactly on the counter.

"You take those signs down now and start letting people in here. What's the matter with you? Why aren't you letting people take refuge in the lobby?"

"Sir—do you want me to call the manager?" It was obvious the girl didn't know who he was. That was okay. He didn't know her either. Young faces. Couldn't tell one from the other. No character in the smooth faces to go by. No history written there. Plenty of snip, but no history whatever.

"Call the manager," he said. "That's a good idea."

She left in hostile confidence and went in the direction of the lobby. They followed. She went behind the check-in counter through a door, telling them they had to wait so they waited by that door. Presently she reemerged, went past them with a snub and back toward the restaurant. Big Mike Mehelic came out then.

"L.John! What's going on? 'A guy talking loud,' she says. I might have known."

"I'm not talking loud. Not yet, I'm not. What's this making old folks and the babies stand outside? Not taking credit cards? What the hell kind of human being are you?"

"Sssh! Sssh!" Big Mike tried to hold him down. "Come in the office."

Rose was in the office, behind the desk and frog-eye glasses. Going through papers. Looking for files maybe, thought L. John. He knew the office would look like this and Rose would be here doing something of this kind. He had never been inside that office and it all felt like a thing that he would do each day or so, a sight that would always be the same. She looked up at them, looked down again and didn't talk or stop going through the papers. Mike as usual would be doing all the talking. L.John realized that they had their little empire cut up into territories: his and hers. There were parts that were entirely Mike's, but this was not among them. This was Rose's. The office had fluorescent lighting and the potted plants were plastic and they needed dusting. Only the plants though. Every other thing was clean and well maintained.

"Rose told you to tell the help not to take credit vards, is that it? And checks?" said the mayor. He talked to Mike. No use saying anything to Rose Mehelic. She wouldn't answer.

Mike shrugged. "We *never* take checks—"

"Skip it about the checks. What about the credit cards?"

"At times like these its riskier. A lot of pickpocketing. Tricks. You know."

"What kind of tricks?"

"I don't know. They come up with new ones every day. You can't stay ahead of it."

"Well, cut this thing out with the credit cards and let them in. I don't care. Everybody's doing what they can. You will too."

"Like you guys, I suppose? You did a lot to keep the town from being overrun, I see. What if it turns into a riot or a panic or like that? We'd heard there's going to be another storm this afternoon. Worse than before."

Beck moved in on it. "It's your place, Mehelic, and I'm

just advising, but if you let people in here they'll perceive it as their own turf and if anymore try to break in or jeopardize the place in any way you'll have yourself a built-in army. They'll defend it for you. On your own, you'll just get overrrun. Smashed to pieces. No time flat."

"Seems like we'd get a lot of damage anyway."

"Maybe you will," said the captain. "The other way is almost guaranteed."

Mike watched Rose for some silent seconds. She did not look up nor change her countenance in any way and kept busy in her papers and her files. Poor Mike. The spider and the fly. She had got him to marry her for her own purposes like everything else. Mike paid high interest on his money.

Mike looked back at them again. "Naw," he said. "Bad business. Steal us blind. People sleeping in the halls and lobbies for weeks. Who knows what all? I don't argue with the wife on things like this, guys. She *knows* the business. I mean—she's never wrong. Not ever."

L. John pushed past Mike and went directly to the desk.

"Rose, I asked you nice. We just got done talking to a bunch of guys like Red Cross and the army and the Turnpike and all them federal-type guys. Not one hour ago. The army's coming here on Wednesday. And the Red Cross and the Salvation Army, the whole pack of them, and if you *don't* have this place filled up here in an hour with those old folks standing outside now, and the little babies, Rose, I'm going to have those federal operations coming straight to you and have them commandeering the place and turning it into a headquarters or troop barracks or some kind of field hospital thing that gets blood and vomit over the rugs and furniture and don't think they won't do it too. You got a perfect setup here. They'll like it very much. I'm coming back to check. I don't want to see anybody out in front that's old enough to be my mother. And you take their credit cards and feed them too. One hour, Rose. One, lousy hour. It better look like human decency around here."

He turned and left and Beck went with him.

Mike followed them to the outer front doors. "You can't make us do it, L. John. You haven't got the power."

"Anymore than you can stop me telling the army where's

Their entrance attracted the attention of the management almost at once—two soaked and filthy looking kids with a dog in a bowling bag suspended from a shotgun walking in the front door of the still sedate, if somewhat overrun, Edna Hotel. Attracted his attention, even today. The skinny 60-year-old guy with flat-top and bow tie came out from behind the check-in counter at once. The kids had stopped to check out the vending machines in the lobby. Everything was gone. Everything. Cigarettes and candy bars and gum and everything. Even the combs.

"You kids! Get out!"

They didn't though. They stood their ground and let him come to them.

"What's the next time you'll be running buses?" Em said.

"Take that gun and dog and get right out of here. What are you trying to do, start a panic?"

"How far is it to the hospital?" Ed was just as impervious as Em to what the flat top's personal concerns were.

"What?"

"The hospital. Where is it?"

"If I tell you, will you go there?"

"Sure."

The guy gave them a lengthy set of directions. They went over it a couple times. Ed wasn't sure. He didn't know the town at all and wasn't sure if the directions would make sense to him once he set out and actually tried to follow them. Daisy whined and was anxious to get out of the bag, but the flat-top guy would have none of that. Daisy was a muddy, sopping mess.

"I'll find it," Em said, rare impatience showing. "What's the next time you'll be having buses running?" That was what she cared about.

"Your guess is as good as mine, young lady,"

"Could I wait here?"

"Not with that gun and dog, you can't. No sir. Ma'am."

"The gun and dog belongs to him," she said. "How much to Morgantown?"

"Roundtrip or one-way?"

"One-way."

"$10.40 or 9.85. One or the other. I'd have to look and see. You kids get out now. Go on. You better hurry up and get some-

place and get holed up before this blizzard hits. If you're goin' to
the hospital, you better go."

Outside they kept going south on Main Street #219. The
guy had said to keep going down Main Street until they came to
a wide street at the south edge of town. He said there would be
green and white signs saying "HOSPITAL". It would be to the
left. They couldn't miss it, but they better hurry though.

REDFORD HOSPITAL—1:10 P.M.

The roof of Redford's hospital was a repeat of what they'd
had at Somerston atop the armory. Uncleared deep snow. The
pilot guessed again and set down in the largest area devoid of
structures as before, having only Lee's assurance that there was
in fact a helipad beneath it someplace. Whether they had hit it,
they couldn't know, except that the chopper didn't punch through
and go down into the upper floors this time either—the preferred
outcome, always. Woods and Reese jumped down and waded
toward a stairwell door leaving Lee behind with Jennifer. Jennifer
had come around again, but seemed dopier than before. Weaker.
Paler looking. It wasn't quite the stereotypical pattern. A little
strange.

Lee had her hand in his. She rolled her head and peered at
him through sunken eyes. "My hero."

"Aw, shucks," he said. He wasn't smiling.

"Where are we—are we there?"

"We're at the hospital."

"What for?"

"We're in the neighborhood, I thought we ought to say
hello."

"You lie. You've brought me here to have me stuck with
needles."

"I'm middle-class. I've got hobbies."

"For God's sake Lee, I'm fine. I'll be all right. I don't need
any hospital. Take me away from here."

"Let them have a look at you. I'm not jeopardizing a dynamite love life because you're squeamish. Just relax."

"But—"

the best place to shack up if I'm in the kind of mood to do a thing like that, huh? I mean if for some reason I have this place on my mind as opposed to some others I might have thought of. If it wasn't so much in my mind. Look at where you're situated! This is perfect here.''

"Heck of a way to start the family," said Mike.

L.John paused just at the glass front doors. "Isn't it, I was just about to say that.''

"You didn't hear nothing from the kids then?" Mike said.

"No I didn't. One hour, Mike. I'm coming back to see.''

He pushed out through the doors with Beck. The guy with the watch was on the outside now, but still selling. He held it out to them again.

"What about the watch?" the guy said.

"I got a watch," said L.John.   "Go inside. It's okay, now.''

SOMERSTON HOSPITAL—12:45 P.M.

They had waited in the coughing squalor of the hospital corridor for almost two hours and not been seen by a doctor. That was all right—they hadn't seen one either. Chris seemed no better, no worse. Petulant—a little bitchier than normal—even for her. Dan couldn't blame her. He was too. They were dirty, cramped and hungry—hadn't eaten since the day before—and it was getting to them. All of them.

"Wait here with Chris. I'm going out.''

"Where? What for?" Irene was nervous about it. He knew she would be, that she would not relish being left alone.

"Going out to find a phone. Call home. The folks will be half nuts to know what happened to us.''

That was true. The pattern of the past ten years had been that they would set out from the farm just after breakfast. Ten. Ten-thirty. Arrive in Detroit about eleven or midnight and would call. Obviously, there would have been no call, the folks would have heard the weather and about some of the highway problems on the late news, would have tried to call and got no answer, would assume the worst. By now, they would be frantic. A worrier herself, Irene couldn't argue with that reasoning.

"I'm just so afraid that we'll get separated like with Eddie," she said.

"We won't get separated. You stay here. No matter what. I won't be any longer than I have to. Just a phone call. Maybe pick up something to eat."

"Isn't there a pay phone in the hospital?"

"Maybe there is. I'll see."

SOMERSTON—1:00 P.M.

The first five dozen people they asked were not from Somerston and couldn't tell them anything—nto the location of the bus station or the hospital or anything. Somerston had proven not to be the shining orb they'd had in their minds—in Ed's mind anyway. Once in the town, the going was actually worse than coming down the emergency channel from the bypass. When the channel ended it was back to slop and ice-wet feet and Daisy in the bag, suspended from the gun between them. In addition to having been too short-legged she was trying to chase pigs and getting lost amid the junkyard streets of Somerston. Ed's arms were aching from carrying the bundle of magazines, but he was determined not to give them up. He'd had to remove most to get Daisy back into the bag. They had continued to follow #219 down into town and kept on Main Street until they reached the central square around the courthouse. They found the bus station there. It was not a depot in and of itself, but rather one of those incorporated into the enterprises of an old and semi-residential hotel, the Edna, half-populated with pensioners and ferns in pots about the lobby, dark woodwork and gold-leaf bordering around the windows. They found it easily because of a Greyhound and two Trailways buses parked in front and it was obvious, of course, that there would be no buses leaving that day. Inside, the Edna was like all other places, full of refugees. Everything packed solid to the walls. They went inside despite it, perhaps because they'd pilgrimaged ten miles to get here.

"It's a selfish motive. Trust it."

There was a noise outside. Lee looked out the hatch. Woods was pounding on the stairwell door, kicking it and shouting.

"What's the problem?" Lee shouted at him.

"Locked! Would you believe it?" Woods was fuming. What the hell were they expecting nine floors off the ground? "HEY! YOU DOWN THERE! OPEN UP! COME UP HERE!" He renewed his assault upon the steel-clad door.

Presently it all seemed futile. He gave it up. Woods started back and made it halfway to the chopper when the door came open. A tiny nurse of maybe fifty and a young orderly stood out whitely against the black interior of the stairwell.

"Who are you people?" asked the nurse. "What are you doing up here?" She was a tight-lipped meany. Lee could see that much clear across the roof.

Woods returned at once and flashed I.D.s. There was some discussion, several looks and gestures toward the helicopter, then they disappeared below. Lee glanced at his watch. 1:10. Two hours plus to the storm. Three maybe. The brilliant sunshine made it so hard to believe. Jen had drifted off again. The quiet had returned. Almost. There was some sound of automotive movement far below them on the ground.

"She'll be okay," the pilot said.

It made Lee jump. It was the last thing he expected.

"What?"

"I said she'll be okay. Hung over for a day or two, a little dopey, that's it."

"I'm sure she will."

"Yeah—heck, yeah." Pause. "No harm in having her looked over though."

"No."

"Why take chances?"

"No reason."

"You're doing the right thing. Really."

The conversation died, the silence rang again. After some time Lee looked at his watch. Only 1:15. In the silence and the apprehension minutes had swelled up like grains of rice. Jen was still asleep and snoring slightly, the soft and tiny snore that had

always been there. Since they were married. At first he feared
that it might grow and become repulsive finally, but it had remained unchanged throughout the years. Jen was not aware of it
and Lee had left it that way. It had grown instead into one of
those endearing traits, which, if brought to the person's awareness, will sometimes die soon after of the loss of innocence. It
was a comfort to him now, a sense of Jen, a sameness, a con-
tinuation of normal things. He wondered whether it would mean
the same to him now, brought out of their bedroom into these
unfitting circumstances. Funny which things got to be important
through the years.

Lee thought about himself and thought about being forty and
the snarl of a world that lay ahead. Things were getting more
complex and he was getting older. That could get you in the end.
At the rate things had been changing, he had probably lived more
experience than his father and grandfather combined, seen more
things come and go, had to relearn his field three times. Some
things had to stay the same. You'd go bananas. It was important
that she go on snoring.

"She always snore that way?" the pilot asked. Again it was a
startling intrusion.

"What's that?" Lee said.

"Your wife—does she snore a little always or is this new?"

"Uh—no. It's normal." Lee had a rush of anger, but the
fellow obviously was well-intentioned. Lonesome. Maybe a little
scared himself.

"Yeah, that's good then. She'll be all right. You're lucky;
mine sounds like a 747." He sucked his teeth and shifted in the
seat. "What the hell is keeping them? If we don't beat it out of
here we're never gonna clear that storm." Lee shrugged. It was
getting to be a long excursion. He was feeling pressure to get
back to Central.

"You out of Pittsburgh?"

"Yeah."

"How's it out in Pittsburgh?"

"Crazy! Nothing moving in the streets most places. Maybe
not as bad as this though. Still got electric power in about half
the town. That helps. The traffic's piled up near the Pike and

I-79. The big roads, you know. But the further out away you get from the big arteries, the more you just get unbroken snow with lumps, buried cars spaced out here and there. Man! It's just *quiet!* Nothing moving. You wonder what's going on with all them people underneath those lumps there. Nobody's getting to them except in just a couple places. They won't even *think* about the 'boonies' for a week yet. A month if we get much more snow. You hear anything about that? I hear three feet more.''

That rocked Lee. He'd gotten six to eight from Nadel and the National Weather Service—but that was hours back. The way things had been changing, the pilot could be right. Maybe it was just the force of rumor, the energies of people impacted against an obstacle, a problem that they couldn't move. It made him again anxious to get back to Central, get his hands on things again—the unabating need to *do*. Something. Anything at all. Even if it was wrong thing.

"I hadn't heard that. I heard six to eight," said Lee.

"Yeah?" the pilot seemed to brighten. Probably he had been only testing, fishing for new information or emotional support or simply conversation. "Even so, that's plenty." He sucked his teeth and and shifted buttocks. He had been doing a lot of sitting, waiting, since before dawn. "Funny. At the airport—airport's open—I mean—they can fly them in and out, but once they get there, they can't get the passengers to town. Stuck right there. Parkway's shut down totally. Can't get them out from town. No one to board arrivals except the previous arrivals that decided to go back to where they came from. Those are the smart ones, if you want my opinion. I've seen winter storms and shutdowns, once or twice before, but from what I've seen of this one you'd be better off if you were *any* place but here." He shifted cheeks again. "You guys are *never* gonna get this mess cleaned up—you know that, don't you?"

Lee was about to say something—he didn't know just what—when the roof door opened and Woods came out, followed by a guy in white—an older guy, perhaps a doctor—followed by the same tiny mean nurse. Woods plunged straightway into the ruts he'd first made crossing from the chopper. The medicals looked at the snow ahead of them and balked. Woods turned back and exchanged comment with the two white-clads standing in the door like young birds in the nest. After some gesticulation, the doctor followed Woods; the lady stayed behind.

"Man!" Woods hoisted himself up and in. "You would not *believe* that place! Packed to the rafters! Couldn't find a doctor!"

"What's this coming?"

"Well—a doctor. Had to go down three floors. They've got them bedded in the halls, the johns—everywhere. It's nuts!"

The doctor arrived. Lee and Woods reached down and hoisted him aboard. The man was fifty and his face bore testimony to everything that Woods had said. The eyes were bloodshot, cheeks unshaven. He looked gray.

Lee nudged Jennifer. She looked up into the doctor's face. The doctor held up two fingers.

"How many fingers?"

"Five," said Jennifer.

"How many?"

"Five. Two up—three down."

The doctor backed up in disgust, his sense of humor long depleted. "How long have you had her in fresh air?"

Lee looked at his watch, 1:30 now. "Forty minutes."

"And you gave her oxygen?"

"Yes."

"It doesn't figure."

"What doesn't?" Lee asked.

But the doctor addressed himself to Jennifer again. "How do you feel?"

"Lousy."

"Be more explicit."

"Headache. Sick. I can't wake up. Legs hurt."

"It doesn't figure," said the doctor.

"What doesn't?" Lee asked as before.

"Well, with monoxides—unless they're virtually dead, and I mean *dead*—a couple hits of oxygen should stand them up, bright-eyed and bushy-tailed."

"No aftereffects?"

"Shouldn't really be."

"The house was full of gas," Woods ventured. "Maybe she got some of that before she went out to the garage."

"I don't know," said Jennifer.

"Wouldn't you have smelled it?" asked the doctor.

"Maybe not," she said. "I—well I *was* doing a little drinking I remember now."

"How much?" asked the doctor.

"Four martinis." She looked a little guilty. "I *think* four, anyway."

"Touch of gas perhaps," the doctor said. "Hung over definitely."

"For heaven's sake, Jen! What were you thinking of?"

"I'm sorry, Lee! I couldn't get in touch with you, the phones were always busy and Charlie didn't call and then I heard all that stuff going on on the scanner and then the lights went out and no TV, no radio. I didn't know what to do. I guess I went a little crazy. I've been a fool, huh?"

"Yep." Lee hugged her with the arm he'd had about her shoulder, squeezed her hard enough to reassure her. "I'm the fool," he said. "I should've brought you in last night."

The doctor had gotten up to go.

"Should we leave her? Do you want to keep her?" Lee asked.

The doctor shook his head. "I suppose we'd do it any other time. The way things are in there, she'll be better off at home, or someplace she can rest and get clean air. Just let her sleep it off. See your own doctor in a week or so."

"I—I'm sorry doctor," said Jennifer. "I actually forgot."

The doctor turned to Woods on leaving. "If you can get us anything we certainly could use it."

"What do you need?"

"Blood. Oxygen. Anti-biotics. Toilet paper. Five hundred beds. A triple staff. Faith healers. God. A miracle."

Woods rolled two of the Red Cross bundles out onto the roof.

"Merry Christmas," he said. "This isn't much, but then again, it isn't absolutely zero either. We'll be back immediately after the bad weather. We'll bury you with goodies then."

The doctor shrugged and nodded. They left him staring glumly at the canvas bundles as the chopper lifted off for Redford Central.

"God! I feel so dumb!" said Jennifer. "I forgot, Lee. It's the truth. I honestly forgot! That doctor—I don't suppose he believed me, did he?"

"I believe you," said Lee.

He meant it. Jennifer was not a drinker. Four martinis would've put her on her can. In fact, they had.

SOMERSTON HOSPITAL—1:35 P.M.

The pay phone in the hospital had been so full of coins that not one more could be inserted. Braden had gone out and up and down the streets and through the south end of the town and business district of Somerston and found them all that way. Stuffed with money. So stuffed they could accept no more. He arrived at the idea of breaking one of the cash boxes open, cleaning it out to make the phone operable, when he came upon one that had fallen victim to that same idea. Whoever did it wasn't solely after money. A lot of coins were trampled into the floor. He got some clean coins from his pocket, tried no less than seven times. The phone was bent-up looking, but seemed functional. Sometimes he'd get a busy signal, other times he would get nothing. Silence. No dial tone or anything. He gave up on phoning after that and started back toward the hospital. On the way he spent eleven dollars for three apples, one bag of pretzels and half-dozen packages of those little creme-filled cakes from people along the way. You couldn't get things from the stores. Whatever there was came from people in cars sitting in the street with things to sell.

He walked straight into the hospital. There were no guards or anyone to stop or even challenge him, he simply walked in and picked his way among the floor squatters in the hall until he found Irene and Chris where he had left them.

Chris seemed brighter. She was glad to get the pretzels.

Irene took Dan aside.

"Oh, Dan!"

"What is it?" What's the matter?"

"There's nothing wrong with her. She's perfectly okay. Well, not okay, but *okay* not-okay, you understand?"

"What is it?"

"It's her period. Her first period. Didn't know what it was."

"Did she see a doctor?"

"No. She went to the john and then came back and got me, terrified."

"For crying out loud, Irene! Didn't you tell her in advance? Give her some idea of what to expect?"

"Sure I did. More or less. Look, it's tough the first couple times. It manifests itself in lots of ways before it settles down. And she does feel bad, I guarantee you. It's a hard thing to get used to."

He looked at his watch, 2:30. He had heard the storm would come at 3, 3:30. They hadn't time to get back to the car; he hadn't seen anyplace preferable to where they were in the town. Whether Chris truly required a hospital or not was an issue of much lower priority than shelter now. Here they were. Here they had better stay, he said to Irene. She nodded and agreed. If a doctor or medic or whatever ever came they would simply play dumb as they had been before they knew what it was. Let the hospital mess with it. The storm would soon be upon them and they would refuse to leave. They doubted whether they would have to. Nobody was going to force them out into a blizzard.

There was a diversion in the hallways. Some sort of excitement. Peanut butter sandwiches made on flat Syrian bread were being passed among them. A sled-train load of the sandwiches had been sent over from an outpost kitchen at the United Church of Christ. The sandwiches were strange on the chewy flat Syrian bread—but very good with hunger. Very good indeed.

Dan felt dumb about shelling out the eleven dollars. His supply of ready cash was low.

REDFORD CENTRAL—1:35 P.M.

The chopper set down in the parking lot at Central at 1:55. Arch Reese was waiting for them there. Lee and Jennifer got out expecting Woods to follow. He did not. Nor did the pilot cut his engine. Instead, Arch Reese climbed into the hatch behind them.

"Will you be in Pittsburgh?" Lee screamed.

Woods shook his head. "Philadelphia headquarters. Then Washington. Outside the range of this until it's over."

"Courageous of you!"

Woods shrugged. "If Santa Claus is going to come Wednesday, he's got to pack the sleigh. See you Wednesday!" He started to slip back into the chopper, but leaned out again. "And good luck." he said.

Lee would have preferred he hadn't. When you wished somebody luck, they usually need it. Man and woman clung together as the downdraft from the rising helicopter tore at their hair. Woods watched from the doorway. Lee recognized a stab of feeling of desertion. That wouldn't do; the next step would be self-pity and that whole endless maze of games. A mechanism in him set about to wall that feeling over, confine it and keep it harmless as they watched the helicopter go. It rose straight till it was high enough for direct distance travel and went east—a black mosquito in a bright but now slightly clouding sky. Lee took Jennifer inside when it was gone.

The lower floors were still a brawl of bawling infants and haggard refugees. The grumbling mob had doubled, a little more staff and volunteer help had made it in—those who lived in Redford—as more of the streets had opened.

Lee was anxious to get Jennifer a quiet place to sleep, and get himself to work below. Many things to do. He'd take her to the third floor. The sofa in Chuck's inner office would be the best he could do. The inner dorms would be a snoring jam of cops and operators grabbing Z's. No place for his lady.

Three guys from the armory were in Chuck's office setting up that military radio. Lee had forgotten all about that. The private link to Harrisburg, the Governor's Mansion. Chuck was standing by, looking somewhat invaded.

"Why up here?" Lee asked.

Chuck squinted at him over the tops of his glasses.

"You're the radio man. What are you asking me for? Hi, Jennifer."

"Hi, Chuck."

One of the guardsmen looked up from his modules.

"Excuse me, sir. In answer to your question it's a matter of antennas. We had to put them on the roof and there was no reasonable way to run the coax all the way down to the basement. I understand you can be paged anywhere within the building through the intercom though.''

It made sense. So be it. Now to ask a favor. Chuck had the biggest sofa in the building—Jen was six feet tall.

"Chuck, we need your sofa.''

"It squeaks.'' Chuck looked mock-apologetic. Lee looked suddenly a little dumb.

"Not that!'' Jennifer grinned and gave the little guy a playful shove.

"Chuck you're *horrible!* Imagine, Lee! His *office!*—Public Relations—''

Lee kept his eye on Chuck.

A soldier dropped some pieces of apparatus and stooped to get it.

"The tall comedian here is sick and should lie down on something six feet long.''

"What happened?'' Chuck was serious again and guiding them into his inner office.

"Went by the house, it was full of gas, bashed out a set of brand-new energy conserving triple-pane-super-expensive storm windows, left the doors wide open, found her in the garage passed out in her car with the ignition on. The gas tank empty. If she weren't such a procrastinator about keeping up her car, I'd be buying a black suit now.''

"How would you look in black? I wonder.'' Jennifer put a finger to his lips to end this talk.

Lee bit the finger.

"Lonesome.''

He untangled himself from her lanky arms and made a double jointed pile of her on the big, plush couch. Chuck produced a quilt from somewhere. Lee spread it over his gorgeous and ungainly woman and tucked it close around her chin.

"How's that?''

"Super!''

He and Chuck began to leave the room. Jennifer was murmuring, already drifting off—still pretty dopey from her toxic overnighter.

"Lee?" Jennifer spoke with her eyes closed.

"Yeah?"

"Charlie knows the number here?"

"By heart," he said. "At least three of them."

HOSPITAL IN SOMERSTON—2:00 P.M.

The flat-top guy in the hotel had told them exactly right. They had gone south on Main Street #219 and come finally to the sign at the edge of town and now stood outside the small Somerston Hospital. People were thick around the driveways and the entrances. A hospital security guard showed up from nowhere and stopped them at the door on account of the dog. The shotgun didn't seem to bother him. They retreated to the corner curbstone. Em would wait outside and watch Daisy and the gun. Ed was medium suspicious. She wasn't going to run away. She wanted him to get the other money and finish up the sale. The price the flat-top guy had quoted was more than she had combining Ed's deposit money and her own. Not enough to get a ticket and eat for a week, if need be. She wanted it to work out as much as he did now and besides she wouldn't know his folks and they would not know her, so how else could the thing be done? Ed couldn't get around that logic. He was satisfied about Em, but there were other reasons that he hated to go in. It was risky several ways. Number one was that after having lost him overnight his folks would not let go of him again. He'd have to stay. It would be like Butch Cassidy turning himself in. That would be the end of it right there. They might be around this town for days and he'd be chained to one place like a backyard dog.

Em mulled it over. She kept looking at the sky. It wasn't bright out anymore. The sky was clouding over. It was getting colder.

"Well, someone's got to come out for the dog," she said. "You saw they won't let no dog inside. You'll probably have to move your family."

"That's right," Ed brightened. The dog! It was terrific leverage. Thdy'd have to come out for the dog.

"You tell them I ain't falling for taking no dog off their

hands. If nobody comes out for the dog I'll leave her. I got more dogs than I need at home already. Pathetic type of dog like this type here without much hair will only freeze."

"Okay." Ed was soaking it all in. She was loading up his mind with dynamite ammunition.

"You better hurry what you're going to do," she said.

Ed still had the armload of nude magazines. He got Daisy out and stuffed the magazines into the bag. "Keep these hid when we come out," he said.

Ed found them pretty fast and with surprising ease. They were in the hallway on the ground floor and he ran into them two minutes through the door. Why not? The idea that they might not have made it or would for some other reason not be here had not occurred to him.

"EDDIE!" His mother screamed, grabbed him and kissed all over his head and got tears in his hair. He knew she was going to do that. Another part of why he didn't want to come in altogether. Now he stuck it out—it had to pass. Nobody kept up that kind of stuff up very long. The worst part was the people looking at them.

His dad pulled him out of it. His dad was looking kind of choked up too.

"I got your note," Ed said.

"What happened to you? Where did you spend the night?"

"I got in a camper with some guys. Some guys took me in their camper. What's the matter with Chris?"

"Mother, if you tell him I will never speak to you again," said Chris. "I swear to God. Not *ever!*"

It's—well it turned out not to be as serious as we first thought."

"You finally get your period, huh?"

"Mom!!!!"

"Eddie, you're atrocious! I don't ever want to hear you say a thing like that again!"

"So what? They teach about it at school. Films in living color. Everything. It's natural!"

"Shut up about it, Ed."

"But—"

"Knock it off, Ed. I mean it."

His Dad did, in fact, mean it.

"I got the dog outside," he said. "They won't let her in."

"Daisy?" Chris was overjoyed.

"They won't let dogs in. Hey, Dad, come outside, I need to talk to you a minute."

"What about?"

"Just come out. I need to talk to you about a thing out here. Come on."

"Where?"

"Just outside. Come on."

Em was waiting at the curbstone where he'd left her with the dog and bowling bag and shotgun. Ed introduced her. She nodded soberly at his old man and shook his hand like Gary Cooper. Courteous and distant and one simple shake.

"I need part of my money, Dad. I owe this kid twelve dollars."

"Twelve dollars? What for?"

Ed went through the whole thing. Em listened to it all coming out of him exactly as she thought it would. Especially the part about not getting the eight dollars back, expecting to be picked up by the heels and having those eight dollars shaken out of her. But the kid's dad was okay. The kid's dad was onto him.

"He won't go back on his deal," said Dan. "You keep the money. Thanks for helping him get down."

"Hey! It's my money! I can do with it what I want."

"Ed, we're low on cash. I have to commandeer your money for the family till we're out of this. No telling how long that's going to be."

"Yeah, but that's *my money*."

"Sure it is. You'll get every nickel of it too. When we get home. Ed, I spent eleven dollars and got three apples and some twinkies. Twelve dollars is a big share of our cash. You know I don't carry a lot of cash. They won't take checks or credit cards or anything."

"You shouldn't be spending anything on food," said Ed. "They're giving soup and sandwiches out free up in the town. A bunch of places."

"I know. They sent some here. I didn't know it then. Come inside. There's supposed to be another storm. We're staying here."

"They won't let Daisy in," said Ed.

Dan looked at the sky. He could see his breath again. It was getting cold.

"We can't leave her out here," Ed went on. "She hasn't got enough hair. She'll die."

It was never straightforward with Ed. Every situation was an intricate ecology of compromises. There was no way that he could be so dumb as to let Ed get separated from the family again. Not after that same mistake had just been so improbably forgiven. For several moments nobody thought of anything to say.

"Well, I better go," said Em.

"No, wait. I'm coming, too."

"You are not!"

"I got to, Dad. I'll find a place and then come back and get you."

The kid was more than normally resourceful. Dan wasn't that concerned for the well-being of Ed himself, but Ed was dreadful to keep track of. He was like a spy from some other family finding out everything there was to know about you. Always experimenting, getting strange reactions out of life. Ed would probably be able to accomplish what he said he would. He'd probably get them someplace to recline on silk pillows and be fed fresh seafood and girls with flowers in their hair to bathe their feet.

"Make it someplace close," he said. "Make it within an hour."

Ed and Daisy ran to catch up with Em who had set off on her own and was half a city block closer to the Main Street than they were when they broke away from Dan. She was toting the gun and the bowling bag and magazines and everything.

"Thanks for not dumping out the magazines," he said.

"Take them out or else take this whole thing."

She handed him the bag and he lofted the entire thing. It was heavier in weight, but was a single, unified object and easier to manage.

They reached Main Street #219, again, and headed north into the thick of town.

REDFORD CENTRAL—2:10 P.M.

Lee got a sloppy stack of papers handed to him when he came into the little foyer of the "cage." Emmert singled out a note from the Forest Service, a memo to Eastern that there was a human body hanging from the Number 12 repeater tower. Was Eastern aware?

"And you said what?"

"I said we didn't know. Who is it, Weeks?"

Lee nodded. "Keep it to yourself," he said. "I'll tell you later."

"Everybody saw this, I think. It attracted some attention."

"Then everybody just shut up about it. We'll do something when we can."

"They said they can't get up there. They were out scouting for lost hunters. The snowmobiles can't make it up that rocky steep stuff at the top because the snow's too wet and melting. They saw him through binoculars."

"What else?" said Lee. "What about the storm?"

"The same. 3:30."

"And that's all?" Lee sat down on the steps of the "cage" and took the galoshes off. His feet were wet inside. He had forgotten his intent to get his good boots from the house in the thick smell of sour gas. Maggie's boots would take him through a lot if he could just once dry his feet.

"The backlog has been cleared off up as far as Willow Hill—170.0 They were trying to clear it west as far as where #70 breaks off at Breezeway and Penn Dot is working up from the south on #70 to tie into it and help disperse these cars and stuff all south, but we still have 27 miles to go from Willow Hill. There just won't be time. Of course they're going to go on plowing through the storm, but who'll drive it once it's open? It's too bad too because the ground is bare and dry in Hagerstown. We could get rid of a hell of a lot of these cars."

"Did anybody turn up any fuel for the generator?"

"Chelinski turned up a guy with four barrels of it someplace up by Kregg this morning. Two hunert gallon, but it didn't come to us. We took it to the hospital. They're in tougher shape than we are."

What could Lee say? It was a clear priority.

"Leaving us with—what?"

"Hunert-forty gallons as of two o'clock."

Lee gave his little shop-disaster whistle. That wouldn't see them through the night. It wouldn't see them through midnight. They had followed his orders about the use of lights in the building, saving everything for the electronics, to keep the "brain" alive. Still the fuel was going much too quickly.

"We haven't quit trying," Emmert continued.

"What about repeaters?" It was time that some of them could well be running dry or showing up the "gnomes" in their local generators, working so long now after having lain idle for so long. These power failures usually did not persist so many hours.

"So far we're talking good across the mountains. Something happened between Pittsburgh and West Gate though—can't raise anybody. Whether Numbers 1 and 3 went out or whether the guys are just not in their cars is hard to say, but it's like the finance company just come in and ripped out everything from Pittsburgh to Ohio."

There was a buzz from the telecoms behind him in the "cage." Lee went up and punched the button. One of the new guys that had made it in, Tom Poltz, was looking at him from the Zone 2 console.

"Chief, the Troop "T" captain's on the VHF, the gates at Somerston. Wants to talk to you in particular."

"Patch him in."

"Lee?"

"Tell me stories of success and warmth and flowing traffic."

"Are you crazy? This is total bullshit here! You can't turn these people back! This Woods guy is completely nuts!"

"What are you doing?"

"Exactly what we said. We set up a barricade and PA sets on the ramps and blocked that lane they opened up with the trucks last night. We got the mayor here, the county coroner here, me and Prokovic and LaBarr and all the local vigilantes on their snowmobiles. It's like keeping flies off shit; it can't be done."

"What's the matter, have you got a riot on your hands?"

"Hell no! There's just so many of them they walk past us like we weren't even there. I feel like one of these Hari Krishnas or somebody. We're just being ignored except people asking directions to things in town."

"Have you tried the CB thing? What about that?"

"Lee, the locals have been talking with these guys up on the Pike since way last night already. They got common sense enough to have been telling them exactly what the bright boy said right along: they better stay put in their cars and most of them are. They've got a decent radio net set up that reaches almost to Irwin. They're miles ahead of us. Point is—most people are staying with their cars—maybe 20 percent abandoning. But 20 percent of the amount of people we got out here is overwhelming. You ought to have a look at the streets in Somerston now. You thought this morning was something, you ought to see it now."

"So what do you want to do, cash it in?"

"No. I'm not saying *that!* Some are listening and going back, but suppose it was you and you had walked five miles? The thing seems to be what Woods was saying: keep them from leaving in the first place. Haven't they been putting this stuff on the radio and TV? You know, that whole campaign!"

"I don't know. I just got in myself. Haven't been listening to the radio."

"Where were you?"

"I stopped by the house for other shoes."

"Well, good idea. You needed them."

"You're staying with the gates, then?"

"No point in going into Somerston!"

"It's really *that* bad?"

"Maybe not. Maybe it's just the streets, but it looks like it from here. We may be doing some good, but it doesn't *seem* that way. It seems like we're not accomplishing one damn thing."

"Join the club."

"I'm breaking off. Check out that radio thing."

"I will. You're going to rough this storm out at the gates?"

"10-4. Dig a hole or something. It's clouding up in the west already. Maybe the weather will stop them from getting out of their cars. Then again it just might work the other way. We're going to hang around and see."

"Let us know if you change locations."

"10-4."

Lee rocked all the way back in the swivel chair and cracked his knuckles, gazing at the interphone. He thought of getting Poltz to patch the zones together and make some sweeping general announcement, but there wasn't anything that he could say that everybody on the turnpike didn't know already. With a hundred million dollars worth of communications apparatus it could hardly be said that talk was cheap, but at the moment it seemed worthless.

He punched the interphone and dialed Chuck's extension, to pursue Beck's request and find out what Chuck had done about the media and about the education of the staff at Redford, but Chuck changed the subject before it had a chance.

"Lee," said Lee.

"Good," said Chuck. "I wanted you. These guys have got this radio thing set up with Harrisburg. Turlock's on. He want to talk."

"I'm coming up" said Lee.

REDFORD CENTRAL—2:17 P.M.

What they had was two complete transceivers, two identical narrow-band FM systems on two different frequencies. Duplex. Anybody listening would get only half the conversation. For service radio it was luxurious. You could talk simultaneously, like telephone. It was nice not to have to deal with all that "10-4," "roger" and radio procedure garbage.

Turlock sounded overwhelmed and very tired.

"We've got problems, Lee."

"These are new ones, I assume. Not the ones I know about."

"We don't have the federal declaration yet. It's been an ugly Monday in D.C. People coming straight out of an extended weekend, lethargic and unwilling to face a giant crisis. We set off a lot of bickering. How to go at this? What's best to do? Where to start it? Who knows? Everbody sees it different. Everybody wants to be a star.

"Will we get it?"

"Oh, we'll get it. We'll get the declaration, eventually we'll get help. No problem there. This kind of thing's political hay— chance to do something spectacular. What they're bickering about is who gets to give it to us and how. The governor's gone down to Washington in the faint hope that maybe we'll get a small chance to participate in some of these decisions. Still waiting to hear. What's up with you guys?"

"Trying to get these idiots to stay in their cars."

"Having any luck?"

"I don't know, Sherm. Hard to figure. Have you guys made any moves to get the media behind this—what we talked about this morning—that radio and TV stuff?"

"I don't know. The public relations office here has been talking to some stations, I think. When they can get through. Scattered rare occasions. They're putting out a lot of take-it-easy."

"Sherman, it's important, don't you think? We've got a crisis situation in Somerston. All the exit towns are overrun. The place is overrun. This blizzard's due within a goddam hour!"

"I know—I know! We've been up to here in trying to get the power lines restored. That's been the priority. Two-thirds of the state is blacked completely out! We got half a million sitting on the Pike; millions freezing in their homes, dying in their respirators. Food rotting in refrigerators. There are officially *no* roads open, by the way. The governor has followed the Ohio and New York example. Shut down everything. Now comes the question: how do you get around to put up power lines again? We can't communicate. Do you know a guy walked over here from the phone company this morning to explain why the phones were so screwed up? The goddam phone company couldn't call us on the phone. The State Capital. He couldn't call! That's a first for me, I'm telling you!"

"Sherman—"

"Lee, this thing is shaping up into the worst natural disaster in U.S. history. San Francisco Quake, Johnstown Flood—or should I say floods—Hurricane Camille. This one's going to set the records. It involves so many *people!* It's gone beyond what we were talking about this morning—they *will* send in the Army Corps of Engineers. The special snow guys up from Fort Bragg and it looks like full divisions of the army. They have to. There's nothing else to do. It looks now as if they'll organize along the southern edges of the region and push north as soon as the storm begins to break and come up the major roads at first—probably before it breaks. Whatever comes has got to come from outside; everything within the disaster region is snowbound—as you well know. And they're going to step on toes and break things. They're going to use the dozers if that's what it takes. It can't be helped. We have to open roads. This hit us just exactly perfect. Brother. What a sense of timing. The Russians couldn't have devised it better."

"Sherman, I believe you! I'm not arguing. I do think a radio campaign for the sake of all those people is still a damn valid idea—whether they're in cars, houses, hotels or whatever. Every individual stuck someplace out there is interested in one thing only: direct help. For himself and himself alone. When they hear that Washington has mobilized, each one of them will naturally assume it's coming straight for him. That the army and the Red Cross teams might have one or two things lined up ahead of him just won't occur. When he sees the help arrive, but helping someone else, he's going to get mad and do dumb things. If he doesn't know it's coming, he's going to do dumb things. If we don't structure some of this ahead of time—while they're just sitting there—prepare them for what to expect, it'll be criminal. We have to talk to them. Say something. Talk should be the easiest and most effective thing that we could do right now. This moment. That much I agree with Woods. I agree with it completely. We have to shine the light on ourselves and our activities. We have to let them know that someone cares!"

"I'm sure these stations are already broadcasting on their own. It's big news. They wouldn't miss it."

"Don't you think that if we let the media run free with it they'll paint this into Black Monday, revel in the death tolls, the big numbers. You think that's wise? You think it's intelligent?"

"Lee, there aren't any stations operating in the affected area except two in Pittsburgh, the only island of electrical power between here and Fort Wayne."

"Speaking of Fort Wayne, Sherman, you can hear WOWO almost anywhere along the Pike. WRVA Richmond, KMOX St. Louis. Especially at night. Sherman, when you talk to Washington—and Woods has gone there too, he'll be pulling for this, he better be or we've been stabbed—just remind him of these big clear-channel stations. We can address anybody in the shut-down region with them. The locals have been trying to work it with police and CB nets here and having some success, believe it or not. People can take it if they only know what's happening, but we're still getting too many vehicular desertions. Start talking to them. You said you were going to start this. What happened?"

"This guy really sold you, didn't he?"

"Yes, he did. How are you getting through to Washington?"

"We have another setup like the one we're talking over now. The only place left in the country you can get a phone call through is up in the Dakotas, Montana, like that. This is a region where everybody in the country seems to be living or be from or have relatives. Incredible."

"How bad were we hit in Harrisburg?"

"Nothing at all. Not worth shoveling the walks. We had a couple inches, but it's gone. Melted. We're supposed to get it in this next storm though. Is it hitting you yet?"

"Not quite. Pittsburgh maybe."

"Ohio's into temperature like +4 and 50-mile-an-hour winds. Batten the hatches. By the way, there may be news. There's half a chance this thing won't last through Wednesday. It could end soon."

"How much sooner?" Lee perked up.

"I don't know. All we hear is a 30 : 70 probability it may not last as long, but if so—it's going to be worse. It'll all be there compressed—like playing 33's at 45. My kids do that. It drives me up the walls.'' Turlock broke off in an extravagant yawn. "Whoof! My God, Lee, we been at it every second solid since yesterday. I got a chance to grab a couple hours and I'm going to. Got to. I'll look into that radio business. Call you after a while.''

"Do it, Sherman. By all means.''

Lee turned to Chuck. "Who have you been able to talk to?''

"KDKA Pittsburgh. That's it. I told them what we want. They seemed to know. They said the Red Cross had gotten hold of them before.''

"How did you get through?''

"We relayed through the VHF to Pittsburgh where they had a phone connection with the Gibson Barracks, but now that's gone.'' Chuck shrugged. "We lost the connection somehow.''

Emmert had mentioned the dark spot on the system west of Pittsburgh. When line power to the repeaters failed, a relay would trip instantly and connect the robot to a bank of storage batteries and start a gasoline generator. Maybe the repeaters were starting to go. Pittsburgh surprised him though—the one place west of Harrisburg that still had current. Who knew what was going on out there?

"Have you got a radio?''

"You mean a regular radio?''

"Yeah.''

"On my desk, sure.''

Lee looked at his watch: 2:55. Hourly news coming up. That storm ought to be hitting Pittsburgh just about now. Chuck did not come into the office with him. He had something else to do downstairs. Lee remembered the slip of paper Maggie Pribanic had given him, gave it to Chuck to take down to the trooper at the desk. He instructed Chuck to have the trooper make a copy so that it would not get lost.

Lee slid quietly behind the desk, easing down into the chair so that it wouldn't squeak. Jennifer continued to sleep soundly on the couch, her small, soft snore uninterrupted. Lee switched on the set with care not to have a sudden burst of volume, found the big Pittsburgh station at 1020 on the dial but never heard the news. All his efforts and exertions, lack of sleep and exposure to the gas caught up with him. By 3 P.M., he was oblivious to everything.

SOMERSTON—THE CENTRAL SQUARE

It was simply luck that they found a place to sit. A couple with a baby stood up near them and the kids grabbed the space. Resting places were a rare prize now. In the time it had taken them to get back to the central square the density of people had trebled.

And it was colder. Overhead the sky was grayer. For the first time since the early morning Em's denim jacket was no longer adequate. She blew on her hands and hunched her shoulders against the cold and the glacier of people flowing past. Em's instinct to get clear of large concentrations of people had risen high inside her and she felt irritable and vaguely suffocated. She looked at Ed with his ridiculous fat dog and for the moment hated them as two more living things pressing in on her with needs competing with her own.

"We just going the same way out of chance? Or what?" She spoke abruptly. It was the first thing she had said since the hospital.

"Where are you going now?" Ed was stung a little and being stung made him mad at himself. When it happened he saw that he still had corners in himself where occasionally people would become important to him without his knowing it—his prime weakness, the one big obstacle between himself and getting rich enough to survive his own imagined future. He was angry at himself, as always, for having been surprised, but deftly recovered by going to the next logical stage of discussion without batting an eye, as though it was what he had been thinking all along. He was gaining skill at this, he knew. If he couldn't overcome it altogether he could get to where no one would ever know.

And she was right, on her side. The gun deal that had bound them together had come to an end. They had reached the hospital and hadn't got the money. The gun and his eight dollars were hers and that was it. It hadn't come out happily. She'd gone miles out of her way not once but twice and couldn't benefit by it because there were no buses. Now she would have to eat on the money till they got the town cleaned out and working again. He had his folks. She didn't. He would be taken care of. There was no reason they should stay together now.

She wrinkled up her nose and squinted at the leaden sky, watched a couple gritty little flakes of snow go by, the hard compact kind that came from somewhere very cold. She shrugged and spat, but not tobacco. She had not chewed since entering the town. It seemed like she had to do it to get her mouth cleaned up for talking.

"Where do you expect to go?" Ed was grinning a little. Where was there to go? If there was any other place to go the people would be going there.

"Beats hell out of me," she said. "Someplace out of here. This whole thing looks bad to me." Hole up someplace. Further out though. Something bad is coming up. Too many people."

"Like what for instance?"

"I don't know. Too many people, that's all."

"Stampedes and old grandmothers getting trampled and stuff like that?"

"I don't know what exactly. When you get a lot of people bunched together in the same place it's bad. The more there is, the worse. It's a hard-fast rule. I'm gettin' out."

"Where?" Ed was grinning openly now. To him it was a moot point. Academic. "Back up to your truck? Stand out in the fields? That's crazy!"

"You need to get some more of an idea about the amount of surprises contained within the world. Things ain't always what you think."

"Like what, for instance?"

"Well, I don't know. That's the thing of it. They wouldn't be surprises."

"Aw, I heard that old crap before. It's dumb. You get the junk when you think that way."

"You get the junk anyhow. There's more junk than good stuff. That's why it's junk. It's raining down on ever'body all the time. You got to sharpen up your eye to see it through."

"What?"

"The junk. The shucks. The garbage."

That impressed Ed deeply. She knew exactly what he meant about the junk and how that's what you wound up with if you weren't super-careful all the time. Most kids didn't. Most grown-ups either. But Ed knew all about that part of it. What he didn't know was how to ferret out the goodies straightaway without foraging through all that other stuff first. The way she talked she had more advanced information than his own. Ed smelled sharpened skills. And profits. He was vastly interested.

"Stamps and rare antiques and miser money?"

"Naw, that's TV junk. I mean mostly what you need to get you off the hook. Out of trouble when you need it. You don't need no more'n that. That'll do the job. But you don't know what it will look like or where it's coming out of. You got to train your eye to see."

"I don't get it."

"I fell off a barn one time and the whole way down I thought I was going to die and didn't." She thought some more. "And then one time I had these bills for feed t' pay and needed more and work came up from no place and I got square. That happened more'n one time." She thought again. "And then that business about runts and that."

"Runts?"

"Like runts of the litter. Cats and pigs and animals and stuff. Most people don't know it and they never pick 'em, but they're smarter. Way, way smarter. I had a hunting beagle promised me for work I done these people? Well, they never told me of the births till all the good ones was sold off and just this runt female in the basket. I took it on account of that is what I figured on for my Pa's Christmas, this was the *night* before, and so I took her—smartest dog we ever had or knowed of. Best dog, too; better than a person. Cats the same. Seen it a bunch of times. Always keep the runt and let the others go. If they survive they're gonna be exceptional; they got to be. They're given something. Helps them make it to the tit amongst the others."

She paused, then looked hard at Ed. She looked him up and down.

"I don't suppose you're to your full height yet," she said.

"Aw, heck no. My old man's six-one."

"Yer Ma's side?"

"Big too."

Em shook her head, spat out of habit. It seemed the knell of doom. The end for Ed. She didn't say a thing.

At last Ed couldn't stand it. "So what?"

"I've thought about it some. Napoleon was little. Alan Ladd. Hitler. Little guys."

"Because I'm going to get big I can't make it, is that it?"

"Lot of times it's these little guys that's looking for a fight. The pushiest. The bullies. Bantam roosters and the like. Bears thinking about."

"Baloney! Rockefeller's tall. He ain't a midget or nothing. John Wayne. Lot of big guys. Stinking rich. Loaded. Standing up on tippy-toes so as not to get suffocated by their money."

She nodded, gave it her usual sober thought.

"Goes to show, " she said. "You can't always have it figured, can ya?" She paused. "It's true of runts though. The runts is smarter. Ever' time."

It was really getting colder now, breezier and kicking up in small gusts with more of the hard little snowflakes in them. Ed had his hands jammed hard into the pockets of his jacket and rocked back and forth, kicking his legs against the wall. Em stood up suddenly on the wall to see above the crowds.

"I can't talk for you, but I'm getting off this main street here, and goin' out to the west."

Ed stood up too to see in that direction also. The people were all coming toward them from the west on old Route #31 and almost none going in the other direction. The side streets they could glimpse a little of seemed less overrun.

They backtracked a block on Main Street #219 going south because the influx from the west on #31 was so heavy and because the northern half of town was so much more worse than it had been before and all the flow of it would be against them. It was against them anyway when they stopped going south and turned the corner. It was tough going no matter where you turned.

MILEPOST 109—THE GATES—5:30 P.M.

The storm had not hit all at once, but in the quantity of time between 3 and 5 P.M. the world had gone from balmy sunshine to a shrieking, bitter ice blast, a vicious screaming from the pitch of night that tried to remove your hide, that seemed to come at you with equal hatred from all sides.

Beck looked at his watch: 5:30. Christ! This night would last forever! But it was the half-hour at last; his shift was up. He left the barrel fire that they were keeping by the toll booth and returned to car 337 parked just beyond the other side. They had managed to get it over from the westbound earlier and it was now their only refuge. The booths themselves had no heat or light and offered insufficient space for comfort.

The captain squeezed into the car with Stokes, Prokovic and the mayor and displaced Officer LaBarr out to the barrel to do his fifteen minutes. Fifteen minutes at a time was plenty. Perhaps they would discontinue the watches soon. The storm seemed to have pretty much accomplished what they had not been able to: it stopped the flow of people into town.

As the weather worsened, the lines from both the east and west slopes dwindled proportionately, became intermittent and they saw hardly any of them now that it was dark and painful to expose oneself to the weather. Stokes and Pribanic were stuck now. There was strong reason to doubt that they could find their way back into town until the weather lightened up. In any case, the shifts were among the captain, Prokovic and LaBarr and not the stubby mayor of the town of Somerston. They didn't want to go. And it did no harm to have two extra bodies radiating heat within the car.

The captain slammed the door quickly after LaBarr and blew on his stinging hands. From inside the car they all were blind. It was dark and frost had grown thickly on the glass—the frozen condensed moisture of their breathing. The captain fired the motor and would let it run awhile to make up for the heat lost when the door was opened. No more. The car had slightly more than a half tank of gas. They could add that to the list—another reason to cut out the watches.

The captain wondered where all those people had gone. In fact, the captain wondered what the hell he was doing there himself.

SOMERSTON—5:30 P.M.

The worsening weather was having the effect of clearing people off the streets and driving them to shelter as it had done on the Pike—whatever shelter was at hand and what there was was getting tight. People were jamming into doorways, empty cars, sheltered alleys. Trash dumpsters. Anything. It was dark and freezing cold now. The kids found themselves still in the blasting winds at the northwest edge of town, starting to backtrack to the south again having found nothing suitable for Ed's whole family and dog. They had left the square originally and gone west. The town had petered out quickly to the west and south in farm fields and farm-type things like barbed wire and tractors and outbuildings and the naked winter vegetation standing darkly out of the snow. They had then turned north and crossed #31 and explored the northwest quadrant which had developed much more strongly than the south and seemed to have more to offer. But other people had come first. They found themselves caught out in the storm and hurting for it. Ed had given up thoughts of getting his family and bringing them to someplace all together. There were no such places. They were safe and warm now. It was *Ed* that Ed worried for.

Em led. She had the flashlight she had packed into the bowling bag. The night was so thick and vicious that he could just make out the beam. They were linked together by the shotgun on their shoulders, the dog between suspended from the bag as always. It seemed to Ed they had been on this snow safari for a thousand years. He didn't know where she was leading. They were more or less feeling their way from car to car. What did she have in mind? At last he'd had enough. He shouted for her to hold up a minute.

She shined the light beam in his face, about as far as it would reach.

"What?" she shouted.

"Where are we going now?" Both of them were screaming to surmount the wind.

"Barn!"

"What barn!?"

"Big wood one by the road, remember?"

Maybe he did remember. There were a couple of them hard by the road. Just a ditch and one strand of barbed wire separating them. They had passed a big one on the way—maybe it was that one—but it was near the edge of town and it seemed to him they would have passed it by now. He said that to her.

"No," she said. "I don't think so."

"Well, where?"

"Close here someplace. We got to get off the road. Follow that bob-wire now."

"Aw, man—"

"Can't see. This light won't make it. We have to."

"What's in your dumb barn?"

"Don't know! How should I know? Got to beat this!"

"Won't it be stuffed with people as the other places?"

"Don't know till we look at it."

She started off again. He followed. She left the road and headed as near due west as she could reckon and they crossed the ditch. Within a few more yards they came to the strand of barbed wire. The cold had caused the snow that had partly melted during the day to harden and become rock-solid and dependable to walk upon and this provided at least one advantage.

A toss-up now. Decision to be made. She thought the barn was south of them, but it might not be. In that case they would follow the rusted strand of wire a half a mile or more before they were sure of their error. It was hard to gauge how far you'd gone. They could go back and forth a dozen times until they wore themselves down and froze—thinking they had gone a mile when it was really just a couple hundred feet or so. The night kept getting worse and she knew that it had thrown her sense of distance off already. They had to get to shelter quick. It had to be one way or the other.

She didn't think they'd passed the barn.

"Which way?" he demanded.

"That way!" She pointed the beam south.

"No!" he said. "We're past it!"

"I don't believe it," she said.

"Well, you go that way then," he said. "I'm going this!"

She went south and despite what Ed had said he followed.

The fence led almost at once into a thick stand of bare sumac that proved impassable and they were forced to let the wire go and circumvent the thick and stubby branches, which caused further doubts about the direction. Em did not recall this vegetation. There had been trees and bushes and so forth, but they had not paid attention to them. The sumac got thicker and forced them so far out from the strand of fence that they were in the ditch again and Em lost sight of it, out of reach of the flashlight beam. It seemed the sumac would go on forever. Then it retreated from the ditch and they were able to reach the wire again quite suddenly. They followed the strand for ten feet more and came up against the corner of the barn.

It was sudden because the wire was stapled to the barn and continued beyond the edge of it. She played the beam over the planking and could not discover doors or windows, but then the beam was short and penetrating poorly into the weather. There was more sumac down along the barn so they decided to go under the wire right there. She went under and then Ed passed the gun and dog to her on the other side and came under the wire himself. They felt along the wall of the huge barn—a great wall of ancient sagging unpainted wood that seemed to go on forever. The north end was featureless. They found no doors or windows but the door appeared at last, around the corner and in the center, opposite the road and fence.

It was padlocked.

"Can we shoot it off?"

Em shook her head. "Come back in your face. Farmer'll hear it. Come and shoot you a second time."

"Well, what?"

She took the shotgun, stuck the barrel of it through the padlock, using it as a lever to twist the hasp out of the old wood. It came with a crunch, a groan, and out. She slid the door ajar about a foot, just enough for them to wriggle through, and slipped inside. Ed followed quickly, staying as near the light as possible. It was the only light there was and seemed the center of the world now. She rolled the heavy door shut behind.

Within the barn it was another universe entirely. The wind was gone—the sand-blast stinging on their faces—but it was even blacker than before and the sound had changed. It howled outside and clawed and tore at the old barn and made it sway and creak and groan in the darkness like an ancient ship in heavy seas. The kids stuck close together. Ed set the bag down and Daisy got out but stayed around their feet and did not venture into the unknown blackness. Em cast the beam of light like a rod, illuminating little round fragments of this new world—deep and spooky clues and pieces. Heavy solid beam rafters. Half a loft above them. Old machinery and unused stalls and one end of the barn stacked high with bales of straw and some alfalfa. Headlights of an old tractor flashed at them suddenly like the eyes of a great beast in the darkness.

"Yee," said Ed.

"Tractor," she said.

"I know," he said.

"How come you said 'Yee'?"

"I thought it was an animal or something for a second."

"Won't be no animals in here," she said.

"How do you know?"

"Wouldn't have a lock on it if it had animals," she said. "It's storage. Nothing more."

They inched through the barn exploring it with stabs of light. A center-door barn with the aisleway forming a "T" extending equally from them in both directions as they came in deeper from the door. To the right of them, the south, was mostly the hay. To the aisleway to the left were stalls containing sacks of feed and lime, empty sacks and some machines. The stalls had once held horses, she pointed to where great beams had been half gnawed through, now worn and sculptured looking.

"Horses don't eat wood; that's crazy!"

"Bored," she said. "Ever chew on pencils when you're bored in school?"

"Sure—I guess."

"Same as horses. Fifty years gone by and anybody knows a thing about a horse can see these stalls and know whoever had 'em was an S.O.B. and that's all that's left of him and them poor horses. Didn't love 'em enough to let them be free."

"So?"

"Nuthin'. Only if I had a choice of leavin' that behind or nuthin', nuthin's what I'd leave. He kept them in too much."

They peered over the edge of the last stall and when she shone the beam into it a cat jumped up and past them, startling both. It's eyes flashed momentarily and then it tore into other darkness elsewhere in the barn. Daisy barked after it, but didn't chase; she stayed near their legs, a coward. Em shined the beam in pursuit but couldn't see the cat. It was a huge barn with lots of stuff inside it. There could be a million cats, you'd never see them.

"I thought you said there wouldn't be no animals," said Ed. He had been badly shaken; now he was mad in the afterwave of the adrenalin.

"Cat," she said.

"I know it was a cat. You said there wouldn't be no animals."

"Cats ain't cows and horses. Can't keep cats out of a barn. Not with God's own promise, anymore'n you can keep out rats and mice."

"Rats?"

"Can't keep rats out. Not altogether. Want some cats around to keep the rats down. That's what it's doin' here."

Ed looked nervously around into the blackness, imagining a million beady little eyes peering at him from as many directions. Every time she moved the flashlight beam he thought he saw movement, something scuttle, dart for cover. It could be shadows just as easily. That was worse because you couldn't tell.

"I hate this place," said Ed.

He was freezing, dancing up and down. She was feeling the cold too. He could hear the chatter in her voice when she spoke sometimes. The still cold seemed as agonizing as the wind in its way. Maybe it was the old principle: When you got used to an improvement, at once you became dissatisfied. And that was the whole force behind human progress. His Dad had told him that and he had been watching to see if it checked out and so far it had. What he was after now was warmth. Then it would be a soft place to sleep and on and on. By morning he'd be wanting crystal chandeliers. His Dad was right. It was a force all of its own. You couldn't stop it.

"What should we do? Should we build a fire or what?"

"In this old barn with all this hay and everything?"

"Well, what are we going to do then—stand around all night and let the rats gnaw off our ankles? I'm cold!"

She led to the south end of the barn and examined the high-piled bales of hay more thoroughly with the flashlight. The bales were piled two stories high and like an ancient pyramid of Egypt made of straw. There was a narrow space between the stacks and south wall and a dirty, frosted-over window hidden there. They moved some bales to hollow out a little space, a kind of cubby-hole roughly rectangular. A little room. She broke one of the bales apart and spread it on the floor. They crawled inside and there was just room for the two of them and dog. She dug out the blanket and examined it in the flashlight. It was pretty much caked up with mud, but mostly dry, and that was the essential thing. There wasn't much to worry them about the dried mud. The carcass of the turkey had come unwrapped from the foil in the bag and was about as dirty as the blanket and the bottom half was frozen. The top half had been kept thawed by the dog. They tore off pieces and fed them to Daisy. None of them had eaten since the morning. The kids were hungry but the turkey was too smeared with mud and looked a little green and strange. The dog ate half of what there was and Em balled the rest back up in the foil and restored it to the bag. They rolled up back to back in the blanket. Ed cradled Daisy in the cavity of his abdomen.

"I'm going to shut the light off," she said.

It was total, absolute, awful darkness.

"Turn it on! Turn it on!" he said.

She turned it on.

"What's the matter?"

"The rats!"

"The rats won't get you."

"What makes you so sure?"

"Barn rats got a lot to eat. They don't need to eat on you."

There was logic in it. Ed needed logic in that answer. It felt better.

"I got to shut this light off. There won't be any batteries."

"Okay," he said.

She shut it off and the awful, rock-solid darkness pulled at his eyes again as if they could not get used to anything whatsoever to be seen. Eventually he saw a very faint outline of the window.

"I wonder where that cat is."

"Cat won't bother anybody. Go to sleep."

Gradually, Ed felt warmer. He listened to the powling and the groaning timbers. He listened to Daisy, her stomach growling like the timbers. Maybe she'd get sick on them from the spoiled turkey.

"I hate this place," he said.

She didn't answer. He could feel her back against his and she breathed slow like she was sleeping.

He guessed he didn't hate the place as much as before. He hated it, but not like before.

REDFORD—7:20 P.M.

Lee awoke in darkness, taking several minutes to sort out the darkness within from that outside himself. There was no light at all and just the sound of wind. He felt a blanket over him and leaned forward to switch on the lamp on Chuck's desk. Jennifer was no longer on the couch. He'd figured that when he'd felt the blanket. The watch said 7:20. The radio crackled softly. There was no station. She hadn't turned it off. That would have awakened him. But there was no station. He turned it up. Static. A background of jumbled distant stations, whistlings. The dial was still 1020. He turned carefully around that part of the dial a little. KDKA was off the air. More of Pittsburgh must have lost electric power. The world was caving in all over.

The desklamp had told him Redford Central still had juice. Maybe they'd got lucky and found gas. Lee got up and tossed the blanket on the couch. The hall and offices outside were lit with candlelight. They were conserving fuel as he had ordered. He snapped off the radio too.

In the outer office, tiny blue and red lights glowed from the military radio apparatus. Two of the armory guys were sleeping. The other smoked in semi-darkness. Jennifer was not there. Chuck was not around.

"Has anyone called on that thing?" Lee approached the smoking soldier. He felt compelled to whisper for some reason. Everything felt like a funeral, a church at night or something. It had to be the candles.

"No sir. Last was two hours." The soldier whispered too.

"What was it?"

"Mr. Ellis took it. Said not to bother you."

"Where is he?"

"Below someplace. He said he'd be downstairs."

He was in the "cage" with his feet up. Lee pulled up a chair and put his feet up too. They looked out across the floor at tiny colored lights and candles. They had come up with a lot of candles. A Christmas reindeer burned between them on the counter of the "cage." It was a funeral for Christmas, Lee decided.

"What have you done with my wife?"

Chuck punched #8, the public phones monitor. Jennifer's voice. Talking to a young woman. The young woman made him think of Charlene. Talked like her a little bit, like bad things didn't really happen.

"—but you think they're probably all right then? I mean—well you said there haven't been a lot of deaths or anything, so they'd be all right."

"I'm sure they probably are."

"Probably!" The young woman laughed. "Say, you're a great help, aren't you?"

"Best I can do. I'm sorry. But listen—don't get overly alarmed about them spending one night in a car. Blizzard or whatever. I've done that myself. In fact, I got pregnant that way.

And they're broadcasting all kinds of information. About safety in cars, I mean.''

"I know. I heard the radio. Well, I guess I'll believe you then. Thank you.''

There was a momentary pause and the young woman was back.

"Do you think there will be a white Christmas?'' she asked.

"Not a chance.''

"I know! Isn't that the way? Well. Bye!''

Click. Then a man's voice at once.

"Hello?''

The man's voice was both young and responsible, very serious. You could tell, no matter what, he wasn't happy.

"Eastern Turnpike,'' said Lee's wife.

"Eastern Turnpike?''

"Yes, that's right. Can I help you?''

"Uh—I suppose you have a lot of cars stuck out there.''

"Yes we do.''

"There is no way I might reach someone out on the Pike, is there?''

"No.''

"It's very bad. His brother has died. He killed himself. We need to reach them if we can—''

Chuck released the button. Lee was glad. Neither of them had any reason to eavesdrop on that. Chuck arched his back and shifted in the chair. The chair squawked for oil.

"Wanted something she could do,'' said Chuck.

"She gives them too much time,'' said Lee.

"She's doing well. She has good instincts. Let her be.''

Chuck was like a small dog that would bite you if you tried to pat him. Lee said no more about it. Chuck had a little thing for Jennifer. He always had. The two of them looked out on the floor by light of candles. They looked at Judy. She was always what they looked at when they sat like this, even though Chuck had a thing for Jennifer.

"Where'd we get the candles?'' Lee asked at last.

"Truckload of Christmas items.''

"We bought them?''

"Merry Christmas."

There was a pause.

"Someone should have wakened me."

"Chirstmas is a month away," Chuck said. He put his feet down on the floor, leaned forward on his elbows to try that position for a while. He spent his life trying positions.

"I don't know. I shouldn't have slept so long. Has there been anything from Harrisburg?"

"Not much."

"Have we got the federal declaration of emergency yet?"

"If we have, I haven't heard about it. The teletype is out."

"What about the rig upstairs?"

"Nobody's called. What can I say?"

"Nobody's found us gas?"

"There isn't any Santa Claus."

"This place is going to hell on a handcart."

"Make that a dog-sled."

"What's going on in Somerston?"

"Don't know. We can't talk to the west side of the mountains."

"Number 12 again?" The repeater must have run dry by now. It figured.

"And Number 7. And 3. And 15, etc., etc. We're about 60 percent blind. These repeaters are running out of gas. That's it."

"What about us?"

Chuck looked at his watch. He shook his head. "Joe said there was an hour, maybe two. That was an hour back."

Lee sat up suddenly. "Jesus Christ, Chuck. Quit making me drag it out of you! Lay it out."

Chuck heaved a sigh and cracked his knuckles. "It's plus-eight Fahrenheit. Wind gusts up to fifty miles an hour. I walked out with Ollie when he brought in the guy with the Christmas stuff. It's like a sandstorm. It hurts. Like your skin's on fire."

"What does Tri-State have to say?"

"Nothing. But then more of the phone lines have come down. The rest are twice as overloaded. Probably what the N.W.S. was saying before the teletypes went out—morning. Nothing new."

"What do you mean morning! What about the morning?"

"The storm breaking? You didn't know that? Tomorrow morning?"

"Hell, no! I was asleep, remember?"

Chuck punched the telecom. "Judy, have you got those last sheets from N.W.S?" He let up the button with a shrug. "I thought you got them. I guess I'm getting punchy. Cabin fever."

Judy stood up at the console and picked up a stack of notes and memos from the top. She brought them to the "cage" and handed them to Lee. Lee received them with his arms.

"We're looking for the weather."

"Oh. Right."

She took hold of the stack with Lee and began leafing through to show him where they were. She had surprisingly strong hands, hard forearms. Like another girl from many years before. He hadn't thought about that girl in many years. Then Judy found the sheets and pulled them free.

"Here. That's the last. 6:45."

Lee looked at the clock. 7:50 now. The N.W.S. sheet bore out what Chuck had said. Precipitation an additional eight to twelve inches overnight, high winds, overnight low plus-four. Storm-front to have passed through Pennsylvania sometime before dawn. Clear and cold through Friday. He couldn't believe it. Maybe there *was* an Easter Bunny.

"That is fantastic! What a break!"

"Well, I thought you knew."

"Hell no, I didn't know! How could I?"

"Yeah. I guess I'm getting punchy." Chuck yawned and stretched. He always stretched a certain careful way, as if he had stretched once and broken something painful in his body.

"It's your turn in the barrel," he said. "Now I lay me down to sleep . . . et cetera. I'm going upstairs."

Chuck got up carefully and began to leave.

"What about our PR?"

"Something's going on. I got through briefly to KYW: that's it. They had been contacted by the Red Cross P.R. in Philly and seemed to know what to do, so I guess it's happening.

Somebody's working something from someplace. Lemme go, Lee. I'll fall right on my face.''

"You haven't slept at all?"

Chuck shook his head.

"Get out of here."

Chuck left. He walked like the last part of being drunk, when it's just being very very tired and no fun anymore. His feet slid along the floor.

Lee turned to Judy. "How much of Zone 2 can you talk to?"

Judy shrugged, "I don't know. It's hard to tell. I can talk to Aurora sometimes. Sometimes no. It's hard to tell."

"Everything this side of the mountain?"

"No. There's blind spots."

"How do you know?"

"Ollie. He's been going up and down the eastbound in a plow trying to find gas. I lose him sometimes. He found the candles. It's weird, huh?"

"What?"

"The candles. Like a mass or something. Like an Italian Christmas."

"Where is Ollie now?"

"I don't know. He went out two hours ago. I think he's at the tunnel."

"You can't talk to Somerston?"

"No."

"No idea what's going on there?"

"Well, Aurora hears them sometimes. We can go through to Aurora. There has been hardly anything for hours. Aurora says they can hear them now and then. They're mostly talking to each other."

"Saying what?"

"Keeping tabs on one another. Where they are. Who's got gas. That's about all I'm doing too. Keeping a list of who's where. There's a lot missing. A lot of plows and patrol cars nobody had heard 'boo' from for hours. Some since last night. God! To listen to the VHF you'd think there's nothing going on out there. Most boring day in history. Nobody's talking. Everyone's just huddled up trying to keep warm and sleep.'' She shook her head, looked at her fingernails. "Your wife is down here, did you know that?''

"I know.''

"She's really tall.''

"Yes.''

Judy didn't say anything. She looked at her nails.

"Can I get coffee?''

Judy lightened up a little. "Yeah. There's coffee. We kept the coffee on. We thought we ought to despite the lights and everything.''

"Right. We ought to.''

He followed her out, watching the way the uniform fit her. He wondered if she looked any better out of it than in. It was doubtful. In the back he got the coffee and saw Jennifer. She made smiles and faces attempting to communicate, but was unable to get free of the phone. Lee grinned back and drank his coffee.

REDFORD CENTRAL—8:30 P.M.

Jennifer sat down at the phones again. She had been at it steadily since six and it was now after nine. When Lee had come back into the equipment room for coffee she had joined him. They had asked each other how they felt and talked about the house a little—standing wide open and deserted, windows busted out. Lee doubted there would be much looting with the storm at such intensity, the streets impassable. It was to be cold tomorrow. Maybe they could sweep out the snow that had blown in before it had a chance to melt and wreck the rugs and furniture. They did not talk long. Just long enough to have a cup each. Lee had two. Lee had waited for her to find a chance to break away and both felt compelled to get back. Jennifer pushed down the insistent, flashing button.

"Eastern Turnpike.''

There was no answer. She had a live line. She could feel the depth of it behind the ear-piece.

"Eastern Turnpike. Hello? Is someone there?"

There was a little pause, more faint static, the sea shell hiss, the quiet roar.

"Mom?"

It took a second to believe it. "Charlie! Charlie where are you?"

"What are you doing in at Central?"

"*LEE! My God, it's CHARLIE!* I've got her on the phone!"

Lee was halfway back across the main communications floor. Her cry spilled the coffee in his hand. It burned, slopped down his pants leg, burned his leg too. He threw it whole hog into the nearest shit can and ran back to the phones. He punched up track eight on the recorder. Their voices filled the candlelit air.

"Where are you?" Jennifer was laughing and a little crying too.

"Somerston."

"Somerston? That's crazy!"

"You don't know the half. Clifford's goddam car broke down."

"Charlie!"

"I don't care. I'm just so damn pissed off I just don't care. We passed the wreck up at the tunnels yesterday and got halfway down the other side. Then comes this terrific rapping noise from in the engine. We coasted down the hill and limped through the ramps. I had to pay. Clifford had no change, right? Right! So then we make it halfway into town, in that incredible traffic, stopping, going with this machine gun underneath the hood. Smoke is pouring out by now. Bang! The car stops like it hit a house. My head goes into the windshield."

"Charlie! Are you all right?"

"We were doing a blinding seven miles an hour. Anyway, the car would not start. It just would not turn over. Not at all. A cop comes and we shove it off while thousands curse us and shake their fists requesting that we die. And it's raining and rain-

ing and raining and raining. Clifford takes off to get help with
the cop and that's the last I saw of him, and if the bastard's still
alive someplace, that's why! I sat in that car six hours and it got
cold and colder and the snow started and finally I gave it up and
went into town. I had to pee. The hell with it."

Lee ran back to the repair bench and grabbed up the phone.
He punched the outside button.

"Why didn't you call us?" Jennifer was beginning to get
some control of her relief.

"I've been trying to all last night and all today. You would
not *believe* what's going on here! I never saw so many people in
my life! Every one of them is standing in a ten-mile line leading
to a telephone. It's crazy! It's like some kind of thing that happens in China or someplace like that, but not the good old
U.S.A! *WOW!*"

"Where are you now?" Lee spoke for the first time.

"Dad?"

"Hiya, Baby."

"Have you been here all the time? Why didn't you talk? I
hate that!"

"I was listening. Where are you?"

"Somerston!"

"Where in Somerston?"

"United Church of Christ on North Sixth. God! You can't
imagine what it's like here!"

"But you're indoors?"

"Yes."

"That's good. Don't lose your place. Don't go outside."

"I'm wise to that, don't worry!" She paused. "There are
others waiting for the phone. They're pressuring me to get off.
It's so great just to hear your voices! What's Mom doing at Central?"

"He brought me in, the house was cold and filling up with
gas. He was a regular old-fashioned hero."

"You're kidding! You mean it's like this at home too?
What's going *on*, Dad?"

"Just a bad storm. Baby. Real bad storm. Uh—look. I don't
see any way of getting you back here before tomorrow. Can you

tough it out one more night? You're not hurt or anything like that, are you?''

"No. Sure. I guess I can. I'd give anything if I could brush my teeth. God! I feel so *grungy!* My hair is total grease!''

"You're warm where you are? The place is heated?''

"Oh, yeah, Mom. In fact it's stuffy. I was in the armory till ten this morning, then they moved a bunch of us in here. It was really crowded. I've been helping them get people to the hospital. They have a snowmobile thing going between here and there.''

"Ten o'clock?'' Lee's voice rang with irony.

"Yeah. What's the matter?''

"I missed you by an hour!''

"You were here in Somerston? You're kidding!''

"Around noon. We were in the armory. Can you beat that?''

"Wow!''

"You stay put and we'll get you over sometime tomorrow. The storm will break by morning and we'll get you over here.''

"Okay.'' She paused. "Well, I guess I better get off. A lot of people waiting. It was really great to hear your voices.''

"Don't go out. If they make you move or anything else happens, go to the courthouse. Get in touch with Mayor Pribanic or Mrs. Pribanic. You should do that anyhow. Yes. Go to the courthouse in the morning. Tell them who you are and wait for me. Good people. They'll take care of you.''

"Okay. The courthouse.''

"Yes. Stay the night. Wait the storm out, then go to the courthouse, got me?''

"Gotcha.''

"We love you, Baby. We'e been half nuts to hear from you,'' Lee said.

"Me, too.''

"See you tomorrow,'' Lee said.

"Wow,'' said Charlene.

"What's the matter?''

"I feel so—I don't know. Selfish. Guilty.''

"What for?''

"I mean—God, Dad—there's a lot of *people* still outside.

Out in the streets. It's horrible out there. Freezing! What's going to happem to them, Dad?''

"They'll huddle up in cars. They'll be okay. They're broadcasting all kinds of things to do."

"Will they?''

"You just stay inside.''

"But—''

"God damn it Charlie, stay inside. I don't know those people. I got just one kid. Those people will make out somehow. They always do."

"Well . . .''

"Promise me!''

"Well—''

"Promise me!''

"Okay.''

"You promise?''

"Promise. They're pushing at me to get off. It's fair. I have to go."

"Good night dear.''

"Night Mom. Night Dad. I'll be okay.''

"See you in the morning, Baby.''

"Yeah. Sure good to hear your voices. It's like another planet here.''

"It isn't that much different here.''

"You guys are there. Together. And I'm not.''

"Just hang on until tomorrow. You promised, remember?''

"Okay. Tomorrow. Bye now.''

"Love you.''

"I know. You too. Bye.''

"Bye, Baby.''

Lee and Jennifer sat looking at each other. Jennifer ignored the calls for a while.

"She's inside and unhurt. She'll be okay,'' said Lee.

"I know.''

"She's got shelter. She's out of the weather. That's the main thing.''

Jennifer just nodded. She looked at her hands.

Then the generator engine died and started up again. It died once more and then did not start up again. All the little lights went out on the electronics, on the big map and the consoles. From the main room came the sounds of the operators pushing back their chairs. Lee had never heard that happen here before. Redford Central had shut down. The candles burned as if nothing had changed. It would soon be getting colder.

SOMERSTON—8:30 P.M.

Em awakened in the darkness. Her eyes came open and saw nothing. Daisy had begun to growl low and deeply in her old fat body and the growl would break as the dog took a breath and then come back again immediately and each time a little higher, a little more in earnest. Em listened and heard nothing but the growling and the wind and endless creaking timbers of the barn and didn't move at all. All at once she heard the barn door rolling open and the wind rush in and the voices and scuffling feet of people. Daisy's growl heightened and it seemed that she would bark, Em didn't want that. She elbowed Ed to wake him to take care of his dog.

"What? Hey what's the matter?"

"Sssh! Quiet your dog. There's people coming."

Ed sat up in the straw, stroked and patted Daisy, put his hand around her muzzle and hugged her close.

"Shut up, Daisy! Quiet!"

"Quiet yourself too," she whispered. "You stay here with your dog. I'm going to have a look."

She crawled out to the edge of the great pyramid of bales of straw, through the narrow channel between it and the south wall of the barn until she could peek around the edge. The voices grew louder and she could perceive a little light as she got closer to the center.

Twenty, maybe thirty, people coming in. Maybe a third of them had flashlights. She perceived them in jagged silhouettes, captured momentarily in the erratic, swishing beams of half a dozen flashlights. They stomped and cursed the cold and beat themselves with their arms and she could see their breath-steam, no faces, but there were women with them and some kids. Some other dogs ran among their feet. Daisy barked behind her and she tensed, but the new dogs were barking too, and none of the new people noticed.

Ed crawled up behind her and looked. Daisy was whining in his arms. He held her tightly, semi-punitively.

"I couldn't stop her!" he whispered hoarsely.

"It's okay. There's other dogs. Be quiet."

They watched and more people came until there were what looked like several dozen. Maybe a band of them had gathered up out of the cars or other buildings, driven out of somewhere that was even less satisfactory than this old drafty barn. Somerston was just across the road; hard up against it. There wasn't anything gradual about it. It seemed for a while as if the people would never stop arriving, but then the doors rolled shut, the wind stopped whipping in and the furious piling-in activity slowed down. The mob milled in a ragged vortex in the center of the barn.

They watched them probing the interior with the flashlight beams, jabbing into the upper rafter regions and the things on either side and listened to them talking. A lot of "whews" and "boy it's good to get out of that wind" cliches and feet-stomping. A handful of the men began to prowl and scuffle up and down the main aisle as the kids had done and when one of them came near, Em punched Ed to alert him, and they slid back into their cubbyhole and waited. The light shot over them and around above their heads a little, then was gone and they could hear the footsteps going back toward the center of the barn, the voices murmuring.

"What are we hiding for?" Ed whispered. "They're not Nazis or police or something. They look mostly ordinary to me."

"Sssh!"

"Well, what for? Maybe they got food or something."

"We're better off right here."

"What for?"

"I don't know what for. We are, that's all."

"One of your cowboy nature instincts or something?"

"Go on out there if you wanna, but don't steer them onto me."

"How come?"

"My business. You go out if that's what you want but you keep your mouth shut about me."

Ed thought about it. She hadn't given him a reason other than her own example, but she was really interested in staying hidden, and no kidding.

"What's the trouble between you and people?"

"When you get them in bunches, I don't like 'em— 'specially in times like these."

"What's to stop me telling when I'm out there? What's to stop me then?"

"Nothin'. It's entirely up to you."

Ed made no further comment. Neither did he leave. Their attention was suddenly drawn back to the mob of people in the center of barn now—the noises they were making. They were breaking boards and piling things up in the middle—boards and straw and gunny sacks. Matches were being struck.

Em cursed under her breath, "Them idiots is buildin' a fire!" and they ducked. Some of the flashlight beams turned their way again. A couple of the men came toward them, took bales off the pyramid and carried them back to make a ring of seats around the blaze. The flames grew quickly, fed by sprinklings of loose straw. The wood was dry. Flames and people and their shadow-children danced in the black draftiness. The people settled down around the fire, sat on or in front of the bales, and settled down and sounded safe and cheerful and warmed their hands. It made a picture out of blacks and reds and oranges and looked nice and like you'd almost want to be there.

"You think this whole place will burn down?"

"Could happen easy."

"But not absolutely sure."

"I wouldn't be sittin' here," she said. "I'd be divin' head-first out that window."

"You said the place would burn down for sure."

"Nuthin's absolutely sure," she said.

9:10 P.M.

The fire stayed under control. Em had watched it the entire time. She had not taken her eyes away from it since the new people had come into the barn. Ed had watched awhile and then crawled back into the cubbyhole among the bales and had fallen back to sleep. It had been a long day of the worst kind of exertions. Falling asleep was easier than not, but Em had stayed awake and watched the people and the fire. The people had talked awhile and, then, the talk had dwindled and a lot of them had gone Ed's way and drifted into sleep, having had the same day too. It was quiet and just a couple of them were talking lowly and keeping up the fire. The fire was not as high as it had been at first. Some of them recognized the danger of the fire and had talked about it and were trying to be careful and had reduced the size of it. Maybe it would be all right, thought Em. Maybe she *had* been overcareful and they could have had a fire themselves, except that the people would have seen them instantly and she still would not have cared for that to happen. But the barn was a barn and very drafty. The wind howled worse than ever and the timbers groaned like some wooden galleon and she was cold and thinking now of crawling back into the cubbyhole with Ed and sharing half the dog and blanket. She wanted to in the worst way, but couldn't give up watching.

She had all but made her mind up that it would be okay to do it when the two dogs at the fire raised their heads and growled, then barked and she heard Daisy waking up behind her.

Suddenly the great door of the barn rolled open and there was an outcry from the people in the circle. A blast of wind rushed in and blew the fire up in a sudden, vicious gust of glowing embers, sparks that flew and lighted everywhere in the straw and started little flames throughout the whole interior at once. The whole barn was afire in less time than it took to realize what happened.

Ed was stirring when she got to him, half awakened by the dog.

"Get up!" she said. "Let's go!"

"What's happening?"

"They set the barn afire, the way I said. Let's go!"

She took the shotgun and bashed out the window with the butt of it and kept beating at it till the glass and sticks that held the grimy panes together and everything else was gone. It was bright orange all around them, showing up the ceiling, now, and walls behind the pyramid of hay bales. There were shouts and screams from the other side.

She beat with the gun butt until there was no glass left in the wood to cut or catch them. The wind from outside clawed at her face and flung little particles of the glass against it stinging.

The window was a little high. Chest high on Ed. He'd need a boost.

"Come on," she shouted. She held her hands down cupped for him to step in and he didn't argue. He stepped in and she boosted him and he went up and out headfirst into the whipping windy blackness. She lifted Daisy and looked out to find Ed but couldn't see him, called but either didn't get an answer or couldn't hear one. She held the dog through the window and dropped her straight down, then climbed out herself with the gun.

She landed on top of Ed.

"Why didn't you answer?"

"Answer what?" He had Daisy with him. They were a pile of three in the whistling frigidity. Then a light came on. Ed had brought the flashlight. And the blanket still around him. She was glad to see the light.

"Never mind. We got to go. We got to get away from here. There ain't but very little time!"

"Go where?"

"Anyplace but here. Grab onto me!"

They had overlooked the bowling bag, left it behind. Em took the dog because she was bigger and gave Ed the gun. They felt their way along the wood wall of the south end of the barn, colliding with obstacles a couple of times despite the flashlight. The weather seemed evern tougher than before. Ed hooked his hand into her belt and stumbled along behind. Finally they came to the familiar strand of wire and more of the nubby stubbs of leafless sumac. The dog was proving just too clumsy. She had Ed hold the light while she wrapped the dog in the blanket, made a sling of it over her shoulder. Then both of them went under the wire and fought through the thicket of sumac until they found the bottom of the ditch. The wind still blew from the west and her idea was to go south now, following the ditch, because the wind would blow the fire across the road and east and into Somerston and it would be a furnace. She figured you would never get away from it going with the wind. They had to break off and cross the wind or get upwind of it to be safe. She remembered about the ditch and that it went beside the north-south road at the edge of town. She did not want to go west. That was totally unknown except that it was open fields and undeveloped. North they could get caught by the blastfire of the burning barn in just the time it took to traverse the length of it, so they were going south and staying in the ditch. It had to lead them to something eventually.

It had to.

REDFORD CENTRAL—9:10 P.M.

Lee did not know where his car was. They had moved it. He had left the keys with Judy when they'd flown to Pittsburgh and the men had come to plow the driveways later and had moved it. Into the parking lots. Judy said that's what they'd told her. He had not thought to look for it among the comings and goings of the day, had no use for it. It simply wasn't on his mind then. Now it was. Minutes after the auxillary had run out of gas the deadness and the deafness and the blindness of the silenced communication center had pressed in on him with suffocating claustrophobia and he had to get near a working radio. It was a necessity, like coming up from underwater, an urgency to breathe, to clear the ears and hear. He had to have it and he had to have it now. The candles and the coughing and the sound of babies from the cafeteria took exactly twenty minutes to have him pushing through the east-end exit with a flashlight and a hundred feet of nylon line.

Outside the door, it was black and vicious; everything that Chuck had said it was. No light of any kind from anywhere. The driving particles of ice went for the eyes. The exit came out

under ground, opening into a concrete stairwell, considerably
sheltered, although filling rapidly with gritty snow. Chuck was
right again. Like sand. Exactly. Hard little particles of ice. And
cold. The cold air hit his lungs like wood smoke and he choked
and tried to suck the next air more slowly.

Snow drifted over the stairs in a single wind-shaped dune.
Beneath the drift the slush from the warm day had frozen into
jagged shapes. He slipped several times climbing, bringing last-
ing pain to knee and shin, seeming always to fall upon the same
side, the same leg. He reached the top more by the power of his
arms than legs, bracing against the wall and using the steel hand-
rail. He could feel the coldness of the steel through the leather
gloves. It had an aching deepness to it that seemed to suck the
warmth from the forearms up to the elbows. The warmth did not
return when he let go.

At the top he tied the line to the railing and paid out several
feet. The 6-volt lantern was a farce. With it he could see perhaps
two of his own footprints disappearing quickly in the blowing
snow behind him. He ventured out a few yards, then began to fan
out gradually in a series of stumbling lateral sweeps. He would
pay out a few feet each time making the fans until the line gave
out. He would not let go. There would be a strong chance of not
finding his way back without the line. If he had to, he would go
back for more. He fell, got up and promptly fell again. The wind
was vicious and the ice beneath the powdered snow more ragged,
ruggeder even than in the stairwell. The ice could not be seen.
Wheel ruts fossilized in ice which could not be anticipated. The
snow had bones. He inched forward into the whipping gale, trying to be careful.

The line ran out and still he hadn't found the car. Where the
hell had they put it? He groped his way back along the slender
rope and fell again, wondering if it were the same spot as before.
Next time he fell, he told himself, he'd fall on his left hip. Three
times on the same side was starting to tell. He wondered if it
were possible to react in time, to think that fast. His hands found
the door. It was easier with the line. He wondered if there were
enough of it in the shops to reach the full length of the parking
lot. That would be something like a hundred yards. He hoped

those idiots had not put it so far out, was sure they had. Murphy's Law. Of course they had.

Jennifer caught him in the corridor.

"What happened to your face? You've been outside."

Lee shrugged and continued toward the shops. He did not want to be mothered just now. "I thought you were working on the phones," he said.

She looked down. "You went out in those stupid sneakers? Again? What happened to those boots you had?"

"I was just going to the car. Make one call on the radio."

"Well, did you?"

"What?"

"Make the call?"

"No. I couldn't find the car. I'm going out again."

Lee had not stopped moving. Jennifer had dogged along beside. They were back in the equipment rooms now. Lee was rummaging in lockers full of parts and junk. Jennifer was still on top of him.

"Where are they?"

"What?"

"Those rubber boots you had. Galoshes. Whatever."

"I don't know."

"Where did you have them last?"

"I don't remember."

Jennifer bit one of her fingers suddenly. "I remember. I took them off you. God, it seems like years!"

"Well, I don't remember. It doesn't matter." Lee was preoccupied. She disappeared.

Lee found another coil of the line amid random lengths of wire and coaxline in a box beneath the benches. There were no technicians anywhere around. Probably asleep. Why not? He hoped another hundred feet would do it. He had not seen any more.

Jennifer caught up with him at just about the same place in the corridor, Maggie Pribanic's big galoshes with her.

Lee was miffed, unwilling to give time to this.

"I thought they were upstairs."

"I brought them down with me. Put them on."

"Jen, Jesus—"

"Put them on. I don't want your toes in a bottle."

Lee thought about the way it was outside, the falling and the stinging and the pain. He put them on.

The galoshes seemed to help. The line helped greatly going up the stairs, much easier than the first time. He followed the line to it's extent again, trying to reckon a straight line out from the building, straight out without the fanning. He had explored this much already and it wasn't necessary. When he reached the end he joined the new line with the old and resumed fanning. He could see nothing. It was like walking off the edge of the world.

Then he walked into the car. It was so heavily encrusted that he had to break the ice from the registration plate to be sure. There was another car behind it and cars on either side, but he had somehow found the Bonney on the first try. He tied the rope line to the antenna. It was necessary to remove one glove to get the keys and get them in the lock. Whoever moved the car had also locked the door and ice had frozen in the lock and cracks. It was glazed solid, cemented shut. He got the key inserted and it turned part way but it wouldn't trip. He put his glove on quickly. Any direct exposure of the skin was to be regretted. His hand burned inside the glove. He balled it to a fist and pounded on the ice around the door, around the latch. He beat the door until his bones seemed ready to come loose within his hand. The latch gave sluggishly at last. The key turned all the way. He tugged at the door. It still would not come open. He took the handle with both hands and threw his full weight into it and still the door did not come free. Lee threw his weight repeatedly until it gave and landed him on his back, on the boney ice again. He retrieved the flashlight from the snow, stood up and got inside. He swung the door back and forth and slammed it several times to free it, then shut the door and put the keys in the ignition. In the 6-volt flashlight beam the windows were iced solid. The wind raged outside trying to get at him. In the still cold Lee's ears hurt like crazy.

He sat there for a while just resting. Then he stomped the gas pedal twenty times. He counted the times. He had found that out about the Bonney, that she loved a flood of gas when it was really cold, and it was really cold. Then he held the pedal down and turned the key. The engine ground slowly, laboring heavily. The oil must be thick as honey. It growled lowly, then picked up a bit. He stomped the pedal furiously and it caught a little. It was rough, the car shook and the engine would not rev. It died. He waited momentarily then tried it again. The engine caught and ran. He revved it hard to whip the oil up and get some warmth going in the cylinders.

When he had raced the engine till it would idle on its own, he turned the dashlights on. Three-quarters of a tank of gas. He thought of siphoning the tank for the auxillary. He thought of siphoning the gas from all the cars that had come in and dismissed it. With so many of the repeaters down they couldn't talk to anyone except the east side of the mountain, Everett, maybe Kregg. Twenty-five or thirty miles down east. He could do that much from the car. And who was there? With the gas he had he might be able to run through the night. He could siphon other cars to run the Bonney and keep it up for days, if need be.

Lee took a scraper from beneath the seat and got out of the car. He chipped the ice off VHF, CB and AM antennas and got back in again. The engine was idling smoothly. He allowed himself the heater for the first time now, switched the VHF on and listened.

There was nothing on the VHF. He cut the squelch down to zero, till the atmospheric noises came through. It was exceptionally noisy. A great deal of electricity in the air. Some distant things then; he couldn't make them out. Activity beyond range. Short little bursts. Widely spaced and almost lazy. A catastrophe in hibernation. Sitting in the solitary blackness of his own car, he knew what it was for millions upon millions of other cars. As lonely as he'd ever been and damn glad he knew where Charlie was.

He tried CB next. It was usually impossible to tell what was happening on all 40 channels. Not tonight. Some women gossiping on seven, but they seemed to be at home and not out on the road. Locals not talking of the storm. Just gossip. Bullshit. Laughing. The 40 channels were much quieter than he expected. He had expected a hopeless jumble of overlapping calls, the usual. Maybe that had happened earlier until the people had simply given up or run their batteries down completely or were finally just sleeping. The usual wasn't happening. Now it was an occasional probe out into the howling blackness. Sleepy. Someone just announcing he was still alive.

The the VHF blasted all at once and scared him. He grabbed at the volume, rolled it down. The fright turned to anger and subsided.

"Aurora to 2237."

Gap. Static.

"Aurora to 2237. Call back, Ollie. What the hell?"

Fred Barger, tired and crabby, getting hoarse. The signal was powerful and clear, a spark of life up on Aurora. Time passed. There was no reply. Barger tried once more, then Lee picked up the mike.

"Aurora this is Rider. Do you copy?" He didn't know if he could raise the maintenance facility without the repeater. It was roughly line-of-sight. Very roughly. And the same side of the mountain. Also it was twenty miles of blizzard. Ice. Trees, Rocks. And the steel administration building was between them.

"10-9?" Sounded like Barger. He either hadn't copied well or was responding to something different. "That you 2227? We didn't copy good."

"No, Aurora. This is Lee Rider down at Central."

Another voice replied. A growl of cynical familiarity.

"Hello, Rider. Who the hell you talkin' to?" It was Old Ollie.

"What's your "-20," Ollie?"

"Damn if I know. Should be gettin' someplace close to the Howard Johnson's at 138.2"

"You coming down the eastbound?"

"10-4! Hey listen. If you can raise Aurora you're a better man than me. Pass on some four-letter-commentary, compliments of me, and tell 'em keep their goddam ears on if they don't want them knocked off."

"Can't you hear them?"

"Negatory, Rider. What do you suppose the foregoing little speech was all about?"

"They've been calling you."

"News to me. We didn't hear a thing. Listen, Rider, what the hell is going on? We can't raise Central, can't raise nobody. You at Central? You don't sound like Central."

"We ran out of gas. I'm in the parking lot. I'm in my car. Who's with you?"

"Miscenic."

Lee thought about it. Miscenic. Yes. The big guy. The big patrolman at the tunnels Sunday afternoon.

"Hello two-two-three-seven. Call back, Ollie." Barger broke in again. It was loud and clear, five-by-five. It was crazy that he could hear Aurora so well and not be heard by them. The VHF was like that. Skipping, bouncing. Big blind spots. No way of predicting just what it would do without the blanketing repeaters.

"Hear that?"

"Never mind. What are you up to? What's going on?"

"We're going down to the Howard Johnson's for another loada gas. Barger wants another load. Goddam bird wants everything that he can get!"

"What gas?"

"We come up with one of them gas-driven generators, them little ones you pick right up and carry. Me and Luther tied it into the wires of their gas pump. It works. Be our second load now."

"Dammit, you guys! Didn't you hear our appeals? We're out of gas down here!"

"Sure we did! We sent a guy down with a thousand-gallon load of aviation gas. What happened to it?"

"We never heard of it."

"He never got there?"

"Hell, no! When did you send him?"

"Hell, a couple hours anyway."

"Negative. We certainly did not."

"Musta got lost I guess. Shit! Things really come and go."

"Well, to hell with taking gas back up the mountain. Bring it down here where we need it. How much can you get me?"

"Rider, I am driving number thirty-seven plow. We have one clean 50-gallon drum. Me and Luther attracted some attention down there before. Lot of spooky people out there in the night with guns. Hunters. Creeps. Who knows? They were getting out of cars and coming over last time. I got Miscenic with his magnum, but it's only me and him. We're not going to try for it if we have to shoot our way out. To hell with that shit!''

"Give it a try.''

"Suppose Miscenic has to shoot somebody?''

"Suppose he does?''

Fifty gallons would revive the brain of Eastern Turnpike and at least keep that much alive until well into the morning, well into the sunlight and beyond the storm. In Ollie's pause Lee could hear a shrug.

"I hope we can get past Everett. All packed up across the road down there. Cut-overs, runaways—them two miles from 138 to past 140 is a goddam junk yard. All them illegal turn-arounds from yesterday.''

"You're in a plow. Plow them off!''

"You're really set on getting that gas, aintcha? Well, we'll try but don't hold yer breath. We're not makin' any time tonight.''

"Where are you now?''

"Can't see Dick Shitt out there tonight. Not mileposts, nuthin'. I honestly don't know. I think about 136, but I really just don't know.''

"I'll be here in the car,'' said Lee.

Then there was silence and the howling wind. Lee observed that moisture from his breath had condensed and frozen on the windows. He jacked the heater up a little higher. He was glad that Jennifer had made him put the boots on.

SOMERSTON—9:20 P.M.

Em had been leading, following the ditch away from the barn. It rose on either side and when you were getting off the track, you felt yourself going uphill on either side and it kept you centered. She had thought they must come to a cross-road eventually which would lead to shelter. Some structure. Anything.

They had been able to see the great orange of the burning barn behind them for a time, but even that was gone now. Just the darkness and the wind and their own privation.

Suddenly the ground was rising in front of her as well as on the sides. She stopped and Ed collided with her. She took a few tentative, exploratory steps in several directions and found the ground to be indeed rising in all directions save the one by which they'd come.

"What's the matter?"

"I don't know. The ditch is ending. We may be coming to a road."

She went forward gingerly. The ground rose more steeply until it was a sharp climbing angle, making footing difficult because of the icy crust. She had had the flashlight off to save the batteries, turned it on now, but it showed her nothing but a bank of rising snow. It could be a drift or an embankment rising to the level of the road. She hoped. He slipped and fell behind her a couple of times. She was kicking at the ice-crusted surface to make stepping holds, but he didn't always find them. And they didn't always hold a second time. She came to the end of it. The crust stopped at an edge and fell away in front of her. She probed the depths before her with the flashlight and saw the curved rim of a heavy concrete culvert. They were apparently standing on the rim of a large drift that had formed sand-dune fashion in a wind-vortex at the end of the culvert. There was a gap of several feet between the culvert's end and drift, swept continuously clean between by the roaring currents of air. Ed caught up with her by painful inches. She tried to warn him not to come, but he was beside her before she knew. Their combined weight cracked the edge and they tumbled down into the crescent cavity. The water in the bottom of the ditch had frozen. There were rocks and awkward items of human debris.

Em scrambled and recovered the flashlight. It was a big, dual culvert maybe five feet high. She guessed that they were at or under Route 31 where it entered the town. She shone the light down through the culverts, found them glassy-bottomed—solid ice floors. She gathered Ed and the dog and urged them forward into the right-hand tube.

Inside they could nearly walk erect. They traversed the first tube from one end to the other and found the floor not solid ice, there were large sand or mud bars in placed—little islands on which, she thought, they might build a fire. But the wind shot through the tubes as though they had been designed for it.

They crossed over into the other tube and found conditions identical and just as unsatisfactory. The cold was penetrating and all but unbearable, aggravated by the wind. They tried huddling in the blanket on one of the sand bars for a time, trying to make it do, but finally the truth of it was overwhelming.

"I read about a thing once," Ed said.

"What?"

"The eskimos can live in solid snow. They dig out caves in solid snow sometimes when they get caught out in blizzards. It's the wind that gets you."

"What do they do?"

"They dig up snow or dig a cave in it and just crawl in and pile their dogs on top of them."

Em thought about it. It sounded vaguely familiar. The muscles in her back and legs were tying up in knots from shivering. Charley horses. She decided that there wasn't anything to lose.

"Come on," she said.

They retreated to the north end of the tunnel and the great drift they had fallen from. It was soft beneath a hard crust of ice and with the butt of the shotgun she broke an entry hole into it facing the culverts. Ed held the light. She dug into it dog-style until a small cave had been hollowed out. They tried for a fit and found it small and kept digging till all three of them could snuggle in. The snow was soft inside the crust and she tunneled deeper and to one side. They plugged the hole from within so the wind could not get at them. It seemed okay, out of the wind. Then she realized it would be no good. The snow would melt from the heat of their bodies and wet their clothes. The single blanket by itself would never do. She told him that.

Ed unzipped his jacket and brought forth the magazines.

"You still got those?" She was incredulous.

They spread them and made a floor and rolled up on it in the blanket with the dog between them.

She cut the flashlight. It was fading, getting dim and yellow anyhow.

She wondered if she would ever again feel what warm was. She thought about the way she hated August and September and muggy nights she slept with nothing on and an electric fan blowing on her just so she could sleep.

It seemed like some kind of a story told to her as a child. Nothing she had ever really done herself.

MILEPOST 138.2—9:39 P.M.

The big plow had come fifteen miles down off Aurora. Fifteen miles in something like an hour and a half. It was the third trip for the driver in the dark and storm but it had not improved his time. The trip was blind. Even Ollie Chelinski could not learn terrain he couldn't see. Wrecks and desertions were becoming much more frequent now. Sunday's break-overs at the turn-arounds had all tried to go back east the way they'd come, had piled up between Everett Barracks and the Howard Johnson's at the foot of the long mountain at Mileposts 138.2 and 140.2. Ollie dropped the gearbox into neutral and brought the big orange truck to a stand. Miscenic, the big patrolman, played the spotlight toward the medial, looking for a milepost. The snowy beam revealed a station wagon upside down, belly blanketed with snow. Little caps on each of three wheels. The fourth was gone. Ollie recognized it.

"I know where we are," he said. It was the first trip for Miscenic. Ollie and Luther Green had gotten by with taking out the first two barrelfuls of gas without a body guard. It had attracted enough attention from the cars surrounding the gas pumps that he had left Luther in the tunnel and brought the big cop down this time.

"I reckonize 'at station wagon. We'll hit that 138 post in another twenty yards."

Ollie threw the gearbox into low and nudged forward at a crawl. Miscenic swept the beam ahead of them. The headlights gave them thirty feet, no more—the spotlight just a little more into the driving whiteness. Frozen shapes began to loom everywhere in front of them, passing ominously through their little smudge of light at a grinding mile an hour.

"It's like the goddam bergs," the cop said.

"What?"

"Icebergs."

"What the hell you know about icebergs?"

"I was in the navy on a breaker. That's exactly what it looks like. Sort of."

"Keep that beam up! Forward! Forward!"

There were vehicles on either side now. Another had come into the beams directly in their path, ten feet ahead. Ollie hit the brakes. The plow skidded, even at the negligible velocity. They rammed it.

"I thought you could get through to the Ho-Jo all the way," Miscenic said.

"Get out and see if there's any goddam patrons in that car!"

Miscenic handed him the spotlight, picked up a 6-volt lantern.

"Hold the beam."

Miscenic bumped against the door, dropped to the running board and was momentarily out of view. He emerged into the beams again holding down his hat, face inclined against the driving wind and pounded at the window of the car. Ice fell away, the cop peered in with the lantern. He looked for a while, then came back to the plow.

"Empty. Nothing in it."

"Gotta get it clear."

The big cop shrugged. "Hell, it's busted up already. Smashed in on the other side. Why not?"

Ollie backed up, dropped the plow in first again and gunned it. The crashing impact stopped the plow. The wheels ground stupidly beneath them. The car was frozen down into the hardened slush of Monday, cemented to the road in solid ice. Ollie threw it in reverse, backed up ten yards and came forward harder. It stopped the plow again, threw Miscenic against the dash and Ollie on the wheel. When the plow pulled back again the heavy blade had crushed in the whole side of the car and burst the glass. The car stood halfway up on two wheels. This time the plow went through, carrying the demolished car into another one just behind it. Ollie backed up a little. There was a passage to the left, now, and they took it. In the next half mile more vehicles had to be pushed out of the way. None of them had people. They saw no people at all.

At the Howard Johnson's they could do no better than the high-speed lane. The Ho-Jo was at the exact bottom of the ascent and had become the unofficial marker for the beginning or the end of level land, depending on which way you came. The road was flat now, but the restaurant was not visible through the storm. They drove on until it seemed they should be opposite the service station and the gas pumps. They had judged it short and came through the bushes just above the pumps. Cars were everywhere and there were people in them now. They had one 5-gallon can and one 2-gallon and could fill the drum in eight trips. Ollie carried them. Miscenic had the little generator. Ollie found the pump again. The pump had been pried open with a crowbar or a tire iron. The lock was broken and the metal bent, a panel gone. The mechanical guts were filling up with snow. Ollie dug the snow out, found the wires. The cop pulled at the rope to start the little generator. It started easily because they'd put it in the cab to keep it warm. It made sparks when they clamped the jumpers from the generator on.

"Jesus," said Miscenic. "What about them sparks like that? Around this gas?"

"We won't make sparks, that's all." Ollie felt the gas pump with his hand. He felt the electric motor running inside it. With the screaming wind and the engine of the little generator there was no way he could hear it. But he could feel it with his hands. They were in business.

"Try it," Ollie said.

The big patrolman lifted down the nozzle and held it out. He squeezed it squirting out a little bit of gas. "Okay," he said.

"Don't jiggle them wires," said Ollie. "Don't let them wires get touched together."

"No." Miscenic stayed far from the wires.

Ollie screwed the cap off the 5-gallon can and held it up.

Miscenic put the nozzle in and filled it. When it was filled a little of the gas squirted out on his hand. It soaked through his glove and made his hand so cold it hurt him.

"Watch out getting wet with gas," said Ollie. "Freeze you quicker than with water."

"No kidding?"

Ollie screwed the cap back on and got the 2-gallon up and open. Miscenic used his left hand now; had the gas hand in his pocket with the glove off.

"They didn't tell you that in the Navy?"

"Yeah, I just forgot about it."

The 2-gallon can filled up quicker and Miscenic got his left wet too. He hung the nozzle up and put both hands in his pockets.

Ollie picked up both cans and the 6-volt lantern. He left Miscenic at the pump and started for the plow. Miscenic lit his own flashlight for company when the little guy was gone. It was as dark as hell.

On the fourth filling two guys came out of the storm and watched them.

"We seen your lights," the one guy said. "What's that, a generator?"

The big cop nodded. Ollie kept his face toward what he was doing.

"You getting gas up outa there?" the guy asked. Then he didn't wait for them to answer. "Hey, that's dynamite! Maybe we can get some too."

Miscenic shook his head. "Police business," he said. "It's an emergency."

The guy that did the talking grinned at the other guy and then looked back at the big cop. "Hell, everything's a damn emergency. I mean—it's all one big emergency. What the hell."

Miscenic didn't answer. Ollie picked the cans up and went off. The two guys stayed there.

They were there when he got back and there were more of them. Some were hunters wearing hunting clothes. There were eight guys now. Some of them had gas cans. Miscenic was filling their cans. Nobody was talking. He finished one as Ollie pushed into the circle. One of the new guys pushed him back and told him to wait his turn like everybody else. Miscenic intervened. He explained about Ollie. The first two guys confirmed it. They let Ollie by. He filled Ollie for the sixth time. While that was being done three more came up behind the others, saw what was happening and left again. As Ollie picked the filled cans up to go, two of them came back again with gas cans of their own.

"Hey, you guys! I said I'll fill a couple and that's all. We can't stick around all night." Miscenic had his cop voice on but gentle, not wanting trouble.

None of the men made any move or reply. A couple of the first arrivals viewed the later ones with visible resentment, but nobody said anything. Miscenic began filling up the next man as Ollie moved away. Ollie passed two other guys following his trail up to the pumps. Two more guys on the road itself got out of their cars and followed him back from the plow when he had dumped his load into the drum. This would be the seventh load.

A wall of men surrounded the cop and gas pump now. Ollie had trouble pushing through again. The men had gotten very strict about the order. Miscenic finished filling up a guy as Ollie was again identified by him and by a couple of the other guys who recognized the maintenance man from other trips. One guy offered to pay for the gas. Miscenic kept a face of stone. He waved the guy away and brought Ollie forward. He filled Ollie for the seventh time and Ollie moved away and kept his face straight too.

Ollie came back for the last time. Neither he nor Miscenic said a word about it being the last time. Some hassle getting in and Miscenic filled him up. Ollie stood up with the filled gas cans as Miscenic cut the engine on the generator. Five hunting rifles came up level.

"Leave the generator," said one of the rifles.

Miscenic looked around. He made no move.

"Start it," said another.

He started it. He and Ollie moved carefully away without the generator.

They didn't pour the last two cans into the drum. They left them on the bed beside the drum and got away as fast as they were able.

For the next two miles there were more cars in the way than ever. Ollie had not come this far down from Aurora, hadn't passed the service plaza. A trail had not been blazed. He drove right through them, smashing, ramming. Then it was clear, and reasonably easy for a couple minutes, a semi-open place between the Ho-Jo and Everett Barracks. Miscenic looked back from his side. There was an orange glow—dull, but you could see it. He tapped Ollie. Ollie saw it in the mirror. They stopped and watched it for a while, but there wasn't much to watch. Just an orange glow.

"Looks like they let them wires together," said Ollie.

He dropped the plow in gear again and they went on their way.

REDFORD CENTRAL—10:00 P.M.

Ten o'clock. Lee still shivered in the Bonney listening up and down the AM dial, a lot of stations were just simply missing. The ten o'clock news from WRVA Richmond said half an inch had fallen in Washington, D.C. New England and the Lake States to the Mason-Dixon line were like the parking lot around him—a blowing frozen waste. It bore out the N.W.S. predictions, the storm passed into the Atlantic by mid-morning. Tomorrow would be cold and clear. Then back to the talk show, which was awkward because the guy was winging it, making a hero of the station by not accepting calls in deference to government and phone company pleas, filling time repeating that, ad infinitum, along with a plethora of survival items for home and car. Stressing to stay out of the wind. Not to stray from house or car. To stay dry and on and on. Lee snapped it off. Well, good. They were doing it. Wood's big radio campaign. They were talking to them and everything would be all right tomorrow. Lee wasn't sure he liked that. Tomorrow was too soon. Tomorrow's when the work would *start*. Perhaps they shouldn't paint the picture quite so rosy.

Then a sudden pounding on the glass beside him. He jumped, startled. A flashlight moved behind the iced-up glass. He tried to roll the window down but it was frozen. He creaked the door open and shined the flashlight into Judy's face. Sliding over to the other side, he let her in, quickly so as not to lose all the heat. The seat was cold on that side. She was out of breath and leaned her forehead on the steering wheel, gasping in the warmer air.

"Jesus Christ, my God," she said.

"I don't believe this!" She gulped more mouthfuls of the warmer air. She was shivering and sucking air for some time. Then she raised her head and turned to him. She was still panting. Snow was driven deep into her hair. It made it frosty and artificial looking.

"Shake your hair out," Lee said. "You'll be wet."

She shook. It made a little snow storm in the car. "God! It hurts to breathe that stuff! You can't get it past your throat." She breathed breast-expanding lungfuls of the warmer air a few more times.

"You have to go in," she said. "Harrisburg wants you on the army thing."

"Okay. You stay here. Get dry."

Judy glanced around. Her eyes glistened in the dashlights. The thought of staying out there all alone was scary.

"Wow! I dunno—"

"It's all right," said Lee. "Listen to the radio. Ollie's in a snowplow trying to get down with gas. If he calls take the message, tell him where I am. Tell him I'll be right back."

They got out on her side because the rope was there. After he was out she got back in again. His hand slid along the line and he didn't fall this time.

Upstairs somebody he didn't know in Harrisburg said there was a shortwave call from Washington and they were patching him to that. He waited. It was Woods.

"Hello. How are you?" Woods said.

"Free of mosquitos," said Lee.

"Every cloud does have a silver lining, itsn't that so? Listen. We had a sketchy report come in by ham radio about a fire in Somerston. Do you know about that?"

"No. Are you serious?"

"Just one report. Vague. Didn't get it all. It wasn't certain.

That guy got some skip thing on CB. Caught a few calls from the area. Called our ham net in Pittsburgh. They called one here. He *thinks* the area. Then it went out again.''

"We can't talk to anybody there. We're dark. We're out of gas for the generators; no electricity. Sixty percent of our communications are that way.''

"By the way, the media are putting out that information for us. Have you heard any of that?''

"I have. I was listening in my car. It's good. I'm glad. We need it. We needed it this afternoon.''

"A lot of stations are off the air.'' Woods seemed unwilling to address Lee's low-key barb.

"I know. I heard Richmond. You can hear it very well here. My AM radio is nothing special. They should hear it everywhere.'' Lee didn't press it. He guessed Woods had his reasons.

"This thing on Somerston was to the effect of the whole town burning, not just an isolated fire.'' There was a pause. "From what we saw this morning, there'd be little they could do—couldn't move through the streets to fight it—nothing. If that's the case, there wouldn't be much you could do, would there?''

Lee hesitated. "Not on twenty seconds notice—''

"I know,'' said Woods. "I can't think of anything and I'm in the business. It's just that being so much closer you might come up with something, might know something we'd not have thought about. We'll be coming there tomorrow.''

"Here?''

"Bright and early. Communications is the big pain in the ass. We're down to putting notes in bottles. You're so well set up there it's a natural.''

"It's still on about clear weather; that's not going to change on us, is it?''

"No. Clear and cold. Supposed to hold through Friday. We can fly tomorrow.''

"Break for everybody.''

"Yes and no. It means we have to move a lot of stuff a whole lot faster. The way they're going *at* it is that divisions of the Guard and Army Engineers from the states to the south and west will bore in from the edges. Open up a few of the major roads to begin with. Then all the relief people in the world can roll in behind. But there's one less day. There isn't going to be the time to pussyfoot around with all the goodies. They're just going to plow them clean—everything into the ditches. It has to be to get those first few roads. We have to make a start." He paused briefly. "I want to know if this is happening in Somerston; I need confirmation. There's a decision to be made about Route 219, whether it will be one of those first roads or not. If the town's burned down, it will be. The military will go up Route 219 and I can send up a trailer town behind them. Temporary housing. I'm thrashing around in bullshit here. Not knowing what to do. You can imagine how many directions we're being pulled. I need that confirmation."

"Okay. I'll find out someway. Make you a deal. I'll get your confirmation—you bring me gas tomorrow."

"So, you're sitting in the dark there?"

"Almost. We lit some candles."

"How much do you want?"

"240 gallons runs us twenty hours more or less." Lee said nothing of the fifty gallons coming down with Ollie. If it ever made it down with Ollie. Fifty gallons was next to nothing.

Woods voice came haltingly, writing. "No . . . problem. Communications are priority." Then he spoke more briskly. "Look. I'll let you go. I have a lot to do, you have a lot to do. Leave any message with Harrisburg. I'll ask for it. No need to talk to me." He paused. "If you must go out, stay dry. Don't wear those idiotic sneakers."

"How is it there?" Lee ignored the sneakers altogether.

"Cold. The ground is dry. Well, I say 'cold'—cold for Washington. 35 degrees."

"Must be very difficult for you."

"You wouldn't believe this, but I'd rather be out there. Up to my neck in snow instead of bullshit."

"You're right. I don't believe it."

"Well, you're right. You shouldn't. I don't envy you at all."

"Bring me gas tomorrow."

Lee fell only once on his way back out to the car. The same hip. No, he told himself—he couldn't think that fast. Or maybe it was that his mind was now on Somerston. The hip was getting sore though. It was only one fall, maybe he was getting better adapting to this somehow.

Judy screamed when he pounded on the glass. She was terrifically embarrassed when he got into the car, but Lee knew why and said so. There was no warning whatsoever, no sound of footsteps coming through the whistling wind, no light outside except the pitiful 6-volt lantern that only showed in the last few inches and the glass was iced and caked with snow. Just bam-bam-bam out of the dark beside your ear. He told her it had scared him too.

"I guess I got the creeps out here," she said.

Lee nodded. It was creepy, he agreed.

The tension broke with a small laugh. "I almost wet myself," she said. Neither of them thought of anything to say and they didn't say anything for some time. They just sat there grinning. Moisture from two adults breathing frosted up the glass at a terrific rate until it looked like the inside of a refrigerator. Lee speculated to himself whether it would eventually fill the car completely. He wondered how many days that would require.

"Hear any calls?" Lee said at last. He didn't think there would be. She would have said so.

Judy snapped out of the temporary freeze of mind. "Oh! I heard Ollie. Calling you. I called back but he didn't copy. They apparently have gas and are trying to make it down. They're past the Exxon at 140.2. He said he wasn't giving out his '-20' after saying on the radio that he has gas, but I figure that's where he must be. He was mad we didn't answer."

"Yeah," said Lee.

"I heard Aurora Maintenance trying to get Ollie. They can't hear him but he hears them. I can't reach Aurora either. Maybe if we were on the other side. I think our signal's bouncing off the building."

"Boy! We can't do anything without that Number 12 Repeater, can we? Didn't you send Jimmy up there? He still hasn't come back down, or has he?"

"No. He hasn't." Judy had not been around when he got the memo about Jimmy and apparently Emmert hadn't told her. Lee decided that he wouldn't either.

"He'll probably just stay up there until it's over," Judy said.

"I guess he will," said Lee.

ON THE EASTBOUND—MILEPOST 123—12:08 A.M.

Plow #37 had made it into Central and Lee had joined Ollie and Miscenic. They were halfway up the mountain again, as near as Lee could tell. He pressed the button of his watch. Red digits came up 12:08:18—bright as hell within the dark cab of the plow. He worked his shoulders free from between Ollie and the gargantuan patrolman and leaned forward. He picked up the mike again.

"Plow #37 to Aurora Maintenance. Come in Aurora Maintenance."

No answer. They had lost contact with Judy sometime ago and now were in a radio no-man's-land somewhere halfway up the mountain, still unable to raise contact with Aurora or with anyone. The plow had made it into Central but the gas had not. In the course of the bashings and the rammings the drum had tipped, the contents spilled. Evaporated. Fifty gallons simply blown away into the swirling black wind and neither Ollie nor the big patrolman smelled the fumes. The gas was gone and Central still lay mute behind them in the glow of candles. Judy manned the outpost at Lee's car.

The plow was trouble. Impossible to steer. Ollie wrestled constantly with the wheel, fought with it like some living thing that had come up through the floor to kill him. Lee's left side was getting sore from whipping elbows. The bashings and the rammings had deformed the blade mounts too and broken one of the hydraulic rams. The blade could not be raised. It bit too deeply into the drifts, shoving up a constant pile in front of them, the tires ground at the ice, the rear end fishtailing constantly. Lee fought to hold the mike. He tried again.

"22-37 to Aurora."

"Aurora to '37. Ollie where the hell you been? You sound weird. What's the matter?"

"Lee Rider. I'm in the plow with Ollie. Don't ask about it. Too much of a story. What I want to know is, can you talk to Somerston?"

"10-4. Jesus, Mr. Rider. We been trying to call Central for the last two hours. What's going on? They got fire in Somerston. The whole damn town."

"That's what we heard round about. Who were you talking to? Beck?"

"10-4 again. Him and Officer LaBarr is there. They're at the gates at 337. They're talking panic situation. People by the thousands running out into the fields to get away. They wanted us to get in touch with you; we couldn't. What's wrong at Redford?"

"Central auxiliaries are out of gas. We're going to have to drop back down to radio range of Central and pass this confirmation on to Harrisburg. Then we're coming up."

Ollie backed out of the forward push, swung the plow about-face and went down, trying to stay within the lane they'd cut and not push up more snow.

Lee raised Judy minutes later. She knew what to do. They swung the plow around and started up again, still following the track. Lee confirmed that they were on the way. After that, a talkless ride, into the light beams full of snow.

They shut the plow down outside, out of the way. If they had to have a plow they'd take one of the others. #37 needed some shop time. Ollie's conduct with equipment was running true to form.

Aurora Maintenance was a great surprise: inside an oasis of warmth and light in all the blackness. They walked the mile of it seeing no one till the far west end. The feet of sleeping crewmen protruding from the cabs of some of the machines. A few refugees. Lee had expected more. A great many more. There was room here. A lot of room. There wasn't great warmth, but warmth. Dim light, but light. Aurora had healed considerably. Paradox. Outside of Zone 5 it was probably in better shape than anything else on the system.

Talk to Beck. That was first. Lee found Barger in the office cubicle. A couple dozen patrons sat against the cubicle on the floor outside. The office was two hundred feet from the west end and had been saved from fire, windows cracked, a little blistering on the fire end. No more. Sipping coffee Barger crouched below the level of the windows on the inside so as not to be seen by the people outside, but he offered coffee to the three. It was black and steaming. They accepted.

"Keep it down," he said. He passed cups to them keeping one eye on the people outside. He shrugged at Lee's somewhat admonishing grin.

"There's not enough for us and them," he said. "We got the work to do."

There was nothing coming from the VHF. Lee thumbed the squelch down and the static came. The set was on and working. He turned the squelch up again so the receiver wouldn't speak until there was an actual call. Not as far. Everybody had a different idea about the squelch. Some time passed, then the set barked at him. Everybody jumped. The tunnel was so quiet.

"Hey, LaBarr. What is your 20?"

Silence. Maybe it was Beck. It sounded like him.

"Call me back, LaBarr."

Silence. It was Beck. Lee took up the mike.

"Lee Rider, John. I'm at the tunnel. You still at the gates down there?"

"Lee? 10-4. In 337. Where the hell have you guys been? I can't raise anybody! Did they tell you what the hell's going on down here?"

"Affirmative. We got it via Washington. Woods. The Red Cross guy reported it on ham radio. They wanted confirmation. I sent it. They will send help directly."

"When?"

"Morning."

"Morning? Great. We'll stack up all the frozen bodies for them. All they have to do is—ah, fuck it, Lee—morning isn't good enough! It isn't good enough at all!"

Lee's mind grabbed for ideas.

"The people have run out of the town?"

"Hell, yes, they ran out of the town! You would too!"

"Where are they now?"

"Mostly north of town. Between us and the town. The fields, the ramps and everything. We walked down to have a look. You can't see anything from here. It started someplace on the west side. It would start on the west side naturally. And the wind took it. They all just ran out of town."

"Can you see it? Can you see the fire?"

"Big orange glow, that's it." he paused. "Christ, Lee— what do we do? This is terrible. They're standing out there freezing to death!"

"Where's L. John?"

"In the car with me."

"Stay near the radio," said Lee.

Lee sat down opposite Miscenic, Ollie and the tunnel chief on one of two filthy and dilapidated sofas brought in by the men. They looked like "hear no evil see no evil monkeys." Three in a row. Everybody sipped coffee below the level of the windows. Lee sipped his. Then he turned to Ollie.

"That D-8 'Cat' still up here?"

Ollie looked up from his boots. "You management are keeping up the payments, aintcha?"

"Not the kind of item somebody just walks away with," said Barger.

Lee was on his feet abruptly. He chucked the plastic coffee cup aside and stepped out of the office cubicle. He looked down the mile-long maintenance garage, down the twin rows of caged light bulbs on the sides, the blackened end and salt where the fire had been the day before behind him. He made rough mental calculations. Barger followed and came beside him.

"Where you getting all the gas?" Lee asked.

"Ollie brought two drum-loads from the Exxon before going down for you," he said. "We siphoned maybe 120 gallons out of stuff like water trucks and rollers we're not gonna use. We never started burning any till sometime around five o'clock when we got the wiring back together. We're good for forty hours, maybe more."

"What happened to the patrons?"

Barger shrugged. "We was ass-deep in them till three-thirty, four, when it got cold. We didn't have this going by then. It was getting colder than a witches whatzit when the storm hit and they drifted back into their cars. They saw we didn't have as much for them as their cars had, they went back. They went someplace—where else would they go?''

The big Mack plows stood along the walls before him, with boots protruding from the windows.

"These plows got gas?''

"Sure. We're keeping up the plows. If we need anything it's going to be the plows.''

"Get these guys awake and run a train back down to Redford, open up the Civil Defense stores and clean them out. Bring everything up here. All of it.''

"What you gonna do?''

"Garage sale. Go! Get moving now! How many plows?''

"Seven.''

"Send seven then. Get moving.''

"You want everything?''

"In one trip. That's all there's time for. It's an hour down—an hour back. Get going.''

The Fiat-Allis dozer was bigger than his remembrance of it. Like a house—so big he couldn't see all of it. The hulk of something lost in dark and murky waters. It was as Ollie left it, pushing up against its hill of snow, down the tunnel's throat to keep it there. The tracks were higher than his head. He reached up to find the height with fingertips and couldn't—found them overlaid with thick ice. The "Cat" had stood through Sunday night's deep fall and all day Monday through the warmth and melting. Icicles as thick as thighs had grown like glass wisteria down among the mechanisms to the pavement, ice so thick he doubted that the "Cat" would move. It looked forgotten here a thousand years, an awesome thing left from an ancient war.

"How the hell do you get up this thing?'' he screamed to Ollie. Lee skirted the back of it, beneath the cab. He saw no set of steps, no ladder. Nothing. The wind was screaming through his clothes—worse on this side of the mountain, where the wind came from.

Ollie threw a grappling hook up on the track and pulled the rope. It came down in a minor avalanche. Also the second time.

And the third. At last the weathered monkey pulled himself up onto the track, stood up right and around and shouted down to Lee.

"You wanta turn this go-cart over, Rider, go get Barger to send out a half a dozen of them clowns with torches. Warm up the block." He turned and going higher, disappeared.

The plows were rolling out toward the east end, thundering inside the long garage.

Lee relayed the demand to Barger, glad to be out of the wind and cold. His ears and fingers stung. His toes were killing him. He followed Barger and his men to the supplies, scavenged work gloves to put over his own, then asbestos gauntlets to put over those. He could barely make a fist, but he was going to make a twelve-mile journey through this night in the open cockpit of a dozer doing maybe—what—two miles an hour? Five? My God, that could take hours!

He returned to the "Cat" dressed in everything he could find: two hooded sweatshirts under the coat, work goggles, two pair of wool socks over the sneakers inside Maggie's boots. And the gloves. Even so the cold cut through his jeans the minute he stepped outside. The "Cat" was running, now—idling with a purr like God's cat purrs. Barger's men were leaping down, shutting off the torches. The rope from Ollie's grappling hook let up into the cab now. Lee couldn't see into the cab. He took hold of the rope and began to climb up the side.

The mufflers blatted thunder. Heavy machinations from the inside shook the big machine beneath his feet, a heavy clunk as gears fell into place. The engine seemed to strain, to fight against restraint, then the "Cat" exploded ice. Lee slipped, fell back into the snow. A shower of the crystaline debris. It had broken free. Lee scrambled to his feet as the enormous treads began to roll, the "Cat" pulled backwards from the tunnel. He dived for the medial as the blade swung wide, the D-8 spun in place and came to face downhill. It stopped. A light was moving in the cab. It shined his way, passed, and then came back again.

"Rider! Is that you?" He realized he must look like *The Thing from Planet Z*. Ollie wasn't sure. Lee waved. He heard the voice but couldn't see him.

"Yes!"

"Well, come on then."

"That thing got a VHF?"

"What?"

"A radio! Has it got a radio?"

"Hell no!"

Barger had come out, had been watching. He handed Lee his walkie-talkie.

"You bring this back or I have to pay for the sonofabitch," he said.

Lee nodded.

"Hey, I mean it," Barger said. "Two hundred and seventy-eight, eighty-five. I'm serious. It's happened to me once before."

"I'm sorry," Barger said. "I got to think of Christmas coming. The kids and that. What am I supposed to do with all that stuff from Redford when it gets up here?"

"Unload it. Keep it here. Can you get the plows out this side—through the damage?"

The crew chief nodded.

"Good. Send them down this side when they're unloaded."

"What the hell are you planning to do?"

"The tunnel is twenty feet wide."

"Sure, what of it?"

"A mile long. More or less. You could give eight thousand people each a space of two by seven feet to sleep on."

"You're bringing eight thousand people up here? How?"

"Walk them. How else?"

"Rider! Get a bucket and a piece of hose. We're gonna need to steal some juice to keep this thing alive." Ollie was yelling from somewhere above them.

Lee started back into the maintenance to get the hose and bucket. The crew chief dogged his heels.

"You're going to walk them? That's twelve miles! Uphill twelve miles!"

Lee shook his head. He agreed with Barger. It was nuts. Completely crazy.

"Can you think any closer place for them to go?"

They got the hose and bucket and came out again. Barger

seemed to spend the time in thought. He had nothing else to say. Lee thought about the fire and Charlie. He took the rope and climbed up onto the track and then into the cab.

The crew chief watched them grind away.

AURORA—WESTERN SLOPE—1:58 A.M.

It was like having your own dinosaur, your own great, powerful and terrifying beast that went where you commanded, that crushed and destroyed what you wished mashed out of existence. It was not like any of the other forms of self-transporting machines Lee had ever known. No steering wheel: a pair of levers, each of which controlled one of the giant tracks—slowing or completely stopping one relative to the other, thereby causing one side to go slower, turning the gargantuan machine. It had a throttle, which meant no gas pedal. You turned a knob that set the engine speed and it stayed that way until you changed it. If you had a heart attack and died, it kept on going until it ran into a granite mountain or ground into the sea or finally ran out of fuel. Ollie said that that had happened. It was known. There were stories every now and then. But it was not for transportation, not a thing for pleasures or for comfort. It was for putting asunder what God had wrought. It was strictly business. It rode hard. There was no give, no softness to it whatever—no up and down, no sway, no resilience. It beat its way forward into the storm with precision series of concussions, of forward rapid jerks, iron-hard jackhammer blows. Lee had to stand. The open cab had only one stiffly padded seat. Driving it kept both of Ollie's arms and legs so fully occupied he could not have shared it. No way. The dozer was so massive and so incredibly powerful that it could be tearing through a house and if the operator didn't see it, he wouldn't feel the difference. They were twelve to fifteen feet above the ground, and pushing up a hill of snow at least that high in front of them. They fought to see what they were driving into. The head beams were obliterated yards ahead in swirling snow. Lee hung out the right side keeping tabs on the steel medial with his 6-volt lantern, guiding them by it. At times it would be gone, would be drifted over—other times entirely exposed. Mostly it was just not visible, obscured by driving snow.

The rolling hill of snow ahead of them disgorged vehicles from time to time. They would jut up suddenly and then plunge sideways like leaping porpoises or salmon. Behind them they were leaving a twelve-foot swath of nothing—a deep, square channel between walls of snow. Ollie tried to dump to the left, to the outside and not over the medial and onto the standing westbound. There were people there. East and westbound sometimes separated widely on the Pike, but not here—not on the mountain where each foot of right-of-way had been sorely won. Some went over onto the westbound side. Not as much as to the left, but some. There was nothing they could do. Nor were they stopping to check out the cars in front of them. There just wasn't time. Cars still on the eastbound were supposed to be evacuated anyway.

Lee looked at his watch again. 1:58. They were maybe halfway down the mountain. Ollie had said twelve to fifteen miles an hour for the "Cat." Who knew for sure? There wasn't a speedometer. What for? But at twelve miles an hour, they should be close to halfway down the other side now. Halfway down the mountain. Halfway down to Charlie. Maybe. Maybe no.

It was cold. He was cold. The clothes he'd jammed into at the tunnel didn't do it. The open, unprotected cab, so high above the ground, was no help either. He listened to the pavement cracking under them. Was it just the snow or his imagination? Oddly, he thought of summer—whether the urgency of this night could be communicated in some stifling committee room, where the lazy drone of bees came in through open windows, a committee wanting to know just exactly why it had been necessary to destroy twelve miles of eastbound pavement between Gate 10 and the Aurora Mountain Tunnel at about a million dollars per. It was cracking under them like puddle-ice did when you stepped on it in late October mornings on the way to school.

Whether he could really hear it above the noise of howling wind and clanking treads and engine of the great machine he didn't know. He guessed it didn't matter anyhow.

REDFORD CENTRAL—2:10 A.M.

Barger's plow train made it into Redford Central at about 2:10. Nobody knew for sure. The clocks had gone with the electric power and nobody's watch agreed exactly. But the trip down had gone faster following in the wake of Ollie. They had encountered drifting, but the obstructions remained shoved clear. No cars had been moved to block their way. Ollie had blazed a proper trail.

They had passed what appeared to be a fire at the Exxon or the Howard Johnson's at roughly Milepost 138, Fred Barger wasn't sure. Whether it was actually one of the buildings or a car or some kind of a bonfire he didn't know. It was twenty, maybe thirty yards and you couldn't see a house afire beside ths road in this kind of weather.

There had been men out in the road as they rolled by. Not many, but a few appearing suddenly in the headlights and these scurried to get out of the way and had made no difficulty. Barger hoped it would go that easy on the way back up again.

Barger found Joe Emmert and Chuck Ellis in the Main Communications Room. Chuck had given up trying to sleep and come downstairs. They had the civil defense stores cleaned out and loaded on the plows in fifteen minutes. Cots and blankets and food mostly. Medical kits. They left the radiation survey instruments behind. Fred had brought two guys with each plow. The technicians and operators had nothing else to do. The whole thing took a quarter of an hour.

Jennifer caught up with Barger as they were going out the door. She wanted to know if Somerston were actually on fire. He told her that it was.

"I'm going up with you," she said.

Fred stammered something about the inadvisability of that, the danger and so on. It didn't work.

"Where's Lee? Is he in the tunnel? Where?"

"He's on his way down to Somerston, Ma'am. He left at the same time we did."

"Let's go," she said.

That was all there was to that. Jennifer pushed by him, fought her way up the icy stairwell and climbed into Fred's plow. She didn't know it was his. It was the first one in the row.

MILEPOST 109—2:40 A.M.

The dragon reached the Gates at 2:40. They couldn't see the gates, of course. They would have missed them altogether except for numerous little clots of dancing, arm-slapping people appearing in the headlights, then a patrolman running alongside wildly waving a flashlight. Ollie throttled down. He did something to the big machine that left the engine running while it stood in place.

"Who the hell are you?" the cop shouted up at them. It was Beck, the captain. Lee didn't look himself, he realized. The goggles, extra clothes. He must look like something from a cheezy science fiction flick.

"Me, John! Rider!"

Both of them climbed down, first to the track, then to the ground. Lee's legs were now so stiff with cold he had to think about each foot as he put it down, like walking on stilts. He dropped to the scraped surface of the road, then moved away to clear a landing spot for Ollie.

"What the hell are you doing here?" The captain was leading them among the dancing slapping people.

"What do you expect to do with *that* thing?"

Lee looked for the fire, the burning town. Away from the Caterpillar's blazing head beams, he could just catch a dim and distant flickering of orange. He guessed they were getting closer to the gates, the ramps. The crowds were getting thicker, harder to push through.

"Where's everybody else? Where is Pribanic?"

The captain hadn't heard him in the howling wind. He stopped them now and seemed momentarily disoriented. He took a few paces in each of several directions, came back to them and signaled them to come on again.

"What did you say?" he shouted.

"Where are we going?"

"Trying to find the goddam car! Get out of this rotten wind. Hang on!"

They found it and all three of them dove into the car. They were the only ones in it. Beck fired and ran the engine for a little heat. Lee came back to his original inquiry.

"I thought you had Pribanic with you?"

"Did."

"Where is he now?"

The captain shrugged. Not a flippant shrug. A scared shrug. An overwhelmed shrug. Lee had never seen him shrug that way before. It was not encouraging.

"These patrons started piling up around the car," said Beck. "We had them mostly turned back by the time the storm came. We got out to get them to go back, do like we had been telling them. The mayor, too. He was doing the best with them, does good with crowds that guy. We found out this new bunch wasn't from the cars. A lot of them had no idea what was going on, they just went where everybody else was going. Then we started hearing about fires. One fire. Two fires. The whole town on fire. He and LaBarr went down on foot to check it out. We left Pribanic in the car with Prokovic. I wanted somebody on the radio. We went down and seen it and when we got back and called it in on the radio they were still here. The mayor and Prokovic. So then I put Prokovic and LaBarr to hang around the gates. The mayor was real quiet, wasn't saying anything. I didn't think about it. All of us were tired. So then I got a call from Prokovic on the walkie-talkie. They were having trouble with an old guy at the in-bound booth. I went over. When I got back the mayor was gone. That's all."

"What happened to the old guy?"

"Died. Dead. Heart attack, or something. We stuck him in the snowbank with the others. What you gonna do?" He shrugged that shrug again.

"Others?"

"Oh, hell yes! Lee, it must have been a goddam flat out stampede. We got there after. By then it was a standing crowd, but there was another crowd underneath it, not-so-standing.

Trampled. Old people mostly. Kids. I been a cop thirty-one years. That's one I hadn't seen yet. God, their mothers wouldn't recognize them." He shook his head. "Now they're standing out there freezing in that shit. I don't know what to do!"

"How long ago was that?"

"Couple hours—" The captain shrugged again. "Oh, you mean when the mayor was gone? 20 minutes—half an hour."

"Your men are at the booths now?"

"Prokovic is. LaBarr went down #219 to see if he could find the mayor." The captain's look changed slightly—less overwhelmed—more irritation now. He turned on them. "What the hell are you guys doing here, anyhow? Just what the hell you think you can accomplish? It's over. All we can do now is wait for them to die. Stack them up in piles tomorrow." They sat in silence for a while.

Lee felt an object on the seat beside him, picked it up. One of the electronic *bullhorns*.

"Have you got more of these?" he asked.

"Sure," said Beck. "Two more in the booths. A couple of the 'townies' have them. Ones like them anyway."

"Townies?"

"Somerston guys. Fire department. Local armory. Like that. I mentioned it this afternoon. What of it?"

It was good. A plus. An extra. Lee hadn't been thinking in terms of help outside the Turnpike personnel.

"Still around? You know where to find them?"

"Some of them. A dozen maybe. Things got scattered since the fire."

"Got any road flares?"

"Sure. Full case in the truck. Always have them."

"What about you?" He turned to Ollie.

"There's a case of flares up on the dozer. In the tool chest. Underneath the seat," said Ollie.

"In all the equipment? In the plows, too?"

"Should be. More up at Aurora, in supplies. Shitloads of them. We was saying how lucky it was the fire never got to those. Boy!"

"Okay, look—I don't know if we can do this, but I can't

think of any goddam other thing to do. We're going to gather up Prokovic and LaBarr, your 'townies,' you and me and then we're all of us going down the ramps with these bullhorns, get these people gathered up and moving in a line. We're going to march them to Aurora. Ollie's going to turn that 'Cat' around and lead them back up to the tunnels—like a locomotive on a train. We'll put a guy on with him lighting flares and throwing them off every couple hundred feet or so to mark the way for the people further back along the line. They won't really need them with that channel we just cut, but I think it's important. Reassures them they're going the right way, that something's going on."

"Them flares don't last forever," Ollie said.

"When Barger gets back to the tunnels he's got orders to bring plows down here. We'll keep them going up and down along the line all night, keep them throwing out new flares. Barger could be at the mountain now. If not, any minute. Whoever talks to him first pass that along. He knows he's supposed to come down here. He doesn't know about the flares. Tell him to bring down all he has from storage. Tell him not to start them till he's down and working uphill."

The trio sat in silence for awhile. The wind rocked the car. Beck shook his head. Ollie sucked a yellow tooth. Same doubt that Fred had at the tunnel, same doubt Lee himself had now.

"Eleven miles," he said.

"Don't tell them it's eleven miles," said Lee. Then moments later. "Suppose you tell me what else we can do?"

Beck took a couple seconds to adjust to the idea. He shrugged again. The hopeless shrug as before, but maybe just not quite as hopeless.

"Let's go." he said.

They got out of the car.

EASTBOUND MILEPOST 138—2:50 A.M.

On the way up they lost the #7 plow, the last in line.

They got away from Central by 2:35 and were making better time back up the mountain. The plows had all been carrying full loads of salt and cinders when they left Aurora Maintenance. Barger had his men "salt and cinder" all the way down so the beds were emptied by the time they reached Redford, leaving room to load the civil defense stores on. On the way back up now, the tires were biting in. They were doing almost fifty miles an hour, making super time. Jennifer Rider sat between Fred Barger and big Miscenic, the patrolman in the lead plow, peering anxiously ahead into the snow-swirled beams. 50 miles an hour in present conditions was really much too fast. She said nothing, tonight the speed of light would not be fast enough for her.

So far there had been no bad surprises. They were still on level land, had not passed Everett Barracks or the Ho-Jo and the road was much improved by salt and cinders and the passages of seven of the heavy plows. They kept in single file, some twenty yards apart, and barreled on and on like bobsleds in old Ollie's rut.

Now the snow mounds that were cars began appearing to the left of them. They were coming into the tough miles, the tangled miles from Everett to the Ho-Jo. Barger picked up his mike and ordered the plows behind to drop speed to thirty-five, then dropped his own machine to that, giving the other guys time to comply.

They went a couple hundred yards at thirty-five. Then men appeared in front of them. Right in the road in front of them. Fred hit the brakes. The plow skidded sideways, came to a stop crookedly in the plowed channel. Jennifer caught glimpses of the figures scattering into the darkness on the sides, jumping. Diving. The images included rifles. Guns. Barger grabbed the mike, barked a warning to the guys behind. #47 hit them from behind. It wasn't much. Not serious.

"Back up! Back up! Gimme room! I'm stuck into this goddam snowbank, here!" Barger fairly screamed into the mike.

"I can't! 44's stuck into the back of me!" a voice came back.

"What the hell's going on up there?" another voice.

"Patrons in the road here," Fred said. "Be careful there. There's a lot of guns around. I don't like the look of this."

Jennifer felt a jolt and plow #47 pulled back from them.

"Okay, #49. Yer clear."

49 was them. The lead plow.

Fred worked the gears, the big plow pulled out of the snow-bank slowly. As the lights again swung forward there were the men. Maybe a dozen. Then more came from the dark on either side. Half of them had guns, were dressed like hunters, were waving. Three approached the plow.

Barger picked up the mike again.

"Look out here," he said. "I'm looking down the barrels of a half a dozen .30-.30's here." He took a large revolver from inside his coat and wedged it on the seat between himself and Jennifer. Miscenic did the same. He set it upside down with the butt forward so that he could grab it easily and fast. Miscenic too. He put a finger to his lips to Jennifer then spoke into the mike again. The guys were almost there.

"Let's all keep a level head here," Barger said into the mike.

The guys outside were pounding on the door. He rolled the window down.

"Hey!" said the voice outside. "What the hell's going on? When are you people going to come and get us out of here?"

"In the morning," Barger said. "It's going to clear up in the morning. Listen to the radio. It's on the radio. Go on back and keep warm in your car."

"I ain't got a car. My car's burned up. Anybody tell you guys this whole service area down here is all burned up? The whole goddam place is burning down! There's people dying there!"

"What do you want?" said Barger.

"Help!" the guy said. "Jesus Christ! Nobody's doing nothing!"

"What can I do?" said Barger.

The guy was thrown by that. He shook his head. "I don't know," he said.

"You want a ride up to the tunnel?"

"What's the tunnel?" said the guy.

"There's a tunnel up there. We're putting up a shelter. We can haul some of you, get through the night there. Best I can do."

"Sure!" the guy said. "I gotta get my family."

"Keep your mouth shut," Fred yelled after him. "Just your family. Don't spread it around. We ain't got that much room."

"Awright," the guy said. "Wait for me!"

"Hurry," Fred said.

He leaned out the door and shouted to the guys in front of him that if they wanted on to get on fast, then pulled back into the cab and rolled up the window. He picked up the mike again.

"Listen you guys. We're giving a lift to some of these patrons. Up to the maintenance. The minute you get what you think's enough you pop that clutch and roll, you got me? Roll! We got a real explosive situation here. We can not take them all. Once rolling we don't stop for nothing. This next mile here's gonna be a lulu. When I get rolling just follow me."

They sat in the cab—feeling it shake as people climbed onto the plow. More and more seemed to come out of the darkness. Mostly guys. A few women and kids only here and there. Then it was a small mob. Pressing. Crowding them.

"I don't know if this was such a hot idea," Miscenic said.

"Hey, I don't either," said Barger. "But I can't blame them."

"Nor can I," said Jennifer.

"It's not their fault," Barger said.

"On the other hand it's dumb. No way you can be fair," the big cop said. "You're creating a panic situation."

A couple minutes went by. The commotion increased outside the plow. Then Barger got out. He stuck the gun back inside his coat and got out of the plow and took a 6-volt lantern. His plow had taken all the passengers it could possibly hold. They huddled piled up high on the supplies from the survival stores. More were trying to climb on. Things were falling.

"Hey! That's it! No more! We can't take any more!"

Jennifer heard outcries and defiance.

"Go back!" Barger was yelling now. "There's six more plows back there. Get on one of them others!"

She heard more of the commotion, more shaking of the plow. Then the door burst open. Barger jumped behind the wheel. He revved the engine and the plow went forward. More people appeared in the headlights. He leaned on the horn and kept blasting.

"Grab that mike!" he yelled.

Jennifer grabbed it. "Just push the button?"

"Yeah," said Barger. "Take the goddam thing and let 'em know we're rolling. Tell them that you're #49 and I said roll."

Suddenly four guys were in the light in front of them. Barger didn't stop, he hit the gas and the horn. The guys dived to the side. Then there were shots and the glass splattered by his ear. Twice more and then a bullet entered at the side and through the windshield in front of him. He stomped the gas full down. Jennifer felt the back of the seat press into her.

"Jesus Christ!" the VHF spat. "These fuckin' people's shootin' at me!"

Jennifer had forgot to make the call.

Barger grabbed it from her.

"Okay, you guys—this is #49. It's hit the fan. Roll out now! Now! Don't stop for nothing or nobody. Roll!"

Barger laid the gas down even harder and #49 thundered forward, the heavy engine laboring to catch up with the gas pedal. The VHF spat half words. Pieces of words. Expletives. More refugees in front of them. Showing in the headbeams. Barely time to dive out of the way.

The the VHF broke out again.

"Help me! Jesus God! I'm shot, somebody! God!"

Then suddenly, in front, a new group. Five, maybe six. They showed up all at once and when the screaming came out of the radio. There was a crunch, then the plow rode bumpy for a couple seconds—two distinct episodes of bumping. The front axle, then the rear.

Jennifer put her head down between her legs and screamed.

Fred Barger didn't stop. He didn't even slow the plow.

MILEPOST 118—3:00 A.M.

The vicinity of Milepost 118 stood exposed in driving wind and on quite bare ground at a place where features of the west side of the mountain shaped the wind and drove the snow away. They had heard and seen the giant bulldozer going by. It had roused the sleeping occupants of several cars. A plumber in his van. A party of hunters. Two cowboys and a woman. They got out to see if anything more would come. All had sat where they were now since Sunday and had watched things getting worse. Too far to walk to Somerston. Four miles from the tunnel. And what was there at a tunnel? They had first taken comfort from the things being told them on the radio, but as time went on it seemed much longer until Wednesday. Then they said Tuesday. What to believe? Look at Watergate. Look at Viet Nam. None of them had spoken to each other before now.

"What do you think that was?" the woman asked. "What's going on?"

"I don't know," said one of the hunters. There were five of the hunters from the same car. They were different sizes. The smallest did the talking.

"That's that bulldozer they had up here Sunday night," the plumber said. "They're taking it back down, I guess."

"What for?" said the woman.

"I don't know," said the plumber.

But they saw that where that bulldozer went there was nothing left standing in the way. Behind it was a clear and open road.

"I'm fed up with this shit," said the plumber. He went to his truck and got an acetylene torch. He lit it in his van, away from the wind, then set it to a strong flame that the wind would not blow out and came back with it to the medial rail. He readjusted the flame to a sharp, bright jet and set to work to cut the rail beside his truck, to cut a passage to the eastbound side.

SOMERSTON—3:10 A.M.

Lee found the mayor at the fire's edge, as close as anyone could stand and bear the heat of it. He didn't turn or otherwise acknowledge Lee. He just kept facing to the fire with both hands in the pockets of his Harry Truman overcoat. The face was expressionless, a spectator among the many except that this one stood out further, in front the wall of people ringing the town. Stood closer than the rest, less mindful of himself, watching his own history burn away.

Lee stood beside him and together they watched the town burn for a little while. The wind drove flames from right to left across Main Street—all the way across—a solid blast of flame, like horizontal rockets. All the snow had melted and it boiled on the streets, boiled anything that lay in the streets. The cars Lee could see were red hot hollow shells with nothing in them. Some others closer and less directly in the flames had burned out too, were black and paintless and had black things in them. The wind changed momentarily. Lee caught a glimpse, a body sprawled across a hood and cooking there, tissues bubbling spurting little jets of flame. He saw it for a second. Just a second. Then the skull exploded from internal steam. The body jerked a little, that was all. A sound came like an aerosol exploding in a trashfire, the wind changed back again and he could no longer see it.

"L.John." Lee touched his elbow.

The mayor looked at him, then back at the fire.

"Which is the United Church of Christ?" asked Lee.

The mayor pointed to the left, the east. It had been a frame structure, a wooden box. The walls had fallen outward the roof caved in and it was mostly a foundation and a mass of embers, hot enough to melt the cast-iron radiators. Lee's heart sank. He thought about the thousands who had gotten out. All around. Why not Charlie among them? Better than an even chance. Still his heart was not as high as before. There was the chance it could have gone the other way.

He took the mayor's arm and urged him back.

"Come on, L.John. There's a lot to do."

The mayor offered no resistance, didn't say a word. He went where he was led. It didn't matter.

They blended into the growing stream beginning to take shape now, following the red flares burning in the snow. A trail up to the gates and through. Away from the flames and crashing walls. Lee could hear the barking bullhorns once again.

"FOLLOW THE FLARES!" That had become a slogan of the night.

The captain and the others had left the refuge of the car and gathered the remaining volunteers at the gates, told them what to do. They had passed out flares and all began to work down the ramps toward Somerston and fanning out into the fields. Lighting flares and calling out the cry to follow through the bullhorns. It was not as chaotic as they had anticipated. The people seemed unhesitating, eager for any show of leadership. Sheep without a ram. Ollie turned the dozer and they organized the beginnings of the line from there, working down the ramps and onto #219. Ollie put the dragon in the lowest gear and began a heavy and immensely steady crawl back up the mountain. And the people believed the flares and the big noise and power of it and had followed. Not a line, it was a narrow mob behind a giant orange machine following a row of small, red, smoky flames. They did n't know that it was going to be eleven miles. Nobody told them. Not on this end. Perhaps after—at the tunnel. Once it had begun to form, Lee made for Somerston as directly as he could.

He had a bullhorn and two coat pockets full of flares. He started lighting them again one from the one before and setting them out as he and L.John moved back toward the gates.

"FOLLOW THE FLARES, FOLKS! WE'RE GOING FOR SHELTER! FOLLOW THE RED FLARES."

AURORA MAINTENANCE—3:10 A.M.

The plow train arrived at Aurora Maintenance short one plow, the #51 plow. Last in line. Had it been the third plow or the second they would have lost whatever was behind because there wasn't room to get around. The place it had happened was narrow and congested. But Fred Barger wasn't feeling lucky. Jennifer was feeling nauseous and hyper from adrenalin. She had a slight case of the shakes, could not forget the feeling as those bodies went under the plow. She wouldn't ever.

They pulled up short of the far end, the burned and blackened end, he looked at her to see her judgment of what he had done and she looked back at him but couldn't think of what to say. As they got down from the plow a man jumped from the back and came forward to tell them people had fallen off while they were moving. He didn't know how many. He thought some women. Quite a way back, just after they had started. Fred walked away and went into the office box. He called down the other side of the mountain.

He raised Patrolman LaBarr through a walkie-talkie. LaBarr was afoot on the long rampway from the eastbound to the gate, urging people forward, keeping up the flares.

"What do they want?" Jennifer heard Barger say.

"They want you to bring the plows down here," LaBarr said. "You're supposed to patrol this line of people on the way up to the tunnel. We're throwing down a trail of flares and they want you guys to help us keep them lit. Bring as many as you have down with you. Watch out on the way down because Ollie's in the lead with that bulldozer. He'll have to cut you out a place where you can get around."

"Where is he now?"

"111." It was another voice. A different transceiver.

"Ollie?"

"10-4. I'm at Milepost 111. I think I'm doing four miles an hour. Start lookin' for me between 112 and 111. Slow down because yer seeing distance is about ten yards."

"You're sure that's what we're supposed to do?"

"10-4," said LaBarr. "The captain and Mr. Rider both said whoever talked to you first to tell you just exactly that."

"That's what they said. I heard 'um." Ollie said.

"All right." Fred sounded persecuted. "I got to unload and take on fuel first." The crew chief paused. "You really walking all those people up from Somerston?"

"And you're supposed to bring down any kind of vehicles that would be better to haul people," said LaBarr. "We're holding back these old people and people with problems. Anything suited to carry people. There will be a lot of them. I'm talking hundreds."

Jennifer remained at the tunnel with the big patrolman to organize the people and the cots and supplies. She wanted to go, but Barger had no one to see to this. LaBarr had said there would be hundreds. Just of the old.

MILEPOST 111.8—3:30

They met head-on at Milepost 111.8. It was not much of a contest. The plumber and the cowboys and the women and three other cars that still had gas and had been able to pass through the medial where the torch had cut it away, had crossed over and come barreling down the eastbound into the dozer's headlights and the blade before anybody knew what hit them. Five 60 mile-an-hour impacts in succession didn't slow the dozer, didn't even make a decent jolt. Summer rabbits thrown against a speeding car. It would have simply continued to grind massively forward with the glacial force of low low gear, matter-of-factly pushing the debris aside in a straight and implacable line. But the engine of the car containing the cowboys and the woman tore loose from its mountings and was vaulted high over the engine of the dozer, spinning raggedly in space like some errant planetoid and Ollie never saw it. It landed on him in the open cab and killed him there. The kid for the Fire Department in Somerston dived clear and landed in the deep snow on the eastbound with his flares, got up and got the hell out of there.

The dozer cast into a moderate curving to the left, a wide circling pattern, crushing into the westbound, gouging into it and plowing a clean channel through the imprisoned traffic. The line of refugees from Somerston began to bunch up, momentarily confused. The orange behemoth disappeared into the darkness on the westbound side and for a time could not actually be heard above the howling wind. Distant crashing metal, crumpling metal now and then. Lost in the whistling blackness then. Complete silence for a little while.

The young man with the flares dug out of the snowbank, came among the milling refugees. Where was it? What had happened to it? He heard the crashings on the other side at intervals and then began to hear the engine sound again getting louder and then a grimy white volcano of car bodies scrambled in snow boiled up in front of him. The crowd began to scream. It ran back upon itself, back down the mountain. He ran down the mountain too. As fast as legs could go.

GATE 10—3:40 A.M.

By the time Lee had worked back to the gates with the mayor, a growing crowd of older people had been more or less stockaded there, held out of the line of marchers up to the tunnels by Beck and a handful of the volunteers. Lee was mindful of L. John and was looking for a scheme for getting him to shelter. Apparently no step in that direction had been taken. He found the captain at the inbound gate.

"Hello Mr. Mayor," Beck said. He looked relieved that Lee had found him.

"Hello," said L. John. That was all he said.

"Have you heard anything from Barger?" Lee asked. "Are they coming down?"

"LaBarr says they were at the tunnel. He said they were going to unload and gas up again and then come down."

They both were yelling above the wind. It seemed to Lee he could not remember talking without yelling.

"How long?"

"I think about a quarter of an hour. Maybe more." The captain addressed a huddling little herd. "Crowd together, folks! Crowd as close together as you can. We have trucks on the way."

"What about that flatbed for the dozer?"

"Walled up in the snow. We siphoned all the diesel out for Ollie."

Lee took Beck aside. "I want to get him out of the wind. He isn't fighting it. It'll get him. Where's the car?"

"Same place as before. There's some in it now. Bad-off cases. But you may as well just wait for them to get down here with plows. You'll never get around that dozer."

"He's got Barger's walkie-talkie. I'll have him cut a place to pass."

"I thought about that. Can't leave here myself. You can take six, maybe eight at a time. But get right down here after. We've got to set up some kind of a continuous patrol along this thing to pick up dropouts, keep an eye on things."

The captain continued to wave and shout people on, playing his 6-volt beam along the line. He stepped forward and singled out a younger couple with a baby, had them wait with the small herd.

"Tell Barger to get his butt in gear," he said when they were alone again. "When you get up there see what other kinds of trucks and things we can use to help these people out. If this has got a prayer we're gonna have to stay on top of it the whole way.''

Lee agreed. He led L. John toward the car.

Behind them they could hear the captain and his bullhorn.

"FOLLOW THE FLARES, FOLKS! JUST FOLLOW THE FLARES!''

MILEPOST 112—4:10 A.M.

Instead of meeting the expected head beams from the dozer coming up at #112, Barger's plowtrain ran into a solid wall of snow and upturned vehicles. Barger and his men pulled up in line and climbed the wall. There was no way of going around. It crossed the road entirely.

At first they could see nothing. The wall cut off any benefit which might have been gained from the plow lights. It was like standing on the rim of some black and frozen crater. Their sealed-beam lanterns penetrated only yards into the driving snow, bringing nothing useful to their senses.

Barger heard a sound of movement and of metal below him in the darkness and played his beam in that direction. A door was opening, a station wagon sticking like a tombstone from inside the crater's rim, the wall of snow. He heard groans, now, cries for help and he dispatched his men to pull the people from the wreckage and to look for more on both sides of the heaped up wall. A woman in the station wagon came out with a bloody nose, but mainly these people were unhurt, just tumbled up among their belongings like so many dolls. The few cars that they had a chance to open were that way. The snow seemed to have had a cushioning effect which minimized injuries. And there were muffled cries from deep beneath the snow, from cars they couldn't see or find.

Barger fought his way along the crater's rim. Treacherous beneath him. Solid in some places, airy powder in others. He found footing on another upturned car and stood a minute listening. He thought he heard a new note, deep and heavy above the wind and the idling engines of the plows. Yes. No. Yes, definitely. Big engine. That was it. It had to be the dozer. He had thought that all along. What else could it be? Where? What had happened? What was going on?

Then he saw it. In it's endless circling, the headlights turned directly up the eastbound now. He saw it coming. For him. Momentarily he wanted to bolt and run back to the plows, but then he saw it was continuing to turn, going round and round. The lights swung slowly to his right and disappeared again. It crossed back onto the westbound, thundering by about thirty yards below and in front of him and now was gone again.

Lee had crept about a mile along the line of marchers in patrol car #337, keeping to the outside more or less and depending upon the flashing lights and horn to clear the way. How could you call that a line? More like a river of humanity flowing uphill through an artificial bed cut by Ollie's dozer, like driving cattle through an 11-mile rectangular chute. Didn't need flares to guide them; there was no way out of that channel, with walls as much as ten feet high on either side. Psychologically the flares were gold—smoky, smelly, sputtery. Pin-point islands of red flame coming out of the gloom at intervals that came just as doubt was beginning to overtake you. Vastly reassuring. They would keep the flares alive no matter what, Lee decided. More show of official-looking lights, more vehicles like #337. Privately the flashing lights and sirens had always irritated Lee, had seemed overdone. Hysterical. Now he saw that in the midst of the enormous confusion they communicated instantly and without ambiguity that authority was there. That order had not evaporated altogether. Whether or not that was effectively so was not questioned. It looked like leadership, like intelligent activity. The lights and flares were bastions of credibility inducing them to march and to continue marching, doing as they were shown, believing it. Woods was right about that. Belief was everything. Any symbol, any sham they could pull off to hold this march together, should be used. For eleven to twelve miles they had to.

Then in the headlights people were coming toward them, crowding, confusing, flooding back down toward the gates again. LaBarr appeared waving a flare. Lee stopped and rolled the window down.

"Something's cockeyed up ahead," LaBarr yelled at him.

"Something went bananas with the dozer."

"You call Ollie? He's got a walkie-talkie."

"No good with the VHF." Lee hadn't thought about the VHF. Not with a carload of six old people and the intricate driving. His volume control had been rolled down completely. He put it up so he could hear. A motor sound, an open air sound interrupted by blackouts, mike overloads from wind noise and mechanical shocks to the mike itself. No voice. Nobody talking. Listening through a kind of window into something violently ongoing, something mindless and enormous and inhuman in the presence of an activated microphone.

Then someone tried to make a call, a garbled, splattering, wowing, buzz of distortion, completely unintelligible. The steady motor noise was blanketing communications. Nobody else could talk either. Somebody else had just tried and didn't make it.

"I think it's on the dozer," said LaBarr. "I think that's where it's coming from."

LaBarr climbed onto the hood. There was no room inside. The people were retreating more thickly now. In droves, more hurried. Greater urgency. LaBarr lit and waved a new flare from the hood and barked at the crowds through his bullhorn.

Then the VHF cleared for a moment. The motor-noise stopped. Lee heard Fred Barger clearly. That must have been the garbled voice.

"Plow train leader to #337 or Gate 10. Does anybody copy?"

"10-4," said Lee. "This is Rider in 337 at about 110. Where are you?"

"Milepost 111.9 and stopped. Me and five more plows. Something went bananas with old Ollie. Dozer's locked into a left-hand circle maybe thirty yards across. Going across both lanes and crossing over in the westbound. Working downhill your direction a little more each time. Ten more yards out of that westbound every time she goes around. We got a ten-foot wall of junk and snow across the eastbound here. We can't get down."

Then strange noise from the renegade was back again. He heard Barger try to call, the howling, garbled mess of two equal FM signals on top of one another. The motor noise kept coming.

Then the road cleared. All at once there were no refugees in front of them. The way was clear and vacant. Nothing. LaBarr set the bullhorn down and braced his hands on his knees as they went forward.

After a quarter of a mile they came to a wall of snow and wreckage just as Barger had. Lee stopped and got out. He and LaBarr played flashlight beams up along the wall. Quiet. No big diesel engine. Nothing moving. Nothing but the howl of the wind, the snow whipping their faces. They listened on LaBarr's walkie-talkie. The sound was there. The strangely pinched sound of an enormous thing, strained down to something scratchy, thin and tinny. As they listened it began to come alive. The tinniness began to flash out, imperceptibly at first, becoming fuller, deeper, more complete. The wall began to burst and roll to the left of them before they realized that it was the real sound now, imposed on the walkie-talkie sound and the wall of cars and snow began to avalanche, to well outward and tumble down on them. They ran back out of range. Lee dove into the car, backed a couple hundred feet further down the mountain. The upheaval in the wall passed to the right and quit. The entire wall had moved ten feet in their direction. Lee left the car and rejoined the patrolman. The dozer had gone by. It was silent on the other side of the crater wall again. Dark. Some people squirmed out of the snowbank. LaBarr and Rider helped them out and urged them back away from it, back down the mountain. Amazingly, no one seemed injured.

The radio went clear again, the bulldozer sound was gone. Apparently an intermittent fluke, an erratic thing. Barger's voice came through again.

"2245 to 337 do you copy, by?"

"10-4, 2245," said Lee. "We've come up to it, Fred. We saw it going by."

"It's doing what I said? It's working downhill?"

"10-4. Now who the hell is going to stop it?"

"Uh—I hate to say this, but I don't think we got one man over here knows how to run one of them things. Myself included."

"Terrific!"

"Maybe we'll just have to wait until it runs out of gas,"
said Lee's walkie-talkie.

LaBarr shook his head. "Negative," he said. "We fueled
up at the gates before he started. Siphoned thirty gallons out of
that flatbed they haul it on. It'll probably run for hours."

"Negative on that," said Lee. "LaBarr here tells me that
they gassed it up down at the gates. It's good for hours. Do you
see it? Where is it now?"

"10-4. It just went by."

"If you can't stop it, you can at least get your men over on
this side. You can dodge the damn thing can't you? It's not moving *that* fast."

"I guess if we have to."

"Of course you have to! Get over on this side and get these
patrons out of westbound cars. It's chewing them up like a mess
of hashbrowns. There's only two of us on this side."

When Lee let up the button he heard the dozer sound again,
the garble of somebody trying to punch through the interference.
He didn't know whether Fred had copied him or not. He waited
for the dozer-voice to quit but it did not.

"To hell with it," said Lee. "C'mon!"

They clambered up the crater wall. LaBarr fell through a
soft place between cars. As Lee reached down for him he heard
the dozer coming around again. He yelled for LaBarr to hurry. It
was bad, the footing tricky. LaBarr slipped several times against
the car he was climbing. The crater wall was tumbling over them
like surf as LaBarr scrambled up. They dived outward headlong
and blind, hoping for the best. Tumbling over and over now in
snow and then quiet finally. Stillness.

Lee's first thought was air. He fought upwards. They were
at the edge of it, under less than two feet of dirty snow. The
huge machine was still above them, just beyond the wall but
moving by. It had moved their portion of the wall as much as it
was going to this time.

They got up, beat the snow off and started trying to find better footing. They could hear cries from people in cars under
them. There wasn't time now.

Lee topped the edge and skidded down the other side to the

crater floor. LaBarr came behind. The floor was not entirely smooth. Chunks of debris and dark shapes came into their lantern beams, some shapes Lee would as soon not look at. They ran up behind the mindless giant grinding on at walking speed, following the tracks until the tail lights and reflectors showed in front of them.

The big treads catapulted chunks of snow and wreckage at them, flinging up debris in brief trajectories, snow and ice and even some sizeable metal objects, a thundering, rock-steady monstrosity. They found themselves dodging constantly, trying to keep close to the tail between the treads where there was less debris. A roughly triangular area of sanctuary. They jogged in the crotch of safety, trying to stay in it, difficult because the under-clearance of the dozer was high and Ollie must have raised the blade a foot or so. Debris passed under and between the treads unscathed. No way to see it coming. They stumbled frequently and fell a few times.

The cab was high above them. No steps or ladders were provided. This was crazy, Lee decided. They were getting nowhere. He left the relative shelter of the center momentarily, enduring the debris to check the right side, to shine the flashlight beam up toward the cab and see whether the rope, that Ollie had cast up to the cab in order to climb up, was there. It wasn't. He tried the left. No rope either. He pulled back into the center with LaBarr. They jogged and hurdled obstacles emerging from beneath the dozer for a while longer. Then Lee stopped short. The great machine just ground on.

"No good," Lee shouted.

"What do you want to do?" The trooper shouted back.

"Come on!"

They retraced their steps, ran back to the wall across the eastbound where the dozer would be taking a new bite next time around. It was out of sight now and they could only hear it through the walkie-talkie. Lee searched the inside face of the crater wall, looking for a way to climb, a portion of the wall composed more solidly of metal than of snow.

"You stay here and keep a lookout," Lee said. "If I screw up on this get Barger, and if he can't make it, then draw straws or whoever has the most illegit kids or whatever. It steers by levers. Pull one back and it turns that way, the side you pull back. I watched him driving it. That much I know.''

"Like a tank!" LaBarr said.

"You drive a tank?" Lee brightened at the prospect. Almost all the patrolmen had military service, most had been marines, a lot of combat veterans. The state police force attracted guys who hadn't made out badly in the military. If LaBarr had learned to drive a tank, then Lee was in no hurry to play untrained hero, LaBarr got the job. But LaBarr shook his head. "My Old Man," he said. "Drove tanks in World War II. Told me they use levers."

Lee gave it up and began to scale the wall. If he waited at the top, at the very edge when the dozer made its pass, he might have a chance at leaping to the roof of the engine housing, as the blade cut away his perch from under him. Might. He saw no other way of getting up into that cab.

He reached the top and waited. Waiting gave him time to notice that his ears were hurting like a sonofabitch. His feet too. If he could get into the cab maybe he could steer the damn thing off the mountain, drop it 300 feet down the rocky cliffs of the ravine. Maybe he could even find the kill switch. Maybe, maybe, maybe! Where *was* the goddam thing? He felt like he was waiting for a bus. He squinted against the driving ice. Still nothing. Cold pain. Stinging pain. The wind filled up his ears and was all he could hear. He wondered about people in the cars beneath his feet, whether they were alive or dead. If alive, would any of them survive the next pass of the dozer? But he felt nothing there, heard nothing. He could make out LaBarr's lantern dimly. It seemed miles below. He waited.

Then it came. He could feel it shake the ground, shake the pile of junk he stood on. The shaking came before the hearing and the hearing before the seeing, and when it was so loud it was all that he could do not to dive down the other side and run like hell, he saw it. By the time he saw it, he had seconds.

The car under him began to move. Big headlights glared directly under him. The dozer's hood was perhaps a foot higher than the rocking, side-slipping surface upon which he now stood.

If he jumped and slipped, he'd go down onto the monster track, be carried forward and then under. The hood was mantled with a coat of ice and snow. Not a goddam thing to hang onto.

Then he saw the stack. The straight-up stack, on his side and toward the back, directly before the cab, it's raincap beaten continuously open by the steady pulses of exhaust. It would be hot. It would be all he had. Then his platform gave way beneath him altogether and he jumped.

He landed hugging the exhaust stack for all the life within him. At first it burned his cheek. He pulled his face away, then managed to get the overcoat lapel between his cheek and the stack. He hugged it for dear life. Waiting. Thinking what to do. He could feel the heat beginning to come through four thicknesses of sleeves. He wished to God he'd put the sealed-beam lantern in his pocket. It was in his hand and in his way now. With enormous effort he flung it toward the cab and got one leg up on the hood in the same violent thrust. The lantern bounced down into the floor of the cab somewhere, the light all but disappearing. He could only see a tiny reflection of it. A little glow. He could not see anything around him or below. He thought about the 2-inch thick steel plates of the great track grinding invulnerably below him. He didn't need a light to see that.

His right heel began to lose its purchase on the roof of the motor. He concentrated to bring as much muscular force as possible to bear precisely down on the heel, to create as much traction there as possible. The rubber of Old Maggie's galoshes held. He raised his hip with aching deliberation until he could slide it up onto the hood as well. He could smell the smoke of fabric now. His overcoat. The shoulder and the sleeves and the lapel were smoking. He let go of the stack, spread-eagled himself face down across the hood and clung there momentarily, trying to determine whether any of his clothing had begun to smolder or was merely scorched. After seconds he inched forward to the cab until he could get hold of one of the roll bars forming a cage around it. Holding carefully to this, he swung his heavy boots around and let them down into the cab.

He found that it was only half a cab, half of it was filled with some large object and he could hardly stand. Underfood was slippery, like walking in an inch of oil on a shaking floor. The 6-volt lantern had slid under the big object, he could see its glow somewhere below, obscured by the large object. He reached under, felt around, brought it out. Dripping blood. The gooey, oily stuff, an inch deep on the floor was blood. The object in the cab was mostly motor block and partly Ollie. Blood all over the 6-volt lantern in his hand now. Dripping thickly. He stood frozen momentarily, then shook out of it enough to function. He thought about the levers.

The motor block had come in through the front, had bent the left hand lever into a permanent position about a quarter back, causing the left track go slightly slower than the right, setting the machine into this broad circular pattern. It was frozen. Would budge neither forward nor back and if there were a kill switch, it was somewhere under the intruding motorblock. But the problem was the left track was still moving, still driving at a moderate rate. Not shut off. Had it been fully stopped he could have simply pulled the other lever back and pinned it, stopping both tracks dead, and then just let the fuel run out. But the lever wouldn't move. Jammed solid. He threw his weight into it and accomplished nothing. That meant he could make sharp right turns with the other or go straight by balancing, but could not turn left in greater degree than he was turning now. He looked out across the hood and could not tell where he was, could not see anything and had lost all sense of direction. No idea of where to turn to send the monster bounding down into the ravines.

Then he thought of the walkie-talkie. It was pressed between a part of Ollie and the seat in such a way the press-to-talk button was held down. There was more blood on his hands than he had realized. He wiped them and the walkie-talkie off onto his coat, being careful not to foul the radio. No telling if there were any life left in the batteries, a walkie-talkie left in steady TRANSMIT for perhaps a solid half hour? How much could be left? He called and got LaBarr.

"Have you seen Barger's guys?" aked Lee.

"10-4, Lee. What do you want?" It was Barger breaking in.

"Let me talk to Barger," Lee said so that LaBarr would get out of it now.

"I'm up on this machine," said Lee. "Ollie's dead. Some kind of a collision. I can guide it. I can make right turns or go straight. I can't go left more than I'm going now. I can't shut it off. I want to drive it off the mountain, across the eastbound and down the ravine. I don't know where I am now. Can't see. Set me up some kind of signal at three o'clock on the cirlce, on the eastbound when I'm going due east. Pointed up the mountain I can make a right turn then, and drive her straight off the mountain."

"You can steer it, huh?" said Barger.

"Yes a little."

"You think you could steer it around enough to clear some of the eastbound of these walls before you run it off the cliff?"

"Hey! This is a first for me. I never ran one of these in my life! I've got one lever!"

"Lee. These walls! Ten feet high! Unless we break them down I can't get my plows through, you can't get the people through and what's it all for anyhow?"

Lee thought about it. Yes. What for? "If we can work it so that I can do it all in sharp right turns. That's all I got. Right turns."

"I think it can be done," said Barger. "Listen—"

Lee had to ride the beast around again. Another bite out of the westbound. He hated that, felt every inch of it. He was to watch for five flares in a group, then get ready. LaBarr would fire a shot into the air and he would pull the right lever back all the way, making a dime right turn onto the eastbound, punching through the lower crater wall. He would straighten for about five seconds, then pull the lever and bring the dragon fully about and go straight up the eastbound and across the "crater" to punch through the upper wall. Then another sharp right and off the mountain. That was the plan. He waited with his doubts and listened to the crushing metal under him.

Now he saw the flares. Five in a row. He tensed. Waited, the gunshot came. He pulled the lever back as far as it would go.

"NOW!" screamed the walkie-talkie.

Lee felt the world turn under him, the wall swirling dizzingly by in the head beams.

"STRAIGHT NOW!" screamed the walkie-talkie.

He let up the lever halfway. Was that enough? He couldn't work the walkie-talkie too.

"MORE!" It screamed. He let up to move. "OKAY! ENOUGH! NOW PULL HER AROUND AGAIN! ALL THE WAY!"

Lee pulled all the way back and again the world whirled under and around him.

"STOP!" It barked. "STRAIGHT NOW! I'm in FRONT OF YOU WITH A FLARE. FOLLOW THE FLARE!"

Lee didn't know how accurately he'd turned or hit the eastbound or cleaned out the wall or anything. He was going entirely by directions given. Everything around him looked the same until he saw the flare.

The small red flare stayed ahead of him for what seemed hours. There was little junk piling up in front of the blade now. They were crossing the crater floor. No voice came from the walkie-talkie for a long, long while.

"All right now," it said at last. "I'm veering off to the left. You don't follow. You keep going straight again. You go through the wall and then you do a "90" to the right and then go straight again. You'll be going straight off the mountain. Get the hell off just as quick as you can." There was a pause. "Okay. We're coming to the wall. I'm veering off now."

Lee saw the small red smudge go to the left and then the wall reared up in front of him and he went into it, scarcely feeling the impact. Cars reared and plunged in front of him

"Okay! You're through!" the walkie-talkie barked again.

Lee pulled back the lever and spun slowly on a dime.

"Okay. That's 90. Let 'er go!" the talkie shouted.

Lee let the lever forward till it matched the other. The dragon ground inexorably forward.

"Get off!" the walkie-talkie barked.

But Lee couldn't. If he let up on the lever the bulldozer would fall back into it's broad, counter clockwise rotation and might not be close enough to the ravine and would come back on them again and they'd be back where it had started all over again. No. He'd have to ride it out. Ride it as far as he could. Ride it to the edge.

He had no idea how far the edge was, had no idea how broad the berm was, how far it was before the mountain simply dropped away. He was piling up cars and snow so high the headlights were now buried and he could not see a thing. He just rode it. On and on. The land stayed level for what seemed forever, then at last began to rise. He felt himself going upgrade slightly, heard the crack and splintering of wood, some pines fell backwards and bounced off the roll bars. Trees were bouncing off the cab now and he was still going up. He held fast to the lever, trying to keep straight and waited. Then the dozer leveled out again and then was going slightly downhill and then *really* downhill and he jumped, just dove blindly from the cab. He landed feet first on the tread, jumped again, went through pine branches and landed buried in the snow. He heard the breaking of big trees and crashings going faster and faster and then the sound of the motor was gone and the crashings disappeared far away and were covered by the wind. Finally, far below, a great veiled explosion and then that was all.

He had no trouble finding his way back to the road. The trail was amply marked. When he got back he found his work a little ragged, but the walls were breached, the plows were rolling through. He hopped one for a ride across the crater on the running board, down to the warmth of the state patrol car #337 to pick up where he'd left off.

AURORA MAINTENANCE—6:08 A.M.

An hour and a half before dawn it quit snowing. The wind continued to be strong for twenty minutes more and then it too died quietly and everything was still except little spraying gusts that came for a while, sporadic mavericks rushing to catch up, but those died too and then everything was very still and cold. Lee looked at his L.E.D. watch—6:08. Two hours since the bulldozer and now the first of the long line of refugees was just arriving at the tunnel. In the absence of the wind the crunch of footsteps in the hard crust of scraped-over snow crackled like grass-fire down the long, long line. The motors of the plows thundered far below, none near the tunnel at the present moment, echoing in the ravines and silent forests up the mountain. When the air had cleared of swirling snow, the flares became visible in an endless line down the mountain—pinpoint stars of red strung on an unseen cord, winding out of sight below him in the distance and forever.

After his battle with the great machine Lee had resumed the trip up to Aurora in car #337, had rested at the maintenance and left the settling of his passengers to Jennifer. By then a couple dozen cots had been set up and there were places for them. Jennifer took charge without comment at her husband's appearance. She put L.John in the office cubicle. She led the others away and got them settled too. Lee went into the supplies and found other clothes. Overalls. A maintenance jacket. He rolled his trench coat and his jeans up in a bloody ball and pitched them into a dumpster, hosed off Maggie's big galoshes, walked up and down in the snow outside and came back in and hosed them off again. He needed the galoshes and was intent on returning them, but not caked with blood.

For the remainder of the night the plows, patrol cars and even some of the snowmobiles worked up and down the eastbound, regathering the marchers and starting up the line again, patroling up and down. Picking up attrition. Despite efforts to single out the older and the seemingly ill or weak, some fell by the wayside. There were just too many; the statistics were against them. They weren't doctors and they weren't God and they couldn't get them all. If alive, they drove them to the tunnel; if dead, they cached them in the outside wall of snow and put up branches from nearby pines to mark them. They would keep beneath the snow.

Now at 6:08, Lee leaned against the blackened west entrance to the maintenance and watched the first of the marchers coming by, picking their way among the ruts outside the tunnel. He sipped coffee and took a break now. His back and hip were aching and his toes hurt like hell. Maybe he'd lose a couple. Frostbite. His cheek had given rise to blisters where the exhaust stack of the dozer had burned him. The cold felt good against the cheek, the only place it did feel good. He sipped coffee and leaned his back against the wall, taking stock of what was left of himself now. He decided he was beat to hell, but not irrevocably damaged, except maybe for a couple of toes. The toes hurt though. Woods had said that was a good sign. Woods! Bah! Who knew what to believe where Woods was concerned?

At 6:08, it had begun to smooth out and was settling into routine. LaBarr had relieved him of car #337. Beck was still down at the gates with L.John's volunteers. Officer Prokovic had simply disappeared. They hadn't heard from him in hours.

Still almost two hours before daylight. Less than twenty days until the shortest daylight of the year. How many shopping days till Christmas? Lee sipped his coffee, watched the faces, waited for the dawn. What a night! There was a still part of him that did not believe day would ever come.

DAY THREE: TUESDAY

AURORA MAINTENANCE—DAWN—TUESDAY.

They came as promised in the morning. Not at first light, but later when the overcast had burned away. At first light there was not a flake of snow and it was still and brittle cold and very, very gray. It would be two hours before the sun came fully through and the airplanes and the helicopters and the rest of it appeared in earnest.

From the west end of the tunnel Lee had watched the first light come and the people coming and still coming. He had looked at every face and not seen Charlie and the faces kept on coming and still no Charlie. The ragged line would keep coming well into the daylight, well after the arrival of the sun, the helicopters and the airplanes and the rest of it till deep into the afternoon. Lee was more tired than he thought it possible to be, his face so long in need of sleep and washing that it didn't feel the cold except a little on his forehead and his eyes, refreshing and preserving him a little.

Jennifer came out from what she had been doing inside and watched with him shortly after dawn. They watched the smoke that rose straight up from Somerston. Smaller columns stand like pines—making one larger, seemingly fluted column far away beyond the trees and from far below in the valley. It came up straight, and then spattered against some difference in the higher air and broke toward the east, passing to the south of them. It had been a surprise to Lee. Somerston was not where he had thought it was, had taken it for granted to be all these years. It made no practical difference, it was just not where his mind had placed it when emerging from the tunnel all these years. But the column was irrefutable proof. That's where it had to be.

"How is Pribanic?" Lee spoke first.

"Same," she said. "Sitting in the office on that wooden chair. Won't take coffee. Won't let you do anything for him."

"Does he talk to you?"

"Yes, but he doesn't look at you. He acts like he's ashamed, like—oh, I don't know! I want to ball him out for pouting but I can't. How could I? How could anybody get so utterly invested in a *town*?"

Lee shrugged and sighed and shook his head and didn't answer. Something lost to him and Jen. There had been too many towns. All for terrific reasons. Too many just the same. He thought about the new house standing open, full of snow and couldn't get distraught about it. It was a nice house like a lot of houses. Maybe if they lived in it for sixty years. They watched the trudgers for a long time after that and didn't talk. There was just the crunch of feet on brittle snow, the sound of plows from far below.

At 8:30 on the nose a single light helicopter passed directly overhead and kept going west until it was gone from view. That was the first one. Maybe it was Woods going back to Pittsburgh. Who could say?

At 9:15 a plow came up along the outside of the line and stopped in front of Lee and Jennifer. It was Barger.

"That's it," he said. "The tail-end of them went through the gates a quarter hour back." He paused. "How are you making out up here?"

Lee shrugged. He couldn't think of anything to say and so he answered with a gesture that said so. His mind was on Charlene, but there was nothing to say about that.

"You want to go down to Somerston? I can take you down if you want to go," said Barger.

"Yes. I do." Of course he did. His mind was locked on Charlie now. He thought about the Mayor, too. L. John would want to go.

"How bad is it? Is there any of the town left at all?"

Barger nodded vigorously. "Oh, hell yes!" he said. "Three quarters of it. Wind blew it across from west to east. The northern third is gone, but it didn't spread south hardly at all."

"What about the courthouse?"

"The courthouse is okay."

"Wait there," said Lee. He went inside to get the mayor.

They passed the end of the line about three quarters down, a little below of Milepost 112. The sun was peeping through the overcast here and there. A lot of military helicopters passed over head from behind them and went on west. People were emerging from the westbound cars in increasing numbers, watching them go by in the plow, squinting up at the sound of the helicopters, watching for whatever might be going on. There was a lot of life beneath those mounds of snow. A lot of cramped and scraggly human beings. L.John regarded the emerging people distantly from between Lee and Barger in the plow but made no comment. Forest and terrain were such that Somerston could not be seen from the turnpike until wihin yards of the gates. They could see the straight-up rise of smoke, that's all.

At 112 they stopped. They were in the crater of the dozer now. Patrol car 337 and two other plows were there together. A dozen guys worked around the plows, loading them with bodies from a cache in the bulldozed wall of snow. Lee got out, leaving the mayor in the plow. Barger got out too. They found Beck supervising on the other side of the patrol car, when they came around it. Lee and Barger leaned against the car, on either side of him. Nobody said anything for a while. They watched the bodies being put into the dump beds, stiff as boards. They didn't seem like people. No sense of people about them. You could not pick up people by both ends like logs and stack them. It did not seem real.

"What are we going to do with them?" asked Lee. A simple question seeking information, asked without emotion. They had to have a place to put them. That was that.

The captain sucked his teeth. He kept his hands in his armpits.

"The idea now is to get them out of sight. Out of here. It's going to be getting pretty busy. Westbound's waking up fast."

"Where?" said Lee. His mind was too tired for speculation. Let somebody else supply the answers.

"We thought about the old Bypass Tunnel. Hidden. Nothing in there now but salt and gravel, old machines. What the hell?"

What the hell indeed? It wasn't bad. From the Pike you had no idea that there was an abandoned tunnel below the newer bypass. An obsolete two-laner but still three quarters of a mile from end to end. A lot of bodies—a lot of anything—could be stashed in there.

"Who's *we*?" asked Lee.

"Oh, me and that one-armed guy, that civil defense guy. What's his name. We can't find the coroner or the mayor."

"We have the mayor," Lee said.

They were working on the ramps as best they could with no other equipment than two plows. Barger pulled his own plow to the side at the gates. They got out on Lee's side because the snow was too deep on the outside. Fred has pulled as far to the side as he could get and could not get out now. Fred was showing signs of wear, Lee observed, like himself.

The little mayor had remained silent all the way, had gazed through the windshield with unseeing eyes. He had to be urged to awareness to leave the plow, and did what was asked without comment. That made him look older, caved in and worn down. Lee raised his arms to help him down and he accepted.

Then the little guy stopped, halfway down from the cab, still in Lee's arms. He looked at his town. The gates were higher than the town, the turnpike built up almost a hundred feet above it and the view was clear. The fire had razed the northern third. It had burned across from west to east and not spread south at all, like Barger said it had. The hill on which the Orthodox church stood seemed to have acted as a barrier, prevented the spread at the beginning, when it counted, and the fire could not backtrack thereafter against the power of the wind. The church had not burned down this time. But the main thing was the courthouse.

It stood starkly out all by itself with ruins all around. For whatever reason, whether that it was brick and stone, that so many of the great elms about it had been broken down, or the fact of distance—sitting isolated in its private island like a Mexican *El Centro*—it was there. Intact and standing.

The mayor blinked a couple times, then let himself down all the way and disengaged himself from Lee. He took his eyes off the old edifice and looked at Lee briefly and a little strangely. Then back to the courthouse once again. He straightened his Harry Truman overcoat and walked away without a word. He walked through the gates, through the straggling remnant of a mixed guard of town volunteers from the night before. The mayor walked a full foot taller and he walked straight for the old courthouse.

Lee and Barger exchanged glances, then Lee went after him. Fred followed.

Most of the highway businesses remained. The Mehelic

Highway Motel had busted windows, but was there. Mehelic Feed and Implement was gone a hundred yards further down and everything from there to the courthouse. The blackened steel parts of tractors, hayrakes stood among ashes. Most buildings were just black rectangles in the snow. Brick walls standing starkly here and there.

The mayor was keeping up a ferocious pace, his chin up high. Lee and Barger kept a hundred feet behind him, best they could manage. The underfoot was slippery and there was incredible debris. They could not catch up with him.

Pigs were still around. Not as many, though. They ran into a little pack, three of which were feeding at a spilled bakery truck, cracking rock-hard frozen pies between their jaws. #219 from the gates to the courthouse was devoid of people. Almost. One here, another there, emerging hollow-eyed from the second night in a car. Probably not their own.

They walked a few yards further on. Lee just kept walking, trying to gain ground L. John. They were well into the town, a block behind the mayor. More of the black bodies. Bodies sat behind the wheels of blackened cars. Bodies to be stepped over. No live people getting out of these cars. And it was dogs now, a couple worried looking dogs among the blackened things.

Around the courthouse, among the fallen trees and on the walks people in greater numbers were going in and out, but mostly coming out to see in what ways and to what degrees the world was altered. A mess of kittens venturing from their nestbox for the first time. Cautious and stiff. The little man marched up the steps disappearing among them, reappearing, then finally vanishing inside and out of view altogether.

Lee had sheltered something in his insides up to now, shielded himself against it, anesthetized himself against the pull of it and not admitted to himself how desperately he wanted to get inside that building and to know. In the last few hundred yards the pull became greater than his fear of disappointment. He began to jog, then run—despite the ice, despite the debris and the dogs and the bodies and the people. He bounded up the front steps and inside. He didn't fall. Didn't run into anybody. He considered that an accident.

"Oh. Well, good. Mike! That's it. Mike's his name. He's acting for the coroner. We think it's a good idea until whoever gets in here with refrigerated trucks or whatever the hell they use. It's supposed to be cold weather all week long. Is that so?"

"I got no information. Don't ask me."

"Well, I heard that someplace. I dunno. Christ, you look like shit, Lee."

"Yeah," said Lee. They leaned against the car for a while in silence watching the guys load up the bodies, thinking what it would turn into if it suddenly got warm. Lee thought about two tunnels now—some twenty-two miles apart: one for the living, one for the dead. Some kind of balance in that somewhere.

"How many do you think?" he said at last.

The captain made a helpless flurry with his hands and put them back into his armpits. They must be bothering him a lot, decided Lee. "How the hell do *I* know? I just work here."

"I guess," said Lee. He didn't know why he had asked that. What would a number do for him right now?

"They'll be finding bodies for the next five years," Beck said. "Next ten years!"

"I guess," said Lee.

"We got to get a lane plowed up to the bypass, yet. Some of the Guard guys and the electric guys are working on it. Just barely getting started."

Lee shook his head. There was another of those silences in which they watched the loading of the rock-hard people on the plows.

Then Lee snapped out of it. "Well. Got to go on down."

The captain nodded.

Lee sent Barger to the plow, said he'd be coming in a minute. He wanted private words with Beck, and waited until Fred was gone.

"What?" said Beck.

"You've met my kid, haven't you? I mean you know what she looks like."

The captain looked at the white ground, kicked at the snow. "You didn't run into her, huh?"

"No."

There was another silence, but they both looked at the ground not at the bodies.

"Sure, I know what she looks like," said the cop. "What the hell, Lee . . ."

"I'd want to know it before Jennifer," Lee said.

"Stop it, Lee. It's kind of early to be throwing in the towel."

"I'm not throwing in the towel. I'm saying *if* that's how it is, you come to me first. *IF*! That's all I'm saying."

Beck shrugged. "*If* I'm around. *If* I happen to be at the exact place, all right? This thing is spread all over. It's a big, huge thing!"

"Okay. Skip it!"

"*If* I recognize her."

"Forget it. Never mind."

"They don't always look much like themselves when they're frozen solid that way." He nodded at the bodies. "But, *if* I see her I will let you know."

"Fine," said Lee tersely. He turned and started for the plow.

"I'm only being straight with you, that's all."

"Never mind!"

"For crying out loud, Lee. You didn't need to ask a thing like that from me!"

Lee stopped and turned and looked at him, then nodded. Of course he didn't. Another group of helicopters racketed above them heading west. They watched them go. Lee looked back at Beck again and nodded. He hardly knew his own mind anymore. He turned to go.

"Cut it out," said Beck. "Go find your kid."

"10-4," said Lee and climbed into the plow.

Somerston came normally to view at Milepost 110.1, the first leveling of the road, the first break in the trees—but the snow walls rose so high on either side they could not see out of the channel. Just the tree-branch markers where more bodies had been stashed. The straight-up columns of smoke remained all that they could see until the gates. Another mile.

They had let them come into the courthouse during the night. Lee was surprised. Different the day before. Day? More like years. Memory images going black around the edges. More crowded here than at the tunnel, tiptoeing between people on the floor and stairs, from stepping stone to stepping stone, narrow footpurchase in the tiny spaces between them. It was like that on the second floor as well, and on the third, and on the fourth. They had opened all the floors. The fire must have divided the stampede, some going north, some south. He wondered whether they had let them in the courthouse with the fire in progress. If so—a monumental risk. He searched frantically among the floors and saw no Charlie. They filled the rooms and hallways. Ellis Island when his grandfather had come from Ireland, in the holds of the slavers, et cetera. Lee felt hostile and defensive against people concentrated in such squalid numbers. It was getting to him. It was alien and wrong, something vastly un-American about it. Something of his own was taken away.

The attic door was closed and didn't stop him. None of the refugees were in the narrow stairwell, none up in the attic. He dodged the beams and hanging objects in the gloom, making his way to the north window where they'd found L.John before.

"Who is that?" came the voice. L.John. Somewhere behind.

Lee stopped.

"Hey? Who is that there? You can't come up here?"

Testier than ever. The man behind the voice was well restored.

"Lee Rider. Where are you?"

The voice had come from the south side, opposite where he had been going.

"Ah! Okay, Mr. Rider. You can come. You didn't let any of the ragamuffins up behind you, did you?"

Lee found him after winding around chimney shafts, old desks, and piled up dusty things toward the voice. He found the mayor less directly than he might have.

He was at another of the gable windows—this one facing south—with his old brass field glasses as before. The window stood wide open. His giant wife was with him, shyly picking strings and straightening the Harry Truman overcoat.

"No. I'm by myself," Lee said. "Hi, Maggie. The boots saved my life. They really did. I want you to know that. Can I keep them just a little more?"

"Oh, Mr. Rider!" she blushed enormously. "Sure!"

L. John needed a shave—needed food and sleep too—but he was all right now. His size was back inside him. He was tired and shaken, but himself—almost as before.

"It's okay," he said. "We can get over this." He gestured to the courthouse underfoot. "The records are the families. The rest you can replace okay. We still know who we are."

He handed Lee the field glasses and pointed out the window, looking south down #219. "Take a look at that. What is that? That's something coming."

Miles down the road and over the crest of the horizon spouts of sooty diesel smoke, high feather-plumes of gray. Snow-blowing equipment—like in the Rockies, the snow lands.

"Army. L. John. We told Washington about the fire. They said they'd be here in the morning."

"Maybe they can haul these surplus populations out and we can get the town back in some kind of shape again."

Lee didn't answer. He knew that it would be many, many weeks before the refugees were entirely gone from Somerston—years before the town was built up again. And not the same. Not quite the same again. Not ever.

The Army convoy was still several miles below the town. It would be a while. Lee let the field glasses pan slowly down, following #219 from the south edge of town up to his toes. Beyond the edge of town the snow was white and deep and virginal. Unmarked by any passage. As his slow pan progressed up and along the main street there was more and more activity, more people leaving buildings and converging in a growing river of the curious coming northward.

He singled out the women—the young women—and watched each of them a little while. What had Charlie worn? Was it the navy peacoat or that tan wrap-around thing or what? He hadn't thought to ask. He wondered if he'd recognize her walk. People were not walking naturally with the rough underfoot.

A block below the courthouse square he saw her. Suddenly a flock of army helicopters had come low, racketing around the courthouse, casting shadows on the snow and his eye had followed one despite himself until it caught on the young woman. The shadow passed without him. It was Charlie! In the navy jacket. And she was making for the courthouse as he'd told her.

He was waiting at the top of the front steps as she came up the walk. She had gone on the snowmobile train to the hospital before the fire, accompanying an old woman.

She wanted to come home at once or even to the tunnel but Lee thought about the things between them and Gate 10. They'd wait until he could get them a helicopter back to Redford.

SOMERSTON—9:30 A.M.

The sun was fairly well up in the sky before the kids awakened to the light filtering down to them through several feet of snow. Then their heads poked out of the drift like woodchucks coming up for spring. The rigors of the day and night before had exhausted them so thoroughly that it was possible for them to sleep late even under such conditions. Eddie had one black eye.

He felt around the eye. The bright light on the snow had both of them squinting and squinting was painful to the eye. She regarded him with more than normally severe sobriety.

"What does it look like?" he said.

"Well, it shows."

"I wasn't doing nothing," he complained.

"We have a difference of opinion there," she said.

"I wasn't."

"Well, you never done no more of it though, did you?"

They found the culverts did run under #31. They hoisted Daisy up and wrapped her in the blanket and got up onto the road and for the first time were aware of the devastation of the north end of Somerston. There had been a lot of town there and there wasn't now. Blackened standing brick walls. A huge area of black ashes, snowless ground, and the hulks of cars.

Em let out a long, low whistle at the sight of it. They looked north and saw the stone foundations of the barn and some metal things which hadn't burned, the tractor and iron implements.

"You think it was the barn?"

"Tell you this much; I'll be glad my whole life it wasn't us that had to have a fire."

The south end of town was very much alive with army trucks and army people and the huge, olive things thundered by them on #31, shoving cars off right and left. They dodged their way into the town with a growing throng of people who had spent the night somewhere along the road, mostly in the cars that were being shoved off now. The army was at least checking and evacuating the cars before pushing them into the ditches. It was maybe six blocks to the central courthouse square and when they were past the hill with the white church, they saw that much more of the town was left than it seemed from out on #31. The army had cordoned off the north end of town to regular people and no one was being allowed to go that way, so they hung around the square watching for whatever might turn up. It was chaotic at the square now. The army guys seemed to know what they were after, but nobody else. It was noisy and a mess.

"I guess I better go down to the hospital and let my folks know I'm okay," said Eddie.

"Yeah. You better."

"Well goodbye," he said. He couldn't think of anymore to say.

"G'bye."

AURORA TUNNELS—10:30 A.M.

By 10:30 the sky was bright with sun and dark with helicopters. As Woods had promised, Somerston was overrun with relief agencies and military. The Army Corps of Engineers had made it to the junction and were pushing left on #31 out to the fairgrounds to erect a field hospital and trailer town to house the displaced. National Guardsmen became suddenly plentiful in and around the remainder of the town. They were doing exactly what Woods said they would. A squad of soldiers went ahead evacuating people from the cars and then plowed them off. There was no discussion. They just got them out and plowed them off. Behind the spearhead a convoy of covered trucks and then trucks hauling trailers, mobile homes. From the courthouse they could see no end of it.

Woods was waiting for them at the tunnel with Jennifer. Lee had sent Barger to the gates to radio the tunnel from the plow, to let Jennifer know that Charlie had been found and was okay—but it was still a big reunion. Lee counted it among his assets that his wife and daughter had grown into such good pals. Woods had come first to Redford and was told where to find Lee. He then took his chopper up the mountain and was again told where to find Lee. This time he waited at the tunnel with Jennifer and sent the chopper for them. He radioed for other helicopters to bring relief people and supplies to the east end of the tunnel. They would set up a more complete shelter and field hospital in the Maintenance. Woods liked the tunnel. It was a natural and he wanted to see it well begun. His pilot picked them up at the west end again with Lee and Charlene aboard now. Woods looked a little dark around the eyes, but otherwise was bright and clean shaven when he and Jennifer climbed in.

They took off at once. Lee signaled to the pilot to swing south around the mountain to avoid taking the women past the body on the Bald Knob tower.

As the chopper rose and swung south, Woods fished out the pipe and started to repack it.

"I'm impressed," he said. He nodded at the tunnel. "I wouldn't have thought it could be done."

Lee said. "Maybe it shouldn't have."

"No. It was the right thing. It was great."

Woods had struck a wooden match and was firing up now, raising clouds about his head.

"I wish you wouldn't do that," Charlie said.

"Huh?" Woods looked up. The pretty face was marred with disdain.

"That. I wish you wouldn't smoke that here. It smells like shit, it really does."

"Charlie!" Jennifer feigned shock. Jennifer was the most outspoken woman Lee had ever met and that was partly why he'd married her, but she was no match for her daughter.

"That's okay!" Woods held up a hand. "She's right. I'm sorry."

Woods smothered it, capping the bowl with the box of matches.

"She needs her nap," said Jennifer.

"Well, I'm sorry—but I just spent two whole days and nights packed in with people like some kind of stockyard and I want some air. Who are you anyway and what are you doing in our helicopter?"

Lee could not surpress a smile. He introduced them.

"She's hungry," he added. "I'll give you twenty-five to one. She gets that way when she's hungry. Since she was a kid."

Charlie still looked cross. She thought about it.

"Well, I'm sorry. I can't help it. I've had just too much people. I can't help it."

Woods fished in his pocket and came out with a rectangular object in tinfoil. He extended it to Charlene.

"Here," he said.

"What is it?"

"Peanut butter sandwich."

"You're kidding!"

"No. Go on."

She looked at it a little hesitantly, then lunged for it and tore the tinfoil away. She ate the whole thing while they watched. From his other pocket, Woods took out a thermos and poured coffee in the lid. She took that too. Nobody said anything. They watched her wolf it down.

She finished it and everyone stayed silent for a while.

"Oh, go ahead," she said.

Woods was perplexed.

"What?"

"Go ahead and smoke it. I don't care."

"No. It's all right. We'll be there in a couple minutes. I can wait."

"Go ahead and smoke the damn thing," Charlie scowled. "You're making me feel guilty!"

"Don't! It's not required," said Woods.

"Smoke it. Will you please? I mean it. If you don't smoke that goddam thing then I will!"

Woods came up with another tinfoil rectangle and held it out to her.

"No," she said. "I hate peanut butter. It's just that I was starved."

"It isn't," Woods said. He continued to hold out the sandwich.

"Oh? What is it?"

"Tuna. Or egg salad. One or the other. Take it."

"Will you smoke?"

"I won't smoke. No."

Woods started to retract the sandwich.

"All right," Charlie grabbed. "You win."

She ate half the sandwich and saw that Woods was looking at her. Then a smile broke over her and then they laughed.

Woods looked at Lee. "It works. You weren't kidding."

"You have to feed her," Lee said. "It's a matter of survival."

That afternoon Lee took the women home to see about the house. They gave it up and came back to Central after shoveling out the worst of the snow, carrying it out in cardboard boxes, locking doors. Lee closed the main switch, but left the gas turned off. Redford would remain blacked out until the Monday following when Army Engineers would restore the power lines across the bypass. The women set up housekeeping in Lee's office, bringing some things with them from the house. They would live at Redford Central until Monday.

And Charlene seemed not to mind the crowding terribly. Lee noted in the days to follow that wherever Woods was, Charlie was there too. Woods had given her a volunteer position, or maybe he had an inexhaustible supply of sandwiches. When he flew someplace, she went with him. She seemed to take an inordinate amount of interest in the work. All right. There was plenty of it.

L.John's kids turned up late Wednesday night. They were in a hospital in Cincinnati. They had spent Monday and Tuesday in the little green MG, stuck in a place on the highway unprotected from the wind and were found with severe hypothermia and with their legs partly frozen. Rider had turned Maggie's note in to the police desk at Central. The car had been found and he got the notification through the state police desk there. He arranged to have L.John, Maggie, Mike and Rose Mehelic flown out on an Air Guard helicopter. It picked them up in Somerston and landed them in Cincinnati an hour after sunrise.

The kids were sleeping, heavily sedated. They couldn't see them right away. L.John talked to the doctor. Mike had lost a leg below the knee and could lose the other. Maggie could lose one or both legs too. It was too soon to tell. The mayor went back to his wife and relatives and told them, phoned around town and found lodgings and ordered a cab.

They were walking out to the cab, across the hard crunching snow and ice of the hospital parking lot. Maggie walked her usual, unconscious pace or two behind and she was crying—just a little so as not to annoy. Mike Mehelic was crying too. Rose's face was hard as always, like a chicken. What was behind it you could never know.

He stopped them at the cab.

"When we get back," he said. "Whatever happens— nobody knits afghans. Lap robes. None of that. You tell the women."

SOMERSTON

Eddie did see Em again. The Bradens were stuck in Somerston till Thursday until evacuation routes had been established and there were buses and army caravans going south. Dan sent Irene and the kids down to Morgantown where they were to catch another bus east and go back to the farm. Em was on the bus. They didn't talk or sit together on the way. At the depot in Morgantown she told him she had sold the gun to a guy in the army because she had to. She had eaten most of the eight dollars and she thought she'd have bus fare to pay. They weren't making people pay to get out of Somerston if they were unable, but she didn't know that it was going to be that way. And she didn't figure she'd be seeing him again.

"That's okay," he said. "No hard feelings." Eddie had picked up a hundred forty odd dollars trafficking on the blackmarket in the streets of Somerston during the days they waited in the town. He still had the eye. It was a beauty.

"I'm glad," she said. "You take care of that dog now. Get her fixed before the next time."

"Okay," he said. "I will."

Em found Evan J. at home—full of liquor and apologies. The funeral had been yesterday. Molly and the foal were fine. Evan J. would go up and see about the truck next week some time.

Dan Braden would stay another week in Somerston trying to reunite himself with the family car, then return to the farm. He would fly to Detroit the week before Christmas, when things were opening up there enough to get around a little and when his company got back in operation. The family would return late in January. They would never find the family car.

BALD KNOB—THURSDAY

They got Jimmy Weeks down Thursday.

It had to wait for Thursday. It was madness everywhere and there were many, many things that had to come before. Even then it had to come as secondary to the mission to restore the Number 12 repeater to service. It had to wait on the availability of a helicopter with a cable-winch because there wasn't any place to land and because the trails up to the Knob were still impassable. Two guardsmen armed with automatic weapons and a generator went up in the chopper with Lee with supplies to stay until the regular electric power was restored, to guard the place and keep their generator fueled and running till Number 12 was on its own again. High priority, but it was Thursday before they could free a helicopter from life-rescue activities. With Number 12 in shape, the Turnpike VHF communications would be fully operative again.

Lee went up with them to show them what to do. He could have sent one the techs, but went himself. He wanted to get Jimmy down. He saw that job as his alone.

The body hung beside them, just outside and opposite the helicopter's open hatch—arms stiff above the head, the whole position rigid and unchanged. The weather had stayed bright and cold and clear. A lot of people said that they were lucky for that and perhaps they were, thought Lee. If that's what passed for lucky now, the standards had come down. The army fellows were lowered first, then their equipment, then Lee was in the sling.

He showed them where to disconnect inside the shack, where the power line came in and interfaced with the apparatus of the repeater. It was a relatively simple thing to do, to disconnect with the switch main and tap in with the cables of the army generator at the switch box. The repeater's own auxiliary needed work, the batteries had died laboring to restart the gasless generator engine and would have to be replaced—but this would do for now. They set it running, Lee checked the electronics briefly and made a call down to Redford and to Somerston Maintenance on the other side. Number 12 was back in operation. The VHF was open all the way.

Then they went outside again and stood looking up the tower. The leader soldier ran to catch the sling and signaled to go up again. When he was opposite the body he signaled to stop and be maneuvered closer to the tower. It required four passes because the wind across the Knob was gusty. The pilot struggled constantly to keep the chopper steady. The guy smacked hard into the tower on the last try. Some icicles broke off and made a little avalanche down through the girders. Lee and the other guys stepped back a little, but it didn't amount to much. The guy up on the tower had caught hold though and was working at the body. The sky was bright and it was hard to see from the ground. Silhouette with no details—a shadow picture. After a time he swung out on the cable, signaling to be let down. He slipped out of the sling and came up to Lee, his nose bleeding from the impact with the tower. He wiped it on his glove and wiped the glove on his fatigues.

"Can't work him loose. The leg is frozen—wound around. Wedged in like a rock."

Lee said nothing. The other guy said nothing. The three of them looked up the tower.

The nose bleed guy shrugged. "I could saw it off," he said.

Lee thought about it. The hanging body was becoming something of a landmark to the constant air traffic back and forth across the mountain, lately to the point of wisecracks on the military UHF. Lee had heard a few of those. Didn't like it. He wanted Jimmy down. He nodded and the guy took some kind of folding saw from one of their survival packs.

First the body fell. It came down like the rigid and insensate thing it was. Then the leg. The leg came down inside the girder tower and they had to work it out like some kind of money puzzle. The body landed in deep snow, sending up a whoof. The other guardsman went after it like a bird dog for a duck. When he picked it up, there was a lot of snow stuck to it and the arms were stuck up high above the head like Jimmy was surrendering. They put it in the sling and stuck the piece of leg inside the jacket with the foot protruding from the collar, zipped the jacket up to hold the leg and sent the whole thing up the cable to the hovering chopper. It went up like some kind of ludicrous acrobat with upraised arms, complete leg arched back rigidly in a stupid circus pose. It turned on the cable this way then that as if in deference to some unseen cheering throng. At the top the winch-guy took it in like a sack of spuds and sent the cable down for Lee.

Lee kept his gaze directed out the window. There was nothing in the chopper to wrap Jimmy in. The winch guy had gone forward with the pilot and Lee was alone in the fuselage with the body. It rocked awkwardly about the floor with the movements of the helicopter, unable to be laid flat in it's absurd pose. Bodies per se didn't bother him. He was almost getting used to them. He had talked with Beck a little earlier. They had 706 stashed in the old bypass tunnel and plenty coming. But Lee had known this kid and death had hardly left him dignity. Lee preferred to keep his gaze directed out the window. He'd find some way to cover or to thaw him before many others saw the body.

Below him they had opened up the eastbound tube through Aurora and a single lane was moving through. The backlog had been cleared as far as Breezeway. They were turning them around and sending westbound patrons back and south. At least those who stayed with their cars. They gave them gas and sent them east or south till things got better. The vacant cars were being towed to large stockades and catalogued laboriously by make, model, registration number, state of origin. The army had commandeered strip mines, fields, parking lots—any level space to put them on and there were thousands upon thousands. They were trying to stockpile them as close as possible to where they had been found and were doing the same with people too. The fairgrounds west of Somerston had been turned into a trailer town—eleven hundred so far. More on the way. There were twenty-three such instant towns along the Pike alone, but Somerston was the biggest concentration, crowded with homeless locals too. The army was hauling cars out of the streets and lining them up in the fields around the town. The enormous job of reuniting people with their cars was just begun. There would be those who'd not be home for Christmas, those who never found their cars, cars who never found their owners. It would at last boil down to a final residue that would never be resolved. In any case, the streets of Somerston were starting to be opened. Redford too. Soldiers everywhere. Some scattered looting, but the impassable roads were keeping that down to a minimum. Lee had taken Jennifer back to the house each day and so far they had not been robbed. There was still no power and they still couldn't live there.

Woods had set up quite a thing at the Aurora Maintenance. Hospital. Shelter. That was still going strong. Charlie was spending lots of time up there with Woods. Woods was right about the three-day syndrome though. The first three days they had been full of sacrifice and brotherly love. It was turning now. The subtle shift. "When do I get mine?" Scattered reports of little altercations breaking out. Arguments and shovings. A growing pettiness. The crowding. The boredom setting in.

Woods was right about a lot of things. They were overrun

with "help" now—agencies he'd never heard of. Donations. The trailer load of chocolate-covered marshmallow Easter bunnies sitting down at Redford now. The guy drove up and parked it there on Wednesday—said all he knew was he was told to deliver it to "the disaster." Had no idea of what it was. Didn't care. Left the trailer, drove the tractor off again. Similar thing at Irwin. 200 gross, size 44 bermuda shorts. Things like that. Popping up all around. The kind of help they didn't need. Woods said it happened everytime. Tax write-offs. If you didn't take it, you were an ungrateful bastard. They'd turn it over to the Salvation Army.

He and Chuck had talked with Turlock yesterday. Eastern saw no end of litigation to result, probably going well into the next century. There was some question about Lee's "Death March" up the mountain. "Death March!" Of course they couldn't call it "Life March," could they? He thought again about that stuffy, summer committee room. It meant a cloud to live with till the thing was brought to something either way.

Finally, he'd spoken with Nadel just briefly that same morning. The immediate thing was whether the clear skies would hold and for how long. It looked good for the coming week. A lot could be accomplished in a week. They talked a little about his projection for the coming year. Nadel, as always, would not be pinned down, but he did say that the high air patterns, the Arctic jetstream, were swinging further north and south than last year, slightly enlarging upon the pattern that caused such radical extremes of weather in these recent years. The indications all were there . . . .

Lee watched the world of white pass far below, the black ant lines where man and his machines were confined to go, the brown fuzz of the winter forest. They all were talking about the phenomenal timing of it, the coincidence of it, the astronomical coincidence and size of it. They all were talking about how leaves would be full on the trees before the bulk of it was cleared away. The indicators all were there. . . .

It was going to be a long hard winter.